HUNT THE FAE

HUNT THE FAE

VICIOUS 2 FAERIES

DARK FABLES WORLD

NATALIA JASTER

Books by Natalia Jaster

VICIOUS FAERIES SERIES

Kiss the Fae (Book 1)

Hunt the Fae (Book 2)

Curse the Fae (Book 3)

FOOLISH KINGDOMS SERIES

Trick (Book 1)

Dare (Book 2)

Lie (Book 3)

Dream (Book 4)

SELFISH MYTHS SERIES

Touch (Book 1)

Torn (Book 2)

Tempt (Book 3)

Transcend (Book 4)

Cover design by Juan, coversbyjuan.com
Map design by Noverantale
Typesetting by Roman Jaster
Body text set in Arno Pro by Robert Slimbach

For all the bad-boy heroes out there—and for the authors who created them

The
Solitary Forest

The Heart of
Willows

Juniper's
Campsite

The Skulk of
Foxes

The Passel of
Boars

N

W · E

S

The Bonfire
Glade

The Seeds that
Give

The
Swarm of Rats

The Faerie
Triad

Mind the trees. Touch the roots. Hunt your fears.

THE HERD OF DEER

PUCK'S CABIN

THE GANG OF ELKS

THE ROOTS THAT TAKE

THE FAUNA TIMBERS

THE WICKED PINES

THE REDWOODS OF EXILE

THE CLAN OF BADGERS

DARK FABLES WORLD

THE SLEUTH OF BEARS

Chase your desires. Miss your target. Hit your mark…

From the Book of Fables

Once in the dark forest, a Stag hunted a Doe…

Prologue

No matter how true your aim, he won't go down easily.

I should know, because I've tried thirteen times to hit the mark, dead center in his chest. Books have instructed me how, Fables have taught me how, and practice has shown me how. I've made a study of it.

One, how to hold my weapon.

Two, when to catch him alone.

Three, which body part to target.

But it takes more than tutelage and training to best this Fae. He knows when to expect an ambush, because he's fluent in my methods. He knows how I operate, from the way my fingers curl around the crossbow, to how my spine flexes, to the split of my legs as I hide behind a tree.

He sniffs me out, the same way he inhales damp soil. He detects my movements, the same way he hears roots unfurling in the earth. He senses me like he senses the woodland, like he senses temptation—deep and carnal.

No matter how sharp your weapon, his words will be sharper.

I should know, because I have the scars to prove it. So if his voice cuts to the quick, it's my fault for letting my guard down. It's best to remember such lessons for the next time.

One, he'll deal a verbal blow.

Two, he'll watch you bleed.

Three, he'll smile while it happens.

They call him the ruler of the woodland. He's a satyr of the dark forest, a vicious creature bred amongst thickets of moss and rings of mushrooms. He dwells amidst the pine needles and the broad, moaning trunks of oak trees.

Tales speak of his sensuous grin and mischievous antics. They claim he feasts on blushes and laps at a lover's sigh like nectar. And such companions talk of his seductions, every conquest left in disarray, the debris of their hearts splintering along the woodland paths. Those tales are even more wicked if his catch is a mortal—and a virgin.

No matter how quick you move, he'll catch you first.

I should know, because every time I've backed my enemy into a corner, he has trapped me in kind. But of all the creatures in this wilderness, and for all his cleverness, this arrogant Fae should know better. He should know I'm a fast learner. I don't make the same mistakes twice. I might be a human captive in Faerie, and I might be trapped in his land, but I'm not his toy.

One, stalk him.

Two, do it quietly.

Three, expect a trick.

These are my newest rules. They're keener, shrewder, and wiser than what they used to be, because I've learned my lesson. I've learned what I'm up against, because before I started hunting him, he was already hunting me.

As to how it all began—well, that's a long story.

1

I aim for the heart. From behind the shrub, I nudge my crossbow bolt through the crochet of leaves, the weapon's iron tip ready to fly. A remote figure is approaching, its weight shuddering the damp earth under my feet. Whatever creature this is, it's big.

And it knows I'm here. I can tell from its pace. There's a sensibility to its gait—thoughtful, considerate. My nostrils flare, drawing in the pungency of bark and fungi offset by a candied aroma, the sort that will rot one's teeth.

Well. I've never liked candy. It's a frivolous delicacy that makes me gag.

But there's one type of being in this world who dotes on all manner of treats. That fact reminds me this isn't a normal woodland. There's nothing human about this forest, except for me.

So much for entering the land of Faeries without incident.

Daggers of grass splay from the soil while exposed roots thread in and out of the surface. Ribbons of blazing white clouds peek through the eventide canopy, bringing to mind pale tresses that flap in the wind.

Lark.

Teal shadows remind me of eyes in precisely the same shade, the irises gentle and comforting.

Cove.

My chin trembles. I glimpse past the oaks to the path I'd taken here. It had begun with The Faerie Triad, the dividing line between my world and this one, where an oak, ash, and hawthorn stand sentinel. Then my route had continued into The Colony of Fireflies, where floating insects glow among the yews. Beyond all that, the spot where I had said good-bye to my sisters less than minutes ago resides.

I lock my jaw. I don't have the time or luxury for bereavement. Cove and Lark are gone, taken from me and parceled out into their own horrors. Worrying about them won't benefit any of us.

My fingers grip the crossbow's trigger. Perspiration beads across the nape of my neck. Three steps into this trek, and a predator has already made its proximity known. I gauge its direction, estimating from which recess it will appear, at which degree to aim my weapon. One pull, and the bolt's iron will accomplish the rest.

True, this is hardly the wisest precedent to set. Fauna are sacred here, I've only just arrived in this woodland, and felling one of its inhabitants will do me no favors among its kin. However, if up against a famished animal, I'd prefer to keep possession of my limbs. Most especially, my cranium.

Only shoot if it attacks, I remind myself.

Only shoot if I have no choice, I lecture myself.

Several twigs snap to my right. The noise bites into the silence. My breathing accelerates as I fight to keep the crossbow steady.

A gargantuan silhouette disturbs the underbrush. Offshoots crack beneath an unseen girth, the noise splintering through the weald. The sound lacks the telltale reverberation of paws, as well as the scrape of talons. Rather, it's the punch of hooves.

Bushes quaver out of the animal's way—east of this trail, thirty paces off. The ground continues to shake, jostling my boot soles. I sink onto my belly, my archery poised, and peer into the vegetation.

How many times have I been in this position? How many times since I was six years old? How many times have I regretted it?

Candles perch along the branches, as if they've germinated from the boughs organically. Flames bud from the wicks, sprinkling auroras of gold that penetrate the teal darkness with faint light. It's not enough to illuminate minute details, but it's enough to strike true.

The hedges split. The creature stalks forward, one hoof crushing a toadstool and squishing the fungus to a pulp. Fables almighty. I keep still, hold my breath.

I can do this. I grew up doing this.

I have read a thousand comprehensive pages about the fauna of this domain. I know every meticulous fact and cautionary tale and—

The shadow launches at me, tearing through the shrubs. I disarm, leap aside, and roll across the earth. Muck clogs my mouth, the putrid taste of feces assaulting my palate. I hack up the mire, snatch my weapon from the grass, and vault to my feet.

The animal turns and gallops my way again. It's some predatory metamorphosis of equine, the entirety of its shape indecipherable despite the oaks' candles.

I race through the trees. The massive figure pounds toward me, its panting breaths pumping through the wild. My heels slip across a puddle of sludge, and I stumble into a creeper that snatches my hair. I yelp, fist the lock, and give it a tug. The instant those threads rip from my scalp, I flee.

My cloak flares around me, the hood thumping. I check over my shoulder, then swivel as a bulbous tree root materializes. I skid on my heels too late. My toe catches on the root, and the world careens, broadleaves wheeling in my vision. I tumble down a dry ravine while bracken slashes my skin.

The slope evens out, and my body rolls to a stop. I cough up gritty lumps of soil, my lungs burning. My crossbow, quiver, and supply pack lie on the ground beside me. I totter to a sitting position, stunned that I hadn't broken a bone. Then I swerve toward the incline, but the animal is nowhere in sight.

At the ravine's base, the original path emerges. It weaves into a candlelit cluster of towering oaks, fallen acorns, and teal toadstools, white dots speckling the spongy, phallic caps.

The visuals hone my senses, pulling me from my stupor. I can't have returned to the path that easily. At this juncture, I should be lost.

Yet the strum of music hints otherwise. The sumptuous glide of strings filters through the branches, causing leaves to flutter in tempo. The tune teases my skirt, sidles up my spine, and strokes into my ear.

One must always beware of glamour. I rise and inventory my defenses. My clothes are inside-out, so that's taken care of. As an extra preventative, I reach for my pack. Extracting a string of dried hawthorn berries, I shove them into my skirt pocket, which…does nothing to staunch the enchanted melody. The notes keep pouring from their source like blood from a wound.

My face scrunches into a glower. There must be an explanation.

At all times, humans must be polite to Faeries. Hence, it's rude to keep them waiting, especially if that human is a prisoner. I withdraw an envelope from the opposite pocket, unfold the leaflet, and reread the contents.

For your trespass, be our sacrifice—to surrender, to serve, and to satisfy. Under the vicious stars, three sisters must play three games.

Bookish Juniper, your task is delightfully sinful. Mind the trees. Touch the roots. Hunt your fears. Chase your desires. Miss your target. Hit your mark.

Welcome to The Solitary Forest.

Fables curse them. I glower at the ambiguous, riddling missive that had greeted me just inside this realm. What does it mean to miss my target yet hit my mark? Frustrated, I return the sheet to its envelope and stuff both into my pocket.

The sinuous music hums through the landscape. The strings curl their fingers, crooking, beckoning. Since the trail winds toward the lyrical tones, this must be where the lane had intended to lead me.

I harness my weapon and supplies and pursue the trail. It leads into an oak arcade where branches arch over the path like a ribcage, the boughs scrolling into the murk. Eventide leaks through the mesh, a patina of blue-green blending with the candlelight and enhancing the route.

Branches croak as if speaking in an arcane tongue, from the veins of their roots to the lungs at their bases, and up through the cracked throats of their trunks.

My eyebrows slash downward. The ominous arcade narrows. Once I'm through, the oaks suddenly dissipate. In their place, evergreens pump with more candlelight, embossing the needle leaves. The trees of this domain must be impervious to the heat.

I slow my pace, picking around batches of mushrooms. The fungi appear harmless, clustered in bouquets rather than circles. Nevertheless, I can't be too careful. I've studied the Fables' appendices about Fae rings and read what happens when a person steps inside.

The overlapping sounds of revelry grow denser, louder. But not just any kind.

The lusty echoes of rapture invade my ears. Moans tangle and overlap, rhythmic and excessive. My arm hairs prickle. I'm no expert, but I've shared a home with a rather promiscuous sister. Moreover, I've researched the clean Fables as well the obscene narratives. Woodland Faeries are notorious for making this sort of racket.

Communal grunts and whimpers drift from a grove at the path's end. I sidestep the entrance, paste myself against the nearest trunk, and process the signals gravitating from around the corner.

The air reeks of intoxicants: myrrh, sweat, and some type of charred herb. Heady, gaudy, overindulgent fragrances. The kinds of cloying scents bred for spoiled, capricious beings.

How exceedingly primitive. Contending with a four-legged predator had been easier than what I suspect awaits.

The echoes of those licentious cries thread around my knees, tugging me closer. My captors could sniff me out, but a huntress knows how to stay quiet, undetected. I creep my head around the pine tree and peek into the grove.

My mouth unhinges. My fingernails dig into the crevices of bark.

It's a den of debauchery, straight from the halls of an Unseelie court. Candle tapers writhe from the boughs. And sprawled beneath that blazing display is another type of spectacle.

Figures lounge on pillows while others lean against the trunks, loll across the offshoots, or perch on the boughs with their limbs swinging. They possess hybrids of humanlike features, animal traits, and a facet synonymous with their kind: pointed ears that stab the air.

Solitary Faeries.

Brownies, no taller than cattails, their flesh woven of peat. Sap drizzles from a female's bottom lashes as if she's weeping.

Leprechauns—some merely scruffy and unshaven as lumberjacks, the rest leering through the copper hedges of their beards. All of them are handsome in a rural way.

Statuesque dryads, flora enmeshed in their hair. One of them boasts a mane of birch leaves. Another, a set of braids entwined with daisies.

Satyrs and fauns with horns and antlers of varying shapes. Thickets of fur cover their lower halves, sometimes to the waist, enabling them to wear nothing at all. For others, the fur ends at the knees, at which point the Faeries don trousers or sashes of ivy.

Many of these figures are breathtaking, their angular faces rivaling the beauty of their animal features. Badger tails swish from their backsides. Porcupine quills spear from around their wrists and ankles like spiky bangles. Elk antlers splay from their skulls. The markings of a chipmunk adorn the upper half of a male face.

Musicians take up residence in the branches. They strum fiddles, violas, lutes, lyres, and other stringed, paddlelike instruments I've never seen.

Before my eyes, images wrought from storybooks come to life. My lids peel back, my eyes dilating with astonishment. Most of all, heat scorches my cheeks.

From their respective positions, the Folk watch the exhibition taking place in the venue's center. Two male fauns flank a female—a wood nymph, based on her curvaceous form, the laurel circlet askew on her pistachio head, and the vines arcing from her eyebrows. One of the fauns stands behind her and sucks the flesh of her throat. She gasps, throwing back her head while reaching up and raking her hands through his tawny hair.

The other male hunkers on bended knee. With the nymph's thigh hitched over his shoulder, his face vanishes into the slot between her legs. And when this happens, the female cries out.

Numerous Folk enjoy the scene. The rest tend to their own partners. They embrace and fondle one another, their tongues flicking and their bodies jutting, bouncing, and thrusting.

Their states of undress vary, from partially clothed to fully disrobed. Gown straps and untied shirts hang limply off their shoulders, the wools, leathers, velvets, and other unrecognizable textiles wrinkled. Breasts glisten, handfuls of females doing nothing to shield their busts, nor the sprigs of hair at the apexes of their thighs. Several males remain exposed, their pectorals rippling, their private flesh erect and on display.

I avert my gaze, my face roasting to cinders. It's not the same as examining fauna genitalia, in order to identify the animal's sex—not that I had expected it to be the same.

Only one figure appears unruffled. He reclines in the shadows, observing the entertainment from a high-backed chair constructed of bark and stinging nettles. His head flops to the side, the half-light blotting out the nuances of his face.

From this vantage point, I can only make out a few hints about him, including his red hair. Molten waves sweep his shoulders, the coiled ends licking what's visible of his jaw. Indeed, a smooth and rakish square jaw and a pair of naughty, quirked lips.

My teeth grind. I know who he is, because I know that horrible grin. I know it from a hundred perverted legends whispered between mortals. What's more, I've seen it in the flesh, in my distant past. I've seen it up close, so much closer, far too close.

I inch nearer, focus harder. Leather hugs his athletic frame, neither bulky, nor slender. A vest of buckles and straps cinch across his chest. Buckskin breeches accentuate his thighs and end at the knees where—

A nymph sidles over to him. Decorative yellow petals clutter her dark hair, and a matching dress woven of the same flora clings to her frame. A gradient of pigments dusts her upper eyelids—from the yellow of her ensemble, to celery, to caterpillar.

She rests a palm on his shoulder. He slants his head a fraction, giving her half his attention, the other half still angled toward the vulgar display.

He listens to whatever the nymph whispers in his ear. The more she says, the more he pays attention. Eventually, his shadowed face slides fully toward his informant, heeding her words. An enticement, perhaps?

Whatever the female tells him, he consumes the information like a glutton tipping back wine—greedy and enthusiastic.

Those masculine lips tilt into an impish smirk. With a flourish, he raises his arm and snaps his fingers. The single sound jumps off the trees, silencing the moans and musical strings. Everyone stops to glance at him.

The petal nymph backs away while pressing a fist to her tittering mouth. My blood chills, dread crawling up my spine. I huddle deeper into the evergreen.

The male's attention slides across every Solitary in attendance.

At length, he leans forward. The candlelight brings him into stark relief. My breath stalls. I see eyes like melted sable, the lashes lined in white and black streaks. I see stag antlers rising from his head, the barbed prongs looping to the back of his scalp. I see those inflammatory locks framing a wily, wanton countenance.

It's the face of a troublemaker, one that has haunted my dreams.

His tenor rings out. The lilting accent has swagger to it, along with a touch of mockery. "It appears we have a guest, luvs," the Fae announces. "A rather tardy guest."

Then the ruler of the woodland swings his head. And he looks straight at me.

2

A pair of calloused hands seizes me from behind. The owner's platter-sized palms dwarf my biceps, clamping around them like manacles. I grunt in protest as my captor yanks my wrists behind my back and shoves me ahead.

Candlelight floods my vision, the metallic flames twitching erratically. My boots scrape the ground. I fight to stall the inevitable, my heels grinding into the dirt and mowing through grass.

The assailant marches while pushing me forward. I wriggle and twist my head over my shoulder, then promptly swallow my objection.

Big. Very big.

Two bulky arms made of steel. Four other limbs, including massive hindquarters. An olive-green coat, plus a long mane and tail of the same color.

An equine body. A dark male torso and face.

The centaur takes offense to my awe. He slits his eyes and jerks me back around. I stumble, much to the amusement of my audience. Pitiless chuckles pinch my ears, and I compress my lips until my molars ache.

The centaur gives one last shove. I careen forward and hit the ground with a thwack. My knees and hands smack the forest floor, breaking my fall. If not for the shock absorption, the landing would have fractured my nose.

My crossbow, quiver, and pack clatter. I crane my head, my eyes stumbling into a pair of hooves. But to the contrary, they don't belong to another centaur. Unlike the hooves of a horse, these ones are narrower and cloven.

Smooth, tan fur covers a pair of calves, a line of scars peeking from the right one, the kinds of scars made by the teeth of an iron trap. Those calves disappear into the buckskin breeches I'd noticed earlier. From the knees up, the leather molds over a set of toned, humanlike thighs and a tapered waist.

My gaze charts a path from that vest ornamented with buckles, to a fair complexion, to the gleaming, brown eyes looming over me. The spokes of his antlers pierce the air, the tips sharper than his ears.

If the red hair and antlers hadn't confirmed his identity earlier, the hooves certainly do. Of all the Fables I've studied, my least favorites have always been about satyrs. In the whole of Faerie, their infamous depravities are legendary, as is their addiction to lust.

Whereas fauns are rumored to be the attractive ones, satyrs are the libertines. Pretty is too dainty a term for their racy looks; provocative is a more accurate definition.

The ruler of the woodland bends forward in his chair and inspects me with a slanted head. "So our guest of honor has arrived at last," the satyr murmurs. "A merry welcome to you, luv." His accent is as jaunty as the music, as rustic as roots, and as roguish as his grin. "Do forgive my comrade's roughhousing. Cypress isn't accustomed to humans your size, much less apprehending them from behind." He quirks a sadistic brow. "I, however, am acquainted with many sizes and shapes, especially from behind."

I gather that's supposed to impress me. "Unaccustomed."

"What was that?" he queries. "Don't be shy."

"Unaccustomed is the proper word, according to the laws of grammar. As in, Cypress is unaccustomed to humans my size."

Intrigue brightens his face, a field of white freckles dancing across the bridge of his nose, visible despite his skin tone. This close to him, the essence of cloves and the sweet bite of pine nips my nostrils.

"Hmm." He leans back, ropes of bronze earrings dangling from his lobes, the chains outfitted in leaf charms that jingle with his movements. "I've always wanted a tutor. Do you school your lovers in bed, too? Instruct them on the proper way to moan?"

Guffaws resound, poking me from all sides. I stiffen, having forgotten the crowd of onlookers.

The satyr chuckles along with the rest of the Fae, his shoulders shaking. He waves his arm, fingers swatting the air. "Sorry, luv. It was a joke, though from that healthy scowl of yours, I gather you don't fancy jokes. Here, let me educate you on how they work: I say something funny, and you laugh. Go on, try it."

"I'm not a puppet," I retort, then think wiser of my attitude. "Thank you very much."

"Ah," he exclaims. "She's on a roll, correcting me for the second time. Do me a favor and gainsay me again, and do it slowly."

My ears tingle, sifting through his words for a trick. A favor is the last thing I'm about to exchange with a Fae.

Although I fail to detect duplicitous loopholes—he wants my blush, not my compliance—I do catch the snide lilt. Even his ridicule sounds flirtatious, his sarcasm erotic. This is precisely the type of scornful teasing that chips away at the flesh, until all that's left is shame.

I'd rather not dwell on how I know this.

"That reminds me," he says. "We can't summon our newest human to this realm without making introductions. I'm—"

"Puck," I say. "Ruler of the woodland."

"Why do humans always forget to include Seducer of Innocents and Ruiner of Morals? It's not that hard to remember," he complains, then flaps his hand in a rising motion. "Come on, then. Stand up so I can see you better."

I don't stand up. I'm dragged up by the centaur named Cypress, who snatches my shoulders and hauls me to my feet.

Puck takes his time, his eyes burning a trail up and down my form. My green hair is a nest of stems. My skirt is torn at the hem, gunk stains my cream blouse, and dirt crusts along my hairline.

Sometimes my sisters rib me about being fastidious, not to mention capricious, not a hair out of place. I have no idea why. A clean appearance is a clean mind.

Nonetheless, I'm grateful for my tarnished appearance. Tempting a satyr leads to doom, seduction, and a loss of one's maidenhead. Although Faeries rarely trifle with mortals intimately—they would sooner bed slugs than lower themselves to the level of nonmagical beings—Puck's rakish ilk have a habit of making exceptions.

If he doesn't find me attractive, so much the better. Thankfully, that seems to be the case, his expression betraying not a hint of admiration. Rather, he appraises me with…a flash of consternation.

My joints tense. Does he know?

Please don't let him know.

I keep my face neutral as Cypress releases me. At Puck's dramatic nod, the centaur divests me of my archery while keeping vigilant of the iron bolt tips. He takes care to avoid touching them, then hands the crossbow and quiver to a dryad standing nearby.

At which point, Puck's equine lackey seizes the pack and makes an example of my possessions. In front of everyone, Cypress empties the contents I'd curated for every contingency: a pouch of salt to ward off enchantment; piddling trinkets—such as a posey of dried bluebells and a twilled spool of ribbon—intended for negotiation; a cotton blouse; a knit sweater; spare leggings; undergarments; a pair of woolen socks; a waterskin; the hardwood case protecting my reading spectacles; and a few other items.

Most importantly, my pencil and prized notebook. The latter comprises years of scholarship about Faeries, Fables, and their fauna.

The centaur tosses each item to the ground, my privacy on display and at the mercy of the Faeries' inspection. I fix my gaze ahead. I will not quail, I will not shrink, and I will not plead. That's what they want.

Puck snatches my notebook off the ground, the tome bound in lambskin vellum. He scans the front cover, then scoffs and—how dare he!—chucks it to the dirt like so much rubbish.

My retinas kindle with heat. He notices my reaction, soaks it up like a washcloth, and draws some unspoken conclusion. "Do you like juniper berries?"

I blink. "Excuse me?"

"Juniper berries. I think they're dellllicious. What about parties? Do you like those? We've arranged this revel to welcome you, though seeing as you were late—bad, bad girl—," he scolds, wagging his finger at me, "—we started without your blessing. I trust you don't mind? Fuckery waits for no one."

Against my better judgment, I wrinkle my nose. "In that respect, you appear to be thriving without my company. Don't let me stand in the way. I've taken up enough of your time."

The satyr's eyebrows lurch into his forehead, a fresh thought animating his features. Instantly, I taste the bitterness of my error. The freedom to walk away is a luxury I no longer have. The moment I stepped into Faerie, I became his. I belong to this monster now, and I've just reminded him of that deadly fact.

Puck slumps into his chair, making himself comfortable. He licks his lips, contemplating a potential fetish, savoring it as one would a sugar cube. "Now who said anything about standing in the way? You're in precisely the right spot, and what a fetching centerpiece you make."

I tense. "What does that m—"

"It means take off the cloak."

"What?"

Puck just stares at me, as do the rest of them. Dryads, brownies, leprechauns, nymphs, fauns, satyrs, and centaurs. All these beings of the weald, with their woodland complexions, fur, tails, ears, and claws. They crowd in, fencing off every escape outlet.

My stomach cramps. I'd heard his instruction, loud and clear. Truly, I should have expected it.

If I do what he says, will it stop there? And if it doesn't…

Apparently, I've taken too long, because Puck sighs as though I'm being difficult and flutters his digits at Cypress. The centaur exits the premises, then returns a moment later, ushering a small figure into the circle. The boy thrashes and whimpers, his voice clotted with unshed tears, his black curls matted, and his blue eyes glistening with fear.

Ribbons of burlap hang from his malnourished frame, a tragic excuse for rags. My throat swells, and my knuckles curl. He can't be more than nine—my age when I'd been a homeless foundling, in a similar state of disarray, hungry and skeletal.

Cypress thrusts the boy onto his knees. In my head, I scream for these knaves to let him go. Outwardly, I keep my face blank—until the centaur accepts my crossbow from the dryad, carefully loads it with a bolt while avoiding the iron tip and aims it at the boy's nape.

My mouth opens, a shout ready to catapult off my tongue.

Puck's casual voice intercepts me. "Take. Off. The. Cloak."

Silence descends, frayed at the margins by the boy's muffled weeping. He sinks his teeth into his lower lip, attempting to stifle the sobs.

Fury shoots up my fingertips. Disobey, and I'll condemn myself. Comply, and the satyr might require me to strip further.

My aloofness holds firm, embedded in my face. I move without preamble, seizing the tasseled closures of my cloak and pulling on the ends. The hooded mantle shivers off my shoulders, the short sleeves of my blouse revealing a gilded leaf bracelet entwined around my forearm.

Puck watches me fold the garment and set it upon the ground, his irises pinned to mine. "That's the spirit." He gestures to where I'm standing. "Now that you've made yourself at home, tell us a story."

I frown, baffled. To say the least, I had anticipated something graphic next. This can't possibly be his request. It's rudimentary, and while forest Faeries are penned as flighty, neither are they known for being obtuse. How could they assume this is a challenge for someone with my vocabulary and diction? My wardrobe gives me away as a commoner, yet I hardly pass for uneducated.

The Faeries incline their heads, waiting for me to start. Very well, then.

I clasp my hands in front of me. *"Once, a snowy hare confronted an Elf—"*

"Ah, ah, ah." Puck flaps his digit. "Tell us a story of your own."

"I...beg your pardon?"

"I didn't ask you to regurgitate a tale created by someone else. What I want—what we all want—is a tale of your own making. Compose a fable, if you must. Or a fairy tale will do, complete with horny princes, swooning maidens, or whatever tropes you like, so long as it comes from you alone."

"Surely, there must be something else you'd rather have me do," I stammer, my pulse thudding.

Puck makes a scandalized face. "Are you propositioning me? How bloody forward. We barely know each other."

I shouldn't have given him ideas. Nevertheless, I count off my fingers. "I can recite by heart every tale in the Book of Fables, among other narratives. I can deconstruct analytical theory. I can—"

"Your qualifications are not on trial," Cypress snaps, his baritone so deep it could grow roots.

"That depends on her definition of qualifications," Puck remarks to the centaur while examining me. "Quite the show-off, aren't you?"

Why does everyone call me that?!

At home, it's no different, but my family is allowed. They mean it affectionately, unlike the rest of the village mongrels who make fun of me yet can't tell proper rhetoric from a belch.

I refrain from replying. Evidently, Puck doesn't need me to. "Then by all means, show off some more."

I glance at the boy. The iron bolt pricks his slender neck, the pulse point visibly thumping.

Visions flash in my psyche. A little girl stalking animal prints through the bushes, then aiming her crossbow while crying. A little girl who'd been unable to shoot, who'd spluttered, "I can't."

A little girl being told by men ten times her size that she's worthless. A little girl deciding not to believe them. A little girl proving them wrong.

A little girl, years later, working diligently to sound out letters on a page. A little girl learning to read and write. A little girl growing into a woman.

A woman who has never scripted an original story in her life.

My temple throbs. *"Once, there lived…"* I trail off, sweat coating my upper lip. *"There lived a girl who…who couldn't…"*

But my head turns into a blank slate, words slipping across the surface, unsteady, unreliable. Everything that comes to mind has been written already or doesn't sound good enough, smart enough, sensical enough.

My chin hardens. A blade chips away at my skull, as well as my confidence.

Puck watches it happen, perhaps senses it happen. "Such a shame." He rubs his thumb and forefinger together, then clucks his tongue. "You've come to the wrong place, luv."

A hot pool of mortification floods my cheeks. Did he just call me inadequate?

The Faeries sputter with mirth. The woodland Folk are the craftiest of Solitaries. They know how to woo and beguile. They know how to conceive stories, myths, fables, folktales, and fairy tales.

And they know how to fool humans. The boy isn't on his knees any longer. He's leaning against the centaur, slapping his thigh and cackling. Orange irises replace the blue ones. His clammy, pale skin shudders into its true nature—a vibrant, peachy complexion. A marten tail sprouts from his bottom, and he no longer appears runty but rather the equivalent of a thirteen-year-old lad. Black curls dangle around his face, and intricate orange vine markings spiral wide across his forehead.

My posture buckles. Glamour.

They'd glamoured me.

But that can't be! Not with my clothes inside-out and the hawthorn berries in my skirt pocket. Such talismans ought to have protected me from enchantment.

I stand there, my possessions discarded on the ground, and my archery confiscated. I stand there, the butt of a jest. I stand there, humiliated.

Puck mock-laments, "I hate to tell you this, but you have a bit to learn about us. For a start, our standards for diversions are high."

Outrage singes my tongue. "Oh, I can see why someone of your exemplary caliber would rely on a *human's* recitation for suitable entertainment. How flattering. However, I'd be wary of clinging to those…what did you call them? High expectations?" Then I quote *The Fox and the Fae.* "Choose diversions wisely, lest they lead to downfall."

It's an empty threat. But it feels good to say.

The laughter dies. My audience stirs, wrath darkening their faces.

The satyr tilts his antlered head. "My, my, my. It must be nice to rely on other people's words for every thought you have."

I snap, "It must be validating to assume no thought has value simply because it didn't come from you."

He blinks, taking a while to process the rebuttal. "That's not what I meant."

"Isn't it? Then tell me the last time something else—rather than your ego—inspired you? Tell me *that* story."

Hisses and growls erupt from the circle, some of the Fae skulking toward me. Puck holds up his hand, stopping them. Without warning, he rises and saunters my way, his cloven hooves imprinting the grass. Despite those stag limbs, his swagger rivals the cockiness of males back home.

Mortals used to think satyrs didn't have animal limbs, but the Fables had proven that tidbit false.

In terms of height, he's not a tower. However, neither is he scanty. Because of my small frame, I have to crane my head to meet his gaze. Toned muscles bunch across his arms and flex under the leather vest. Up close, white and black streaks line his eyelashes, and candlelight burnishes the red waves around his countenance.

"What a smart fucking girl you are," Puck compliments.

Then he transforms. His artful facade vanishes, his irises darkening. That posturing grin drops like a veil, replaced by a flash of predatory teeth.

Gone is the cavalier Fae. Now I behold a ruler—a livid, vicious ruler.

This, I didn't see coming. And this, perhaps, is his greatest deception yet.

In my periphery, an equine body heads my way. Simultaneously, Puck snarls an order, low and dangerous. "Cage her until she behaves herself."

As Cypress drags me backward, the satyr gives me a spiteful inclination of his head. "Juniper of Reverie Hollow. Welcome to The Solitary Forest."

Lucid realization dawns. He may like games, but he knows when to stop playing them.

The Faeries had already known my name. Yet as giant hands shackle my wrists, I have time for one final, blessed thought: Puck doesn't recognize my face.

He doesn't remember me.

3

It was a long time ago. One special time, years ago.

If not my green eyes, the matching shade of my hair should have alerted him. However, my voice had been different back then—naive, younger, and softer around the edges. That, plus the passage of time must have blocked out the memory. So long as it stays that way, his ignorance is my saving grace.

The centaur snatches my waist. My body flops like a ragdoll, the candlelit trees somersaulting, a thousand flaming pupils rotating. I land on my belly. Slamming onto Cypress's back, the blow to my stomach thrusts the air from my lungs.

The Faeries cackle. Puck's gaze incinerates my nape.

My limbs dangle, and my skull bounces as the equine trots from the grove. At least Cypress maintains a languid gait along the winding lane, rather than vaulting into a gallop.

Inadvertently, my attention skids in an unseemly, anatomical direction. But rather than encountering certain exposed organs—he's half horse, after all—I discern nothing but an enclosed sac down there. Like a lid, the flap must conceal the equine's reproductive bits, layering over the bulge. That's one less impropriety I'll have to worry about while draped like this.

As we traverse deeper into the wild, the Faeries' muffled glee recedes. Every muscle and joint in the centaur's excessive body—his size triples that of a stallion—rumbles beneath mine. I struggle in vain to find a dignified position, my derrière on display and my ribs smarting from the ride.

"Cease your twitching, moppet," the centaur clips. "It will disturb your balance, and I am not in the mood to retrieve you from the ground, should you suffer a tumble."

"In terms of kinetics, the logical arrangement would be to let me sit astride," I inform him. "That would relieve your discomfort as well as my own."

He snorts at my rebuttal. "The discomfort of a human."

"An unencumbered journey means a quicker arrival."

"Which of your Fables did you memorize that axiom from?"

It wasn't from a Fable. I'm quoting from my Papa Thorne, whom the centaur has no business mocking.

In any event, Cypress speaks as though mortals are incapable of feeling discomfort, the same way portions of my kind dismiss the possibility that animals have the capacity to suffer.

If I value my tongue, I must hold it—leash it, muzzle it. Regrettably, my bladder has other ideas. It swells, the pressure causing my eyes to water. "I suggest you readjust me so that I don't soil your glossy coat."

The centaur halts, processing my words. "Are you lying?"

"I'm not one to degrade myself with infantile tactics. What's more, urine—*mortal* urine—has a pungent odor, and I doubt you'd enjoy a human marking you."

In less than thirteen seconds, I'm off my stomach and straddling his back. A small triumph, but I congratulate myself nonetheless and abstain from thanking him. Faeries loathe gratitude and aspire to favors instead.

Once I'm settled, the centaur twists ahead. His baritone is thick and accented like Puck's tenor, except less coquettish and certainly less playful. "Contaminate my coat, and I will buck you to the ground. Then I will stomp upon your puny carcass until you are fodder for the wild."

I ignore the knot of terror that cinches my chest. Unlike humans, Faeries can't lie. This mammoth isn't bluffing; if given the opportunity, he wouldn't hesitate to squash me beneath his hooves.

He wouldn't, but for one fact. His kin had called me to this weald. I hadn't merely skipped past their forbidden borders out of curiosity. I came at their behest.

I point out, "That would void the love letter your people sent me."

"True," he acknowledges while leaving the threat open-ended.

Something else rattles my attention, stirring up the residue of my memory. The pace and cadence of his trot. The girth of his body. The echo of his hooves. I assess the broad span of his back, the noises he makes while moving, and the trail he leaves behind us, including distorted off-shoots and chinks in the foliage.

The farther we stray from Puck's harem, the quicker my wits return. "You're the one who chased after me."

Cypress stalls, then continues plodding down the lane. I suspect he's impressed, despite his next words. "You were taking too long to arrive at the grove."

I balk. "So you were corralling me?"

"Faeries disfavor tardiness."

"I'm aware of that."

"Especially Puck," he supplies. "And most especially tardiness to one of his receptions."

That wasn't a reception. That was a bacchanal. That was a crass, gluttonous, revolting—

"Puck is not a patient soul. He does not like to be kept waiting. And you, tiny mortal, were dragging your feet."

"In other words, he sent you to fetch me."

"You were hardly a pleasurable errand," Cypress states. "Not until you gave chase. I took liberties. Your aim was off, by the way. Your crossbow bolt would have impaled my hindquarters, not my heart."

I prepare a counter argument. He bucks his rump, forcing my mouth to clamp shut.

Too many offenses fill my head in succession. Bearing witness to public fornication. Having my weapons confiscated. Hearing my intellect reduced to that of a nitwit. Coming face to face with a nefarious satyr.

What has it been? Less than an hour?

What will happen to my archery? Will the Fae destroy it?

Cypress's coat radiates in the darkness, its texture abrading my legs. We resume our trek down the path, passing under awnings of pine. The relief of sitting upright is short-lived as I recall the hawthorn berries jiggling in my pocket. Why hadn't the morsels protected me from glamour?

Mentally, I rifle through everything I've learned about the Folk, ev-

23

erything I've read in the Book of Fables. Every human in The Dark Fables owns a copy; however there is, and always will be, only one complete version. The original volume had belonged to the scribes who'd penned the tales centuries ago, then eventually faded into history. No one can say what became of the wordsmiths or their source material; the original book's whereabouts are unknown to this day.

All the same, the Fables' contents have remained consistent over the ages, apart from amendments and corrections. No, the book isn't infallible, but it's the best we mortals have.

It's *all* we have.

It's all *I* have.

From Faeries to elves to dragons, the ethereal beings of this continent condemn mortals because we don't wield magic. They brand us as the lesser culture, ungifted simpletons to be ridiculed, tormented, and bewitched, either for bondage or entertainment. To them, we have no feelings or value beyond servitude. Among numerous prejudices is this brilliant one: When compared to immortality, what could humans possibly achieve or learn in our limited lifespans?

Well. I may be a captive, but I won't allow the woodland's ruler to contradict my aptitude. I've taught myself how to distinguish falsehoods from hard facts, the reliable Fables from the dubious ones, so I must have overlooked a vital component about glamour.

Puck has duped me once. It won't happen again.

Cypress smells of straw and the dry notes of cedar. I'd been too frazzled to pay attention beyond the fundamentals, but now I notice more of him. An elaborate leather belt of multiple layers sits where his waist meets his withers, and a horned helmet crowns his head. Perhaps he's a warrior or guardian of this land.

The lane narrows and slopes downhill. Pine needles poke my skirt and ankles while the air tickles the slot behind my ears. Even the atmosphere has a foreign texture and current, as if every brush against my flesh is intentional.

At the slope's base, the evergreens fade, replaced by a new species of trees. My eyes stagger across a circular glade bordered by redwoods that tower three-hundred feet into the sky. A majestic tree towers in the center, this particular redwood exhibiting a large, hollowed-out trunk. The recess burrows into the column, forming an empty cubicle.

The closer we get, the clearer my view gets. Gnarled cords of bark outline the entryway. Inside, similar ropes hang from above. Crimson mottles the suspensions, as though the color had once sprayed everywhere.

I've seen fauna blood. I've seen Fae blood.

This is neither.

My pulse drums in my throat. I swing my gaze east and west, but there's no point. I wouldn't get far against the speed of a centaur. If I hadn't toppled down that ravine, he would have caught me.

Running will only divert Cypress, then grant him an excuse to be harsher. Doubtless, Puck gave him leave to do so, should I misbehave.

The centaur clomps into the glade, with candlelight from the branches dousing us in ochre. The tapers cast a sheen on the central trunk and highlight the interior's wooden cords, the bonds dangling like manacles. I know the makings of traps and snares, and I've handled enough of them decipher what this is. Despite the open threshold, that redwood is no mere alcove. It's a cage.

I cannot panic.

I will not panic.

I have never panicked.

With the elasticity of a feline, Cypress twists in my direction—how does his anatomy manage this?—and plucks me from his back. He deposits my weight unceremoniously, releasing me without care, so that my boots smack the forest floor. I grunt, stumbling in place. My hands find purchase on his hindquarter, but he slaps my palms away.

He must have been a granite bust in his former life, dark skin pulling taut over his countenance. His eyes match the olive hue of his coat, while a complex pattern of olive ink encircles his navel. Lastly, a leather hoop pierces his nostrils, the nose ring visible both at the bottom and where it perforates the bridge.

Out of nowhere, a longbow and quiver materialize, shuddering into being across his spine. It's a classification of wood that must be native to this realm. Scrolls carve through the limbs and nocks, and the arrow fletchings glow like beacons.

He whisks the longbow from his back and an arrow from his quiver, nocks the weapon, and jerks it toward the central tree. "In you go, moppet." I suck in a breath and hold it fast. Then I exhale and turn.

The cage gapes at me, its maw waiting to swallow me whole. I suspect this recess has no door for a merciless reason. It's a torment, flaunting to prisoners a freedom just out of reach, all the while exposing captives to the elements and the wild's carnivores. If a hungry animal happens upon this glade, there's no barrier to discourage the creature from a free meal. Hence, the human blood stains.

My heart thrashes about, but my head stays level. I avoid looking at the crimson flecks and step inside—then yelp as my warden spins me toward him.

This trunk is expansive, able to accommodate Cypress's girth. He's disarmed now, the weapons harnessed as he snatches my arms, thrusts them over my head, and seals the bark cords around my wrists. Some form of natural hinge cracks into place, the cords' tether rising into the redwood's crown, into the darkness.

The shackles force my body to stretch. My gilded leaf bracelet flashes—the only bright thing in this darkness.

I flex my shoulders as best I can. "Is this how you treat all your mortal prey?"

"No," Cypress says, a lattice of shadows cleaving his face into slices.

At which point, he vacates the dank compartment and gallops back the way we came. The percussion of retreating hooves assaults my ears, then fades altogether. My senses perk, attuning themselves to the environment beyond the redwood. Claws scuttle across the branches, and the candles wink from the needled mesh, the flames crackling, fizzing.

The funk of rotted wood conflicts with the incense of conifers. The cords dig into my pulse points, the extensions forcing me to maintain a locked position.

I languish there, violated, confined.

Like an animal. Like the fauna I've saved. Like the ones I haven't saved.

I bow my head, inhaling the aromas of home wafting resiliently from my blouse. Baked bread, windy mornings, and jasmine. Papa Thorne, Lark, and Cove. My eyes clench shut, and I take solace in the scents of my family.

26

So much has happened. So much, in so little time.

Only several days ago, Lark was ambushed by a group of trade poachers intent on doing her harm. She'd had no choice but to flee into the Solitary wild—home of the Solitary Faeries. The intersection of the mountain, forest, and river is forbidden to humans. Regardless, Cove and I had pursued Lark there, desperate to protect her.

The trade poachers had wisely aborted the pursuit, aware that incurring the Faeries' wrath is never worth it. My sisters and I hadn't been so fortunate. Less than a day after we'd rushed home from the ensorcelled realm, we'd received separate messages ordering us back into the wild.

A deer had delivered mine. The animal had appeared out of nowhere, trotting onto my family's property with the note in its mouth.

Mortals don't trespass into Faerie without being punished by the Folk, and refusing their will is fatal. My sisters and I had no alternative but to leave home, knowing we might never return. We'd set forth while our Papa Thorne slept, unaware of our departure.

The moment we'd returned to the borderline, our fates had shifted yet again. Additional letters had awaited us there, addressed to each sister and containing vague instructions about our impending fates.

Ergo, the two leaflets in my possession: the first one dispatched by the deer—which I'd filed in my pack—and the other currently inside my pocket.

My sisters and I hadn't been allowed to share the details of our missives with one another. Worse, we'd been forced to separate—Lark to the mountain, Cove to the river, and me to this forest—each of us sentenced to pay a price, customized by the individual realms. Specifically, the rulers of these realms.

Ruler of the sky. Ruler of the woodland. Ruler of the river.

I still haven't figured out how to translate the second letter and its instructions. Based on my present circumstances, Puck isn't in a hurry to elaborate.

What about Lark and Cove? What has become of them? What are the rulers of the mountain and river doing to my sisters?

The scents of my family ripen. I tuck myself into them while the manacles stretch me to capacity.

Outside the glade, hedges rustle. I tense at the unmistakable signs of approach—a towering frame, a proud stance, and graceful limbs. My chest flutters, but I can't tell if it's from foreboding or anticipation, because I recognize the sound of this particular gait.

I wait on tenterhooks. Then I give up waiting and purse my lips, releasing a tentative whistle into the air. This doesn't work on all of them, but it does work on one special creature back home, one living in my family's animal rescue sanctuary.

This being the land of mystical fauna, I could be very wrong. I could be encouraging a predator. But I refuse to be wrong.

I whistle once more, then gasp. "Oh."

The deer strides up to the trunk in a sprawl of rich, russet fur that defies the darkness. It's taller than usual, twice as statuesque as its mortal counterpart.

And its antlers! The crown splays wider than any set I've ever seen, two panels of solid bone that could scoop up a troll. Shamrocks bloom from the spokes, a garden of sprigs growing naturally.

My lungs empty, releasing a puff of awed breath. Stunning does not do this creature justice.

Realization crops into my head. This is the same messenger who'd delivered the summons into Faerie hours ago, only its antlers hadn't been adorned back then, and its frame hadn't been this large.

The deer must have been glamoured, enchanted to resemble a normal one. As it regards me through cautious onyx pupils, I discern the evidence that she's a female.

In my world, a doe doesn't grow antlers. As recounted in the Fables, they do here.

Not only that, but this great specimen has the bulk of a stag. She stands, a soldier of her world.

I meet her gaze, unable to move lest she disappear. Whatever she sees, it prompts her to enter the cage, ducking as she crosses the threshold, her antler shamrocks trembling. My shackled hands itch to reach out and touch her.

I whistle again. The doe inches nearer and nudges the bark cords with her nose, surveying them. Tentatively, I bow my head in a gesture of submission, and she bumps her cheek against mine.

I lift my gaze to hers, a smile unfurling across my face.

"My, my, my," a smarmy voice says from the entrance. "Your face wasn't stuck that way, after all."

4

My smile drops. A new set of antlers crowd the threshold, oil black among the exterior candlelight. He slouches into the trunk's frame, the picture of nonchalance with his shoulder propped against the bark. I don't require additional light to detect the suave indentations of his lips. I feel it as I do the manacles—sinister, unyielding, and on the brink of cutting off my circulation.

For someone who'd ordered me out of his sight, Puck's presence is quite expedited. Thus, I add impulsiveness to his list of unpardonable qualities.

The doe twists toward the satyr. She welcomes the affectionate hand that pets her coat, his palm gliding over her back. All the while, his head tilts in my direction, his expression shadowed. It doesn't matter what I can or can't see from this vantage point, because the weight of his gaze travels, thickening the air. Like his grin, the satyr's attention is a tangible thing, a root burrowing deeply.

Puck murmurs something to the deer, and the creature vacates the trunk. My heart sinks as I watch her go, the disappointment so acute that I fail to conceal it from present company.

Once the animal's gone, I squeeze my fingers around the shackles. I'm trussed up like a hunk of meat. The bonds lengthen my body, and my blouse pulls taut over my bust, enhancing every lurch of breath, every heave of my breasts. The cubicle's chill brings another fact to my attention—my nipples pebble through the blouse, likely visible to his Fae gaze.

My cheeks bake. Never in my life has my person suffered this kind of exhibition. Certainly not in front of a male. If this knave desires, he can strip me bare, and I'd have no means to stop him.

Would he, though? Satyrs may have a reputation for debauchery, but forcing themselves on others? I haven't heard or read the likes of it. As masters of seduction, they lack the need, much less the inclination to violate their partners. From what I know, his ilk prefers their appetites be reciprocated.

Puck shifts, lambent strands of red blazing in his hair. I keep my snarl in check and focus on the glade beyond the trunk, refusing to entertain his whims.

I will not speak. I will not let him goad me. I will not set that precedent.

"Comfy, luv?" he drawls. "My apologies for depriving you of horizontal accommodations. We ran out of beds."

I will not utter a word.

"It must have been your would-be recitation that sent everyone rushing to the sheets. Such a stimulating performance."

I will not take his bait.

"Though to be honest, I'd expected more from a know-it-all."

My tongue ignites. "I'm not incompetent."

Victorious silence descends, in which the smug Fae beams. If he didn't know one of my weak spots, I've just handed it to him.

I've spent nineteen years honing my willpower, and this is the best I can achieve? What has come over me? Him. That's what. This satyr and his stupid, despicable leer.

I'd counseled my sisters about Fae schemes, insisting Cove and Lark mind their tongues. Yet my own resilience has abandoned me. Twice now, Puck has provoked me to take leave of my senses. For some untold reason, I can't resist sparring with this miscreant, nor justifying myself to him.

"Ah," Puck observes. "I see your plucky little mouth working hard to contain the rest. Go on, let it all out. Tell me about your grievances, about us Faeries mishandling you, about our vile and villainous ways. Better yet, tell me how callous and shallow I am. You'll feel much better, I promise."

"You seem awfully invested in my opinions," I challenge.

Acknowledge it, and he degrades himself. Deny it, and he'll sound defensive, which will place unintentional value on my judgment.

Puck registers the trap and frowns, drumming his fingers on the entryway. "By all means, then. Let's move on. Did Sylvan approach you on her own, or did you beckon her?"

"Who?"

"The doe."

Oh. He must have arrived during the latter part of my interaction with the animal. "Why do you ask? Is coaxing her to my side prohibited?"

"That depends on Sylvan." He takes my measure, perplexed, uncertain. "So, which is it?"

"Both, actually. Our interest in each other was mutual." Yet he remains quiet, contemplating that answer while the bonds threaten to nip my wrists. "I demand—"

"You demand. You insist. You request." Puck rolls his eyes. "If you're about to complain, I'd advise against the impulse. It's not my fault you condemned yourself to this hovel. However, since you're indisposed, why not use this time productively? It's a fine hour to reflect on what incarcerated you here, in The Redwoods of Exile. If you had behaved yourself, you could have stayed in The Wicked Pines with us. Why, we hadn't even served cake yet. What do you think about that?"

"I think you like to hear yourself talk."

"Of course, I do. My voice is irresistibly sexy. It hardens cocks and wets clits in a trice," he boasts. "But enough about my attributes. To your point, can you blame me? If I left you in charge of this conversation, things would get taxing rather quickly, what with your didactic *this* and pedantic *that*. And what a bloody waste of academic skills. You're so motivated to be right, you don't stop to ponder what you'd learn if you were wrong. You know, I can't decide if it's impressive or a travesty that scholastic vanity rather than intellectual curiosity—and copulation, for that matter—whets your appetite."

I fire back, "And I can't decide whether it's tactical or pathetic that you can't get your point across without tying someone up."

"Believe me, anyone tied up in my company will enjoy my points."

"Must everything be about sex with you?"

"Let's just say I'm compensating for us both. I saw how you restrained yourself from gagging at the sight of my naked peers."

I scowl. "Well. I don't need your assistance there."

Puck breaks from his position and saunters into the trunk. Consuming the distance between us gives prominence to his features. The streaks lining his eyelashes, the smattering of white freckles across his nose, and that bonfire of hair.

He halts before me, his leather vest centimeters from brushing the frayed trim of my blouse. The trunk's acoustics magnify my inhalations and his exhalations.

"You're a virgin," he guesses.

Of all the crude, filthy…!

I open my mouth, but he lifts a finger to my lips without making actual contact. "Don't answer me."

I wasn't going to. With his digit in range, my incisors have other ideas. They ache for retaliation—to break skin and watch him bleed. How would he taste? Metallic? Sweet to the point of sickly?

Puck's irises flare with dangerous amusement. "And don't do that, either," he warns. "Never bite unless you're willing to moan."

It could be the clammy air, my parched mouth, or the nearness of his finger to my lips. It could be his threat, so easily tossed into this cubicle. It could be the drip of fear that plonks into my stomach. It could be his clothes on the brink of scratching mine.

Whatever the reason, I tremble. "You don't frighten me."

"The night's young," he intones.

It's undignified to lose my nerve, which is what he's after. The wry slant of his features also states the obvious, and my wild pulse confirms the lie, the beat strong against my neck. I'm sure his tapered ears detect the rhythm. Damn him for calling my bluff.

"What a high-strung thing you are, with so much happening beneath the surface," Puck croons. "Do I detect a note of fear thrumming—" he pretends to play an instrument, his arm sliding and fingers vibrating over invisible strings, "—through your insides?"

"I have no use for fear."

"Even with your sisters at the mountain and river's disposal?"

"Leave them out of this," I snap. "What would you Solitaries even know about having a family?"

Faeries rarely conceive children, so it's hardly a stretch that Puck has no experience with the subject. Yet the comment takes a bite out of his facade, which narrows as he grits out, "And just what the fuck would you know about Solitaries beyond the secondhand shit you've read? Hmm? Do you know what it's like to be a wee Fae caught in a deathtrap?"

A reprehensible prickle crawls up my back. I know what massacre he's referring to. I know that singular, harrowing event like it was yesterday— the day mortals rebelled against Faeries.

Puck tucks his hands behind his back and strolls around me, leaves crushing under his hooves. "You're a stripling, trapped in a snare for days, with iron blistering your flesh until you can't feel your limbs. You hear the pained howls of your fauna kin as they suffer without you, calling for your help. You listen to the wails of other Faeries your age, screaming because they're alone and hurting and petrified out of their minds."

His voice strokes me from the right, raising goosebumps beneath my garments. Rounding on my nape, he says, "And when you can't take those sounds anymore, when your sanity tips over the edge—oh no, magic won't save you from that—you learn to take the blisters instead, because enduring those teeth is the only way to stay alive."

He halts insufferably close behind my left side. "To survive, you let yourself burn. And when you're free, you hunt your enemies back. And when you catch them, you burn them the fuck back."

I gulp. "And if you do that, what have you learned?"

"Such virtue. I'd suggest you bite your righteous tongue, luv."

"It must be a considerable weapon if it needs to be bridled. Either that, or you're more fragile than you seem, taken down by only a few words."

He leans in, a line of hot breath pumping into the shell of my ear. "Who's words? Yours? Or the ones you quote from?"

If we start that debate again, we'll go in circles.

"I'd wager you haven't known the amenities of a real trap until now," Puck continues. "Though, we've barely begun with you and your sisters. *That* is why you have every use for fear."

My breath shakes, rage trembling at the margins. If I cower or show he's gotten to me, it will give him another button to push. "You're wrong. My will is stronger than my fear."

"Are you sure about that? And what about your heart?" the satyr whispers, angling his head toward my cheek. "Shall we test both? See how much your will can take? See how fast your heart can beat? See how much they can withstand?"

"Using glamour would hardly make it a test."

"And here, I thought you prided yourself on facts instead of assumptions. I never mentioned glamour. I leave that tacky business to my kin."

"Then how do you explain what happened to me earlier?"

"Yes, well. That was then, and this is now." He hasn't so much as touched a hair on my head, yet his frame radiates heat against my cold, ruler-stiff spine. "Trust me when I say I have natural methods of getting into your head. I'll steal into that cramped, narrow nook inside you, dabble with what I find, shift things around, and then, when the time is right, lay everything I find on the table." His husky breath glides under my jawline. "Now I'll ask again, should we try each other on for size?"

The buttery leather of his breeches grazes my skirt, our bodies aligning in such an indiscreet way that protests desert me. Any additional movement will drive my backside into his pelvis, the faint contours of which prove him very much male.

Under the blouse, ink mars my lower back. *Do not let him see your tattoo.*

Cove had reminded me of that before I ventured into this realm, though I'd already been cognizant of the danger. I shift my hips inconspicuously, double-checking my skirt's waistband and making sure the blouse is still tucked in—tight, secure.

Modesty aside, Puck stands in fatal proximity to exposing this truth. No matter what this lecherous heathen wants from me, I can't let him discover the marking.

I shuffle, putting an inch between us. "I know myself well enough to predict what I can handle."

Puck closes that inch, sealing it off. His chin hovers over my shoulder, his earrings tapping my shirt. "Always? At all times? In all ways?"

I want to say yes, but I can't speak. With him this near, I've forgotten how my mouth functions.

I hadn't expected him to be this shrewd, given satyrs' legendary appetites for shallower pursuits. To say the least, my loathing for him breaks unrecorded barriers. Dismantling people and breaking them down to their finer points is my territory, and I abhor him for infringing on that. He will pay for this. He will pay dearly.

My captor pulls away. "Not to worry," he taunts, swaggering back into my line of sight. "I was hypothesizing for now. I only fuck with one subject at a time."

My gaze clicks toward the blood staining the trunk's entrance. "I'm not the first mortal who's been here. What did you do to them?"

Vindictive crevices dig into Puck's countenance. He plants himself in front of me, his abdomen almost, *almost* flush against my bust. Oxygen siphons from us both, the fabric of our garments in danger of colliding. "For the last time, mind that tongue," he cautions. "Unless you'd like it removed from your mouth. Maybe that will give you an inkling of what happened to your mortal kin, among other dissections."

Bile washes up my esophagus. "You dismembered them?"

"Nature did that, not I. The wild grows hungry, the fauna roam, and if they wander here, it's not for us Faeries to deny animals their feast. However, the humans who did as they were told and played our game? They spent little to no time in here. I'd suggest you follow their examp—"

My spit hits its target, fluid splashing his face. Puck doesn't flinch, though his eyes squeeze closed at the impact. I've shocked myself, yet I can't bear to repent. As he'd spoken, I'd pictured those captives, villagers I might have known, humans who could have been my sisters, if their fates had been switched.

My body quivers but not with dread. I'm shaking from the satisfaction of watching my spittle dribble down Puck's comely nose. He chuckles without humor, then wipes the saliva with a brush of his thumb.

He considers my actions for a heartbeat, then opens his eyes. Those sable irises fasten on to me, a certain kind of madness intensifying the color. "Now that's more like it," he compliments.

I'm tired. I'm thirsty, tense, confused, and appalled. I'm pulling more muscles by the second, my joints howling in agony. And yes, I'm terrified.

"See luv, you're supposed to accomplish three things while you're our guest," he announces. "Pity for you, jumping straight to the nitty-gritty

36

of Act Two isn't how I work. I desire a preliminary first, an appetizing build-up to the main event. So do me a favor and cooperate, or I'll get sulky. You don't want to see me sulky."

"What I want," I vent, "is to see you in a trap of your own."

"That," he seethes, "is a mistake I only make once."

My attention stumbles across the scars branding his calf, a line of puncture wounds made by iron teeth. A memory surfaces, vivid as though it happened yesterday.

Yes. Puck's rant about being confined is warranted. He's been caught in such a trap before. I was there when it happened.

But he doesn't recognize me. He does not.

Because if he did, he would be treating me worse.

I resume a safer train of thought. He had referred to the revels' setting as The Wicked Pines, whereas he'd called this woodland prison The Redwoods of Exile. Evidently, these locations have hosted their share of human victims. Glamoured or not, captives had either danced to the Faeries' tunes, played their games, or languished in this cell. So if debasement and degradation is what these monsters do to mortal prisoners, what are the rulers of the sky and river doing to Lark and Cove?

"By any chance, do you have a nickname?" Puck inquires.

"You don't need a nickname in order to badger me," I say.

"No, but I'll need it for the ransom letter."

Very funny. "What do you want from me?"

I'm not fooled by his quips. I'm here at the mercy of whatever game he wants to play, should I survive a night in this tree.

Intrigue simmers in his visage. He chews on his lower lip, considering something impertinent. I cement my features, then falter when his hand dives into my pocket, burrowing in and hunting through the fabric.

Even now, his elusive fingers manage to avoid physical contact, fishing through the garment with dexterity. Nevertheless, at this angle, our lips threaten to brush. And the nexus of my thighs lurches in a disturbing way.

Puck's nostrils twitch. His gaze darkens, accelerating my pulse.

Finally, he withdraws the envelope containing his welcome missive and exhibits it between his middle and index fingers. "I think you've gotten a hint of what I want."

His lips crook into a devious grin. The sight plucks at a hot, sensitive place inside me—a place that yearns to tear him to shreds.

Perhaps he's a mind reader, because he smiles. "Lovelies."

A coterie of nymphs materializes outside the trunk. Curvy females and sinewy males, all half-dressed in flora confections and wearing laurel wreaths of yarrow, peonies, and other blossoms. The Faeries traipse from between the redwoods, including the nymph in that yellow petal dress, the hilt of a dagger protruding from an open case at her hip. She's the one who'd whispered to Puck during the revels.

She and her clan linger, awaiting Puck's instruction. He addresses them while keeping his eyes tacked to mine. "Make sure she's ready for me."

5

He vanishes before I can question his meaning. The nymphs chortle behind lips the colors of parakeet feathers and slink into my cell, whiffs of cardamom permeating their earthen garments as they fiddle with my hair. Next, they toy with my blouse collar while uttering "*Pretty*" and "*Pitiful.*"

Verdant green stains one female's cheeks, the pigment suffusing as she appraises my body and pats my backside. One of my sisters would have tried to bite the Fae or stomp on the female's toes, while the other sister would have gasped and recoiled. I react by not reacting at all. The nymph's menacing giggle scrapes my ears as she grabs my chin and twists it so that I face forward.

To my relief, the unruly clan tinkers with the bark cords.

To my astonishment, the restraints take effort to unlock.

When the shackles loosen, I buckle with a pained grunt, my limbs as flimsy as strings. The nymphs catch me and pretend to dote in what I presume to be Faeish, cooing and simpering with mockery.

The coterie escorts me out of the glade and back to The Wicked Pines. When we arrive, all traces of Puck's party are gone, including the stench of fornication and the nip of cloves and pine. The satyr's thronelike chair has been carted away, too.

Only the natural environment remains, untainted and broader than I'd realized. The area is vast, a series of groves ringed in evergreens and connected by lanes. The nymphs usher me through the hub's enclosure. On the way, I recall the profane scene I'd witnessed here and my subsequent humiliation.

We bypass several hollows before slipping between a curved fence of pine saplings. Stepping through the entrance, I frown in confusion. The trees encircle the perimeter, and candlelight drips gold across a central well burrowed into the ground. Extra flickering tapers outline the depression, its fluid contents glistening.

It appears to be a pool.

Make sure she's ready for me.

The next thing I know, the gaggle of Faeries swarms me and begins peeling off my clothes, boots, and socks. I sputter and attempt to bat them away, which earns me a scolding and a lot of tut-tuts. At least, that's what their tones suggest, since I can't understand their language.

A set of fingers unties the low ponytail at my nape. My blouse flies from my head. My arms flounder to cover myself, but one of the females switches to the mortal tongue, lecturing me to behave. My skirt and leggings puddle to the floor, yanked off my hips by who knows which of them. My thighs pebble as I stand there in nothing but a thin shift, my bare soles pressing into the spongy earth.

"Wait." I hop backward and slide off my gilded leaf bracelet. I raise the trinket, presenting it to their bright gazes. "Who wants it?"

The offering holds the Faeries at bay. They admire the bauble, their irises sparkling with greed. The one in the yellow petal dress—presumably the leader—lifts a jaunty eyebrow. "Rather generous, mortal. To what do we owe this gesture?"

"It has enough leaves for each of you," I barter. "If you give me a moment of privacy, I can disrobe myself."

To this, she rolls her eyes. "Is that all?"

"How quaint," a snide male remarks.

"Not only plain but prude," a female adds, disappointed. "Whatever does Puck find so marvelous about her?"

Envy laces another male's words. "Ceremonious or not, he's never asked us to bathe any of them before."

"That's because the others didn't stink of purity," their leader concludes. "Her starchy innocence is unmistakable, which makes her a challenge. Satyrs enjoy that, so it's no wonder he wants to pamper this one first."

"Do you want it or not?" I ask, jingling the bracelet.

Frankly, I don't care what made Puck order my grooming. All I care about is whether they'll accept my offer. It pains me to relinquish the bracelet, but whatever the price, I can't let them strip off my undergarments.

The nymphs give me wry looks that ooze judgment. Fine, let them think me a puritan. It wouldn't be the first time I've been called a prissy spinster, and it's best they don't suspect I have other reasons.

At last, the petal nymph mutters something in Faeish and snatches the bracelet. She tosses it to her companions, and they pick apart the embellishments as though the jewelry's made of paper, distributing the ornamental leaves amongst themselves.

They keep their word and exit the clearing, giving me time to undress on my own. I wait an extra few minutes, then check the perimeter. I'll have to trust my senses that no one's spying. I discard the shift, my breasts toppling from the material. I make quick work of my drawers, telling myself I'd had no choice. It was either sacrifice a bauble, or they would spot my tattoo.

If the Faeries were to see it, they would tell him.

A lump swells in my throat, and my traitorous eyes sting. My sisters would have been the first ones to insist I do what it takes to keep the tattoo secret. All the same, Lark and Cove gave me that bracelet.

I suck up the despair. The loss belongs to me alone, not these hellions. I won't allow them to trigger it.

Steam curls from the pool, bubbles squirting beneath the surface. These Solitaries wouldn't go to the trouble of drowning me in a vortex or dunking me into a toxic pit. Not yet.

After folding my clothes and setting them on the grass, I dip a toe into the water. Ripples expand across the surface, reflecting the stars and candle flames. The temperature is overly warm, overly indulgent.

Resentment tightens my face. Back home, we have a bathing chamber. It's called a creek. Although it runs through our property, the water's icy in autumn, winter, and most of spring.

I'm grimy at present but hardly unsanitary, and I'd washed myself thoroughly at home this morning. Make sure I'm ready for him, indeed.

I submerge myself. I keep everything below my shoulders engulfed, the pool's depth and my stunted height shielding me from prying eyes. My palms scoop water into my mouth. Like a fountain, I spit out the liquid, which is something Lark would do.

A melody strays into the hollow. The gentle tune hums from a distant instrument, a stringed one like the others. Except this instrument sounds bottomless, something grown from the earth. Though remote, the notes chart a path to this enclosure as if the instrument knows where to go. My body sighs, ligaments softening as the water laps against my clavicles.

Suddenly, the music goes silent, retreating like a wisp of smoke. An instant later, the nymphs return, having lost patience, the confiscated leaves of my bracelet nowhere in sight. Perhaps the Faeries had hoarded them.

They skip into the hollow and kneel around me. At the sight of the males, I stoop deeper into the bath. One of them scoffs at my modesty.

A tall phial and brush perch on the ground, the glass vessel containing a mint-hued liquid. A female uncorks the fluid and pours the contents onto the bristles, then proceeds to scour me clean. The warm piquancy of brown sugar curls into my nose. The Faeries massage my hair, suds frothing into the roots, then run their wet fingers over my arms.

Being naked, soaked, and touched constricts my lungs. Yet my joints unwind, my eyes flutter, and a sigh coils up my throat. I fasten my lips together, preventing the sound from escaping.

They tend to everything above water, brushing my fingernails and elbows. I take the opportunity to wash below the surface, depriving them of the chance to grope intimate places they have no business going near. Still, heat gushes into my face as I lave myself in their presence.

Years of hunting have strengthened my reflexes. Traveling with a particular faction of hunters as a child has taught me to move with stealth and without detection. I grab the towel the Faeries offer me and slosh out of the water, wrapping the cloth around my bust and hips before fully exiting the pool.

They sidle backward in a flurry, having failed to catch sight of my tattoo. One of them glides a comb through my hair, the teeth drying the strands instantaneously. From thin air, a male produces a suede dress the color of dark, ripe cherries. Aside from the material, the practical leather clasps, and the long sleeves, this frock has the sort of outlandish design one wears to mortal sacrifices or devil worships.

I scrutinize the square neckline. Most of all, I resent the shade. Only strumpets wear red.

Following my undergarments, the clique of Faeries wraps, binds, cinches, buckles, and hooks me into the dress. The material hugs my bust and flares below my waist, allowing my limbs to move freely.

The nymphs return my cloak to me, the garment also appearing from nowhere. After being forced to remove it at Puck's behest earlier, the cloak's presence is most welcome. But as for the rest of my original attire, the Faeries collect the items while ignoring my objections.

They pick the hawthorn berries from my skirt pocket—"Amusing," one remarks—and toss the morsels to the ground. The nymphs crush the berries under their feet before I have a chance to protest. Although the kernels had failed to guard me against enchantment, I'd been hoping it was a fluke.

The second missive I'd received before entering Faerie rests in the other pocket. Recognizing it, they drop the envelope back into the skirt. Presumably, my clothes will end up in a pile beside my supply pack, wherever that is.

Well. If they can steal things from me, I can steal things from them.

Cove used to be a pickpocket before joining our family. While Lark and I taught her our own survival tricks, she taught us one of hers. Channeling those lessons, I exercise a sleight of hand while the nymphs primp me.

Since their leader has been so hospitable and friendly, I swipe the petal nymph's dagger from its case at her hip. Without my crossbow, an alternative helps.

By the time the leader glances my way, I've got her blade—a serrated design—tucked into the folds of my skirt. It's not ideal, but this frock lacks pockets, and I'm not as skilled as Cove, who can maneuver items anywhere on her person, with targets none the wiser. Not that she engages in such crimes any longer.

The Faeries provide fresh socks, along with my boots and cloak. While donning the footwear, I use the laces to affix the knife against my ankle.

The clique pushes me from the hollow in a fit of well wishes. I totter onto the lane flanked by pines. The mirth evaporates, and when I swerve around, the Solitaries are gone.

I wheel toward the vacant trail. What now?

I pad along the route, winding my way through the evergreens. Fog strokes the needle branches. Roots worm in and out of the soil.

Passing one hollow reveals a trio of leprechauns playing a game that involves tossing acorns onto a grid cauterized into the earth. When one of them misses, the gang ribs him until he guzzles liquid from a tankard. Then they spot me through the entrance, their scruffy jaws and beards shifting to accommodate their grins.

"Comely dress, lass," one of them jeers.

"Care to play a few rounds?" another invites.

I march away, increasing my pace as they cackle. They may as well be coughing up thorns, the rasping sound still cleaving my ears.

My feet spirit me around a bend, my boots crunching a weed. There's no telling what's expected of me, or where I'm supposed to go, but I doubt joining those varmints is on the agenda.

The Wicked Pines proves navigable. I tap into my memory and back-track in the direction the nymphs had led me.

In another grove, brownies tidy their surroundings, buffing roots, plumping pillows, and sprinkling petals on the ground. They seem to be preparing the space for a dalliance between lovers.

In yet another hollow, a female dryad strums a lyre while a male faun sways before her, his gyrating posterior attracting her ravenous gaze.

In a third niche, a female satyr lounges naked while a centaur paints her.

I avert my eyes for the rest of the journey, until a groan reaches my ears. My head leaps toward the sound, my attention stumbling past the entrance of a grove where a tent pitches off the ground. I trip in place, speechless. Three Fae males lavish attention on a female within the tent, two of them suckling her nipples while the third member grunts, his body flush atop hers.

Her thighs splay around his buttocks, clinging and rolling. The female's hand dips between the male and herself. "Take out your prick so I can fuck it."

I gasp, but they're too busy to hear it. How can she possibly sustain all three of them? What female has that energy? She'd chafe and hobble for days.

A hot stone settles low in my belly. I can't move, can't look away.

"If they catch you watching, they'll assume you'd like to join," a rascally tenor says.

That voice skates up my spine. I whip toward Puck, his robust figure looming inches behind me, his hair burning through the darkness. Aided by the boughs' candlelight, my gaze sketches his leather pants, shaded a pecan brown, with a vertical gap cutting through outer seams. Thongs cinch up the sides, the bare skin of his limbs and the slopes of his hipbones flexing through the netting.

I scowl. "I wasn't watching. I was—"

He tilts his head. "Have you ever wanted to?"

"Wanted what?" I balk. "Wanted to watch?"

"Wanted to join," he clarifies. "Have you ever wanted to join with another? Join in a pleasure fest? A feast for the senses? A veritable upheaval of the mind and body?"

Certainly not. Yet if I answer negatively, that will inspire him to no good. And if I lie and say yes, he'll call me out.

I hardly require a mirror to know a glare is burrowing into my face. This satyr has a way of bumping me from one emotion to the next.

The moans escalate, taking on a speedy, gravely cadence. I swallow, and Puck's eyes land on my neck, following the contortion.

Raunchy noises resound from behind, the female crying out in bliss. Whatever those males are doing to her, Puck has an unhampered view. I steel myself and prepare to leave the scene, but he dips his head, his inflection as rich as fertile ground. "Is that a no?"

My eyes dart to the jutting shadows extending across the ground. "Debauchery isn't on my list of priorities. I'm a busy mortal."

"What about sensuality? Too busy for that?"

"It's the same thing."

"Take it from a satyr, it isn't. I'd wager my next meal on it."

"Your next meal is hardly a gamble."

His breath coasts over my mouth, the contact throwing sparks across my lips. "That depends on what I'm eating."

Fables eternal. I...I...

I'm not sure what we're talking about anymore, whether it's the proper definition of intimacy or a new kind, one that brushes my thighs and nudges them apart. His is the type of mouth that makes lovers plead for things they hadn't expected, entreaties such as *Faster* and *Please*.

"I gather you don't care for satyr-centric Fables, then," Puck continues. "You know..." He cups his mouth and whispers conspiratorially, "... the smutty ones."

I lift my gaze to his, my eyebrows slamming together. "Is that supposed to be uproarious?"

"Are you laughing uproariously?"

Never mind. "As to the matter of physical appetites, I assure you, there's a disparity between what satyrs like and what I like."

At least, there must be. Inexperienced as I am, I'm certain his tastes would scarcely align with my own.

Puck's timbre seeps into my pores. "How lucky for me to be in the presence of such knowledge. Someday, I'll have to pick your brain, insist that you elaborate on that disparity, seeing as you know so much about it."

In my periphery, the female's shadow arches off the ground, her rhythmic bleats intensifying while the males warble in Faeish. They all sound as if they're being pushed through a sieve, coarse and fragmented.

Pressure toughens in my navel. A savory flavor builds on my tongue, and my pulse leaps with restlessness. Yet I'm unsure if the candid scene is to blame, or if it's the satyr in front of me causing such havoc.

"I know what you're thinking, luv," Puck murmurs. "You know that I know, and I know that you know. But what are you feeling? Shame? Repugnance? Or something else? What might that something else be, hmm? Delicacy? Confusion?"

"You don't know me. And why are we tarrying here? This is—" I wave in the group's general direction, "—is none of our business."

"You're in Faerie," he says, as if that explains everything.

And I suppose it does when it comes to this region. Woodland Faeries exploit their sexual escapades. Amongst their kind, they consider exhibition and observation an enticement, not a trespass.

Puck's right. If this group catches me, they'll simply keep doing what they're doing. They might do it more thoroughly, for shock value. Though, they don't need to test my resilience or endurance. Puck's already accomplishing that. I turn, ready to flay him with a comeback—but he's disappeared. Relief and frustration clash as I evacuate the scene, abandoning the moans and stalking along the path. I glance left and right, following the candlelight spilling onto the route.

Puck pops out from a sapling. "Now you see him."

I skitter back as he evanesces again. A few steps farther, and he peeks around a tree. "Now you don't." Once more, he vaporizes.

I've played hide-and-seek with my sisters, but this is far less innocent. I glare, yet for some reason, the sensation of being watched, of being tracked, trickles down my vertebrae. I traverse the passage, listening for his weight and the faintest break in nature.

When I reach the setting where the debauchery had taken place, I halt at the grove's threshold and scan the area. Puck's silhouette swings into view. I withhold a yelp, validated when I stand my ground.

In the firelight, he grins. "So you play games, after all."

That wasn't a game. That was flamboyance.

I plop my fists on my hips. "You enjoy being a character. One might say you rely on hijinks, clever turns of phrases, and words, words, words to make yourself essential to a scene. I wonder what would happen if you didn't try so hard and actually kept your mouth closed for more than three minutes."

Puck stares at me. A flash of resentment slices through his pupils. Or it might be intrigue.

He walks backward while bobbing a finger, luring me into the hollow. Though the prospect of entering this den makes me cringe, I step inside and survey the location, once filled to the brim with nudity and music.

Two chalices stand on a tripod table, red liquid quivering inside the basins. A single chair perches beside the table, as though Puck had known I'd prefer to stand. He takes his time sauntering to the refreshments. Lifting one of the cups to his mouth, he drinks while studying me.

Lowering the chalice, he swipes his tongue across his lips. "There," he announces. "I counted four minutes without me saying a word. I must confess, I've impressed myself. This calls for a celebration. Care for a drink, luv? It'll relax your tight muscles."

I cross my arms, the cherry red bodice straining across my chest. "I want my clothes back."

Puck sighs and drops into the chair. "So many demands from a mortal."

"And I want my weapons back. And my supply pack, for that matter."

"Anyone ever tell you that when it comes to Faerie business, you should never hit the ground running?"

"None of my acquaintance," I say. "Though the Fable, *When a Fae Gets Cocky*, alludes to it. I've read that one five times."

"A second ago? I was being rhetorical."

"A second after that? I made up the title."

His lips twitch. "Such cheek. I do fancy smart asses. Couldn't you have made up that title earlier, when I asked for a story?"

I grit out, "By rhetorical, may I assume you're too lazy to formulate an inquiry worthy of debate?"

"Me, lazy? Hogwash." Puck sets down the chalice and reclines in the seat, linking his ankles atop the table. Now that we're idle in brighter shafts of light, his gaze lands on my arm, and he frowns momentarily. "What happened to your bracelet?"

The nymphs happened, that's what. But with the long sleeves, how does he know I'm not wearing it in the first place? And what makes him think it's any of his concern?

When I make no reply, he dismisses the matter and links his arms behind his head, the muscles bunching like a cliff range. "You'll get those cute weapons back in due time, along with your pack—if you can locate them, seeing as you'll need those perks for our merry game." He appraises my dress from its hem to its neckline, where the tops of my breasts inflate from the material. "Notwithstanding, if you play in that, you'll get dirty."

"What game?"

"You read the letter."

Mind the trees. Touch the roots. Hunt your fears. Chase your desires. Miss your target. Hit your mark.

I stuff the reply he deserves back down my throat. "It lacked details."

"Bloody true. And there are plenty of those. You know, details." He wiggles his fingers as if speaking about pixies. "By the way, how badly do you want to know? Should I go slowly or tear off the bandage in one swoop? Very well, your deadpan expression says it all. So here it is: You're to participate in the hunt."

A hunting expedition? That doesn't make sense. It's too simple.

"A Fae hunt," I repeat.

"Is there any other kind?"

"With Faeries. I'm to participate in a hunt with Faeries."

"Including myself. Sounds like a riot, doesn't it? Say yes, and a-hunting we will go."

And now he sounds cryptic. "What are you hunting?"

He smiles and tips his head. "Why you, of course."

6

Word by word, I dissect his answer. I follow the shape, depth, and direction of Puck's meaning like a set of paw prints. But it's no use. This particular trail belongs to a crafty predator that's too far ahead of me.

The pines bristle, making candlelight thrash from the branches. Puck transforms as he had when we were last here, right before he'd ordered me away. The Fae regards me neither smugly, nor mischievously. Indeed, he doesn't seem regaled by his own announcement.

Shadows catch the left side of his countenance, forming a black half-moon, while firelight strokes the right side, enameling the slopes of his jaw. The contrast splits his face in two, so that I can't tell which half is a greater threat.

I prefer it when his riddles fill the void. His silence is deadlier.

Me. These monsters are going to hunt me.

The irony is profound. My brain trips over itself, wondering if I've missed a crucial detail, a sign that he recognizes me. An eye for an eye. A form of payback. Star peddlers and fortune tellers might call this karma, if I believed in such nonsense. That's Cove's obsession, not mine.

Still, I search Puck's visage for recognition and find no proof.

I consider three potential reactions to his news. Cove would retreat a step, as though the words have reached out to snatch her. Lark would stride forward and dare those words to make contact, to fight her. I take the neutral option and regard the satyr placidly.

At which point, peevishness hangs off his face like a curtain. He wants a stronger response from me. I suspect that's what he's used to.

Inevitably, the Fae's countenance shifts, his features lifting at the prospect of a challenge. "My, my, my. Speechlessness doesn't go with your mouth, luv."

On the contrary, I'll never let him render me speechless. "What are you hoping to accomplish by substituting my name with a false endearment?"

"I call everyone *luv*, luv. It doesn't mean you're special. But if it makes you feel any better, call me whatever you'd like. My name rhymes with some rather colorful options."

"No, thank you. I would rather be called Juniper."

"Gimme a reason, and if I hate it, I'll consider your request."

I squint at his logic. But thus far, when have I said something that he hasn't flipped inside out?

Yes, there are more practical concerns at this juncture. No, I'm not there yet. Plus, there's nothing wrong with asking him to address me properly. It's an important request. It's my name, for Fable's sake. I don't like the sound of it whittled down, its syllables reduced to something less significant, less worthy of being taken seriously—all with a single, callous swat of his tongue.

But Puck shrugs. "Down to merry business, then. Only don't interrupt. I get cranky when someone interrupts."

It's unfortunate that we have this, or anything, in common. "What do you want from me?"

"Three tasks." Puck retrieves his chalice and swirls the contents. "Three to be completed before the Middle Moon Feast. What's Middle Moon, you ask? You'll find out later." He slides his index finger across the vessel's rim but doesn't drink the contents. "The point is, we'll be hosting that celebration with you as the centerpiece."

"In other words, the toy."

"Whatever. To win, you must attend the feast and show you've completed the tasks." He continues rotating the liquid, teasing flavors to the surface. "Though fair warning: If you win, we won't like you very much."

I study his digits flexing around the goblet's neck. "What tasks?"

"Number one: Hunt an animal that can't be hunted. Number two: Tell a Fable about that animal—one we Faeries have never heard before.

Number threeeee," he enunciates when I try to speak, "prove the tale's moral is true. Simple."

Like hell does this sound simple. "I thought you said you'd be hunting me."

"I did say that, didn't I," he muses. "We'll be hunting you. In turn, you'll be hunting the animal. The goal is to see who succeeds in catching their quarry first. As you can imagine, stopping you from succeeding will give us quite the motivation."

Bile rushes up my throat. "I don't hunt out of cruelty or sport."

"Really? Then I must have you confused with another type of mortal."

The dress's clasps pinch into my flesh. "I wasn't involved in The Trapping, nor am I a trade poacher."

Not anymore. As such, the statement has a rancid aftertaste, like it's been sitting on my tongue for too long.

Puck stares, dissecting my words. "Good answer," he says. "By the way, Faeries hunt for food and furs, not sport or play. Since I'm in a merry mood, I won't take offense to your assumption."

"This makes no sense! You even call it a game. Hunting an animal this way sounds very much like sport to me."

"That's because you're clueless."

"I'm *what*?"

"You're the game for us, not the animal," he corrects. "We're not about to let you catch it. Though if you do, we'll feast on the creature and return the remainders to the earth, from whence it came. That's respect for you; it honors the lifecycle and prevents the animal from dying in vain.

"And the game itself? What it is, how it's played, and who decides varies from the mountain, to the forest, to the deep. All Faeries target humans for trespassing in our realm—among other historical grievances—but in The Solitary Forest? We don't choose the punishment, nor the game. The woodland does."

I scoff. "Regardless, why would the forest create this hunt to begin with?"

"I'm afraid that's your fault. The games are unique for each person," Puck says. "The forest knows your fears and customizes itself to that. That way, you're less likely to defeat us. We did talk about fear, didn't we, luv?"

"Stop calling me that."

"Certainly. Just as soon as you stop wanting me to stop," he singsongs.

One way or another, I will prove him wrong on that account. One way or another, I will get him to trip on my name like a stone. I'll get him to stumble, to slip up when he least expects it, like an accident, like a hard fall, not knowing what's hit him. One way or another, I'll get him to make this mistake.

He holds up a finger. "Disclaimers, rules, etcetera, etcetera. First: If you fail in any of these tasks, you lose. Second: Once you've officially guessed the animal, you can't change your mind and target a different one. Third: When you've guessed that animal, you must take action on its life."

To recover from that last rule, I cling to thoughts of Lark and Cove. "Are you actually going to let me change clothes first?"

"Why? Don't you like suede?"

I balk, realizing only one of us is being sarcastic. "Wait. You can't seriously expect me to hunt in this frock, nor in this color."

"I thought you were a fast learner."

That's not the point, and he knows it. "I'll stick out like a sore thumb to any quarry. I need a palette that will camouflage me."

The satyr perches his lips on the chalice and tips back the fluid, his neck pumping. He watches me watch him, then places the vessel on the table. "Isn't that what bushes are for?"

Every part of me compresses, the skin pulling taut across my face. "In other words, you didn't choose this garment randomly."

"Perhaps not at the moment. But at one point, I did. Things always begin randomly, for that's their origin."

"They're random until they're not. Then they became part of a diabolical plan."

"Are we philosophizing?"

"Unless you have an objection to females with brains."

But Puck's distracted. With my cloak split down the middle, his irises chart a graphic path over the swells of the dress, down to its hem swatting the underbrush.

His attention elicits a drastic effect, jeopardizing my concentration. And scratch that. He knows what he's doing, looking at me as though the textile's edible. Suddenly, the garment feels too thin, too flimsy, too much, and far too little.

"You should wear red more often," he suggests. "I'm told cherries ripen over time."

I dislike moot subjects as much as I dislike loose ends. "When is the Middle Moon Feast?"

He pretends to mull that over. "Ten days from now. A sexy number for any game, don't you think?"

"How many humans have disagreed with you?"

"Find their skeletons and ask them, unless The Sleuth of Bears got to those as well."

Abominable, contemptible demon! His nonchalance turns my stomach to acid. So this is what becomes of the mortals who don't end up shackled in The Redwoods of Exile. My horror is absolute, a wad of hatred settling in my gut.

Ten days is all I have, and if I've interpreted this trickster correctly, they've hidden my archery and supplies someplace in this weald for me to ferret out.

"I'll need water," I persist.

"Oh?" Puck contemplates. "But shouldn't a bookish huntress be able to find what she needs without it being given to her? And now, who said the most desirable things aren't here, within your reach? Don't underestimate what's right in front of you."

I sidestep that riddle. "I'll need my pack."

"And your notebook, of course."

My knuckles curl. When I was prepping to come here, I'd considered bringing my copy of the Book of Fables—an annotated edition that Papa Thorne gifted to me on my thirteenth birthday. But the tome had been too hefty, and I'd had the Fables memorized anyway.

"What is mine, is mine," I say. "I shouldn't have to forage for my things. I need them back."

Puck rises and swaggers toward me, hooking his hands behind his back. "How badly?"

I phrase my reply with care. "You confiscated my possessions. How badly would you like to owe me?"

The satyr consumes the distance between us. He pauses when several inches remain and smiles, a crease digging into his cheek. "Smart girl."

My favorite compliment. Yet I long to scrub it from his mouth before it corrodes into an insult.

"When do we start?" I ask with trepidation.

He smirks again, the question dangling at the end of a noose. Then Faeish unspools from his tongue. *"Joman ánen mede feidimenninaer."*

The crystalline language threads through the boughs. Silhouettes crop up in the darkness, animal figures as statuesque as monuments. The herd of deer stands proud and tall—taller than animals should be capable of, as tall as the doe from earlier. The one called Sylvan.

They form a crescent around us, their antlers sprouting various symbols of nature. Wisteria blooms from one set, stems from another. Seedlings encrust a stag's points. Atop the crown of a hind, a fountain of droplets spills from the tips. From the spiked rack of a buck, flames lick the air.

Pages from the Book of Fables flip through my mind, made manifest in this grove. Eyes cut from mineral rocks. Tails longer than those of mortal deer, several cascading to the ground.

At last, I'm no longer on the outside of a Fable. I'm inside, tucked within a living, breathing book.

This is real. This is anything but.

Sylvan idles in the center. Her gaze catches mine, stealing my breath. But then her image blurs, wet around the edges.

A finger dabs at a spot beneath my lower eyelids. I flinch, and the world solidifies once more. Puck ruins the trance, appearing in front of me and blocking the fauna from sight. He withdraws his hand from my face, pulling back to reveal a bead of saltwater trembling on his finger.

That tear belongs to me. Not to him. Never to him.

His eyes sketch the translucent globe, engrossed in the sight. He's so absorbed, it takes him a while to speak. "I'd like to see more of these from you, luv."

I won't let that happen—ever. "I don't cry."

Puck's attention flickers back to me. "Oh, but you will." His voice tilts upward, as though he's been waiting for this moment. "You excelled at weeping once. Didn't you?"

My gaze snaps to his. The freckles skipping across his nose. The wily set of his chin. The biting scent of pine and the spice of cloves wafting from him. Most of all, his tonal voice—the familiarity of it.

I hear the implication, loud and clear. Yes, I may not cry. But yes, I know how. And yes, this satyr has seen me weep before. And yes, I was wrong to assume. He knows. He *knows* who I am.

He remembers me.

That's not all. More figures step into the hollow. Faeries lean against trunks. Brownies pop from under bushes and bare their canines. The petal nymph and her clique drape themselves like scarves across low, looping branches. Leprechauns and dryads crowd in on us, armed with weapons both familiar and unfamiliar—bows, staffs, hammers, axes, sawlike blades, and throwing stars.

That young Fae who'd glamoured me earlier sneers, his marten tail swishing, orange eyes glittering.

Cypress stands abreast of him, archery hitched across his back, his face as stony as a cliffside.

Realization dawns. The nymphs. The bath. The primping. Puck's reference to ceremony and his obsession with making every moment into an official occasion. His instructions to "Make sure she's ready for me."

After arguing with him about the dress, I had assumed the hunt would commence in the next few hours or at dawn. I had anticipated a specific juncture in the near future. But Puck grins without humor, implying I'm nothing but a silly mortal know-it-all who should have, well, known better.

The satyr cups his mouth and leans toward me. His mercenary breath caresses my ear, his voice as slitted as a paper cut. "Oh, luv. Did you really think I wouldn't recognize you?"

A chalky taste fills my mouth. Viciousness aside, it's even clearer why he's doing this. A long time ago, I gave him a reason to.

Puck straightens. He catches a yew-wood longbow and quiver someone tosses his way, the arrows clattering like teeth. Harnessing the archery, he says, "Well, here I am, feeling generous and nostalgic." The satyr draws out the last word, emphasizing it with a prolonged curl of his tongue. "Since I like the color red, you've earned a favor more valuable than your supplies." He quirks an eyebrow. "We'll give you a head start."

His cult shuffles forward, eager looks brightening their miens.

My feet inch backward, heedful, careful. When encountering a predator, never turn and flee, for that will mark you as prey.

I suck in a breath—then swerve and run.

The pines scrape my elbows and dress as I crash through the grove and spill into the timberland. From behind, a cluster of noises carries to the treetops, the boisterous howl chilling my bones. It's a wild call, the sort hounds deliver to their pack, to signal a target.

In this case, it's the call of Faeries. It's the litany of pursuit.

They're coming for me.

7

The earth shudders beneath me. The wet slap of feet and percussion of hooves grow louder, gaining momentum not three milliseconds after my departure. Although Puck had kept his word, he hadn't specified how much of a head start I'd actually get.

Pine needles rain from above, tapping my shoulders on the way down. Boughs creak and bob, as if bearing a succession of individual weights. Silhouettes flit in and out of the heights, racing across the branches, jumping from limb to limb.

I sprint ahead, vaulting into the woodland. The haunted teals, sportive greens, and glaring golds of this weald flank me in shawls of color. The evergreens spread out, oozing gilded light from the candles. Despite the illumination, I'm lost in a void, my breath wheezing through the night.

My first concern is a practical one: Don't stop running.

My second concern is a passionate one: Let him try and catch me.

The howling sharpens, mutating into whistles and heckles. They disband and spread out while arrows arc from every direction, cutting the air into ribbons.

They're enjoying this.

My ears prickle, interpreting the catcalls. The leprechauns are a raspy bunch, their hollers sawing through the timbers. The dryads' croak, expansive and weathered. The brownies laugh, plying the land with gratified little chirps. As for the lithesome Faeries, their calls lash like whips.

But which noise belongs to him? What does he sound like while in pursuit?

I strain to hear the roguish thump of cloven hooves, but the rhythmic, galloping stomp of Cypress drowns out the opportunity. I twist to gauge their distance, detecting nothing. Veering back around, I skitter on my heels as a pair of lime eyes glow inches from me. The creature hisses and slides out of sight, its claws scratching high into the nearest pine, the fibers of its tail bristling.

Only in this land would such a critter flash a bushy tail ringed in lime fur to match its irises. Only in this land would its sibilant vocal cords overlap and multiply, reverberating like cymbals.

Raccoon? Rabies?

Ridiculous. Fae fauna do not breed such ailments.

Taken off guard, I discover a crescent wall of rock suddenly encircling me. It's a cul-de-sac. The undergrowth jostles, the creepers rattle, and ethereal purrs invade the woods.

"Juniperrrr," they sing.

"Oh lovely, Juniperrrr."

"Come out, come out and play with us, Juniperrrr."

A cold sweat pools behind my ears. I glance at the evergreen where the critter had disappeared, the branches dense with needles and cones. Lark gave me precisely three lessons in climbing. My sister, a former chimney sweep who'd grown up scaling the sooty, congested lungs of flues, had taught me the fundamentals of balancing my weight and lodging my toes into the right crevices.

More heckling. More echoes of *"Juniper, Juniper, oh, Juniper!"*

My nails and toes burrow into the clefts. I clamp on to the trunk and heft myself up, up, up. The hooded cloak drags behind me, swinging like a curtain. An offshoot snags on my skirt, yanking me in place. I may as well be scaling a cheese grater. I bite back a yelp, my wrists flaring with heat where skin must have peeled away, raw flesh stinging beneath.

I don't make a noise, can't make a noise, won't make a noise. Instead, I keep going, conjuring Lark's lessons, her tips about moving quickly and safely.

Boughs multiply around me. Again, those lime eyes find mine and then swivel away.

If it had felt threatened, its choppers would have severed my thumbs by now. I flop belly-first onto a limb, my chest pumping.

I'm not afraid, I'm not afraid, I'm not—

A cluster of footfalls and hoofbeats gather below. I freeze, my limbs tightening around the bough, my eyes widening as I register the distance between me and the forest floor. It hadn't seemed like a towering climb. Am I truly suspended that high?

Outlines swoop into the impasse, then stalk around the tree's base. A laurel wreath and mint-colored braids, impervious to the dark. A scruffy beard. A floral gown. Talons and tails. Orange forehead markings.

The edge of an axe flashes. A staff hacks through vegetation.

Like a novice, I had forgotten to cover my tracks. Not that it would have made a difference against the Faes' honed senses, their eyes cleaving through the darkness. A mortal would not last a day against that—not unless that mortal were a skilled huntress. One who'd grown up perfecting the art of soundless movement, detecting every shift in nature while keeping out of sight, unnoticed by roaming creatures.

A petite human who knows how to avoid a predator's notice. A person who knows how to strike first.

I fill my lungs with oxygen and scuttle backward, folding myself into the evergreen's skeleton. Of all the members of my family, I'm the only one with patience. And no, this isn't me bragging. It's a fact.

I scan the movements below, identifying two nymphs, one youth, and a leprechaun. The petal nymph is among them. Also, the youth with his marten tail. The clan mutters to one another in Faeish, then slinks away.

Five minutes later, they haven't double-backed. I sag—and regret it.

A lone body struts into the area. It pauses, glances around, and draws the same conclusion as the others, comprehending that I'm not down there.

Yet the figment stays put, then tilts his head toward the pine. I duck further into the mesh while my visitor makes himself comfortable and leans against the trunk. From this vantage point, a rail of antlers loops from his head, catching in a shaft of muted light.

My heart thrashes about. Old and recent memories collide.

Did you really think I wouldn't recognize you?

He'd known. From the moment he caught me spying on his orgy, he'd known who I was.

"Youuuu-whoooo," that impish voice sings. "It's no use, luv."

I disagree.

Silence permeates the vicinity, the cacophony of other Faeries swallowed by the quiet, as though a wall has sealed us inside. Puck circles the tree, examining it. He doesn't utter another word, and the longer this goes on, the shallower my exhalations get.

Why isn't he saying anything? This satyr always says something, or too many things. I want him to bait, to cajole, to mock, to threaten. Anything but this precarious quiet, held together by a string that might snap, might unleash a flood of harsher sounds.

The stamp of his hooves syncs with my pulse. Puck retraces his steps and resumes slouching against the tree, a cascade of hot red waves burning across his shoulders.

In nine years, his hair hasn't changed. Evidently, nothing about him has changed.

Resentment and hurt clash with an odd sensation behind my sternum. He never forgot me. Even though we'd been so young, I'd stayed in his mind enough for him to make the connection. I'm not the only one who hadn't let go of that ephemeral moment in time.

To my right, the critter scurries off. While retreating, its pupils radiate, the sheen embossing a smaller branch stretching like an arm toward me. One might compare it to a handle, with gnarled prongs splaying from the end.

During a spring storm when I was eleven, I fell into a nest of errant branches that diced my shins and forearms. My complexion had drained to bone white, and my body had spasmed with pain. Cove had massaged a balm into the gashes while Papa Thorne recited a Fable to me, and Lark performed the tale. I'd bitten my lower lip so hard that blood had gushed from the incision, which had been more dignified than me wailing.

The point is, branches are functional. And if underestimated, they hurt badly.

This forked limb resembles a tool or a snare. Thereupon, I count two ways out of this. One, follow the maybe-raccoon across the boughs and hope to find an outlet, a place to descend without the animal feeling

threatened—and thus, attacking—and without Puck noticing. That's assuming his kin won't cut me off at the pass, either up here or down there.

Still, it's the lesser of the two evils. It's the logical option, the sane
choice.

Or two, take the stupid route. The hasty and reckless sort of action
Lark would take.

The one that I, Juniper, would never take. The one Puck doesn't expect.

I dip my fingers to my boot, thumbing the blade I'd taken from the
nymph leader. The weapon sits wedged between the laces, toothy as a
miniature saw.

I withdraw the dagger, its platinum fangs biting into the darkness,
and grind its edge against the bark, the friction as silent as a knife sinking through butter. The bough gives, severed from the trunk in five clean
thrusts.

I sheathe the weapon, grasp the branch, and clench my eyes shut.
What am I thinking? This is folly. Puck's a Fae with immeasurable strength
and speed. I'm but a mortal and a fraction of his height. At best, I could
break my leg. Worst-case scenario, I'll split my cranium open like a husk.

I sense my enemy pausing to think, to plot his next tactic. Then a
bullying grin worms into his voice. *"Once in the dark forest, a Stag hunted
a Doe…"*

The narrative stirs up a distant, fragile memory. It tugs between us,
resentful, taunting, as if it had never meant anything to begin with.

Wrath flips my eyelids open. I choose the stupid route.

I grip the branch by its stem, target his shadow, and fling myself off
the ledge. The ground careens toward me. The air buffets my cloak and
skirt. Puck cranes his head skyward. Those cruel irises register what's
happening, dilating as I crash on top of him.

My teeth clatter on impact, and my knees thwack into his hips, the
landing dragging him down with me. We smash to the ground. Our bodies
roll several feet, granules of dirt coating my mouth. The satyr grunts, his
limbs and torso tumbling with mine, his girth driving the oxygen from
my lungs. My ribs and spine jostle out of alignment.

My legs flank Puck's waist, carrying him across the underbrush. I flex
my thighs around his hips and use the element of surprise to capsize the

bastard. He thunks beneath me, his chest a hard plate of muscle that hits the dirt with a wallop.

By some miracle, I've maintained my grip on the branch. I wield the stem, aim at his fiery head, and use all my weight to jam the prongs against his antlers. The forked bough drives into the earth, pinning Puck's crown to the floor and trapping him there.

I waste no time, hopping off him and staggering backward. I suspect his mortification will come later. For now, the satyr thrashes, his shock contorting into fury. "Motherfucker!" he growls. "You encyclopedic shrew!"

"What happened to *luv*?" I retort.

Also, I resent the implied defamation. Furthermore, I've never claimed to be knowledgeable about everything.

His shouts carry and alert the nearest Faeries. A dozen footfalls stampede in our direction, trampling the wild.

I spin on my heels and race through the forest. That makeshift snare won't leash him for long. Because I hadn't plunged it deeply enough, he's sure to free himself before his kin arrive.

Bad Juniper. Foolish Juniper.

Risks have no business in this game. A few inches either way, and my fall could have ended differently. I could have been skewered on his antlers, or the serrations could have pared the flesh from my limbs, or he could have anticipated my actions and caught me.

But I hadn't. And he hadn't.

Thank Fables.

I pound through shags of foliage while restraining my grin. I wish that satyr could have seen his face, the way he'd flopped around like a fish.

Briers poke my toes. I leap over a ball of thorns, then dodge a pyramid of logs. Something slices my cheek, something else munches on my elbow.

The Faeries resume their howling. The sounds inundate the wilderness, grabbing the environment by its hide and shaking it—the trees shedding needles. The overlapping noises have lost their jovial tones, ferocity replacing levity.

The Solitary Forest is their playground and hunting ground. They're the wolves. I'm the lamb, the meat of this game.

My eyes cast about, directionless. Not only do I need an escape route but a destination and my supplies.

But shouldn't a bookish huntress be able to find what she needs without it being given to her?

That's an ignoramus's view of things, far too naive for either of us. Not every item contained within the pack is replaceable, and not everything I'd easily hunt down in the mortal world will be effortless to track in Faerie. It will be enough of a trial to find uncontaminated drinking water and harvest rations, without the added challenge of supplementing other essentials.

My waterskin. My spectacles. My notebook.

In The Wicked Pines, the Solitaries had dumped my possessions onto the ground, but what had happened to the supplies after Cypress had carted me away? What about the archery?

And now, who said the most desirable things aren't here, within your reach? Don't underestimate what's right in front of you.

The most desirable things. Within my reach, right in front of me.

His Royal Slyness hadn't been engaging in mockery. He'd been prompting me. If I hadn't been vexed at the time, I might have picked up on the hint.

But why would he provide me with such a transparent clue?

Either way, I accelerate my pace and fly through the woods. Once I've traveled in a direction, I don't forget it. I may not know how to navigate the rest of this realm, but I know a thing or two about retracing my steps.

Dry needles carpet the ground and cushion my footfalls as I vault back to the pine groves. Even Lark would say this is suicide, but if she and Cove were here, they would race by my side, no questions asked.

A familiar network of evergreens splits into circular hollows. They rise tall enough to blot out the branch candles and my compact form. At least in this condensed setting, I won't be exposed with a target painted on my back. I shrink into crawl spaces, recapping the steps I'd taken here.

The nymph parade. The bath and this cursed dress. The corrupt scenes I'd witnessed in each hollow. Puck cornering me, whispering unfathomable things in my ear, daring me to listen.

A pine trunk appears. I slam to a halt, tottering in place before smashing into it. How many times have I lectured myself, and my family, that it's dangerous to let one's thoughts wander?

I peer beyond the tree into a grove. I'm back where I had started, where I'd eavesdropped on Puck's party and where this hunt began. The table and chair are gone, the area vacant, no supply pack in sight.

Certainly not. That would be obvious.

I whip around, return to the lane, and embark on a search. From one segment to the next, I rush through the entrances, combing the areas in the half-light. The hollow where the leprechauns had played a game, the acorn pieces now neglected. The space where a faun had swayed his hips while a dryad strummed her lyre, the stringed instrument presently abandoned on the ground. In each condensed arena, I find the detritus from the Folk's revelry.

Discarded gowns. Slumped pillows. Empty bottles.

What a mess. Sloppy Faeries.

At one entrance, I hesitate. Then I surrender and glance inside, somehow knowing…knowing…and finding. The tent where that trio had been carrying on with each other stands unoccupied. Amidst the debris of blankets, my pack rests on the outskirts. The handle dangles from a low branch shaped like a bench.

Technically, the sight ought to relieve me. I narrow my eyes, reviewing the bag and its location. The perimeter and its crevices. The pack's unnatural angle, as if arranged just so, in just the right way.

Do I look gullible to them? I dive behind a bush and sink into a crouch. Several heartbeats later, I part the needles and resume inspecting the booty twenty paces away.

A quick glance around yields a stone. I swipe it off the ground. Squinting through the bush, I raise my arm, take aim, and hurl the rock.

It shoots across the clearing and smacks the pack's belly. The bag slumps, the faint shift causing a domino effect. A nest of roots vaults from under the soil, overturning clumps of underbrush. The ligaments splay as wide as a dragon's jowls and then snap shut, forming an onion-shaped cubicle around the pack.

Another trap. Another cage.

A snarl builds in my throat. I leap from my hiding spot and hustle toward the pack while whisking out the dagger. Sliding onto my knees, I drive the weapon back and forth across the grille of roots until my arm fits through. My fingers grasp the bag's handle and tug it out.

It's not as heavy as it should be. I jerk open the pack and gawk inside. All seems accounted for, including my confiscated clothes, which the nymphs must have returned.

Actually everything's here save for my notebook. Anger sizzles from my fingers to my knuckles. He'd returned my pencil but not the tome? Damn him!

Salacious croons reverberate from the outskirts. I sheathe the dagger, heft the pack, and sprint out of the hollow.

My ears chart the wild Fae calls, listening for their direction. As my eyes jump across the paths, I notice the arrangement of this place. The Fables teach us that nothing is as it seems in the world of magic beings. Faeries, elves, and dragons. Their domains can't be taken at face value.

In my haste, I'd forgotten one of the bedrock rules: Look closer.

I gauge the area in conjunction with The Faerie Triad, from where I'd initially traveled. When I'd first stepped into this weald, the routes to the mountain and river had vanished, giving way to the rest of the woodland. Consequently, I take another gander at the hollows and their ringed layout.

Fables. There's a reason they'd greeted me here. This isn't merely where they "welcome" mortals or have their fun.

This is the hub of the woodland. It's the center.

All right. Based on the sun's position at The Triad, the barrier between my world and this realm is south. And if The Wicked Pines is the center, that means traveling east had taken me and Cypress to The Redwoods of Exile.

When the hunt began, I had sprinted west. Best not to repeat that trajectory. I swerve northward, the one destination I haven't yet ventured.

Shouts flood The Wicked Pines, and somebody blows on a strange horn, its brass racket pealing into the night. Sweat coats my palms. I make out the cadence of Cypress's gallop, along with a multitude of footfalls.

My crossbow. I still haven't found my crossbow.

By now, Puck must have liberated himself from my snare. Yet I can't identify which gait belongs to him...because he's probably not with the mob. Perhaps he knows not to advertise his presence, lest I acclimate myself to the sound of his approach. But soon, I will learn how.

I whirl and dash across the lane, abandoning this landscape and heading for another. The route converges with a new sector of trees. I careen in that direction, warning myself not to look back, never to look back.

A thunder of hoofbeats ruptures the earth. It reminds me of the wondrous herd of deer that had surrounded Puck, the thought sending a pang through my chest.

Unable to help it, I glance back. Shadows pound ahead, some on foot—or hooves—some hopping across the candle branches, and some mounted atop the herd. I recall Puck's kinship with that doe, Sylvan. Perhaps he has opted to beg a ride from her instead of using his limbs. I imagine him astride the doe, shamrocks growing from her antlers, the pair of them barreling this way.

His kin and their regal transports infest the area, searching its depths for a puny, weaponless mortal. But they haven't found me yet.

Soon enough, they'll see what I've done to their trap. Soon after, they'll realize I'm not there.

My legs pick up speed. I hurtle deeper into this world, putting leagues between us—between him and me.

Yet a new thought occurs to me like a misplaced footnote, marginal yet significant. I'm hunting some unknown animal, and Puck's hunting me in turn. Except there's one thing he left out, one question I hadn't considered until now.

Who's hunting him?

8

The first animal I'd ever struck down had been an omnivore. I'd been smaller, runt-sized with a mangy nest of green hair and a sunken stomach. The rails of my ribcage had stuck out, a ladder of bones climbing up my tiny chest. Fresh into my sixth year, all I'd wished for on that birthday was to end the gnarling in my gut, to fill my tummy with something other than grief.

I'd made a rickety trap and caught a bundle of twitching fur. If my life had been different, taken on a kinder and softer shape, the creature would have been my friend. Perhaps my best friend. Instead, its carcass had roasted on my spit, and the whole time I had eaten, I'd wept.

I'd let the tears fall until my ducts ran as dry as old wells. That's how a gang of trade poachers had found me. That's when they'd decided, in no uncertain terms, that I would be of use to them.

After that, every kill had kept me alive and occasionally on the gang's benign side. The work provided my belly with nourishment, but none of those meals took away my shame.

I banish the past from my mind and surge into the wild, bearing north. Now instead of pines, sprawling elm trees dominate the environment. Moonlight drips through the canopy and frosts the trees.

Part of me longs to stop and study the details, compare them to what I've read. My thoughts leap from the elms to the wild's mystical animals and the Fables about forest mammals, such as bears with claws and merlons of teeth.

I run faster. Oxygen singes my lungs, and my side splits into a cramp.

An eternity later, the howls peter out. I slow to a jog, then hobble to a standstill and bend over. My palms flatten on my thighs as I heave for breath, my spine bowing in and out. Sweat soaks my bodice, the dress's hem stained from cherry to maroon.

The pack slumps from my shoulder. I sling it to the ground and kneel. The first object I fetch is my spectacle case, flipping open the lid. Thank Fables, the hardwood and its padded interior has protected the lenses from shattering. I'd purchased the case from the star peddler's coach several years ago. The merchant had sworn it was crafted by an elf in The Northern Frosts.

Relieved, I snatch the waterskin next, blessed liquid sloshing inside. I wrench off the cap, lift the rim to my chapped lips, and go still. They could have tainted the water, perhaps poisoned or glamoured it.

Indecision stays my hand. I set the waterskin on the grass and search the rest of the pack for trickery—missing or manipulated items.

Everything seems safe. As for my notebook, agenda is the root of every action, so depriving me of those pages is a maneuver. The satyr knows what reading means to me. He knows because I'd let it slip once, back when my lips were smaller and flimsier, still learning how to withhold secrets.

He must have withheld the book as an extra precaution. Not to mention, I had flaunted my intellect when I got here, so Puck must have omitted the tome not only to inflict pain—by taking something precious, as if my sisters hadn't been enough—but to penalize me for pontificating.

To raise the stakes. To test my aptitude. To make the hunt a tad more diverting.

Spoiled rotten and devious he might be, but never underestimate a satyr. They're impulsive only half the time, conniving the rest of it.

Leaves rustle, and hooves punch the earth, the sounds causing my shoulder blades to tense. It hasn't been more than a few minutes, yet I've dallied for too long.

I twist the cap on the waterskin and drop it into the pack. Crawling across the underbrush, I use my feet to scatter debris behind me, concealing my tracks as I go. The bushes convulse as I scramble through and tuck myself in.

Three heartbeats later, an equine body plods into view. The giant figure slows to a canter, then to a trot, then to a halt. I trace the grim lines of his face, the rim of his jawline brushed in moonlight.

Does he exhibit any expression other than stoicism?

How many have accused me of having the same countenance?

Beneath his helmet, Cypress's unflappable eyes prowl across the area. The ink markings around his navel twitch with his movements. His flanks contract, and the whip of his olive tail hangs idly.

I understand this manner of focus and know what it implies. I sink further into the bush's womb.

Cypress inhales, listens. "I know you are there."

The words hit me like a slap. I reach toward my boot, clench the dagger's hilt, and—

"So what if you do?" retorts a churlish male voice.

My head whisks to the side. Another Fae trots in from between two elms, a pair of feisty orange irises popping from his face. His marten tail curves off the ground, fluffy and far too pompous for his juvenile body.

It's the one who glamoured me in The Wicked Pines. If he were a mortal, I would attribute his epicene beauty to youth. However, he could be several hundred years old.

He greets the centaur with a priggish air and flips a stray curl from his shoulder. "You heard me coming," he corrects. "That's no accomplishment."

"So you were trying to be obvious?" Cypress inquires. "Or was your resounding gait purely an accident?"

"Fuck off."

"This is my quarter. You and the nymphs were tasked to The Gang of Elks. You will leave and resume the search there."

"Even if the mortal's going in that direction, she won't make it that far, much less that fast."

Because that isn't the point, the equine draws out his response. "Then let me speak on your level: I was here first."

"And I was here second."

"Flouting his orders will not impress him."

Sarcastic creases etch across the male's face. "What would you know about trying to impress Puck?"

Like a sucker punch, the question finds its mark. A muscle ticks in Cypress's dark cheek. "You were ordered to search—"

"I already said, she won't make it to elk territory. That's too far east."

East. Elks. Good to know.

Cypress's profile cranes toward the sky, his features scrunched in thought as he contemplates the celestials peeking from behind the canopy. "Do not underestimate her. She might cross more boundaries than we anticipate."

I lean into the bush, the better to watch the other Fae, whose tail bristles. "I'm merely scouting farther afield. Foxglove and her clan thought it a sound idea."

Foxglove. She must be the nymph leader who owns the dagger residing in my boot laces.

"Anyway," the male says, "you're giving the human too much credit. She won't get that far because he won't let that happen."

The centaur mutters, "When do we ever know what he will do?"

"I have a merry idea," a voice chimes in. "Why not ask me?"

That tenor sizzles down the side of my body. It's not the approximation of a shockwave so much as a tingle, its effervescence traveling across my flesh.

Compared with Cypress's baritone and the other Fae's braying, this new accent is equal parts audaciousness and lightness. Yet like roots, the inflection penetrates fully, reaching places it shouldn't be able to reach. Places that urge my knees apart.

My head shifts on reflex, attached to the invisible noose of that insufferable voice. Puck strolls from the creepers. Dozens of vest buckles cling to his broad chest, the longbow and quiver slant across his back, and a breeze rustles the fur of his calves.

Without effort, the satyr fills a void that hadn't been there moments ago. His arrival cuts through the glaring contest between his kin, snipping that cord in half, though neither appears surprised to see Puck.

He balances a flat palm on a trunk and tsks. "So do I need to separate you two?" His head slants toward the lanky member of their trio. "And what do you have to say for yourself, Tinder?"

The one called Tinder meets Puck's gaze without preamble. "Nothing."

Although he was supposed to be combing the wild for me elsewhere, his unapologetic response causes Puck to snort. "They grow up so fast."

Tinder flexes his tail. "You could have at least assigned me to The Passel of Boars."

Cypress clips, "He could have assigned you to The Pack of Weasels."

"Very funny, asshole," Tinder retorts.

Puck sighs and gives Cypress a censorious look. "Please, don't provoke him or belittle the weasels." Then he quirks a brow at Tinder. "You fancy animals with tusks over ones without? So be it. Just remember, a pair of sharp ivories doesn't make an animal fiercer. It just means the boars defend themselves differently than the elks."

Tinder watches Puck carefully, eyes slitting in deliberation. The satyr holds that gaze and coaxes, *"Feldun sjünsamlekaet."*

Whatever he'd said, it works. Those sanguine irises glint with admiration. He gazes at Puck like he's the sun rising over the horizon, throwing light and warmth everywhere.

The Fae nods. "I was telling Cypress you won't let her get far. I'm right, aren't I?"

Cypress and Puck's eyes click toward one another. Then Puck crooks his finger, unclasps his archery, and extends it to Tinder. "Mind this for me on your escapade. Won't you, luv?"

I gawk. He can't be doing what I think he's doing.

Cypress frowns. "The imp has a weapon."

That's evident from the set of throwing stars bridled around Tinder's thigh, the astral blades flashing as though insulted. At Puck's offer, the youth's eyes inflate, then narrow. "Handouts are for pissants."

"Be careful rejecting the favors of others," the satyr coaches, his tone neither condescending, nor severe. Rather, it's paternal, affectionate. "It's only temporary, see? I'll reclaim it in a few days. Until then, I have an alternative, and I'd rather play with that shiny new toy for the time being. It's you who will be doing me the favor."

At length, the Fae succumbs with a prideful grin. He accepts the archery and dashes east into the night, his tail slinging into the shadows.

Puck gave his weaponry to him. He gave up his longbow, just like that.

When Tinder is gone, Cypress shakes his head. "You are foolish. What was the meaning of that?"

"That was damage control," the satyr remarks, studying the direction in which the Fae had disappeared.

"You have stroked his ego. You have rewarded him for disobeying you."

"One, disobedience is as much a rite of passage as a first fuck. Two, the lad can handle my bow. Three, don't piss me off any more than the green sprite already has. My antlers are sore, and it's all her fault."

I roll my eyes while Cypress continues, "Take care with him, Puck. He is too eager to pound his chest. He is too eager to idolize you. The more one does, the more one is prone to mutiny should the object of their admiration betray them."

Puck slides his gaze to the towering centaur. "Are you saying I'm in danger of that?"

Concern folds across Cypress's visage. "I am saying if you disappoint him, his allegiance may shift. That is the price of being a ruler."

"I'm aware of that price. I gave Tinder the bow to solidify his faith. It'll remind the lad that I trust him as much as he can trust me."

"The problem is, why should you give him a reason to doubt you in the first place?"

"He's a sapling, which makes him antsy. He'll grow out of it."

The centaur's eyes flit away. "Some attachments do not wane." At Puck's inquiring look, Cypress adjusts his helmet and grates, "She is headed northeast."

My pulse throbs. I retrace my journey here, because how did he draw that inaccurate conclusion? Hypothetically, whatever signs he'd mistaken, they would come in handy. Sadly, I have no way of reading the equine's mind.

"Northeast? Really?" Puck debates. "Last time I checked the chinks in this environment, she was on a collision course with the north."

"I think not, satyr."

"I think so, centaur."

My attention jumps between them. The centaur's helmet tips downward, a steep incline that shields his forehead. Puck's crown does the opposite. The spokes fling backward in a great, flourishing loop.

All at once, the Faeries puff with humor, the sound dependable, unwavering. It's the modulation of two figures who know one another well, who can laugh unconditionally in spite of their disputes.

Cypress's hooves clomp. "The moppet is northeast bound."

Puck's pointed ears seize on one word. "The moppet, huh?"

The centaur makes no reply. But Puck picks apart the nickname the way he'd pluck the eyelashes off a mortal—ruthlessly and for no fathomable reason.

"In any case, she is not in this vicinity," Cypress maintains.

"I never said she was," Puck says smoothly.

Once more, the centaur and satyr regard one another in silence, some exclusive form of correspondence passing between them.

After a moment, Puck straightens from the elm, kneels at its base, and cups the trunk. He angles his head as if listening, a tendril of red sliding over his cheek. He shuts his eyes, inhales, exhales.

Those fingers flex on the root, once, twice, as if the tree might have a pulse. My own heartbeat thunks as if matching the rhythm. And when it does, Puck's eyelids flare open.

A tremendous russet form strides into the clearing, all beauty and grace. The creature's antlers balance shamrocks as she enters the scene. I'd assumed Sylvan had already joined with him, but evidently that hadn't been the case.

By touching the elm trunk, Puck must have called the doe to join him here. According to the Fables, it's one of nature's channels through which the woodland Folk communicate with the fauna. In the mountain, it happens through the wind. In the underground river, it occurs through the water. Here, it transpires through the earth.

Sylvan nudges Puck as he rises and strums his palm along her back. With the agility of a cat, he swings onto her back. While he whispers to her, Cypress tilts his head subtly over his shoulder, toward the bush where I hide.

My breath catches. That's when Puck speaks up, cutting the centaur off from glimpsing for too long, turning too near in my direction.

"Indulge me, then," the satyr prompts, the deer already swerving northeast. "Let's see who's right about this *moppet*."

They soar into the woods in a flurry of hooves. When the turbulence recedes, I count to one hundred before hopping from the bush.

If Cypress had known I'd been here the whole time, why hadn't he said anything?

I don't have the luxury of squandering time to dwell. I recap the exchanges among the three Faeries regarding my whereabouts. Puck had been right that I'd been heading north, but I can't now. As it is, my pursuers haven't afforded me a moment to figure out where to go, where I should hunt this mysterious animal.

Speaking of which, another thought strikes me. Puck had leant his weapon to Tinder.

My head banks between the secure route and the chancy route. I chew on my lower lip, then proceed in Tinder's direction. It takes me an hour of pausing and squinting, using starlight, moonlight, and candlelight as guides to locate the breadcrumbs the male had left behind.

For a Fae, he isn't adept at covering his tracks. Puck had implied that a thousand years is a fledgling age, so perhaps Tinder's youth contributes to this.

At the final stretch, I crawl across the undergrowth and find him bending over a creek and splashing water on his face. It must be time for a respite because his boots stand a dozen paces off, idle beside the archery leaning against a rock. I had planned to knock him out and swipe the weaponry, but this will do much better.

With his back turned, his rear pitched high into the air, and all that splashing, I require less than three minutes to grab the contraband and scurry off. I travel on all fours, moving as I used to when I was six, seven, eight, and nine. With their heightened sensory perceptions, these Faeries pose a detrimental threat.

But how many of their mortal captives had made a living the way I have?

Once, I had poached animals. Now, I rescue them. Both call for stealth. When I've covered enough acreage, I run.

I pass the spot where I'd spied on the trio, then clear another mile and stagger in place, gasps of exertion falling from my lips. Once I've recovered, I level my flat palm above my forehead, fashioning a visor and peering into the landscape.

I have no compass. As for the otherworldly stars, they're useless, partially shrouded and wholly foreign as they are. Those winking astral lights might as well be the stuff of bedtime stories or the props of a magician.

Thus far, the sun has been my only source of navigation. I'll have to rely on that.

As for the region where I'll find my quarry, I don't recall any Fable hinting of an animal that can't be hunted, nor where any such creature might reside.

Is it a mammal? A marsupial? A reptile?

What manner of fauna can't be hunted? Perhaps it's one that isn't fully an animal. Perhaps it's one that's half animal, half other. But that applies to any Fae with fauna traits, and I have misgivings that it's one of the Folk. That's too conspicuous.

What about the geography? The Book of Fables provides humans with information on how to deal with the Folk, how to survive amongst them. It offers slivers about their magic, their culture, their history, and their landscapes.

If I can't identify the creature yet, I ought to determine an ideal region in which to search. Without my notebook, I reconsider every Fable in my mental arsenal, as well as every entry I've penned in the journal—each story that either involves hunting, or uses it metaphorically, or includes it in the morals and lessons. A selection of those tales has taken place or alluded to the northwest. It's a rudimentary guess, low-hanging fruit at best. However, it's the surest option right now.

To start, I need a proper outlook in relation to where I've just come from, a clearer sense of my location and destination. I stash the longbow, quiver, and pack out of sight, wedging them in the belly of a shrub.

After tying the hem of my dress above my knees, I begin to climb. Thanks to Lark, I do so without incident, my sister's tips preventing me from skinning my knees or fracturing bones.

I reach a sturdy branch in the upper story. From there, I peek through the leaves to gauge the woodland valley. Endless treetops carpet this world, their various heights and textures frothing beneath a dome of white, gold, and teal stars.

I marvel at the celestials. The Fables don't mention them being different colors from my world.

A range of cliffs glimmers in the distance, its peaks ringed in halos of clouds. Some kind of tower looms atop one of the bluffs. Strange crossways extend from the crests or embed themselves into the jagged plates of rock—perhaps bridges and stairs. Blazing torches perch within the summits, illuminating a lone raptor slicing through the air.

The Solitary Mountain.

"Lark," I whisper. My sister, who loves birds and wishes she could fly. She's up there, somewhere.

Under my sleeve, I feel the bare place where my leaf bracelet had once coiled around my arm. A long time ago, my sisters and I had exchanged gold-plated talismans: a thigh cuff for Lark, a necklace for Cove, and the bracelet for me.

Are they still wearing their trinkets? Or have they lost them as quickly as I have?

I study the mountainous view until my chest caves in, then assess the valley. North. South. East. West. After checking the variations in elevation and the diversity of trees, I crawl down the trunk and unravel the dress's hem.

Four days pass. I alternate between traveling at dawn and dusk, the hour at which I take shelter depending on the species of my neighbors. I dodge giant raccoons that hiss from the niches, their mystical vocal cords reverberating through the wild. I back away from a hulking silhouette that lumbers on all fours in the distance, fog puffing from its snout—a bear with Fae ears and incandescent green paws that correspond with its pupils.

I would snare rabbits—the ones who maintain their normal size—and use the nymph's blade to skin them, but building a fire is out of the question.

Instead, I sustain myself based on what I've read. Inwardly, I consult my studies for which fruits and nuts to trust, and which to stay away from. Still, handfuls of Fae pomes and berries are foreign to my knowledge, so I avoid them altogether.

Vibrant worms, oversized snails, and metallic ground beetles residing in rotten wood allude to the additional threat of spiders. The branch candles enable me to peer closely at my campsites and check for webs.

Purrs and hums filter from the lush shadows, taunting and tantalizing. They attempt to lure me into recesses, the primal sounds tickling my nape. I clamp my palms over my ears until the noises dissipate.

Periodically, I hear the Folk sniffing for my scent and scouting for my prints. They sing racy, come-hither ballads about chaste mortals and hidden passions, magnifying their voices in case I'm near.

One time, Foxglove appears and joins in, her voice sickly sweet. "I know you took my dagger, mortal. Very impolite of you!"

"Enough of this horseshit. I tire of singing," a young male broods, likely Tinder. "Another day without sighting our prey, and I'll expire from boredom."

"This hunt is about more than keeping you entertained," Foxglove asserts.

He pays her no heed and throws a tantrum, kicking something on the ground. "Where the Fables is this bitch? This could be over if we just—"

"He ordered us not to use glamour," a brawny leprechaun warns.

Foxglove scoffs. "Are you playing by the rules because you're loyal to Puck? Or because, like everyone else in this forest, you're itching to fuck him?"

"Leave me out of that," Tinder expels, his tone a hybrid of offense and fealty. "And you're wrong. Everybody's loyal."

"Which is why we're not using glamour," the leprechaun repeats.

An ominous, contemplative silence ensues. Foxglove's lack of snide reply does little to console me.

I keep refuge in the bushes—shivering, listening. Based on what else I overhear, the Folk are prowling after me in batches and rotations, each group taking its turn. My body sags like a cloth when this lot finally departs.

Intermittently, I scale more trunks to check that I'm questing in the right direction, lest the environment contrives to hoodwink me. Presently, I happen upon an area that contains a Fae breed of trees with feathery leaves that fan out like dandelion puffs. In fact, those stems detach and float away at the faintest breeze.

These trees also prove tough to climb, offering few nodules on which to leverage myself. And it's worse on the way down, especially since I've forgotten to gather and tie the skirt of my dress this time. I slip at intervals until my heels hit the forest floor. Then I pause and stare at the column, my ears tingling.

A shadow bleeds across the bark. A decisive click plays at the nape of my neck.

I stall, recognizing the sound of a crossbow—one that belongs to me.

Not only that, but a draft pinches my nostrils with the intoxicating notes of cloves and pine. "My, my, my," Puck says from behind. "You've been a naughty, naughty human."

9

A set of earrings jingles, the chime shivering up my tailbone.

That cloven weight. That sly pace.

Eventually, I will learn his vagaries and predict his approach. I will practice this art until everything he does and says works against him—and to my benefit.

Until then, I have a problem. It has to do with the concept of proximity. The satyr's body emits a wall of heat that cages me in. His shadow traps my own, consuming my small frame.

By shifting an inch, I extract myself from the trap. My own shadow maneuvers askance of his. I notice the weapon in his grip, its shape balancing the outline of a bolt.

My upper lip spasms into a snarl. "Give it back."

Deadly silence. Then a pair of lips dip to my ear, his words coasting across the lobe. "Take it from me."

My body reacts in an unpardonable way. A brush fire of anger across my jaw. A convulsion up my thighs and a hot rush between them. Hostility festers on my tongue, while another feral sensation contracts below my pelvis.

When the bolt's tip skims the back of my neckline, my eyelids flutter, and my breasts press hard against the suede bodice. I don't understand it. As long as I'm near him, I will never understand it.

I turn to face him. Clad in mahogany leathers, Puck stands alone, without an entourage or a loyal doe.

"Where's your majestic companion?" I question.

Protectiveness hones his gaze. "Not that it's your business, but Sylvan decides when to keep me company and when I can ride her. In other words, she's not my familiar or my pet."

"How dare you. I never said she was."

"Good to know. Otherwise I would have taken it personally."

So when he'd called Sylvan through the roots, it hadn't been a command. It had been a plea.

Puck lowers the crossbow, the ridges of his arm slackening. The bolts' iron tips have been eradicated, replaced by steel. Now only do I recall the bastard mentioning an alternative to his archery, but this is how he's able to wield it without his power subsiding. He's castrated my weaponry!

Rage tightens my stance. I glower at a set of features wrought from the pages of a storybook, from a cautionary tale about monsters that seduce and cajole, where one can't tell the difference between a moan of pleasure and one of agony.

Those folklorish eyes twinkle with menace as they sketch my face. "Do you know what happens to mortals who pounce upon a Fae's antlers?"

An anticipatory knot rolls down my throat. So he's still vexed about my stunt after I'd jumped from that tree and landed on top of him. "The Fables say—"

He holds up a finger. "I'm not asking what they say. I'm asking if you know."

"If I answer correctly—"

"Ah, ah, ah," he husks. "Winning back your bow will take more than a paltry round of trivia."

"How much more? Haven't you done enough while holding it hostage?"

"You're mad at me for repurposing your toy. I understand." His pupils gleam. "Unfortunately for you, I don't give a Fabled fuck."

"I did what I had to do. That's what this hunt is about, isn't it? It's called defending myself."

"And this—" he points at his face, "—is called having a fit."

What a prat. "You had me treed. I needed to ambush you."

"And this is what happens to dauntless mortals in Faerie. They get ambushed back."

"I can't play this game without my weapon."

"That's assuming you haven't just lost."

"That's assuming I can't break free. I did it once already, and I'm a quick study. Ask anyone. I've never had to be schooled twice."

"Such a gloater," Puck drawls. "What else have you been taught, hmm? Are you proficient in anything outside of books and crossbows?" When he tilts his head, a strand of red slices across his cheekbone. "Have you learned what it's like to swoon against a lover? To partake in the sweet and sour of his mouth? To feel his tongue trace the slot between your legs? To writhe as he laps up your cries like syrup?" His breath skates across my flesh. "In fact, have you ever unleashed such a primitive noise?"

Tremors build under my flesh, threatening to surface. If they do, he'll notice.

I detest these questions. I detest the answers that surface in my head. I detest the aimlessness of them, the way my mouth fumbles to respond.

Most of all, I despise what these questions do to my body. And I resent that he sounds as aggravated as I feel.

"Have you ever lost control like that?" he intones, causing a flurry of activity, sparks fizzing in my limbs. "Have you ever spread yourself wide and felt the lurch of a man's body between your thighs? Have you ever given yourself up to rapture? Allowed a lover to thrust—"

"Until I'm senseless?" I blurt out, needing to get the words out, needing to cut off his tangent. I smear as much mockery as I can into the reply, using a phrase from one of Lark's many stories about her dalliances. She'd once said men love to make such a promise when it comes to sexual assignations.

However, Puck shakes his head. "Senseless? Rubbish." His intonation burrows further down. "I was going to say until you're clear-eyed and know exactly who's fucking you."

My palm cracks against his cheek before I register what's happening. Puck's jaw twitches, and that's the extent of it. The slap barely makes a dent in his face, whereas my flesh stings, and my wrist smarts.

I steady my voice. "Don't touch me."

Well. He hasn't once. Not once.

But I'd needed to utter the words, needed them to form a barricade around me. Yet I can't tell if I'm trying to keep him out—or keep myself in line, in control.

His knuckles etch the pink imprint of my hand, caressing the mark that sears his profile. "Touching is for amateurs."

Without looking away, he sets the crossbow on a lower branch, then flattens his hands on either side of my head. He entraps me within the snare of his body, infusing the space with cloves and pine.

"An amendment to the game," he proposes. "You want what's yours? Then earn it back."

"So you can't contend with me any other way?" I counter. "You require another contest to help you?"

Puck chuckles. "Getting ahead of yourself, don't you think? You haven't heard the conditions yet." His gaze stumbles across my mouth and lingers there, tracing its shape. "But since you asked, I'd rather play than fight. As it is, I'm running out of cheeks for you to slap, unless you'd like to get kinky."

"Earn my archery back, how?"

Puck's gaze travels from my mouth to my eyes. "Three options. One, by telling me that overdue story I'd asked for in The Wicked Pines. Two, with a combative round of archery in which you best me. Or three—" his lips coil, "—with a kiss."

Of course. Satyrs.

I make a point to ignore how quickly my stomach drops and make a greater point of grimacing. "And what? If I don't like the kiss, you'll return my weapon?"

"Nonsense," he says. "I'll give it back if you like it."

That makes no sense…until it does. Not only does he expect me to enjoy it, but he expects me to deny it, and he expects me to fail at denial. That's the test.

I've been kissed before. Lark and Cove don't know this, but I once took a willing buck aside and gotten it over with. I'd figured it had to be done, like an initiation, as my sisters had already surpassed that milestone by then. Lark had said yes to a farmer's son; Cove had embraced the cobbler's daughter, since my older sister prefers both males and females.

However, Cove has remained chaste and doesn't blather about such frivolity. Whereas to this day, Lark routinely makes a fuss about kissing—

and flirting and having sex—jabbering about these subjects until I'm red in the face and she's elated with herself.

I had chosen the most suitable of the bunch: the bookbinder's son. I had propositioned him, and when he'd finally stopped choking on his shock, the buck had consented. At which point, I had snatched his hand, marched him behind the glassblower's forge, and planted my mouth on his.

To say the least, it was what I had expected: two pieces of flesh puckered together.

What I hadn't anticipated was his slimy tongue flopping inside my mouth, much less all that saliva and the aftertaste of gravy. Who knows what the boy and his tongue had been searching for, but I don't think they found it.

I had pulled back and given the kiss its due consideration. Then I'd wiped my hands and said, "Well, that's done. You may go now."

I won't discredit Lark's testimonials, but in hindsight, something had obviously gone amiss during that episode. My sister wouldn't gush over an experience so mediocre. That's why I had never told her about the event. I hadn't been able to admit this shortcoming—that perhaps, I'd put my head into it rather than other parts of me.

Since then, kissing hasn't interested me, nor any carnal activities. I've never had time for hobbies.

I say, "My lips are off limits."

Puck swoops in, his mouth stalling a hair's breadth from mine. "Now," he murmurs over my parted lips, "who said anything about kissing you *here*?"

My head swims. Embers flare across my lips, firecrackers bursting when his breath sails there. Plastered against the tree trunk, I want to shove him away, and I want to punch the smugness from his visage, and I want to take one other action.

One that I can't bear to acknowledge. One having to do with the taste of him, the heat of him.

The barest of shudders tracks along Puck's limbs. His gaze catches my mouth, his eyelids sinking to half-mast a moment before he inches away.

The movement knocks me out of my stupor. I scrutinize his question.

What is he talking about? Where else would he kiss me?

Whatever shows on my face, it wipes the hubris from Puck's features. "Fables. Verily, you smell and speak like a virgin. But still—"

"But what?" I demand.

"But you don't know what I mean."

"Of course, I do," I snap. "I know what you're referring to."

Three seconds later, I'm no longer lying. Realization sizzles across my cheeks, burning bright. I do know what this libertine means. One can't have a sister like Lark and not be educated on the ways of the wanton.

Puck's referring to oral ministrations. Although mortification heats my complexion, I refuse to let that blush travel. I tamp down the reflex with a proper glare.

The satyr may have inserted a fraction of space between us, yet he continues to fence me in, his frame enveloping me in balmy warmth and spices. "A smoky voice that crackles and spits embers. Spruce green hair and eyes that flare behind spectacles. That said, your vision seems fine, considering how many daggers your eyes have thrown my way. What are the delectable lenses for?"

So he remembers the wooden case that Cypress had pulled from my supplies. "They're for the notebook that's no longer in my pack."

"Oh, yes. I've rendered you bowless and bookless. And before you ask—no, I haven't read the notebook. Your privacy is intact there. But until you reclaim what's yours, I guess you'll have to use your imagination."

Or I'll just have to use the dagger propped at my ankle. "My imagination doesn't need your help."

Puck's tone comes out hoarsely. "Prove it."

In that case, I'll go with option number two. But although he means for the archery round to be sportive rather than a physical clash, that sounds too much like a deal, which isn't a safe avenue with him.

Wisely, I amend his proposition. I shift my limb, snatch the blade from my boot, and thrust. Thanks to Cove's pickpocket lessons, the weapon's teeth pause just shy of his jugular.

Puck blinks, dumbstruck. Then he beams, elated.

Damn him, he's going to deflect. And he's stronger than I am.

Time for the second phase of my plan. The Faeries may have taken my prized possessions, but they'll never take my words.

Did you really think I wouldn't recognize you?

I flex my mouth until the reply sits there steadily. "I recognized you first."

Taking advantage of his momentary surprise, I drop the dagger and ram my fist into his mandible. Puck curses, but I duck under his arm before he can turn. I vault to the ground, reclaim the blade, spring into a tumble, and roll straight into the bush where I'd stashed my supplies before ascending the tree.

I jam the dagger into the lace sheathe at my boot. I don't require the blade anymore, since I've got something better.

An instant later, I pop up from behind the foliage. Puck swerves my way and stops. He registers the longbow braced in my grip, the arrow nocked and aimed at his black heart. The ghost of a smile twitches across his mien, visible despite eventide.

The snap of a twig rents the air, snatching my attention. When my head jerks to where Puck had been standing, an empty pocket of space greets me. My ears attune themselves to the wild, tracking shifts in the foliage, a shiver across the underbrush.

Yes, he's no longer standing there. But no, he's not gone.

Close. Very close.

Mechanisms click. I know that ticking noise like I know the brisk turn of a page. I aim southeast, toward a cleft in the vegetation, and let it fly. The arrowhead whizzes. Midway, it collides with a crossbow bolt.

A shrieking noise pierces through the landscape, resounding from the impact of Puck's arrow and my bolt. The latter splinters into fragments. The Fae's archery tears through mine as if the bolt was made of parchment, shredding the mortal weapon into ribbons. Wrath boils in my stomach as I behold the casualties littering the grass. I'd used his weapon to destroy my own.

Masculine chuckles skip across the wild. With a growl, I loose another arrow. It zooms toward that laugh and impales a low-hanging branch.

Now the laughter reverberates from a completely different spot. I swing that way and nock another arrow, which arcs into the trees. In turn, a bolt fires my way, its tip an asterisk of winking light.

I duck and roll, avoiding the next strike. Lunging to my feet, I whirl behind a trunk, my back slamming into it hard enough for my molars to clatter. I paste myself to the column, crusts of bark chafing the dress.

My gaze slides to the right and left. In the distance, undomesticated grunts push through the weald, bringing hogs to mind. Or a larger species, the sort that grows tusks.

I pluck another arrow from the quiver. As I do, a crossbow clicks from his end of the woodland. Life narrows to this grisly place. Flecks of candlelight swim through the leaves, bracken clutters the ground like so much rubble, and starlight filters through the crochet of foliage.

It's just us. It's just me and him. It's just this forest and these weapons.

I'd been wondering who gets to stalk him in this game. The rules say nothing about that, but now I know. With his archery in my hands, the answer's obvious.

Because if he gets to hunt me down, I'll just have to hunt him back.

10

The bolt flies my way. I'd taken a quick look but now surge out of range, twisting back behind the trunk. The weapon's tip whizzes past me, abreast of the column.

I dive to the next tree, evading a strike that grazes the hood of my cloak. Puck's cackle vibrates at the edges, tickling the leaves and making them dance.

That's what this becomes, a dance of twists and turns, moves and countermoves. Me, peeking and shooting. Him, dodging and shooting back. Me, ducking out of harm's way and targeting him once more.

Adrenaline sizzles through my limbs, a heady rush washing through my veins. The corner of my mouth lifts into a half-grin.

Puck's nimble hooves caper through the woodland, scarcely making a sound. I strain myself, listening for the signs—a crack, a thunk, a whisper of air.

Fables curse him. He's good.

Matter of fact, he's adept at maneuvering through the shrubs, agile as a critter, silent as a fox. Stumps and overturned logs force me to leap at intervals.

That's fine. One doesn't live with trade poachers for years without learning how to navigate the wild undetected—bleeding in and out of shadows, slipping into crevices, and prowling the paths of fauna.

I move gingerly. Still, I'm no native of Faerie, and my pace lags.

Meanwhile, Puck bounds on invisible springs, prancing from landmark to landmark with the grace of a gazelle. Yet he accuses me of being a show-off?

I scowl, nettled by an outbreak of competitiveness. I triple my efforts, abandoning my spot behind a giant rock and relocating to a tree stump breeding mushrooms, where I crouch as another crossbow bolt skates overhead. In a flash, I nock my bow—his bow—and brace it to fire.

I must be exceeding his good-for-nothing expectations, because the Fae mutters an obscenity from his corner. Hearing the frustrated sound, another smile threatens to engulf my face.

"Is this the best you can do?" I call out, aiming at the cascade of red glinting in the murk.

His hooves stalk nearer, fifteen paces away. "What makes you assume I need to do better?" he taunts. "I do as little or as much as I fancy. None more, none less. What's better than that?"

"You can try speaking in riddles, but it won't work on me."

"Now who said anything about riddles?"

"You're saying this mediocre performance is the extent of your skills?"

"Puuuleeeease," he drawls. "If I roll my eyes any further back, I'll see my own asscheeks. Is this piss-poor display the best *you* can do to goad me? What a subpar human, you are."

My bowstring quakes. The arrow soars.

Puck's outline steps aside as the weapon streaks by, then he turns and regards me with relish. "Now we're getting somewhere."

He rushes my way. I catapult from the stump, roll between his limbs, lunge upright, and break into a run. My nemesis guffaws, his mirth loud and unabashed.

The crossfire travels through The Solitary Forest. Tree to tree. Alcove to alcove. Shot for shot. The satyr's dexterity versus my precision. Nevertheless, because his power is legendary, I'm starting to wonder if he's holding back.

Is this real combat or entertainment? What's the difference for him?

We pass from one artery of foliage to another. The constellations shift beyond the canopy, the half-light blooming from dark teal to periwinkle. This happens until the trees with their feathery leaves vanish, swallowed by a new environment.

I stumble in place. Twig trees spread around me, their trunks spun from thin switches, which form branches sprouting wildflower buds instead of leaves. Around them grows a vast sculpture garden, the same twigs netting into the likenesses of animals. An elk, its antlers splaying outward. A row of opossums hanging upside down from the boughs, their tails hooked around the limb. A porcupine ten times its mortal size, its quills spearing the air.

They're scattered throughout, along with twig sculptures of Faeries. A small female faun with goat limbs, a basket linked over her arm. A tall, regal Fae brandishing a longbow. A statuesque dryad peeking from behind a tree.

It seems our skirmish has inched past another borderline. Young wildflowers bloom from the sculptures, petals raining down at the slightest breeze. The garden feels like hallowed ground.

My boots carry me toward the oasis. But I halt as a bolt's tip prods between my shoulder blades.

"One inch, luv," Puck assures me. "One measly inch, and you'll see how much better I can do."

I wheel around. Puck looms before me, with my weapon fixed and the bolt pointed at my chest.

Appropriately, I respond in kind. Thereupon, his gaze flickers to the yew longbow poised at his own torso.

The satyr smirks, impressed. "My, my, my."

"Want yours?" I ask, gripping his weapon. "Give me mine."

"Oh, goody. Are we finally making a deal?"

"For the last time: No, we are not."

"Spoilsport. Though this—" he bobs the bolt's tip, indicating the longbow, "—explains the hissy fit a certain marten-tailed youth threw, not one hour after I sent him on his merry way. He wasn't too thrilled about reporting the mishap to me. Are you sure you'd rather not bargain with me?"

Best to ignore that. Otherwise, the meddler won't give up.

Eventide wanes, sleepy blue pouring into the garden. The atmosphere smells of a thousand florals—a sympathetic aroma, though I can't say why.

I jerk my chin toward the array of twig trees and sculptures. "What are they?"

"What makes you think I'll answer that?" Puck replies.

I reshape my question. "Where are we?"

His face scrunches into a frown. "We're in The Fauna Timbers, a patch of land dedicated to the fallen. We didn't have the capacity to weave sculptures of every deceased soul; so instead, each bloom growing from the offshoots represents a life lost. Happy now?"

The fauna are as immortal as the rest of their kin, apart from being slain in battle. Over the ages, some legendary animals and figures have been said to perish thusly, but not in mass quantities. Bearing that in mind, only one historical event could be responsible for this profusion of wildflower buds.

How many times have I tried and failed to purge The Trapping from my mind? Although my sisters and I were children when the rebellion occurred, I keep wishing I'd had the power to stop that fateful night from happening. Because if I had, perhaps that would have erased everything I'd done prior to that—everything I did to the animals of my own world, everything I did to earn the tattoo inked into my lower back.

Daybreak's coming. Scarves of white cruise across the sky, the last vestiges of twilight diminishing.

I blow a lock of hair from my face, and the satyr's eyes trail the movement. "I didn't realize," I say. "The Fables don't tell us how you memorialize your dead."

"We do so by planting our kin, then letting them blossom in peace. That is, until they don't have to anymore—the fauna, at least."

"What does that mean?"

"Is that your favorite question?" Puck rolls his shoulder as if suffering a crick in the neck. "By the way, this arrow is getting slippery."

He sidesteps me. My hold on the longbow tightens. I monitor his prowling movements, half twisting to keep him in my sights. We circle one another across the strewn petals, our weapons primed toward the same beating, throbbing organ.

I shake my head. "You never say anything serious."

"That depends on your definition of serious," Puck says.

"In that case, the definition that most scares you."

"I'd have expected you to believe there's only one definition for everything."

That's true. But again: "You don't know me."

The dawning sky reflects in his pupils. "I did once," he professes, the words knitting around my waist. "How long before we drop the farce and acknowledge that?"

He sounds neither gratified, nor troubled that he once presumed to know me—that we share a memory. One that had lasted a short period of nights, zero time in the span of a human girl's life and infinitely less for a Fae. That experience should have been insufficient to make a lasting impact, yet the question disrupts my balance. He speaks as if I've been the only one avoiding this.

I begin, *"It takes two to—"*

The satyr groans, his head flinging back to address the heavens. "If I hear you quote one more fucking Fable…"

"Why does it bother you?"

"Why do you rely on it?"

"Why do you insist on talking in circles with me?" I snap, my hands suffocating the longbow as we continue circuiting each other. "Is it remotely possible for one of our spats to proceed in a straight line?"

Puck meets my glare. "To match your train of thought?"

I growl, he sighs, and we blurt out in unison, "What are you afraid of?"

Our pace dithers. Then at the same time, we halt.

A cage springs open in my throat. "I'm afraid of nothing!" But the declaration crumbles on my tongue, tasting of ash and lies. "In less than a week, I've been ridiculed, humiliated, deprived of my weapon—"

"Don't forget your handy-dandy notebook."

"—dumped on the back of a centaur, groomed like a submissive pet, forced up and down a tree, and hunted like a jackrabbit, and now I'm standing in a memorial garden with my own weapon pointed at my chest by the one person I've had heinous dreams about since childhood. And don't get me started on the hassle of getting candid answers from you. I haven't the capacity."

Puck stares, his index finger stroking the crossbow. "You dreamed about me?"

"It's exhausting!" I vent, ignoring the self-centered question. "You're exhausting. We're exhausting."

"Now who said anything about us being a *we*?"

I clam up. Every time I've sparred with him, I've forgotten how the argument began and what my point had been, because each dispute has led to a new one without the former being resolved first. At this rate, too many dead and buried things are lurching out of me.

He isn't the only problem. I blame this setting for our latest feud.

I hate the sight of these perished fauna and Faeries, the twig sculptures hovering like martyr statues. I hate the sight of Puck standing among them, his antlers like the exposed, inverted roots of a tree, and his hooves resembling those of a stag. I hate him for having wild traits—as if he and his kin are worthier of this earth than my people, as if Faeries have a more intricate and valuable relationship to nature than mortals.

I hate that he's watching me with an unfathomable, smoldering expression, peering as though I'm made of kindling.

I hate that he's also sneering like I'm to blame for this garden, like I had any choice about what humans did to his kin.

I didn't hurt them. It wasn't me.

And I hate my tattoo. I hate that he'd condemn me more if he were to discover the marking. I hate that I would even care what he thinks, when it shouldn't matter.

He. Does. Not. Matter.

"Such a tirade from such a reserved female," Puck muses. "And don't beat a dead horse by insisting I don't know you. I have some history to fall back on, but even if I didn't, your uptight attitude leaves little to the imagination."

I draw on the arrow. "How clever to describe me without actually describing me."

"I'm more interested in how you'd describe yourself."

"Why would you be invested in that? I'm nothing but a toy to you."

"And like any self-respecting Fae, I appraise the quality of my toys." The satyr drags a pink tongue across his incisors. "I also tinker with my food before I eat it. Habit, you see. Why else would I have ignored your hiding spot in the elms while you played spy?"

He'd known I was hiding? Like the centaur, Puck had known I was there, eavesdropping?

"You're supposed to be hunting me," I say. "Are appraisal and conceal-ment part of the rules?"

Puck steps back, the better to regard me. "You really can't stand un-answered questions, can you? Don't see the value in an open-ended thought?"

"Can't bear to be trapped by facts?"

"Facts," he scoffs. "Those pesky little buggers. Facts are relative."

"I disagree."

"Good," the bastard says. "By the way, I *am* hunting you." He closes in once more, swinging the bow from side-to-side, in an exaggerated motion. "This is me, hunting you. And what are you doing? Protecting yourself? Yes, I'm aware of that. Except you've spent so much time running with-out actually doing any hunting of your own. You were tasked to track an untrackable animal."

I broaden my stance. "Once I'm done with my current pest, I shall."

A slow, conniving grin. "That's the spirit, luv," he condescends, strut-ting forward until the arrow grazes his leather vest. "So deal with me."

That husky tone brings me up short. My gaze strays to the hard con-tours of his neck. Indeed, it's a pleasant-looking neck. Too bad it's attached to such an unpleasant face.

My weapon—his weapon—is primed to release. But Puck has disen-gaged, lowering the crossbow to his side.

I won't shoot anyone like this. I won't shoot if not to defend myself.

He knows this, so what's his ploy this time? Why does he sound like he's just consumed several pints of mulled wine? Why do I feel the heady rush of it?

Why is he looking at me like…that?

My erratic breathing rustles the neckline of my cloak. I swallow, then open my mouth to retort—and an oink peals through The Fauna Timbers. The rusty octave is familiar yet otherworldly, extending for what seems like miles. Puck and I swerve, the arrow and bolt poised toward the crea-ture at our feet.

Peridot gem eyes. Triangular ears. Round snout. Four limbs. Straight tail.

It's a baby boar. Short fuzz coats its pigmy body, streaked in brown and black. But the animal bears no tusks yet.

The satyr and I disarm in unison. The male shoat watches us, snorting inquisitively now that it's got our attention.

My pulse slows, warmth rushing through me. Without preamble, I pitch to the ground, prop on bended knees, and marvel at the piglet's peridot orbs.

"Hello, there," I say. "Are you lost? Where did you come from?"

A masculine outline lowers itself beside me. "He must have strayed from his farrow in The Passel of Boars," Puck says.

Tinder had mentioned that place when I'd eavesdropped on them. I swing my head toward Puck. "Is it close?"

"By human or Fae standards?" he quips, then relents when I just stare at him. "On both accounts, it's close."

The tiny boar skitters over to Puck, squealing with glee and butting its head against the satyr's arm. Puck indulges the piglet and murmurs in Faeish while flicking playfully at the creature's tail. This causes another round of squeals that, any louder, could penetrate every quarter of this wild.

The shoat nestles between us, tucking into the vent between Puck's hip and mine. I glide my palm over its fuzzy head and scratch behind its ears, remembering the sanctuary back home, the haven for animals that my family keeps on our land, the creatures we've housed. The ones waiting for me and my sisters to come home.

I gulp, then laugh as the wee boar snorts into my fingers.

I sense Puck watching us. Mostly, I wish he'd return his attention to the piglet. I don't know how to bear the weight of his eyes on me.

Yet an admission springs off my lips. "I think in straight lines and rely on Fables because I trust them. They'll never veer off course, so I won't get lost or make mistakes. They're safe."

Safer than my own ideas, perhaps.

He's quiet for a long time. I peek at his profile angled toward the piglet, who bumps its snout against his knuckles. Then his sharp features find mine, and he repays me for the honesty. "I want to know your real thoughts, not a Fabled quote or lesson, so I know who I'm up against, to find out if you've changed in nine years, because the payoff is greater that way, and I'm greedy, or I'm selfish—take your pick. But it comes down to this: I want to know your real thoughts because I want to know what *you* think."

"I thought you'd forgotten me," I say. "I didn't want you to remember."

He raises his eyebrows. "At last, something I relate to."

We study one another. The wee one grunts at being left out, snatches my pack, and dashes off.

Puck and I break apart. I lurch to my feet and race after it. "No, wait!"

The satyr falls into line with me. He jogs at my side until the garden, with its trees and sculptures of spun twigs, fades behind us.

The land flushes out into a dense expanse of Fae trees with barbed trunks and spiky leaves. We hadn't gone that far, but we must have crossed another line of demarcation into another sector.

Puck hadn't been exaggerating. If this is The Passel of Boars, it's indeed very close to where we'd come from.

The piglet hits a dead end of bushes. We corner the shoat there and kneel before it. Puck whispers in his language, relaxing the little creature. For a while, it oinks joyously and wrestles with Puck over the pack.

"You're getting nowhere," I boss, curbing my grin. "Let me do it." I take my turn and attempt to wrangle the bag from the piglet. Eventually, I'm able to pry my supplies from its mouth.

Another grunt rumbles from ahead of us, this one louder and larger, coming from someplace above the bushes. We go still, but the shoat trills with pleasure.

Puck considers the approaching sound, then sighs dramatically. "Ah, fuck."

The hairs across my nape stand on end, but I dare not look yet. I stare at the ground and ask under my breath, "What is that?"

To which the derisive satyr replies, "It's the mother."

11

A shadow looms over us, larger than in my world. The Fables tell of mystical fauna in every magic realm across The Dark Fables—Middle Country, the Northern Frosts, and the Southern Seas—and their abilities to shift sizes from miniature to mountainous. Likewise, I'd witnessed this in Puck's doe companion and the herd of deer who'd joined in the hunt's commencement.

As such, it shouldn't be astounding when the sow's outline transforms into a monolith. It should be no surprise when her silhouette bloats, dwarfing both mine and Puck's.

Perked ears, stubbled in whiskers. Bristling threads of hair. Two monstrous tusks that splay into the lances.

My head cranes, tracing the jumbo shadow until I meet a pair of furious, parental eyes. Two bottomless pits of malachite flash, the gemstones reflecting my blanched complexion. The mammoth sow looms atop a knoll situated beyond the shrubs, which accounts for the dead end.

"Juniper," Puck draws out. "Don't move."

The sound of my name uttered from his mouth jolts me out of the trance. I keep my eyes pinned to the shifter. "Do I look like a novice to you?"

"You look like a mortal to me."

"And you look like a lunatic to me." Which is hardly a productive conversation. "She won't—"

"Yes, she will."

"Not if we keep to ourselves," I whisper. "She'll collect her shoat and leave."

"Oh? In that case, my sincerest apologies," he concedes with feigned humility. "I didn't realize you were an expert on boarology."

She's a female. Hence, it would be sowology. Anyway, I can't believe he's bringing this up. "For Fable's sake, this isn't my studious ego talking. We mean no harm. We were playing with her offspring. She'll sense that."

"That would be true, if she hadn't already noticed our weapons."

"There's a hierarchy in the animal kingdom," I maintain. "Of all people, you should possess that rudimentary knowledge. You rule this land."

"Bloody good point. Thanks for reminding me," Puck drawls. "Methinks we're having an inconvenient debate. What say you?"

Perhaps. Nonetheless, shouldn't Puck be able to exert power over the sow? Shouldn't his authority tame her? Can't she sense, smell, or detect who he is?

"Shouldn't she listen to you?" I insist. "By nature, you're her sovereign."

"Everything you've said in the past sixty seconds?" the satyr downplays. "I'd advise you to retract it, unless you want to be very wrong. This isn't the human realm, luv. These are Fae animals, not mortal ones."

Meaning what? His sovereignty is moot?

The jittery male piglet must sense the tension. He caterwauls and careens between us and the spiky bushes, searching for a route to his hovering mother.

Her tusks flank us, jutting so far we wouldn't make it twenty feet without them impaling us. Plumes of air siphon from her snout. The protective sound dislodges an adjacent mound of rocks and causes them to roll across the ground. Her grumble drills into the earth, to an unreachable place below us, perhaps to the other side of the continent.

The stressed piglet runs in circles along the border, more rusty squeals tripping from its mouth. We haven't hurt the baby, but the guarded stance of its mother illustrates her doubts about us.

This being The Passel of Boars, there ought to be more of them nearby. And if they hear this baby's cries…

The repetitive scrape of a hoof across the ground sends a flurry of prickles up my calves. It's the gesture of an animal fixing to pounce. I've been on the receiving end of that sound before, with other mammals.

Puck's knee nudges mine. I offer him the barest of nods and move with deliberate slowness, placing the longbow on the ground. In my periphery, I see that he does the same, disarming to show the mother all is well.

"Stay down," he instructs me. "And for once, pretend I know more than you."

With that, Puck rises to his hooves and shuffles in front of me, shielding my body from the sow. He levels his gaze with the animal, holding its expression. The moment trembles like a leaf clinging to its branch.

From this hunched angle, all I can make out are the massive tusks. Plus, the satyr's leather attire, the unkempt sheets of hair flaying his shoulders, the tapered peaks of his ears, and the spokes of his antlers.

Some form of wordless communication passes between him and the female. I want to explain, to make myself useful. What if Puck's saying the wrong thing, whereas I'll say the right thing? But I don't speak Faeish, and I can't send messages through the landscape like he can.

Adrenaline pumps through my chest. My booted toes grind into the muck.

Out of nowhere, the mother wheezes and rears backward—then springs from the knoll and lands before us. The impact knocks me off balance, throwing me sideways. Puck stays put, as though he'd expected this reaction. Nevertheless, my floundering catches the sow's attention.

She thrusts herself my way on her gargantuan hooves. Puck leaps sideways and lands in a half-kneeling crouch, blocking her from me. His right palm flattens to the ground, his thighs spread, and his head angled downward, the antlers poised like a battering ram.

The baby boar scurries behind its mother's haunches. Puck and the sow pause. I scramble to my feet, waiting as they square off, a primitive lapse in which they sniff one another out.

Like mystical fauna. Like wild animals.

The seconds tick by, the Fae and sow corresponding.

The sow hesitates. Then she growls, the serrated noise akin to a powerful mill grinder, tearing the landscape apart.

And Puck mutters, "Shit."

Then they catapult forward.

The Fae and sow collide in a tangle of tusks and antlers, fisted hands and bucking hooves. I yank an arrow from the longbow's quiver and nock the weapon. They move in a blur, too swiftly for me to track, to aim properly. Meanwhile, the piglet quails in the bushes.

Puck lurches into the air, his limbs scissoring in an intricate pattern as he evades the sow's tusks. His own hooves act as springs, bounding him high, so that he leaps in and out of the creature's path.

At one point, the sow's head swings. Puck throws up his forearm, thwarting the blow of a tusk. He stumbles from the force of it but keeps upright.

In its panic, the piglet careens into a bramble thicket that snags its hoof. The spiky shrub holds fast, leashing the creature in a vice grip. The little one flails, causing the briers to strain and give a few inches of slack.

I glance between the fight and the baby. There's nothing I loathe more in tales than a female standing idly by while the hero does the work. Whatever negotiation Puck attempted hadn't worked, but this might: I shift my aim toward the shackle. The arrow soars, its tip slicing through the restraints and vanishing into the foliage.

The piglet hops from the thicket, free of the manacle. The mother halts, catching sight of what I've done.

Puck's chest pumps for oxygen. A gash rents his leather vest, a red line of blood dribbling there, likely from the tusk.

There's an instant of indecision, of bated breath. My confidence is short-lived as a cavalry of snorts heads our way. I whip toward the sounds, my gaze darting over breaks in the shrubbery. Shame on me for not tracking the signs earlier. A passel of boars and sows appears along the knolls, their withers shaking with rage. Like a wave, they shift from recognizable sizes to otherworldly heights, the tusks protracting into lances.

Puck tears around, snatches my archery off the ground, and runs my way. The satyr pants as he reaches me, "Never mind, luv. Now's a good time to move."

I tote his weapons and fall in line, twisting and charging through the woods. Behind us, an army of swine deploy, their grunts and snorts deafening. They trample the brush, walloping vegetation out of their way, the barbed trees convulsing.

The chase knocks me off balance. My side smacks into a boulder, white hot pain seizing my left shoulder. I yelp but hobble upright, my arm dangling at a precarious angle. I can't wield the bow.

Puck helps me straighten fully, then claims the weapons, arming himself with both sets of archery. His Fae legs are faster than my human ones. Yet he keeps pace with me as we veer through the woodland—and the ground collapses.

The soil gives, caving in beneath us. We drop like stones.

The fall is quick, and we slam into a foundation carpeted in pillow moss. I shriek, dizzy with pain.

Grains of soil cake my teeth. I hack them up, then flop onto my back, my body screaming in agony. I gawk at the hole above, where a tide of hooves stampedes by. The passel lunges into the timberland while driving a thatch of foliage over half of the gap.

Puck goes limp beside me, our weapons scattered on the ground. I struggle past the throbbing in my shoulder and inspect the area, its dirt walls embedded with roots. The depth is considerable enough for the boars and sows to have missed us, but the opening is too high to reach. The pit resembles a den or oubliette. Either way, it's a cage.

"Huh," the satyr coughs, gawking upward. "Alone at last."

No. Not just alone but trapped.

Trapped together.

12

Pain stabs my shoulder, probing bone and cartilage. The womb we've landed in tilts, going fuzzy around the edges like the pages of a book when I'm not wearing my spectacles. Another cry struggles to break free from my mouth, but I don't allow it because if the sound were to reach Puck, who knows what he'd do with it. The satyr might pocket the noise for future use. He might bring up this moment of weakness whenever he sees fit to bait me, to mortify me.

I won't let it out. I won't let—

"You might as well let it out, luv," Puck says, hauling himself to a sitting position next to me. "If your face turns any more purple, you're going to implode and end this game prematurely. I'd rather not have my fun spoiled."

"Go. To. Hell," I grind out.

Puck scoffs. "Hell doesn't exist in Faerie. Hell is for humans."

I have no time for his prattle. My arm's nothing but a limp cord at my side, pleading with me not to move.

The Fae utters something cautionary, the words gauzy in my ears. Ignoring whatever he's saying, I try inching myself toward the nearest wall. Sweat puddles across my forehead, and rolling waves of nausea assault me, so that I fail to reach my destination. Instead, I flop back down.

Fact: I'm going to faint.

An inconvenienced sigh filters through the space, along with the oppressive scent of pine and cloves. From my position on the ground, I blink and see Puck kneeling over me. His earthen eyes stare down, the irises glossed in melted brown.

I cringe. "What do you think you're doing?"

He scans the dislocated shoulder. "I've been asking myself that question since you barged into this land."

"I didn't barge in. You and the other two demon rulers of this wild forced me and my sisters here."

"Those demons are my brothers."

"I beg your pardon?"

"Ugh," he complains. "Now that your body's out of alignment and I'm feeling magnanimous, you resort to begging? You couldn't have waited until I was back to my usual devious self? All you had to do was last another few minutes, and I could have taken advantage."

"I didn't barge into your land."

"I heard you the first time. Too bad for you, it's nothing but semantics."

"Nooooo," I draw out, because clearly he's an imbecile on top of being a goblin. "The definition of semantics is—"

A sturdy palm braces my upper body, and I hear a pop. A coarse sound rips from my lungs. It multiplies into a thousand cries and fragments through the ceiling hole.

The instant my shriek fades, the pain abates, evaporating from my body like mist. I shuffle upright and flex my arm tentatively, twisting it this way and that.

Puck sits back on his haunches and wipes his hands. "Watching you flail around like a stubborn fish was becoming tedious. Besides, I'm not about to win this hunt by accident." The Fae snaps his fingers with sudden insight. "Or just be uncharacteristically lazy and consider it a favor. That works for me."

To think I'd been tempted to break from tradition and thank him. "I'll do no such thing. You did yourself a favor, not me."

"Bloody true. What good are you if you're not a challenge?"

We split apart, taking refuge in our respective sides of the recess. Roots weave through the dirt walls and dangle overhead like snipped arteries. Unfortunately, the fibers aren't long enough to grab, and despite the partially shrouded ceiling hole, whatever tree they belong to isn't visible from above. I fail to discern even a single projecting branch we could use as a brace to extricate ourselves from the pit.

When I suggest Puck use his leaping skills to exit the hole and find a way to lug me up, he sneers. "I can jump high, but not that high or that vertically. Also, there's this concept called momentum, which requires a running start. Do you see how wide this place is?"

Oh, fine.

The Fae retires to the opposite wall, one leg extended, the other steepling as he drapes a toned arm across his knee.

A lull descends over the cramped space. I may as well make use of our detour, until I figure out how to ascend from this trap. I check my arm once more while mulling over each unresolved question stacked in my head. Logic and tact suggest I begin with the simplest query.

"You could have used magic to do this," I say, indicating my shoulder.

"What? You mean this magic?" He wiggles his fingers as animated sparks of gold crackle from the tips. "Magic is boring. I fancy working with my hands, the way humans do. They're fetching hands, good for fetching things."

"I would very much like a straight answer."

"If I speak any straighter for you, my words will have an erection." I just stare at him until he concedes. "Fables almighty. Don't tell me you're objecting to the merits of manual labor. You don't strike me as shallow."

"Magic would have been practical."

"Ah. Practical," he reprises, his tongue sculpting the word until it changes shape and sounds like a vulgarity. "I bet that's one of your favorite words."

He says that as though it's a bad thing. And yes, the adjective is among my top five favorites.

I fan out my dress so that it covers my ankles. "What about materializing wherever you want? You have that ability, don't you? Why not transport yourself aboveground and toss me down a makeshift rope?"

"Because it takes a shitload of energy for Faeries to manifest all over the forsaken place. That's stamina I currently don't have, thanks to the boars and sows. As it is, declawing your crossbow bolts of their iron tips demanded not only a special Fae brew but also proximity to the weapon, which stole a chunk of my endurance."

"About that," I seethe. "I should lop off your fingers."

"Please," he drawls. "Tell me you wouldn't have done the same thing to my longbow. Tell me you wouldn't have castrated its magic if you'd found a way."

Good point. Moving on. "Your declarations smack of humanity. Since when is magic boring and manual labor the ideal to a Fae?" I interrogate.

"Since me," he replies. "Or rather, the earlier me. When I was young and rosy-cheeked, I didn't have a problem with humans and their magiclessness. No, my beef came later when they stormed the lands of my kin. Otherwise, I would have gone on liking them, including one girl in particular, had I met her under livelier circumstances."

I clear my throat. "You've invested a considerable amount of time making assumptions about me. I wonder why you go to the trouble."

"To get on your nerves, of course."

"My nerves are welded of steel."

"Care to prove it? Let's see." He drums his chin in contemplation. "Which bundle of nerves should we test? Which ones will resist an attack?"

My tattered bodice clings to me, the suede no better than an adhesive, no less constricting than his own garments. The Fables weren't wrong when describing the insidious perversions of satyrs. Puck's nomadic eyes rove over my figure, the look meant to strip one's dignity as well as one's modesty. His stare has the disturbing effect it intends to have, propelling tingles across my knees. In the private regions between my hips, blood circulates. I feel a jumpiness there, a fretfulness that doesn't make sense.

My response comes out too fast. "You're wasting the last of your energy."

His response comes out too slow. "Does that mean you're indeed impenetrable? Or just plain hollow?"

"Do all satyrs have a remarkable ability to say so much, yet express so little substance? Or is that your particular defect?"

"Such impoliteness toward a Fae."

"You started it."

"You continued it."

Yes. Against my better judgment, I did.

I glower, those tingles flaring into cinders. "The hypocrisy and entitlement of Faeries is truly legendary, to expect politeness from mortals in exchange for glamouring and brutalizing us over the ages."

His smile collapses. "That's one way of looking at it. Or politeness in exchange for poaching our fauna and maiming our young. That's another fucking way." He lounges against the wall. "How am I doing so far? Does that count as—what did you call it?—substance?"

Nine years since The Trapping is no time at all for an immortal. As far as he's concerned, the wound is still fresh. My chest hitches whenever I think of that era, so I understand his sentiments well.

Typical adversaries would swerve away from one another. Instead, we stare until the staring wears itself out. In this dank and sunken pit, and without a moderator, we'll get nowhere constructive. If centuries of inequality, vendettas, and prejudice between magical beings and mortals hasn't been resolved yet, the satyr and I won't achieve anything here. To be sure, not while trapped, hungry, and thirsty. Despite this intermission, we have other pressing matters.

Puck seems to draw the same conclusion. He squints at our surroundings, his eyes sketching the roots' patterns, his ears perked as if he hears something.

"Stop that," I lecture a moment later when he gets impulsive and plucks a random plant stem from the ground. "Leave it alone."

"Not that it's any of your business, but the wee sapling asked me to relocate it," Puck defends. "The bud has big dreams of being replanted aboveground with the rest of the grownups, and as its servant, far be it from me to deny nature's wishes. Though, if you insist." He sets the stem back where it was, its roots reattaching to the soil, and holds up his flat palms. "Happy? Because the plant isn't. Fact is, it's mighty pissed off at you now."

I blink. "You said servant."

"I say many things. Many things and even more things, and some of those things lead to other things."

Yes, I initiated the subject. But does he ever shut up? "You said servant," I reiterate. "Not ruler."

"That, I did. You have a problem with it?"

"I've never had a problem with nature."

"Has nature ever had a problem with you?"

This is dangerous terrain. I know what he's getting at.

Faeries won't give candid answers unless one either gets lucky or formulates the questions cleverly. Otherwise, these tricksters will skitter around the facts, being truthful without being entirely honest. They'll find a way to respond without responding, to redirect the conversation to their benefit—to the recipient's discomfort or disadvantage.

I amend my words. "You consider yourself a servant of the forest?"

"Ruler. Servant," Puck lists. "In my context, they're one and the same."

I can see the legitimacy in that statement. Kings and queens lead their kingdoms, but those monarchs also have a duty to serve to their people.

"Your mouth's not moving to correct me," Puck muses. "Interesting."

"Not interesting," I say. "I simply believe that to be a sound ruler, one must humble oneself to their kin."

"Including the flora and fauna?"

"Not every human sees nature as their property. We may not have magic, but that doesn't mean we're less connected to the land than you."

"And what connection do you have to nature?"

"I'm still learning."

"I would call you a wise woman, but: one, it would be patronizing on my part; because two, you already know you're smart."

"And three, I'm not in the market for your compliments," I contribute.

Yet at the very least, he values intelligence, if not humanity at large.

Lark had once asked what would attract me to a partner. We were playing a truth-or-jest game at the time, the three of us huddled in our caravan at midnight.

I had said my illusive partner would have to be a scholar. Cove had smiled, but Lark pretended to snore, so I'd tackled her until we laughed and forgot the game.

Actually, *partner* is my preferred term. Lark's had been lover, which... just, no. I can be drawn to someone without such extracurricular activities.

Wings flap overhead. Beyond the hole's exposed half, feathers splay from an avian figure cutting through the clouds. The owl swoops across the sky and vanishes. Based on its trajectory and the geography I've puzzled together thus far, the raptor had been flying toward the chiseled peaks of The Solitary Mountain.

Lark.

The foundation trembles beneath me. I hunch over, pressing my ear against the ground and listening to the distant hiss of water. The rumble of liquid eddies from someplace far below, a hidden river gushing under the earth, flowing into a serpentine network of mystical caves and canals.

Cove.

A sour lump swells in my throat. Thankfully, Puck appears lost in his own world. For once, he's watching our surroundings rather than me, his eyes tracking the roots. If he hears the thoughts of a little plant, can he hear the roots? What do they tell him?

What do the fauna say to him? How does he reply?

In The Redwoods of Exile, Puck had shown a kinship with Sylvan, handling her with tenderness and reverence. He'd ridden the doe into the elms where I'd spied on him, Cypress, and Tinder. So by my estimation, Puck must have a bond with the creature.

Does that extend to all the animals of this weald?

"May I ask you a question?" I broach.

Puck swings his head my way. "No, you can ask me three. So long as you agree to a condition."

"A condition," I repeat, stressing that fact for all it's worth. "Not a bargain."

"Yes, yes, what you said. And my condition is simple."

"Nothing is simple with you."

"This is: Call my brothers demons again, and I'll toss you back into The Redwoods of Exile."

Earlier, he had mentioned his siblings, but I'd assumed I hadn't heard him correctly. Since when do the rulers of this wild call one another brothers?

Puck reclines further, enjoying my astonishment. "Didn't you know? Cerulean, Elixir, and I are brethren. By the way, you haven't yet agreed to my merry condition. You don't want to keep me waiting, seeing as my cooperation comes with an expiration date, and why are you gawking at me like that?"

Am I gawking? I'll take his word for it.

I think of my adopted sisters, who are the same age as me—each of us nineteen and only several months apart. Lark is the youngest, I'm the middle child, and Cove is the eldest.

I think of how we became a family despite having different bloodlines, different backgrounds, different everything. I think of how Papa Thorne gave us a home and became our father, and how they all became my lifelines.

I think of how my sisters and I can predict one another's sentences, how we bicker one moment, then clasp each other in hugs the next. I think of us sitting around our papa's chair while he recites Fables to us, though most times I've had to correct his narration.

I think of my sisters scouring the woods with me to rescue animals, including orphaned or injured creatures and victims of trade poaching. I think of my family sharing that passion, working side by side, running the Fable Dusk Sanctuary together. I think of our connection, our unbreakable bond.

Then I think of what Puck had just said. The protectiveness in his words. The threat he'd issued. It's the warning of one who won't stand to hear his kin insulted.

I contemplate how many times I've voiced that same threat to other people when they snubbed or offended Lark or Cove, and how my sisters have done the same for me.

"Huh," Puck says. "I must have revealed something profound. Or are you finally learning to appreciate my robust physique? You know, they say Cerulean is the sexy-pretty one, Elixir is the violently beautiful one, and I'm the ruggedly handsome one. What say you, mortal?"

Oh, the reply this deserves. Yet all I can concentrate on is what he'd stated before that. "I didn't know they were your brothers."

"By loyalty, not bloodlines. We're brothers of history and brothers-in-arms." The satyr's expression hardens. "Sharing a dark past tends to link people that way."

The Trapping festers between us. However, I leave that memory where it is, refusing to pick it up. It's too heavy, and this chamber is too small.

It's bad enough I have to share space with this villain. If I believed in destiny, I would say fate has a malevolent sense of humor.

"Boy oh, boy," Puck sneers. "Such reserve. Such willpower. If this subject doesn't chop through that scowl of yours, I've got no idea what will. You've been graced with a smoky voice, yet you squander it on lectures and quotes that don't belong to you. What exactly are you passionate about, enough to speak from the pit of your stomach? Enough to shout yourself hoarse? Have you ever screeched? Sobbed? Moaned? Cried out?"

I just did when he fixed my shoulder!

"And your shoulder doesn't count," he censures.

"You wish to know my opinions outside of a book?" I snap. "You wish to know what incites me? You and your brothers don't have the monopoly on suffering. My sisters and I grew up as foundlings, toiling on the streets to survive."

Puck's eyebrows crinkle, but I keep talking, keep speaking. "Though that's not what makes us a force to be reckoned with. It's what we learned from it and who we became afterward. Lots of people develop a bond from mutual turmoil, including my neighbors—the villagers, farmers, and tradesfolk you've terrorized, abused, and indentured since the dawn of time. In short, shared trauma didn't write your brotherhood into the history books." Animosity spews from my lips. "Your actions afterward did."

Puck peers at me in uncanny silence. Because we'd spent a limited number of nights together as children, he doesn't know the particulars of my past. Back then, I never told him about Lark, Cove, or Papa Thorne, just as I never told him about the prequel to those years: my upbringing as a trade poacher.

"You were foundlings?" he asks. "You're not blood-related?"

"Yes," I answer to the first question. "And no," I answer to the second. "Nor do we need to be linked by birth. In my life, the people I share blood with don't matter as much as the people I'd die for. Those are the important ones. *They're* my family."

The Fae stares at me, fixated. With his irises gleaming in the dark, I might go so far as to call him inspired, as if he'd never considered this before, as if he wants this to be true. I think back to The Redwoods of Exile when I'd asked what he could possibly know about family, and I recall his venomous reaction to that.

What's his origin? Other than brothers-in-arms, does he have an actual family? And why is he peering at me like I'm a figment?

I've never been on the receiving end of such an invasive look. I don't know what to do with the rest of this moment. Males gawk at Lark this way. They don't consider me in any way, and certainly not because of something I've said.

Puck isn't one of those males. Regardless, he's about to open his mouth and spoil the companionable silence. "Very well," I say. "I won't call your brothers demons."

That extinguishes whatever private thoughts he'd been entertaining. "Excellent," Puck says. "Back to your questions."

"What has become of my sisters?"

"Ask Cerulean and Elixir, not me."

"Fine, so who rules which landscape? What games are my sisters playing? Do they have as long as I do to win?"

"And that's more than three questions."

"I know," I say. "I can count."

His lips twitch. "Cerulean is ruler of the sky, Elixir is ruler of the river, and you know who I am, of course. Did you just roll your eyes at me?"

"No," I fib. "You were saying?"

"So I was. And you were bullshitting; I saw those eyes roll." He shrugs. "Your sisters are playing games that don't involve hunting or satyrs, and they have as long as those games last."

"That's it?" I balk. "You won't disclose anything else?"

"Apologies, luv, but I've got no authority outside my domain. Solitaries are prone to wagging their tongues, so news does travel fast. All the same, no one's allowed to prattle outside their own terrain, lest it sabotage the proceedings. My brothers and I decided to honor that amongst ourselves, too. Hence, I have no idea what your sisters are going through. I don't even know how the games are chosen in the mountain and river. We've deemed it sacred to each landscape, however unanimously fated we are. It keeps us focused on our own lands, less vulnerable to diversions."

Then I'll have to find out for myself. In the meantime, I slump. "If you prevail over this environment, you should know the way out of here."

"Because I frolic underground all the time? Oh, come on," he insists when I give him a look. "You left yourself open for that one."

My mouth quirks, on the verge of a full-fledged smile. It's a disturbing habit of his, getting me to react this way.

Puck notices. He doesn't say anything, but his lips tilt as if he's accomplished something magnificent.

"I meant," I clarify through my budding grin, "that if you govern this realm, you must know its layout."

"Nature doesn't work that way. Not where you're from, nor where I'm from."

"Elaborate."

"I'm not a king. I'm a defender and guardian, albeit a powerful one. Ruling the forest means representing and serving it—that's my responsibility. Consider me its highest subject. I'm the 'hunky face' of The Solitary Forest, nothing more. Ultimately, nature reigns supreme and makes its own rules."

Fair enough. And true.

"It's as much an adversary as an ally," I reflect.

"If it wants to change those rules, it can," Puck agrees. "If it wants to keep secrets from its residents, it will. If it wants us to work a little harder, it'll do that, too. What's more, I'm a busy satyr. I can't know all the nooks and crannies of this woodland."

"All right, so what were you doing earlier? When you were staring at the roots?"

"I was bribing them. They value gossip, so I said I'd empty the skeletons from Cypress's closet if they gave us a tip out of this hovel."

"The roots gossip?"

"Less than dryads and more than leprechauns."

I've read several texts about the trees in my world, how they're more alive than one thinks. How the roots burrow so deep and far that some connect with neighboring trunks. How the trees share food and water through that connection, and how they take care of each other if one of them is sick.

The same applies to Fables about Fae trees. But until stepping into this land, I hadn't known the trees were able to correspond in other ways, too.

"They communicate with you?" I ask. "You can understand them?"

"All Fae can understand them, as we can understand the fauna," Puck says. "But only some trees have the wherewithal to communicate."

Envy prickles my skin. That, and exasperation. "We've been down here for thirty minutes."

"Thirty-one."

"My point is, you could have attempted to confer with them from the start."

"Meh. I suppose I could have," he acknowledges. "It's all your fault for distracting me with such edifying conversation. You're too tempting to debate with."

"Will they help us?"

"Only if we help ourselves. P.S., you'll be pleased to know that was a direct quote from them."

I wish that were a quip, but his tone says it's not. I stand up, brush the dust from my dress, and resort to pacing.

Is the cavalier satyr merely going to remain sprawled there? Yes, he is.

Also, he reads my mind. "You know, my head won't work any differently if I'm off the ground or lounging on it."

Very well. That is, until I notice him tracing the shape of my footfalls, the imprints, and the unbroken lines of my tracks. He's archiving them for later.

I scuff the prints with the toe of my boot, but Puck just snorts. "Too late."

Indeed. If he'd been standing, I would have done the same with his hoof prints.

To the matter at hand, Puck claims the roots will assist us only if we assist ourselves. Bracing my hands on my hips, I glance at the ceiling and then trace the roots netting through the walls. I peer and peer and peer, but my inspection yields no potential outlet.

Puck pats the ground. "Might as well sit your ass down and get some sleep. A rested mind is a wise mind."

I click my head toward him. *"If a Hare Confronts an Elf."*

"I recognized the tale when you parroted the first sentence in The Wicked Pines. Call me a hypocrite for doing what you do best. Or if I've started quoting others, maybe you're having an influence on me. But I'm probably just too tired to be witty without help."

"I sincerely doubt that."

Nonetheless, I lower myself to the floor and fish the waterskin from my pack. After a few gulps, I toss it to Puck, who catches it with one hand. When he looks at me quizzically, I say, "I owe you for the shoulder."

He inclines his head. "Now you don't."

Those plush lips strap around the nozzle, his throat contorting as he tips back the liquid. I avert my gaze from his puckered mouth. All the same, the slosh of fluid leaks into my ears, followed by his thirst-quenched grunt.

Using the pack as a pillow, I curl up atop a patch of moss. The satyr uses additional water to bathe his hands of grime, a squeamish and coddling act that catches me off guard. Afterward, he loafs against the wall, crosses his hooves, and shuts his eyes.

Silence filters into the pit. A crochet of shadows weaves across the soil. Though I refuse to be the one who falls asleep first, I have a disconcerting hunch that Puck isn't ready for slumber, despite what he'd said.

I recall that one and only time we spent together as children. The recollection coaxes my eyelids to sink. Sleep weighs me down yet calms my breathing—just like that memory always has.

13

Nine Years Ago

In the field at night, I stalk the rustle of leaves. It's a hushed sound, a whisper of noise brushing the woods. My bare toes pick around the wild debris, fallen nut shells and shredded bark.

Also, molehills. Some people can't tell what kinds of mounds they are, but I can. I know lots of things at my age.

I prowl across the terrain, vigilant of muck and careful not to get myself dirty. Nevertheless, it's a challenge. It's one thing to travel through the woods in hard boots and sturdy clothes like my woolen skirt and leggings. It's another to scuttle in the dark wearing yards of frail cotton. The nightgown falls to my ankles, a fussy white film of material billowing from under my hooded cloak. The gown swishes around my feet, snagging on the occasional twig and collecting stains. My mantle wards off the stinging midnight chill, and my crossbow taps against my spine.

This outing had been an accident to begin with. My sisters and I had been engaged in an outdoor wildlife game. We'd been playing hide-and-seek while wearing our favorite animal masks. Lark had worn a bird visor. Cove had donned a serpent. I'd selected a deer mask and a headband of antlers.

Papa Thorne had told us not to venture out after dark unless the animals in our sanctuary required tending. They're safe against the dangers of eventide because magical beings never harm them. Conversely, humans are fair game.

The Folk come out at night, the villagers say.

The Folk are vicious, the cottagers say.

Although there's never been a report of Solitary Faeries harming children—I'm not a child, by the way—Papa insists that we keep our wits about us and stay inside when the sun drops below the horizon.

The game had been Lark's idea because we hadn't been able to sleep. We'd eavesdropped on Papa and his neighbors whispering on our porch. They were reflecting on what happened several nights ago when the villagers penetrated the border to the Solitary wild, exacting revenge on the Fae with a surprise attack.

For all intents and purposes, the townsfolk had laid siege to the Fae fauna, not the Faeries themselves. The Folk are too powerful for humans, but since they'll fade from existence without their wildlife, this option had given my people an edge. It had been a viable alternative.

They'd called it The Trapping. Papa Thorne hadn't condoned the plan, but it was him against our whole town.

The details of that attack had spooked my sisters. Not me. Rather, the account had drawn a frown across my face and produced a quick lurch in my chest. Visions of wounded and trapped animals harken back to a life before my family, so that I hadn't been able to rest, either.

Hence, the game. We'd needed levity, and Lark is an expert at that. She always knows what to do when one of us requires a boost of spirit.

Still, breaking Papa's ordinance hadn't been on my list of options. But since democracy had won out—two against one—I'd complied.

Inevitably, we'd lost each other during the game. This is why I'd suggested a different game. No good can come of hide-and-seek across the plains at midnight.

Elderberry bushes shiver. In the distance, a nightingale sings. My unshod feet pick through the dense region as I scan the ground for signs of my sisters.

The deer mask tickles my cheeks, and the antler headband digs into my scalp. I should remove both items, the costume nothing but an impediment and bait for predators. Moreover, it's clear Lark and Cove aren't in this area. They must be nearer to where we last saw one another, north of here and closer to the open fields.

Meanwhile, I've trekked farther than I had meant to. These woods are a crescent, curving south of Reverie Hollow. I stop and tarry, peeking over my shoulder. Beyond the canopy, the outline of jagged bluffs takes a bite out of the night sky.

The Solitary wild. The land of Faeries, with its mountain, forest, and river.

It looks subdued from here, like any environment does from afar. It's when you wander inside that scary things happen. Things with teeth and claws.

I swerve to head back, then halt. The leaves shudder, trembling like animals raising their hackles to shake off an army of flies.

The remote scrape of metal has me turning halfway. The faint commotion urges my feet to move, to whirl and leap across the ground. My heart stutters, fear tapping my chest.

I don't want to know. I don't want to see. I don't want to find.

Yet I do. And I do. And I do.

I know that ruckus. I know the sound of a trapped animal.

Whatever creature it is, it makes no other sound. No brays, squawks, or grunts. I race faster, hurtling through wood sorrel. My crossbow jostles across my back, and my cloak flares, batting foliage along the way.

This is folly without shoes. I slow to a jog and then halt, my gaze lurching between fragments on the ground and the source of the noise. Instantly, the scraping of metal stops. Milky film laces the tree trunks, and the blues of eventide drip through the branches, spotlighting the surrounding thicket.

Perhaps I was mistaken. But no, I'm never mistaken.

Juniper of Reverie Hollow is never mistaken.

I swerve this way and that but fail to detect another disturbance, nor a single twitch of briars. That can't be right.

Forests don't go mute. Not mortal ones.

Crouching, I flatten my palm against the ground. No vibrations, either. I close my eyes and press harder, waiting for the barest of tremors—a galloping mammal or foraging critter.

That's when I feel it. Not the rumble of earth but the weight of a stare.

My eyes blast open—and collide with another pair.

Bushes tangle in front of me, the leaves centimeters from my nose. Through the snarl, a set of lustrous eyes watch me, the black pupils winking with intrigue.

Above that intent stare, antlers loop into view, the short prongs stabbing the air. It's a young creature, based on the size of its crown.

As the poor thing peers at me, I remember the screeching metal. The animal must be wounded, yet it doesn't make a single sound.

My pulse accelerates. I crawl on all fours, inching closer. "Careful now," I instruct, reaching out to spread the leaves. "It is all right. I'm an expert, and I'm here to—"

My words stagger, tripping back down my throat. Staring at me is a juvenile, but he's certainly not a deer.

Those glossy pupils narrow, so rich they penetrate the darkness. The boy is around my age, maybe ten or a couple of years older. He watches me through the foliage, his face twisted my way.

In fact, everything about him is twisted. From the sideways position in which he's sprawled, to the shock of red waves, to the pointed ears and rails of antlers sprouting from his head.

He's a Fae.

We gawk at each other, separated by less than a foot. The Fae gives me a once-over, his features contorting with curiosity of the malevolent sort, mockery of the disgusted sort. I remember the deer mask perched on my face, the antler band nesting on my head. Compared with his real antlers, I feel so very mortal. And churlish. And silly. I whip off the accessories and store them on the ground.

Now we see one another fully in the moonlight. The Fae is even less impressed by me without the costume. He regards my crossbow and very round ears, amusement and ridicule clashing with another sensation, one that pulls an unwilling hiss from him.

Pain. He's in pain.

Any semblance of color blanches from his face, leaving behind a cold sheet of white. His angular cheekbones and square jaw squeeze together, hurt tacking those features in place. In my world, one would need a mason to chisel such a countenance, but the tick-tick-tick in his temple reminds me that he's not a figment.

My head darts from his grimace down the length of his body, which rests upon an oval bed of grass. A vest strains across the small plate of his chest, and breeches hug his waist, the leather ending at the knees where...

Fables eternal. Instead of human limbs, trimmed fur trails down his calves and tapers into two hard shells of bone. Each has a wedge and a slit in the middle, much like a cracked heart. Cloven hooves.

Stories flip through my mind. Specifically, tales about an impish breed of Faeries, the rowdiest ones who dwell in The Solitary Forest.

Satyrs. This creature is a satyr.

I stiffen but keep my face neutral. He could be a faun instead, but his face doesn't suit that breed. Fauns are depicted as conventionally lovely, like archetypes you'd see painted on teacups. To the contrary, his features exceed that uninspiring description and resemble one of those figurines carved from wood—rugged and unrefined.

The jaws of an iron trap feast on one of his calves and puncture flesh, rivulets of blood leaking down his fur. It's a sight from nightmares, from the past, from days and months and years that curdle in my head whenever I'm asleep. I know the shape and sounds of this trap. I've set up plenty of them and then held back sobs while whatever got caught inside suffered.

Two rows that spring into action on contact, its maw clamping shut. Twelve spikes that plunge deeply into its quarry. The snap of ligaments. Feral caws, growls, squeaks, and roars.

Bile washes up my throat. I scramble through the bushes and into the little hollow. With my fingers outstretched, I lurch toward the contraption, aiming for the right latches. "I'm going to help—"

The Fae seizes my wrists and jerks me into him. "Help?" he drawls. "You can help by staying the fuck away from me."

He thrusts me backward. My rump hits the ground, my nightgown and cloak tangling around my legs.

Pride stings my cheeks. I give the cloak's tail a hearty tug and rise on my kneecaps, "Foolish imp. Keep still."

"Tedious mortal. Go away."

"The jowls are made of iron."

"You don't say," he sneers.

Indeed. This hadn't warranted saying. Faeries have magic, in addition to the benefits of speed, strength, and augmented senses. That is, until iron gets in the way. The trap has fatigued him.

Apparently, it has impaired his brain as well. We glare at one another, hovering inches apart. Me, hunched over the Fae. Him, spread out like pancake batter, crimson drizzling from the gashes in his limbs.

"With that attitude, you'll bleed out," I lecture.

"Ha," he replies without humor. "No, I won't. They won't let me."

What does that mean? Who won't let him?

"I wasn't going to harm you," I say. "I know how to open them."

Suspicion cuts through his face. "You?"

For pity's sake. I don't have time for ignorance. I walk on my knees, approach the iron teeth, and fiddle with the closure.

An obstinate hand swings toward me. Without looking up, I slap his fingers away. "Give me three minutes," I state. "If I've not succeeded by then, I'll leave you to rot."

Galled mirth springs from his mouth. "Three minutes," he repeats, his tenor rusty at the edges. "Now there's a merry number."

If Faeries can't lie, does that mean they're incapable of detecting untruths? I haven't researched this yet. But whether or not he believes my fib, I let the proposal squat between us.

I peer down to review the mechanism, illuminated by a feeble lunar beam. What I wouldn't give for flint and tinder.

Oddly, a chain dangles from the trap and links to a fat nail embedded into the ground. That...doesn't make sense. I don't know about elsewhere, but this trap is a Middle Country design, and the poachers here use such additional gadgets only when dealing with an animal of considerable girth and power. A bear or elk, perhaps.

But those animals don't roam in this area. Skilled poachers would know that.

Unless they're not hunting a creature of this world. Unless they're hunting unearthly ones.

During The Trapping, some of the elder Folk had tried to save their animals and were captured. The villagers had distributed the prisoners across the outskirts of town, keeping them locked in cages or affixed to snares, letting them decay on their own.

But…children? They'd taken Fae children, too?

Is he young? If immortal, he could be much older than I'd originally thought.

The Fae seethes, his limb trembling something fierce. Globs of blood coat his fur and stain the grass.

My fingers sketch the trap. It's the blacksmith's handiwork for certain, with the same construction and vulnerabilities I'm used to.

I find the right gear and settle my digits there. "This is going to hurt."

He's quiet for a moment. "Would you look at me, luv?"

The plea takes physical form, its weight reaching out to snatch my chin. I glance up and meet his eyes, the pupils simmering with mischief, malice, and a queer kind of melancholy. I've never beheld that mixture, a sugar-vinegar-water clashing of emotions.

That, plus arrogance, superiority, and nerve. Also, agony.

How does he tolerate that many emotions at once? Doesn't it bother him to feel so much in a given moment?

I think about my small form and how little room there is within. I can't imagine fitting more than one sensation inside my chest at a time.

The satyr does nothing to conceal these emotions. I wonder what it takes to puncture him so badly that he's unwilling to show his reaction. What would need to happen for him to hurt so much, to be so consumed or defeated by something—or someone—that he's unable to express himself?

If being snared by his enemy won't silence him, if having his kin attacked in the dead of night won't stay his tongue, what type of pain would? Or are Faeries simply that resilient?

I hold his gaze, noting the white freckles sprinkled across his pert nose. "By the way? Don't call me 'luv.'"

I punch and twist. A serrated howl grinds from his mouth. "Fucking fuck!"

The lock quakes, the teeth loosen, and the trap's mouth flips open in shock. A growl abrades from his throat and then, like a wild animal newly liberated, the Fae strives to flee. It's a terrible sight, him thrashing backward across the dirt and tottering to his feet—his hooves—before he crashes again.

The welp flounders, buckling onto the grass. He blasts another vulgar oath into the forest, the sound both anguished and inconvenienced.

"Shh," I tell him while casting about. If the villagers had snared him like this, there's a good chance they'd intended for him to expire out here. On the other hand, they could return to collect him, despite the late hour.

He makes a fuss, cursing his heart out while fumbling to rip a swatch of his leather breeches. His hands shiver, those magic fingers slick with magic blood. Craters pockmark that furry leg, blackened red oozing from the cavities.

Immortal or not, battle wounds can cripple a Fae beyond recovery, possibly kill them. That's what the Fables say.

I gain my feet and hop out of the copse, where I gather my costume and archery, then return to his side. Using the tip of a bolt, I prick the seams from the ruffled hem of my nightgown. Once the thread loosens, I grab a fistful of material and yank.

The fabric tears, the noise clawing through the silence. That's when I realize he's gone mute, watching me.

I wrap and knot the substitute bandage around his calf, ruby puddles seeping through the cloth. Thank Fables, the gouges stop leaking.

The Fae gazes at the dressing, then swings his face to mine. His parched complexion beads with sweat, but the pain seems to ebb a little. The rapid intakes slow, and those irises dull from molten to mild.

A strange expression compromises his features. Bafflement? Distrust?

Finally, he settles on impertinence, his lips tipping to one side. "Thanks, luv."

My skin crackles. "You're not welcome."

And well, he's not. I don't like him tossing out such an endearment, yet my stomach reacts differently than my brain. A fizzy sensation bubbles like effervescence in my womb. It's a part of me I don't know what to do with.

I resent him for that. And what have I done, freeing a Fae? If he'd been one of the captured fauna, I would have liberated him without repentance. But this creature? I've just betrayed my neighbors, knowing all the things Faeries have done to them. All the bad and frightening things.

Faeries deserve retribution, the villagers say. Faeries have no hearts or consciences. Faeries are abominations, bred from the wrong side of nature. The dark side.

I should go. I should get back to my sisters.

I shouldn't have helped him. I'll regret this.

"What's your name?" an earthen voice asks, boyish and quizzical.

The question is a finger poking me in the side, demanding my attention. "It's not 'luv'" is all I say.

"That's a shame." The Fae eases out his leg, then reclines further onto the bed of grass while bracing himself on his elbows. "My name's Puck." His smile goes lopsided. "It rhymes with—"

I cough, half out of shock, half just to stop him. "I know what it rhymes with."

That smile widens, carving through the residual pain. "And what does your name rhyme with?"

"Nothing."

"Every name rhymes with something." He grits his teeth at the slightest movement of his injured limb. "If not, just make up a word that sounds similar. Problem solved."

How lazy. "I will not *make up* a word."

"Aww. Need help?"

"And I will not tell you my name."

Not because it's dangerous. The lore was disproved ages ago: There's no harm in humans revealing their names to Faeries. I just won't tell him because I don't want to give this creature that piece of me, nor any piece of me.

But there is harm in Faeries revealing their monikers to humans. "Puck" must be his nickname rather than his true one. Be that as it may, it suits him.

His tongue is as honed as his ears, his attitude as bold as the shade of his hair. I've never seen a red quite so, well, red. It's an inferno, painted in every blazing hue. It's a volatile color. A naughty one, too.

The satyr doesn't nag me about my name, but only because his attention has strayed to my human legs. They peek from the cloak and frayed nightgown hem, the calves as slender as stems, the bulbs of my toes flushed peach.

At first, I think he's appraising me, so I scoot away from him. But then his head pivots from my limbs to his furred calves, his brows crinkling like dual accordions. Surely, he knows mortals don't possess fauna traits.

Doesn't he? Plenty of mortals have disappeared into Faerie. And he must have noted the ones who'd captured him.

Yet confusion distorts his countenance. "What's it like?"

"What is what like?" I reply.

"Those." He juts his chin to my legs. "What's it like to have those?"

"Couldn't you ask any Fae with toes and ankles?"

Puck's stare uproots me. "But I'm asking you."

I blink. What kind of question is that? What answer does he want?

I consider the wreckage of his leg, the shredded skin beneath that bandage. It's a miracle the trap didn't chomp the limb in half. It's a greater miracle that such a flimsy textile staunched the flow.

It would have done worse to a real deer.

It has.

Such a deer would have wailed.

It has.

The sound would have ripped my heart out.

It has.

Surging to my feet, I grab the trap by its chain and dump it beside the nail hammered into the ground. Out of range. Out of thought. I plonk back onto the grass, draw my knees to my chest, and string my arms around my legs.

I really must leave, but I can't just leave. I can't leave anything that's been bitten by those teeth.

Puck sobers. He stares at me, the humor dashing from his face. I care for that even less than his smile and clasp my limbs harder, folding myself in until I'm good and secure.

"Will they heal?" I ask, indicating the wounds.

"Eventually, and not a day sooner," he says, deadpan.

I sigh. It's hopeless trying to get a frank answer from him.

Nevertheless, the color's returning to his visage, rosy petals blooming across the slopes of his cheeks. His leg relaxes, the blood drying. The fur had been bristling before; now, it appears soft to the touch.

Faeries must enjoy the perks of a swift recovery. Later, I will look that up in the Fables.

Or on second thought, I don't want to look it up. I want to get answers directly from him. I want to ask this Fae a thousand questions. And perhaps I won't mind if he juggles his replies. Parsing through the riddles of a Fae would be a brilliant exercise.

I expect this Puck character can handle an inquisition. His manner of speech is more elevated than any village boy. Sharper, too. Again, I wonder about his age and if his kind grow up with a loftier vocabulary. Either way, I like it.

Lark has dubbed my own speech as "fancy talk." But she means it affectionately.

"What about you?" Puck asks, flapping his hand toward me. "Doesn't it hurt to sit so…tightly?"

"No," I profess. "I'm comfortable."

"Are you sure?" Beneath that easy mien, anger festers. "Don't get too comfortable and let me spoil your night. It's a merry one for mortals. You must have so much to celebrate."

No one's celebrating The Trapping. They're too scared.

Or rather, that's not true. Some of my neighbors are indeed rejoicing in the square. I've heard the fiddles and drums.

Puck's droll tone rekindles the reason he's in this pickle, the reason I'm here with him.

I peek at his bandage, needing to be absolutely sure. "Who did this?"

"I didn't do it to myself," he responds.

That's sufficient enough for me. "The townsfolk say you were trying to rescue the fauna."

"Mind your mortal business," he lashes out. "What were you doing out here? Hunting for fireflies? Wanting to see the spoils of your ambush, maybe? To watch our animals writhe in your cages? Hoping to catch one of us yourself?"

My lower back aches. I think about the tattoo inked there, the coal-dyed image marking its territory. "I wasn't hunting Faeries or fauna. I was playing a game with my family."

That calms him down. "I like games. Which one?"

"You shift moods faster than a toddler."

A chuckle bursts from his mouth, his jubilant laughter pealing through the woods. The cheeky sound dances across my shoulders, making them stiffen with alarm. Not in cautious alarm, but some other kind that nudges the corners of my lips.

I've never made a boy laugh. It's a frivolous accomplishment, yet the crook in my mouth deepens.

Unlike me, he's the one who is injured. Yet unlike me, this Fae's draped himself like a careless prince. He's a contrary chap, if there ever was one.

"In that case, I wager you've never met a Fae before," he says.

"So what? I have now," I declare.

"I've never met a human girl. Never seen one, either."

He slings an arm on his steepled knee and inspects the crossbow resting at my side. I've been planning to add iron tips to the bolts, but I haven't yet, which is fortunate for him.

"I have a bow, too," he says. "It's nicer than yours."

"You're trying to rile me up."

"Is it working?"

"Why do you want it to?"

"Because I can't help myself. You removed that bloody trap—no pun intended—without flinching. That kind of hard-boiled resilience rivals the stoutest of centaurs."

"Really?"

"Really."

"So you want to disarm me, just to know what you're capable of."

"Nah." He cocks his head, the antlers tilting. "I want to know what *you're* capable of."

If the corner in my mouth slides any further across my face, I'll be grinning. It's unwise to let a satyr work his charm. The Fables say his kind are a miserable lot. The ancient pages classify satyrs as rakes, the kinds of bucks Lark fraternizes with, only a thousand times filthier. They're masters of flattery and enticement. They do this so well, it scarcely constitutes glamour.

Regardless, they might use such cajolery to trick a human.

I exercise the muscles in my jaw until that traitorous smile is under control. Then I skid forward, the better to see those hooves. My eyes seek to verify this isn't an elaborate hoax concocted by one of the village boys.

But no, it can't be. The children of Reverie Hollow would never emulate one of the Folk and, thus, risk causing offense. Also, none of them would travel this deep into the woods after dusk.

Lastly, they know I wouldn't let them get away with a prank. I never have before.

Midnight blue smudges the sky. "My family will wonder where I am," I prompt.

His face falls, the white freckles sinking. "If you say so."

"All right." I shift in my seat, the grass stroking my soles. "Will you be—"

"Fine by myself?" he guesses. "I'll live. We Faeries tend to do that."

"I don't like incomplete answers."

"Such disregard for wonderment." I glower at his teasing remark until he concedes, "I'll be hobbling before sunrise. Trust me."

I nod but don't move. Neither of us does.

Truly, I have to get back to my sisters before Cove starts to cry and Lark goes on an expedition to find me. I must return before they give up and tell Papa Thorne.

Besides, if this satyr heals quickly, he doesn't need me to stick around. Correct?

I chew on my lower lip. When Puck's eyes track the motion, my heart gives a small bump, a little fist knocking on my chest and asking me to let it in.

"Wanna see what I can do?" Puck breaks the silence and swerves his flat palm over a tiny bud swaying from the ground. The plant's leaves react, curling tenderly along his knuckles.

My lips part. "How…"

Puck withdraws his hand and lifts it, wiggling his digits. With the conspiratorial whisper of an illusionist, he confides, "Magic."

It happens. A laugh pops from between my lips. The noise travels to his side of the recess, and he catches it, his own grin widening. "Now there's a merry sound."

Warmth pools in my belly. I don't know what's happening, but it's happening quickly, perilously.

I clear my throat, but my tone comes out whimsical and combative. "I can tell you the origin of each plant here."

He plays along. "I can tell you the origin of those origins."

This is wrong. It's wrong to keep my sisters fretting. It's wrong to have nursed this Fae. It's wrong to talk to him. It's wrong to break these rules. I never break rules.

But it's wrong to leave someone hurt. And it feels wrong to leave without knowing more, understanding more.

The thought scares me. Puck scares me in a foreign way. It's a thrilling rush to the head, to the soles.

I swing my legs to the side, tucking them under me. It's my favorite sitting position whenever Papa Thorne tells stories by the fire. "Tell me," I invite.

And he does. And I tell him things back.

And because it takes Faeries a long time to heal from iron wounds, we keep telling each other things over the next thirteen days. I sneak out to visit the satyr every night, supplying him with food, water, a change of bandages, and conversation.

Puck confides how woodland Faeries attune themselves to nature, no matter which realm they hail from. My world. His world. Among animal traits, his kind are born with wind, soil, and water in their blood, ordaining them with a special connection to the land. I'd known this, but I hadn't known it extended to mortal environments.

The satyr demonstrates, miming as though he's playing an instrument. He says it's a cello and describes the notes, likening them to the roots and layers of earth, so that I understand the sounds.

His arm slides to and fro, slicing the air while the opposite digits vibrate over invisible strings. The bushes sway, their leaves teetering. Tree roots crackle, their ancient bark stretching. He feigns playing a tune, making the weald dance around us.

The satyr shares his love of music. I share my love of reading.

He tells me the villagers had confiscated his longbow when they'd caught him. I waver, then speculate aloud where they might have taken it—the blacksmith's forge in the village square.

He doesn't express gratitude for this, nor repay me with a favor, which is fine. Having ties to a Fae could get me into even more trouble. These rendezvouses are enough, with their dancing foliage and clandestine whispers.

Magic doesn't aggravate me like it does Lark. I find it practical like any tool.

I say I'm ten years old and ask about Puck's age. He answers, "Young enough to match you in shape and size, but old enough not to answer the question." To which I fling a stone at his antlers, and he laughs.

A satyr who wields a bow and plays a cello. A satyr who brings the wild to life, with irises as rich as the soil and a wavy bonfire of hair.

Can he see my own eye color? Or my hair, cinched into its ponytail? Can his elevated senses identify the shade of green?

He doesn't speak of his family, whether he has one at all. Likewise, I don't describe mine, not wanting to involve them in case these nights go awry.

On the thirteenth evening, the satyr asks more about my penchant for books. I tell him how it feels safe to see nouns, verbs, and adjectives on a page, an assembly of sentences and paragraphs that will never go away, revelations that will never abandon me. Chapters that can be counted upon, trusted and eternal.

My chest swells and unloads itself. I talk for so long, I lose track of time.

Papa Thorne has been teaching me and my sisters our letters. I'm a fast learner, so I've graduated to the Book of Fables. But since I'm not yet proficient—I will be—I've made Papa recite a handful of Fables until I memorized them.

One in particular. "*The Stag Hunts a Doe* is my favorite Fable," I say.

Puck gives a start. "Mine, too."

"Really? You've read the Fables?"

"Some of them. That one tugs on me the most." He pats his antlers. "And not just because I have these things."

"I can recite the story by heart."

"You have my attention. Let's hear it, then."

I hesitate, then close my eyes and convey the tale aloud. When I open my lids again, the distant market bell tolls, a brass call shivering through the air.

Puck watches me. He looks equally fascinated and nettled, and it's the only instant when he remains quiet.

I catch that gaze and hold it. "Do you think animals feel pain the way we do?"

It's the wrong thing to ask. The curiosity in his pupils fades, revealing two black wells. "What? Suddenly you care?" His gaze ticks over to the discarded iron teeth, then slices back to me. "When we met, how did you know that trick with the trap?"

I taste the sourness of his question, an acidic fruit gone overripe and on the brink of turning rancid. "It wasn't a trick," I defend. "I twisted and pressed down. That unhinged the trap."

"Where did you learn to shoot?"

Poachers had taught me. "Does it matter? Humans need to eat."

"Why are you still here?"

Each query is a blister, his interrogation searing my insides. It hurts. These questions hurt, and I don't know if it's because they're risky or because they're coming from him. A Fae. A satyr. The first male, possibly around my age, who I can actually tolerate, who I can stand to be around. I miss the truce we've shared over nearly a fortnight.

Gracious. Has it truly been that long?

The moon is a white onion sinking beneath the canopy, while eventide's fog yields to twilight. I sit up straighter. "I'm here because I *do* care. I'm not one of them."

Puck's face scrunches, from mildly suspicious to ironically suspicious. "I didn't say you were."

My legs unravel, and I launch to my knees. "I would never hurt an animal!"

"If I'd been standing on my hooves, would you have targeted me?"

My lips part, close, part again. My tongue flops around in my mouth, useless. After all Faeries have done to humans, would I have targeted him if he'd been uninjured, running rampant across the forest? After all the meanness and horror, would I have aimed a bolt at his heart? Despite what I think of The Trapping, despite not wanting those animals caged, and despite him intending to free them, would I have released him?

Or would I have hunted him?

The unspoken answer splits me in half, a gorge widening down the center. But in this moment, it's the only answer that exists.

Puck might be young, but he will grow up. If he isn't like the rest of them now, he will be someday. He'll ruin lives, bully mortals, enslave and glamour innocent people, and maim and terrorize them.

In the future, he might prey on my family. Any of his kin might.

I tense, a cold splash of dread hitting me in the face. Isn't that what I've done anyway? Ministering to him contributes to that.

He's not a stray like I was once. He's not a mortal nor a deer.

He's a monster. I've unleashed a monster.

"You would have targeted me, too," I push back. "If I'd been standing in your way, you certainly wouldn't have been nice about it."

"We. Don't. Target. Striplings."

"I was trying to save you!"

Puck pauses, measures his words, then leans in. He drapes his forearms over his knees and flicks the words into the air. "You'll never save anything."

The poacher tattoo burns into my back. I'm on my feet and out of the copse before I indeed put a bolt in him, before I fully regret my actions— the do's and don'ts colliding. I leave before he recovers. I leave before I'm tempted to fix this moment, to find a middle ground. I leave before he's tempted to do the same thing.

What did we expect? He's a Fae. I'm a mortal.

I'm a traitor to my people and a liar to myself. This night was forbidden and a betrayal. It wasn't special.

Yet something else congests in my throat. Something contrary to remorse. Something that feels cheated, with a gaping hole in its center.

My arms flap wide, smacking bushes out of the way. I'd had the foresight to gather my things, hitching the weapon, stuffing the deer mask into my cloak pocket, and jamming the antler band on my head, its ends biting into my scalp.

Indeed, I've been toting the costume with me for each visit. I don't know why, since I haven't been wearing the items on a regular basis. Nor can I justify why I'd kept coming here barefoot like a wild thing, except that Puck had continually marveled at the sight of my toes.

I stomp through the area—then stumble in place, oxygen draining from my lungs. A silhouette appears from around a bend, the spindles of its crown rising high. The russet deer is massive, the biggest I've ever beheld. And I've beheld many.

The creature steps toward me, then halts in the murky shadows. Two points of light reflect in its pupils as the animal towers over me, taller than a common stag. Steam puffs from its snout, all other sounds fading around us.

That's when I realize it's a doe, which can't be possible—not in this reality.

I know the animals of my world. She's not one of them. A mortal doe doesn't grow antlers.

The ethereal creature studies me. I stare, hypnotized. The sight of her seals the rift in my body, the place where Puck's questions had cleaved through.

Then the deer's head tips up as though listening. The shrubs quaver, creepers dancing.

The doe springs forth. She passes me on slender limbs, galloping toward the place I'd just abandoned. As she pitches into the woods, the breeze stirs my hair, loosening errant strands from the ponytail.

My pulse catapults into my throat. I whip around to chase after her.

A twig pierces my bare heel, stinging my flesh. My nightgown billows, the torn hem slapping my calves. When I reach the spot where Puck had been, he's gone. So is the doe.

In the haphazard gleam of twilight, I do my best to scan for tracks but find none. However, I locate breaks in the foliage and detect the faint whiffs of cloves and pine. I follow those clues through the woods.

"You, there!" From the sidelines, two meaty figures barrel into view. They've bustled here in haste and appear weaponless other than a single pitchfork. In the dappled light, I deduce the hooked nose of the local glassblower and a resident farmer who speaks through an overbite. "What'er you doing out here at this hour, child? Are you hurt?"

My pulse leaps, but I have the sense to play dumb. "Hurt from what?"

"Where'd they go?"

"Who, sirs?"

"There." The glassblower ignores my blathering and points at a string of deer tracks, which have appeared too late for me to conceal. Catching sight of the trail, the man snatches my archery.

"Hey!" I trill.

"First, one runt escapes from the forge, and now this," the glassblower rails to his companion.

My crossbow. That man took my crossbow to shoot the deer!

Or he might go after Puck. Or both.

The villagers bleed into the shadows. I hasten in the men's direction and pursue the hoof prints, scuffing the marks as I go, should anyone else turn up. I pass from the forest, through the open fields, and into another boundary of trees.

There, my feet stall. I huddle behind a tree, a strangled sound rushing up my throat. I brace a palm against the trunk, to keep myself from buckling from the scene.

Cages. Traps. Hundreds of them, with their doors flung open, the latches broken. Flayed bodies lay scattered among the crates, some of skin and bone, some of feathers and pelts.

Nausea roils in my gut. My eyes sting as they veer from one fallen figure to the next. Faeries splayed across the ground, young and old, with pale skin or teal skin, with tails and talons. And fauna, broken and battered. All of them, disfigured and lifeless.

This is but one of the locations. And if this is just one, what is the true death toll?

A Fae kneels. His body shakes so violently, I see it from here. That strangled sound I'd been containing escapes, at which point, the Fae's head lashes up. His eyes incinerate a path to my hiding spot, his expression spasming with grief.

And I can't help it. Tears salt my eyes and leak down my face because I'm sorry.

I'm so sorry for my people and his. I'm sorry they hate each other. I'm sorry that nothing can be done.

I notice a handful of animals are still alive, fluttering and hopping and scurrying about. Foxes, swine, a bear cub, and a juvenile elk. Among them stands the deer, poised at Puck's side.

The satyr came here to set them free, like the rest of his kin had tried to do. He succeeded with several, failed with the rest.

I'd helped him do it. Not only had I emancipated him, tended to his wound, and befriended him. I'd also shown the satyr how to unlock the trap. He'd watched me closely when I worked the iron teeth open, and I'd described the method during our argument that first night.

A bolt zips past me toward Puck. The two men must have deviated from the correct tracks before catching up, their shouts drowning out my scream. The glassblower fumbles to load the crossbow and fire, while the farmer hurls the pitchfork toward the doe and misses. The archery impales a branch, startling the animals.

Puck lunges upright, wobbly on his injured leg. He dives in front of the doe, catching the next bolt in his grip and tumbling across the ground. I see the moment he stops and recognizes the weapon.

His gaze snaps toward me, a newfangled emotion smudging his features. I'd known how to work the trap, the villagers are attacking with my weapon, and I don't need a mirror to see the tears on my face.

I'm crying because I care, but he doesn't realize this. For all he knows, fear or guilt are the culprits.

All Puck sees is a girl cowering while her people target his kin with her archery. A girl who'd been nice to him, who'd acted like a friend. A human girl who can lie.

Puck watches me through ferocious eyes. He thinks I flagged these men down. He thinks I led them here. And because of that, he thinks I'd contributed to The Trapping, had possibly assembled the snares.

We hover on opposite sides of the clearing. Surrounded by mauled Faeries and fauna, his livid gaze strikes true.

I falter, landing against the tree. I didn't do this—not this time.

But I have done this. I've done it before. Perhaps that's why I attempt to shriek again, to absolve myself, yet nothing comes out.

The men charge. The doe buckles on her forelimbs, allowing Puck to mount. The surviving fauna clamor, a wildlife stampede recovering from battle.

Astride the deer, Puck casts me one final glimpse. Mischief. Menace. Mayhem. That look is a promise of all three, should we ever cross paths again.

Deliberately, he steers the doe around and nudges her into motion, vaulting into the trees with a stream of fauna in his wake. They vanish without disturbing the overgrowth, as if they were never there. Meanwhile, the glassblower and farmer bellow for reinforcements and hasten after the pack.

Puck and his animal companions will outpace them. I know they will.

I wait until it's quiet before taking a blind step forward. My foot lands in a deer print, my toes pressing into the demarcations. Through my tears, I stare at the vision.

That's when I dry heave, an unleashed sob wadding in my gullet. I crumble beside the hoof print and stay there until dawn trickles over the horizon.

And then I clean up the mess.

14

In the days that had followed, the glassblower returned my crossbow, and I'd continued to play ignorant. I was out there being rebellious, staying up past my bedtime and pretending to hunt Fae monsters. I'd had no idea about the doe or satyr until happening upon the men. For whatever reason, my story had held firm.

Neither of the villagers had told Papa what happened. They'd been too preoccupied with their own lives to make the effort.

I'd kept my visits with the satyr to myself, even from my sisters. It had felt scandalous to do so, and I was particularly quiet whenever The Trapping came up at the supper table. I'd expected Lark and Cove to comment on my silence, yet they hadn't. For some reason, they'd reacted with similar discretion, as if having nuggets to contribute but refusing to share them.

According to gossip in town, a Fae longbow had been pilfered from the blacksmith's forge. Before the satyr had departed with his deer, he must have heeded my advice and sought the weapon.

Over the ensuing weeks, I'd ventured out each night to see if he'd come back. I'd wanted to explain, to tell him I hadn't helped the villagers, hadn't done anything wrong. But he never returned.

Not at first.

Years later, I would hear his voice again. After my sisters and I had returned from trespassing into the Solitary wild, we'd convened at midnight, hunkering in the wagon by our home. The vehicle had been our playhouse since childhood, a place for telling stories and engaging in make-believe.

We'd been discussing what to do if the Faeries exacted retribution on us. Afterward, we'd recited a Fable. But in the midst of the recitation, Lark and Cove had disappeared—simply evaporated.

Paralyzed, I had blinked through my spectacles. Then I'd frowned with suspicion. Marching outside the caravan, I'd met a howling wind rushing through the property. I'd tracked the current to the willow tree hovering over the wagon and called out my sisters' names, but they hadn't answered.

No. He had instead.

"Tsk, tsk," his tenor heckled from someplace in the branches. "With a voice like that, you'll burn down the wild."

I tensed, scowled. "Who's there?"

"Me."

"Me, who?"

No reply. Suffice it so say, I had anticipated he was a Fae, but I hadn't known it was *him*. Not at the time. I couldn't have deduced his identity because only a bulky shadow had permeated the trees, lounging across the branch yet dissolving whenever I shuffled near.

Also, that voice had grown nine years older, nine years broader, and nine years huskier. In that moment, it had been unrecognizable.

I had insisted to know who he was, and he'd sang, "You'll find out."

I had insisted to know where my sisters were, and he'd drawled, "Ask them later."

I had insisted to know what he wanted, and he'd baited, "To antagonize you. And to see what you look like. And to tell you, it's time to play. So be ready." A smile had shimmied through his words. "Be very, merrily ready."

I had been about to ask more, but he'd cut me off with, "By the way, luv. Your spectacles are lopsided."

Astonishment had brought me up short. I'd forgotten about my reading lenses, which accounted for my stunted vision. I had yanked them off, and the world sharpened into blades of color. But he was gone.

And then I'd heard my sisters yelling for me, as if I had been sleep-walking or imagining things. Yet I hadn't been dreaming or hallucinating. The encounter had been real.

The next evening, I received the first missive summoning me to Faerie. It had been delivered by a deer, glamoured to resemble a mortal one. In that moment, a sidebar of facts had occurred to me, far too late.

One, calling out for my sisters must have provided the Faeries with our names. How else would they know to address the envelopes?

Two, the stranger in the tree hadn't been a stranger at all.

Three, only one voice has ever called me "luv."

15

My eyes crack open. I find myself cocooned against a masculine form, my head tucked in his lap. We lie on our sides, inverted from one another and curled in like snail shells. His cheek rests on my calves, his arm flopping over my knees.

Bleary, I hypothesize whether this is a deranged figment of my imagination. But when I glimpse Puck's unconscious face mashed atop my limbs, reality jolts me upright. His head smacks into the dirt, a husky curse puffing from his mouth.

Puck deduces our position and gives a start. He sits up, unintentionally flanking his limbs around me in the process.

My thoughts are still cottony from the memory of our past and the slumber it must have elicited. That's the only justification for why I don't skid away from him. Puck is sluggish, his groan thick and rumpled—an intimate noise that further incapacitates me.

What's the meaning of this? How did he end up on my side of the pit?

"I have an excuse," Puck vouches while scratching the side of his head. "You were shivering in your sleep, and I was too sapped to think straight."

He must have crawled over, intending to provide body heat. In short, he'd misinterpreted. This forest has a moderate climate, and I'm wearing my cloak, so I hadn't been cold. That's not why I'd been shivering.

"That's what mortals do," I yawn. "They twitch when they're dreaming."

This gives him pause. As he inspects my proximity anew, I become acutely aware of his upturned thighs lining my own, the wall of his torso flush with my back.

Suddenly, we're awake. So very awake.

"Hmm," the satyr muses. "If that's the case, your body must have been overwhelmed, ripe from all that tension needing a release."

Although he keeps his hands to himself, his breath coasts over my neck. I gulp, silently berating myself to move. Yet I stay put, inexplicably cemented to the ground.

"Do you know what I do when that happens?" His tenor drops to an indecent volume. "I touch myself."

Fables almighty. What have I done to get stuck with this shameless being? And why won't my legs budge? Why does my ear tick closer to him?

"If my shaft rises, I clutch it and drag my hand over its length. Such as with a female, if she's damp, she fills herself. Have you ever done that?" he inquires. "Ever pressed between your legs and found the seam of your body?"

Of its own volition, an unacceptable rush of moisture courses to that private place.

"If you rub there, it creates friction," he murmurs, the words tapping my nape. "The ache builds and tightens, until your core throbs like a living thing, like a pulse point. Then you hunt down that feeling, scavenge for it within the sweet, wet clutch of your thighs. You massage the nerve endings, especially that tiny stud of sensation at the very center."

My temple pounds. Everything he describes accumulates in my pelvis and nudges my ankles apart. An aggressive, unforgivable urge sparks within me, prying my thoughts open and setting my morals aflame. I want to squirm, to do something, anything to cease these impulses.

"And if you crook a finger into your cleft, you'll locate the root of that tension, and you can chase it, ride it out," Puck whispers. "If you've never fucked yourself, I highly recommend it. Such a lovely way to wake up."

I muster the willpower to twist and meet his feral eyes. "Why are you saying this?"

"Why are you listening?" he wonders.

I don't know why. By nature, this is what satyrs do. Yet revulsion isn't truly what I feel, nor aversion. That's the scariest part.

Likewise, his intonation lacks daring. His features crimp, overwhelmed, muddled.

Some type of potent energy suffuses the pit, hastening my intakes. A breeze slips into the cubicle, rustling my hair.

And then a grizzly noise rumbles from above. Puck and I exchange alert gazes. The distant wild call snaps us to attention, the noise identifiable.

"That alpha's a long way from The Sleuth of Bears," the satyr muses. "His territory is at the southeast end of the forest."

I stockpile this bit of information, marveling that he would offer it so freely.

Thankfully, this particular bear sounds too remote to fret about. Still, another hungry omnivore could happen upon us, shift to its larger form, and snatch us from this den. Wherefore, I scramble away from Puck.

Perhaps neither of us are in our right minds. For my part, I must be caught up in the residue of those dreams, the vignettes of youth, friendship, and betrayal. To this day, Puck thinks I led those villagers to him and Sylvan. I've debated whether to defend myself, but he won't believe me. He'll denounce it as subterfuge, a ploy for lenience during the game.

I stand and resume searching for a way out, helping myself as the roots had prompted. I consult their arrangement while stepping nearer to the opposite side of this pit. One of the patterns veers into an arc and dives into a pair of vertical lines on either side, like a threshold or a door.

In actuality, it's merely the likeness of a partition, yet I feel a ripe sense of discovery, an exploratory thrill. I hustle to the dirt wall and run my palm along the veins, sketching their architecture. "Puck."

He rises beside me, evaluates the movements of my hands, and makes a noise of comprehension. "Huh. That'll do," he says.

We glance at each other, hopeful, boastful. He sees what I see, cracks breaching the wall, parallel to the roots. They indicate a weak spot, an area that isn't load-bearing, one that's penetrable with the right amount of force.

Which means there's something on the other side.

Puck and I retrieve our archery. In unison, we take several steps back, load our weapons, and aim.

The satyr focuses down the length of his arrow. "Care to do the honors, luv?"

Standing beside him, I count, "One. Two. Three."

Together, we let them fly. The arrow and bolt fire into the facade. Hunks of soil, stones, and several worms crumble to the ground, landing at the toes of our boots.

"Again," I say. "One. Two. Three."

We release another set. Clods of muck collapse from the impact and fill the space with the aroma of damp earth.

Once more, I aim. "One. Two. Three."

Puck looses his arrow, and I loose the bolt. Both stems plow through, the projections vanishing into an avalanche of dirt and dust. The gritty explosion forces us to retreat, our limbs jostling backward until the debris settles.

I swipe my hand in front of my face. A gash appears in the partition, coarse around the edges. Ahead, the pit extends into a trench. Several paces beyond the threshold, the ceiling opens to the night sky glistening above.

Puck and I pick around the mound and enter the passage. The entrenchment tapers into a pupil of darkness, but none of the trees aboveground display branches suitable for aiding our exit. The boughs are either too high to access or too slender to bear our weight. We'll need to find one that suits our purpose or discover an aperture that leads to the surface.

As we journey down the trench, a series of adjacent channels appears, each depression bleeding into a void. More roots lace the walls. A few uncertain moments pass before one of the ligaments expands, then contracts, the others following suit.

I grip the crossbow. "What's happening?"

Awareness sweeps across Puck's face as he watches the roots. He bobs his flat palm at me. "Lower your weapon."

"But—"

"Trust me. You'll like this."

Words I usually have the good sense to ignore. Yet after our talk, and after…after the intimacies he'd described to me in the pit…this intermission has unlatched something between us. I waver, then heed his advice and disarm.

The roots continue to bloat and condense. Except now, their cadence relaxes, easing into a sedate tempo. I marvel, shuffling forward until my arm bumps into Puck's. "This isn't recorded in the Fables."

His profile breaks into a grin. "No. It's not."

The satyr takes my hand and guides me to the nearest wall. Calluses mar his fingertips, and warmth emanates from the basin of his palm. Darts of electricity scatter from the place where his digits curve around my knuckles, so that I'm too stumped to resist. Puck lifts my palm and flattens it against the roots, which flex under my skin, puffing with life.

"Now listen," Puck says.

As I do, he watches me expectantly, waiting for me to figure it out. With each inflation and deflation, the roots eject a sighing noise.

Like lifelines. Like pumps. Like lungs.

I gasp. "They're breathing."

He leans into me, as if imparting a secret. "They favor you."

"You think?"

"I know. Otherwise, the exhales wouldn't be relaxed."

Hubris loosens my tongue. "They must know a kindred spirit when they feel one."

"Bragger," he teases.

"I'm…" I chuckle. "Yes, I'm bragging. But wouldn't you, if you found out a tree root liked you?"

"Now who said anything about 'like'?" Puck taps one of the roots. "This one here? It fancies me. Satyrs have that charming effect."

"And who's the bragger this time?"

Our laughter ebbs. We stare at one another, his hand resting next to mine, our pinkies aligned over the breathing roots.

With each swell, the ground stirs. I envision layers of earth shifting and a river farther underground, a watercourse thrashing along the subterranean channels of The Solitary Deep and drowning everything in sight. I picture Cove down there, struggling to keep her teal head above water.

I sober and tug my hand free, the heat of his touch lingering. My companion does the same, white and black streaks creasing under his eyelashes. While stepping away from the roots, I catch him wiggling his digits as though I'd scalded him.

The roots go still. Silence congests the space between me and this satyr.

"Are they holding their breath now?" I blurt out.

Puck's gaze scrolls across my features, mapping out every nook and cranny. "You might say that. They have complex breathing patterns and cycles. In other words, they only go deep once an hour." His mouth wreathes into a grin, his eyes dipping to the southern regions of my dress. "Unlike a certain breed of Faeries."

The recollection of his breath skidding across my nape and the indiscrete touches he'd depicted trespass into my mind. Mortification scalds my cheeks. That, plus another unforgivable inclination, an appetite for something I can't name. A craving that had been dormant until he'd spoken about wet fingers and private sensations.

I point at him. "Listen to me, satyr. Let's get one thing straight."

His freckled nose crinkles far too cutely. "Only one? Boo."

"This penchant for one another ends here."

"Penchant? What does that even mean?"

"Don't play dumb. I'm talking about this connection between us."

"It's called attraction, luv. Say it with me."

Well. "This attraction means nothing. What you said…that I listened… it meant nothing."

"Is that what you felt while I pumped ideas into your head? Nothing?" The satyr encroaches upon my space. His words travel, somehow managing to reach low, scorching a path across my thighs. "Because the arousal I scented under your skirt? That sure as fuck didn't seem like nothing. If you ask me, it was everything."

"That's quite enough," I utter, my voice a tendril of air.

But he isn't finished. "Frankly, the thought of you touching yourself drives me out of my fucking mind, just like the exquisite sight of you wielding a weapon. To say nothing of how it would feel to pleasure you with my own hands. In fact, I wager it'd be the only type of magic actually worth having."

"I said, that's enough. I don't care to hear anymore."

Puck sketches a flamboyant bow. "Ever at your merry service. But since you brought it up, who said anything about it meaning something? After everything that's happened, we were pent-up, caught up in the moment. We were shaking off the final dregs of sleep, and my kind can smell desire at twenty paces. It was a verbal tease, the least of what my tongue can do to you, and I'd barely gotten started. Naturally, a teeny bit of vocal foreplay means nothing. It rarely does to satyrs, much less sex itself." He inches backward, albeit at a gradual pace that I can't say is entirely deliberate. "Lust is practical. Anything beyond that isn't."

At least, that's something I can agree with. I'm hardly a romantic like Cove. "Good," I say.

"Spectacular," he replies. "Are we done, then?"

I nod, yet we idle in place. The scoundrel transfers his attention to my mouth, and my own gaze commits the same crime, stumbling to his plush lips.

At last, we swerve toward the path and traverse the route without speaking. Eventually, I sniff the air. "No discernible scent."

The Fae contemplates that. He grabs a wad of dirt from the wall, crushes it in his fist, and releases the granules. We study the flecks' descent, which betrays not the slightest shift, nothing to indicate a current, nor an exit source.

"There goes that," Puck remarks. "On the other hand…"

"…rule out the possibilities," I fill in.

He concurs. "It's too messy down here to be the work of brownies. They'd have taken a broom to the passage. Leprechauns, hardly. Satyrs or fauns, definitely not. Centaurs prefer the surface rather than the depths. Nymphs would loathe to get their frocks or faces tarnished. Dryads are too busy tending to the upper story."

"So not Faeries," I conclude.

Which leaves the fauna. When our gazes drop to the ground, I feel like a numskull. The irony is offensive, that two hunters wouldn't have thought to do this immediately.

Puck and I kneel, the better to investigate. Handfuls of walnuts encrust the floor, indicating the type of trees looming outside these trenches. Also, a series of enormous, overlapping paw prints materialize once I broaden my gaze.

Upon second inspection, a thread of copper hair shimmers from the wall, and several large indentations imply these otherworldly dwellers had filled this trench to capacity. That would be unusual, if the Fae fauna lacked the magic to shift sizes.

We trade a keen glance. Puck flicks aside walnut shells and stray fibers of moss from the prints, the better to sketch the tracks. He manages to do so without disturbing the pattern, executing the barest sweep of contact.

It's a mammal with five paw pads and four claws. If I had to guess… no, I don't have to guess.

Once more, Puck's eyes land on mine. We hold like that, deducing the enterprising animals who'd constructed this passage, the satyr's knowing gleam matching my own.

"Foxes," we whisper.

How had we missed this? These trenches are dens, sunken to accommodate foxes when the animals grow larger.

Puck shakes his head, chagrined. "The Skulk of Foxes. I should have known."

"I thought Your Woodland Majesty didn't recognize this area," I contend.

"To the contrary, I'm a fan of foxes and their foxy ways. Henceforth, I stand corrected. I've cavorted here plenty, but not after being chased by wild pigs, hiding from a nomadic bear, and contending with a scholarly huntress. I've a headache that's extended to my antlers and hadn't realized which direction the passel had chased us. Let's say I'm not operating on all fronts, so it's a delayed, woozy reaction."

Though the residents are nowhere in sight, this can change at any moment. An indulgent part of me hopes it does.

We continue into the network. At a fork, the prints veer toward what I suspect is my original trajectory, due northwest. Periodically, we assess the imprints and touch the foundation to check for signs of turbulence— tremors indicating we're about to have company.

I appraise the fox impressions in the dirt. "Do Fae animals shift sizes randomly? Or is it a defense mechanism?"

The villagers of Reverie Hollow had prevented the latter by using iron weapons and cages. It had weakened the fauna from shifting, much like it stifled the magic of the avenging Faeries.

Puck jerks his arm my way. The warning gesture alerts me to a low-hanging root the size of a tree trunk, bulging from one upper wall to the other. We duck beneath it as he answers, "It's both, depending on the animal."

"Watch your antlers," I caution, then repeat myself several times, with several more roots.

"Okay, listen. They're *my* antlers," he carps. "I know how to travel with them—fuck!" he hisses when one of the spokes hooks on to an overhead root.

It's the first time I've witnessed a hypersensitive side of Puck. I compress my lips to keep from laughing.

Once we're through, he pauses to rub his crown and catches my expression. "Go ahead. Say it."

With pleasure. "I told you so." I motion to the rack of spokes. "Do they feel pain?"

"Only when someone challenges my masculinity." Puck gives me a saucy look and waggles his brows. "You know what they say about a satyr and his antlers."

Oh, I give up. A chuckle falls from my lips, and he laughs, too.

Our mirth sneaks down the path and dissolves into another stretch of quiet. Walnuts crunch under us. Moonlight and starlight emboss the walls, dappling the corridor in splotches of light.

I glimpse Puck's profile. His hair burns through the murk, the waves simmering around him.

"It's impolite to stare," he banters.

My gaze jumps to his eyes, but he continues to gaze ahead, amusement dimpling the incline of his cheek. "It's also rude to condescend to someone."

The crook smooths out. "Bloody right."

"I'm always right."

Puck sniggers. "Are you sure of that statement, or are you jesting?"

I'm not serious. Or perhaps I am. I don't recognize my animated tone of voice, so it's hard to tell what I was going for. My words have gotten away with themselves, as if someone has picked open a lock and let them run amok.

Had I been serious or joking?

"No," I sigh. "Or yes. Or in fact, no."

"How very Fae of you," he quips.

"I'm human." I snatch his elbow and tug until he faces me. "And proud of it."

Puck goes quiet. He processes my statement without an ounce of mockery or shallow fascination. Rather than stare as if I'm something to be examined, curiosity unravels across his countenance, as if I'm someone to be understood.

"Then let's play a game," the Fae suggests.

I release his elbow. "We're already doing that."

"Tell me about this mortal pride of yours, and I'll tell you about my immortal pride."

"That isn't a game. That's a discussion."

"Yes, yes." He flicks his digits. "Game. Discussion. Call it what you want."

"I will." I turn and stride ahead, saying over my shoulder, "I'll call it a discussion."

From behind, I sense Puck's grin. He skips to catch up, his hooves landing beside my booted feet, and hip-bumps me. "What? No objection to my proposal?"

The hip-bump is something Lark would do. Normally, I would respond in kind. But that would require touching him again.

As we step around an outcropping of rocks, I ask, "Why would I object?"

"I just didn't think you'd want your studious, preconceived notions challenged."

"I echo that sentiment."

"Fair enough."

"And," I add, "scholars like me believe in learning. That's the whole point."

Puck's gait falters, the longbow knocking against his back. "Touché. But what happens if you learn something that isn't to your liking?"

Now it's my turn to falter. I'd rather not reply to that, but in truth, I'd like to know what makes him proud to be a Fae. Where's the honor in being a deviant? A tormentor? A villain? In which case, I hope—beyond hope—his reply doesn't involve the worst kinds of details. The ones chronicled in the Fables and every child's nightmare.

We speak in low tones, our voices seeping into the walls. There are numerous reasons I'm proud to be a human. Yet as I glimpse the fox tracks, I limit myself to one Faeries have built their prejudice upon.

"Like I said before, I have a bond with nature just as you do," I say. "I don't have a tail or antlers, but I don't need them in order to feel connected to animals."

"Last time I checked, humans wouldn't fade without their fauna," Puck retaliates.

So precisely which part of The Trapping matters most to him? That question alone peppers my words. "Do you condemn us for hurting your kin or threatening your existence?"

Puck halts so quickly, I stumble in place beside him. "Don't," he says, lifting a finger and glancing askance at me. "Do *not* go there."

Offended shadows cleave his face. Moreover, hurt creeps to the surface, whether he wants it to or not. I've seen this expression before on him. The iron scars pulping across his calf remind me of the trap that had caught Puck that night, the reason he'd been there in the first place, and his haunted expression during the most gruesome part of that evening.

No, he doesn't abhor mortals solely for threatening his individual existence. His fauna and Fae kin matter to him more than that.

Still, I won't apologize. Not when he hasn't repented for what Faeries have done to humans.

Yowls interrupt my thoughts, a hoarse sound vibrating from an adjacent chamber. We pivot in that direction. A grin replaces Puck's frown, and he sets a finger to his lips, then nicks his head in the trench's direction.

Excitement carries me down the passage with him. We hunch, taking care to keep our gaits light. At another junction, we crouch and peek around the corner.

My intakes stall. A family of foxes rests among a niche of roots. Vibrant red-orange pelts cover their forms, their frizzy tails tipped in black. They look as they do in my realm, apart from their formidable sizes. One of them grooms its adolescent offspring. Another balances its chin on its front paws, its ear flicking toward Puck and me.

We stoop lower and observe their habitat. Or rather, I gawk. They're so stunning to behold, I could tarry here for days.

The scene acts as a buffer. Puck and I exchange appreciative glances, my lips tilting. For a long while, we're content to admire them.

"You're wrong," I whisper at last. "Human lives are linked to the fauna. We need them for food and clothing. Some threaten our farms while others graze the land, ridding it of pests that ravage our crops. And they provide transport and—"

"So they're efficient," he interrupts.

"They're wondrous, too." I watch one of the adult foxes sleep. "I won't romanticize them, but sometimes a mortal and an animal establish a bond. Sometimes we befriend each other, become kindred."

"That's hardly news to Faeries," Puck says. "The distinction is we have an intrinsic connection to the fauna, which you don't. They're sacred to us in a way they're not with mortals. Your relationships to wildlife come with conditions. Ours don't."

"And who gets to define what makes something sacred?" I protest. "You? Nature?"

The satyr's tongue stutters to a halt, quelling whatever he'd been about to say. I take advantage of his silence. "My sister, Lark, climbs into trees every night and whistles with the birds, crafting melodies with them. Whereas my other sister, Cove, is the only person who can get near a water serpent who lives in our pond. She's the only one the creature places its confidence in."

I count off my fingers. "Establishing mutual trust. Helping an animal recover from trauma. Interpreting what the creature needs or wants, based on its gestures or habits. Exercising kindness, patience, and generosity to the fauna. Who says those things aren't as sacred to humans, too? No, we wouldn't fade without them, not the way you would. No, we can't correspond with them through the wind, roots, or water. And no, we don't share magical or physical traits. But nowhere—not in history or in books—are bonds limited to only those abilities. There are countless ways a connection can be special, deep, ingrained."

The satyr peers at me, his features perturbed and confounded. "So which animal have you bonded with?"

"What makes you think it's only one?"

"Gimme a number, then."

"Hundreds of them."

Every single one that my sisters and I have rescued. Plus, the doe waiting at home for me.

Puck slants his head. "You're a busy bee. Do tell."

We study the fox family. Their furry muzzles and the marbles of their eyes. Their paw impressions in the soil. Their pinched faces. Not wishing to draw unwanted attention to ourselves, we back away and retrace our steps.

The satyr and I continue our sojourn, picking our way through uncharted, uneven terrain. I fold my hands in front of me while Puck threads his own behind his back. I waver, uncertain what's safe to share. But then I glimpse his scars and recall what he did to get them, whom he was trying to save. My story tumbles out, my hushed voice unfurling into the passage, the way it once did in a forest, on a secret night when we were younger.

I tell him about the Fable Dusk Sanctuary. I tell him about the orphaned and foundling fauna my sisters and I have rescued from trade poachers. The injured ones we've nursed back to health. The ones who became our family, too.

All the while, a tattoo brands my lower back, reminding me of what I don't tell Puck.

He makes inquiries, probing me about the particulars of the sanctuary. Nothing technical about managing or habilitating the animals, but about communing with them. Do we have rituals? What's my happiest memory of the sanctuary? What's my saddest one? Which animal do I remember the most?

In terms of rituals, my sisters and I say goodnight to our wild residents every evening, while dressed in our nightgowns and carrying lanterns.

My happiest memory is my very first rescue—a weasel native to Middle Country and prized by trade poachers for its pelt.

My saddest is a wounded dormouse, because the animal didn't survive past the first night. When I lost him, I'd balled myself on the ground, unable to speak while my sisters rested their heads on my shoulders.

As for these days, I share tales about the sanctuary doe who's my friend, who bucks her spindle limbs in excitement whenever I approach her pen.

She's listened to my regrets and hopes. In turn, I know what Fable to recite whenever she has trouble sleeping.

"The Wolf and the Sled," I say. "Tales from the Northern Frosts work every time with her."

When Puck makes no reply, I glimpse his troubled profile. It's unlike me to say so much, him so little.

"Your turn," I say, adjusting my pack and crossbow. "What makes you proud to be Fae?"

The satyr gives it an abundance of thought. "Now that's a merry question," he murmurs. Though, I can't decide if he's addressing me or himself.

If I've revealed myself, he must as well. I open my mouth to insist he play fair—but then halt. My fingers grab his vest, just as he tugs on my dress. Simultaneously, we pull one another to a standstill.

We glance at our hands. Buttery leather molds to his waist, yielding beneath my digits. I jerk away from him, whereas Puck uncurls his hand from the suede frock with a naughty flourish.

He points upward, but I already know. I'd seen the gap at the same time he had. The walls around us are bunched into thick clumps, caked to the ceiling, which must have sealed at some point. Regardless, another hole punches through the soil roof. The night sky peeks down at us through a single, sapphire eye laced in walnut tree branches.

The ideal bough hovers overhead, low and sturdy. Puck and I contemplate the gap, the projection, and its distance from the surface.

The Fae tsks. "That's quite a feat for human limbs. What say you?"

I unhitch my weapon. "I say, watch and learn."

The expert climber in my family would deem the soil too smooth, too uniform to ascend, lacking sockets or rocky brackets for leverage. That's why she taught me and Cove a supplementary method.

At last, the bartering trinkets in my pack will count for something. Among the items I'd brought, I thank the Fables for a twilled spool of ribbon. Its length is short but sufficient for this particular branch. Withdrawing the spool from my bag, I affix the cord to the end of a bolt, then load my crossbow. I focus on the bough and fire. The projectile shoots through the gap, hooks over the ledge, and plunges back down.

The tip stabs the ground between Puck and me. I untie the bolt and drop it into my quiver, then knot the ends of the ribbon together. Once secure, I harness my weapon, grip the twill, and haul myself off the floor while planting my feet against the wall.

Of course, Lark had made this look easy when we were growing up. My arms shriek, and my knees crack. I rope-walk myself up the vertical face, praying the fabric won't rip and feeling Puck's smirk plastered to my backside.

I stop. "Puck."

"What?" he queries, innocent. "I'm just standing here."

My heel lodges into the dirt wall, releases a chunk, and kicks it in his direction. A thunk and his muffled curse pulls a smile across my mouth. I keep going and drag myself over the rim, where I plop and catch my breath. Fresh air floods my nostrils with a crisp, herbal zest.

Crawling on all fours to the rim, I speak into the cavity, "You were saying something about human limbs?"

"Oh, but I say many things," a voice coos in my ear.

Yelping, I whip around so fast, my rear smacks onto the grass. Puck crouches beside me, his longbow affixed to his spine. A constellation of freckles dances across his nose.

I gape. "How did you—"

"I said it's a feat for mortals. Not for satyrs." He holds up the ribbon and flashes a grin. "I'm a fast climber."

My gawk scrunches into a glower. "Show-off."

He chuckles. I shake my head, but the chortle comes out anyway.

Then we stop laughing. Something snips our humor in half, cutting it off like shears: the sound of an incoming blade slicing through the air.

16

It's not that I had forgotten I was being hunted by Faeries, or that he was supposed to be hunting me alongside them. It's not that I'd forgotten he was a Fae, or that we were supposed to be fighting on opposite sides. It's not that I'd forgotten we were enemies, or that I was here because of him.

It's not that I'd forgotten the game. It's not that I'd forgotten anything about our present circumstances.

It's that I'd remembered our past.

We had slipped off track, stumbling into the margins of this land. Briefly, we had gotten lost together. This detour had reminded me of who we used to be: a human and Fae who debated and argued yet managed to laugh and listen, to discover more about each other before everything flaked apart, and the real world surged back in.

A blade flips through the leaves, shooting toward the place where we hunker side by side. Time slows. In those fleeting seconds, my eyes cast to Puck, who glances back at me. All the riddling mischief drains from his features, so that only one emotion wraps around his face, as if nothing else fits there. It's an impulse I can't place, except that I reside at the nexus of it.

Puck's hackles rise, the fur along his calves bristling. His fingers brace atop the soil, about to spring—but not toward me. He's preparing to act, to make an unforeseen choice, his defensive stance fixed on the intrusion.

With that, I see a breach in the rules. I see an impending complication, an amendment to the game.

But I need to use prudence, to be logical. Whatever the satyr's planning on my behalf, I don't give him the chance. I take the initiative and hurl myself out of the blade's path. On the way down, I hook my ankle around Puck's hoof—the one attached to his scarred leg—and sideswipe him. Once he crashes and drops the ribbon, I release my hold and tumble across the soil through flower stalks and walnut shells. Scraping to a halt, I lurch onto all fours. Puck rotates off the ground and braces himself, mirroring my position.

The attack weapon vibrates against the neck of a tree trunk, its blade lodged into the wrinkled bark. It's an axe with a wooden handle. A shower of other weapons propels from various sectors, punctuated by the sounds of charging footfalls, galloping thumps, and woodland hollers.

They materialize as a single silhouette, a mass of horns, tufted ears, and flowing hair. Homing in on us, the mass splits into multiple assailants. They attack in a spectrum of colors, from their tinted skin to their painted markings, from their cloaks, to their leaf-strewn clothing, to their jewels, to the weapons fisted in their grips.

Puck's head swings between me and his kin. Again, he catches my gaze. Again, I see him about to take action.

Again, I rob him of that opportunity. I snatch my pack, grip my crossbow, and pop to my feet. Puck does the same. Our limbs carry us backward, the schism between us growing. We watch one another, suspended in a moment that shouldn't exist.

Then we come to an agreement. He nods, albeit his lagging pace doesn't match the gesture.

Nevertheless, I nod back, because this is how it's meant to be. This was always how our detour would end. A momentary truce and temporary partnership—scarcely longer than a Fable—was never going to last. Consult the appropriate tales, and they will confirm this moral.

My expression rehashes what we'd agreed upon in the trench, and his features hurl back the same declaration: It meant nothing.

So why are we dragging our feet?

The Solitaries scatter, bleeding into the wild, camouflaging themselves as they approach. I glimpse axes, hammers, staffs, knives, and bows. I catch the rustle of branches, an attempt to confuse the huntress.

Puck and I survey one another. Indeed, we've spent too much time together, because I feel him counting with me, as we did in the pit. One. Two. Three.

We spring around in unison. I run, blasting through the underbrush, my boot soles pounding into the ground. A cursory glance over my shoulder verifies the satyr is dashing toward the Faeries, intending to rejoin them.

The foliage swallows him whole. His kin shout, their weapons clicking and twanging.

Axes hack into the creepers. Throwing stars spin like asterisks, one of the projectiles dicing through my skirt but missing flesh. Yet pain sears my chin as one of the stars finds its mark, shaving off a layer of skin. My limbs accelerate, flying through the trees.

They'll scent me out, stalk my tracks. They'll win this hunt, and I'll lose my sisters.

Something punts into my quiver, the impact shoving me forward. I stagger into a walnut tree, a star blade tacking my cloak to the bark. I fist the material and yank, tearing the fabric, then make it three paces before a body crashes sideways into me. We smack onto the ground, the body landing on top and pinning my arms.

A marten tail swishes. Vivid orange irises glare down, and a row of teeth snap in my face. "Gotcha," Tinder boasts.

My fingers grapple for the dagger at my ankle but only feel the loose ties of my laces. The upheaval must have untethered the blade from its makeshift harness. Twisting my head, I glimpse the knife over a dozen feet away, too far away. The vegetation has caught it like a snare.

Like a snare…

My frantic gaze darts about. While hunters make their own traps, they also know how to spot ones growing amidst the wild, fabrications generated by nature itself. Spotting a nest of branches beside us, I calculate its proximity, then flit my attention to the Fae. Multiple straps contain rows of stars at his thigh. The weapons suit his lanky stature, which aligns with my petite frame, which is about to come in handy.

I use my weight to flip us over. The branches snatch his tail, clicking into place as he bleats and thrashes. "You mortal bitch! Over here! She's over here! Get me out of this thing! Now!"

Retrieving the dagger and twilled ribbon is a lost cause. I load my crossbow and spin to avoid another projectile, then target the next and blow it to smithereens. Again, I tumble, this time in the opposite direction. Pitching onto my knees, I let a bolt fly, knocking a star from its trajectory.

As for the arrows, they're made of an unfamiliar Fae wood. But where is the longbow crafted of yew? Where is he?

I pivot and flee, the scenery reduced to collages of color on either side of me. Ahead, a veil appears. It glitters like a drapery woven of starlight, though I can't see beyond its film.

A voice yowls, "Stop her before she—"

I dive through the sheer border and plunge to the ground. Flopping onto my back, I gape at the cacophony of Faeries hissing and swearing. Hooves gallop toward the veil at a breakneck pace—four hooves, not two.

From the sound of it, those limbs belong to a massive figure. A horse, likely attached to a humanlike torso. The faint outline of a longbow appears first, along with a pair of fingers maneuvering the weapon.

I scramble to my feet, aim my crossbow toward the pursuer, and shoot.

A baritone voice growls. The figure storms sideways through the starlit curtain, the mist sweeping out of his way. I scurry backward as Cypress flounders, crashing to the floor with a great wallop that shakes the earth. My bolt is lodged in his flank, blood drizzling into his coat. The horn helmet slips off his head as he groans, pain searing across his features. His hands twitch; they attempt to reach for the bolt, but it's too far to grasp, particularly in his contorted position.

The longbow I had thought he'd been wielding slumps across his back, harnessed and unused. I must have been mistaken, but why wouldn't he target me?

Cypress struggles to rise, his hooves tangled in a snare of brambles that bite into his limbs, similar to the one that caught the boar shoat. The centaur mutters an aggravated oath.

I blink out of my trance. For some reason, the other Faeries haven't crossed the spangled veil. In fact, their voices subside in a wave of petulant vulgarities and ethereal complaints, followed by the echoes of retreat. One of them mutters about a consolatory drink and a round of dancing. I can't tell if Puck is amongst them.

Eventide drips into the woods. Although it's the optimal hour, the Folk would rather leave than venture into this area? With me so close, in catching distance?

Nevertheless, I count my blessings. They're gone, and Cypress is otherwise incapacitated.

I whip toward a cobbled path and sprint several steps before pausing. My hands ball into fists. The equine's not my problem. He's no better than the rest of them, an enemy who wants to stalk me to within an inch of my life.

I start and stall once more. I think of Puck. I think of our time in The Passel of Boars and The Skulk of Foxes. I think of the moment when he'd been about to move, to make a choice he shouldn't make. When he'd been about to defy the rules for no discernible reason.

I think of how it's not supposed to matter. I think of how it does.

I think of one question that keeps me from leaving. With a sigh, I turn on my heel and pad toward Cypress. The centaur regards me with skepticism as I approach. I can't help feeling a reluctant camaraderie with that look, standoffish and surly. Those are qualities I understand, traits I can handle.

I kneel before the Fae. His astringent, olive eyes narrow on my crossbow, then on me. "Come to finish the task, moppet?"

"Not precisely," I say. "But just in case…" I remove a bolt, balancing its stem on my thigh, where he can see it lest he get crafty. "Do all Faeries have a propensity for nicknames?"

Cypress snorts, the leather hoop in his nose jolting. "Nicknames," he observes with disdain. "Centaurs do not bestow nicknames."

"Then why do you call me 'moppet'?"

"Because by contrast, true names are sacred to Faeries. Consequently, we give ourselves alternate monikers."

My shoulders lift. "To know a Fae's true name is to have power over Faeries, for in their true name resides their spirit." When Cypress just stares at me—as horses do, I suppose—I say, "I've researched full volumes on the matter of magical names."

"Bravo." Despite his derision, Cypress's tone converts to something less hostile. "As to your question, we do not utter true names flippantly.

We wait until establishing a camaraderie born of trust. Otherwise, we would be pirating power from one another left and right."

"But I'm not a Fae. Sooooo why 'moppet'?"

"You are obsessed with analyzing the reasons for everything. It must be exhausting."

"I don't know which mortals you've been dealing with, but how I'm addressed matters to me."

"I call you a moppet because that is what you are—a youngling compared with my age. It is purely a label, neither a nickname, nor a true name. In that way, it emphasizes your inferiority."

That explains why Puck took note of the moniker when he conferenced with Cypress by the elm trees. "I would rather you didn't call me that."

"I am sure of it," Cypress replies. "Be that as it may, that was not the question you came here to ask, with me at your mercy. Get on with it or leave before I disentangle myself from these brambles and make good on the hunt."

I nod toward the bolt lodged in his body. "There's one problem."

"But it isn't yours," he grates, rivulets oozing down his flank. "Be assured, I shall not spare you."

"Like you didn't spare me days ago, when I was hiding near the elm trees?"

The centaur huffs. "It was too early in the chase for victory."

He can't lie, so he means what he says. Yet that's not the whole story.

Come to think of it, what was Puck's excuse for protecting my hiding spot instead of exposing it? What's been his excuse for many things he's done since this hunt began?

The behemoth creature next to me winces, his frame spasming in the thorny shrubs, the bolt digging a small crater into his coat. "Enough of this," he hisses. "What do you want?"

I want one answer. "Why were you unarmed?"

The centaur could have targeted me past the veil, yet his longbow had been pacified. He must have been harnessing the weapon, whereas I'd confused it with the opposite.

"Centaurs do not kill in their territory," Cypress says.

My fingers twitch around the bolt. "Territory?"

"You are in The Heart of Willows. It is neutral ground in The Solitary Forest and sacred to my kin. We do not spill blood beyond the veil, unless we are under attack."

Eventide glazes the woodland, highlighting the details I hadn't noticed. The knee-high emerald grasses and the incense of thyme, crisp and invigorating. The drooping trees and curtains of willow vines, also saturated in emerald from their roots to their crowns.

The Heart of Willows. This is his home.

"Is that why the Faeries didn't enter?" I ask.

"There is little point," Cypress explains. "If there is no fun to be had or game to be played, it is not worth their time. They will find amusement elsewhere until you emerge from hiding."

Which, I'll have to do eventually.

Candles grow from the forest floor, bookending a cobbled lane. The walkway curves and dips down a hill, toward a cluster of firelights and the mysteries beyond.

I glance at Cypress, my grip on the bolt relaxing. The equine's wound drips, crimson staining his fur. His dark torso inflates and deflates, each breath distorting the ink markings encircling his navel. His limbs push, attempting to free themselves from the nest.

I store my weaponry and move quickly, grabbing the bolt and ripping it from his flesh. Cypress grunts, the pain grinding from his throat while I rip fabric from my tattered dress and press the material to the gash. After yanking out the long tassel closure of my cloak—which causes the garment to fall off my shoulders—I use the slack to secure the makeshift bandage.

Since I don't have Foxglove's dagger to cut Cypress loose, my hands will have to suffice. It's arduous work, pulling and twisting the brambles to unlock the cluster from around his hooves.

Cypress bucks free. I lurch back, avoiding the brunt of his kicks.

He teeters off the ground and rises, prompting me to do the same. I brace myself but find him balking at me, confusion warping his face. He swings his head between the brambles, the cloak discarded on the ground, the dripping bolt in my hand, and me.

"Why did you do that?" he demands.

Indeed. The equine hadn't stayed his weapon out of benevolence, but out of duty. So why save him?

Because if this is neutral territory, he won't hurt me. Because I've never harmed an innocent creature since I was a child. Because I'm not a poacher anymore. Because despite the game this forest has concocted, I'm a rescuer these days. Because I won't let these Faeries strip that identity from me.

Why did I pull the bolt from Cypress's body instead of letting him bleed out? Why did I help him?

"Because I knew how," I reply, which is also true.

The centaur's expression transforms. He glances at a location over my shoulder, weighing something in his mind. Finally, he nods to himself and collects his helmet, straightening it atop his head. "You will come with me."

I squeeze the bloody bolt. Had Cypress been twisting words when he'd said this was neutral territory? "But—"

"Your own wound needs tending, moppet," he clarifies.

My fingers rise to the cut on my chin, where the throwing star had whizzed past. The laceration stings. Now that I have time to focus on it, I feel the crusty residue of dried blood on my skin.

"It isn't dire," I state. "And I've been delayed long enough."

"You have done me a favor on my land." Cypress stares me down. "You will come, and I will repay you."

A favor. Of course, the Fae wants to repay a favor, likely in excess because that's how they are, because a grander compensation outdoes the first one.

The centaur departs without a backward glance. I shoulder my archery, stuff the cloak in my pack, and then catch up to him. We hike down the stone path. At the bottom of the hill, a bridge laced in willow vines arches over a stream, the eddies reflecting a tapestry of celestials.

A vast settlement of emerald willows and gleaming leaf tents spreads across a valley. Majestic pavilions and yurts, fully constructed of the same willow vines, loom as high as the trees themselves. The drooping vines form walls, the structures ranging in size, from wide to compact. Each residence pulses with topaz light, while the tributary and willows thrive around them, intersecting with the stone lane and its candlelit trail.

"It's beautiful here," I say.

Cypress tosses me a proud but chastising look. "Did you expect it to be grim?"

Grim because of its remoteness and the fact that a dispassionate centaur hails from here? Yes.

One moment, we're alone. The next, we're surrounded.

My pace slows, my head banking east and west as a colony of centaurs appears, their broad bodies trotting, cantering, and promenading into view. Some pause on thresholds or glance from pastures where they lounge, observant rather than visceral—a sure departure from the woodland Solitaries I've encountered thus far.

Sleek coats of pearl, obsidian, and malachite. Piebald fur, splattered with tobacco brown and aquamarine hues. Ink markings twinning around their limbs. Cascading tails that coil or plait into intricate patterns.

Some of them wear belts with overlapping layers—like Cypress does—or leaf sashes. Some balance helmets or laurel circlets. Some are stocky, some curvy, and some slender.

None of them approach, despite Cypress's gash and my presence. They study us as we arrive at one of the pavilions.

Cypress clomps through a leaf-curtain, saying, "Wait here."

Alone, I peek at the settlement. The pastures and candle paths. The ponds and stream. Recesses where trees umbrella overhead to create idyllic little picnic plots.

A multitude of centaurs presides over the landscape. They speak in low tones, practice hurling bladed stars and shooting archery at target markers, or thumb through books.

The rest consider my presence. The shabby dress. My rounded ears. The crossbow and bolt stained with centaur blood. I shuffle closer to the threshold where Cypress had disappeared.

From within the pavilion, glass bottles clatter. Cypress reemerges wearing a gauze cloth strapped around his flank, replacing the cord from my dress as a compress. The textile sparkles at the center of his wound.

"Pixie dust," he explains. "For my injury, it will suffice. I can apply it to your laceration, though the side-effects are potent for humans, particularly ones of your diminutive size."

"I'm fine," I say.

"If you insist. The offer will stand. In the meantime, throwing stars leave an inflammatory bite at the very least. Should you require an opiate for the pain, we can spare a bottle of toadstool essence."

"I'll manage. It's a scratch."

Hunting accidents. Puncture wounds. Animal bites. Razor claws. Slashes. Stitches. Parasites. Fleas. Coming from a home that functions as a refuge for animals, I've survived worse.

Cypress inclines his head. "Very well."

My head swings between his bandage and our audience. "Do they know what I did?"

"Centaurs are perceptive, but they do not react hastily. They see I am alive, and we are together. That is enough to draw a peaceful conclusion. They will not condemn you." The equine hands me back the tassel cord and juts his head toward another edifice. "Come."

I reattach the closure to my cloak, drape the mantle around my shoulders, and shadow him across the pasture and into a yurt with threaded vines for walls. Grass and a cluster of large pillows surround a bed of logs. A blaze springs to life when we enter, the timbers pulsating.

"Sit," Cypress says, motioning to a pillow. "Please."

I falter to hear that hospitable word drop from a Fae's mouth. My limbs sink to the cushion, its plushness relieving my aching backside.

The centaur lowers himself carefully, stretching out his front limbs and tucking rear ones beside him.

A skylight gawks at the constellations. Above, one of the celestials shifts, arcing from its spot in the firmament to a different region. Then another star leaps to a new location.

I blink, but it's not an illusion. The stars are mobile, swimming through the expanse.

"In Faerie, the stars have their own lives to lead," Cypress volunteers while glancing up. "However, it is a private existence for them. Thus, we cannot always witness it, not even from the heights of The Solitary Mountain. The privilege of viewing this spectacle depends on your location. In The Heart of Willows, this is possible."

I know the sound of pride when I hear it. The upward slant and sturdiness of it. "So this is where you're from?"

"All centaurs grow up here," he answers. "We are wanderers—nomads of The Solitary Forest. Still, this is our hub, where we return for periods of rest. I come here when not serving the wild at Puck's side."

He says this fondly and faithfully. Interesting that for such an impassive being, the satyr's name raises the sides of Cypress's mouth.

"I'd thought you lived with him in The Wicked Pines," I say.

Promptly, the centaur's lips falter as though a leaden object has landed there. "Faeries revel and copulate in The Pines. They do not keep houses there."

I shift on the pillow. An unbidden vision of Puck doing to a random Fae what he'd described to me in the pit springs to mind.

My chin stings when I talk. "I'm surprised the satyr doesn't want to be buried in that place."

"Pick another companion if you wish to criticize him," Cypress warns from across the flames. "Do not engage me thus and expect support. Unless, of course, you have vast experience in such activities."

"Why did you bring me here?"

My question diverts him. "First, tell me three things." He dips a finger into the fire's ashes, then runs that digit across the grass, drawing the inside of a tree trunk, complete with grains, rings, and a central knot.

"Assume this represents an elderly tree." The centaur taps the inner portion, sketched to resemble a dense area. "What is this?"

"The heartwood," I say, baffled.

"And what is the heartwood?"

"The oldest part of the tree."

Cypress's mouth slides into another half-grin. "And which is the wisest part?"

I waver and think of myself as a little girl, poaching and then abandoning that existence. I think of starting a new life with a family, a life in which I save things rather than trap them. I think of meeting a boy with cloven hooves, then encountering him years later. I think of who I was before I'd entered this weald. I think of who I might become once I leave.

My gaze sketches the drawing, then raises to Cypress. "There is no single, wisest part. The wisdom comes from the sum of its parts. It's the whole trunk."

A prolonged, deliberating moment follows in which the flames crackle. They polish Cypress's countenance, bathing him in a stark light. "I brought you here because you helped me. Once more, why did you do that?"

"I told you why." But truthfully, I didn't tell him. "You gave me no choice."

"You spared me. You did so in my home, when you could have left me there. You mended my injury using a piece of your clothing, spending that which is essential to you. Those are choices."

"Not to me."

"Puck was right," Cypress muses. "You are stubborn."

"That satyr's been talking about me behind my back?" Against my better judgment, I clear my throat. "What did he say?"

"Why does it matter?" When I refuse to answer, Cypress dismisses the subject. "Aside from Puck, I am the fiercest hunter in the forest. Did you know that?"

"And I'm the fiercest huntress in my village," I declare.

"Hence, why would you spare a Fae who poses such a great threat—such an impediment—to you winning this game? Why not eliminate that obstacle?"

Because of all the reasons I went through before, none of which I long to share aloud. Not with anyone. "Because I have a conscience." As an added bonus, I toss out another reason that's also true, one he's likelier to understand. "And because I wanted you to owe me."

Cypress considers my response and then rises, towering over me. "Wait here."

He disappears while I sit there, flummoxed. In the meantime, recent events finally catch up. My tongue is dry, my throat drier. While I wait, I rummage through my supplies and retrieve the waterskin, guzzling its contents. Liquid drizzles down my jaw, beads plunking onto my lap.

The magnitude of my journey resurfaces. According to map I've drawn in my head, I've made it to the forest's northwest region. But I've been so busy running from my captives and navigating this environment alongside Puck, that I neglected pursuing my task—hunting an animal that can't be hunted.

I need time to breathe. I need time to rationalize and theorize.

Cypress returns, pitching me an apple and promising more later. Ravenous, I consume the fruit to its core.

The Fae settles in his previous spot, his hands bearing a flat object swaddled in cloth. "Nomads and wanderers tend to bond with their peers. You have your own version of such people in the mortal realm. Those who travel The Dark Fables. Your ancient scribes, for instance."

"The ones who penned the Book of Fables," I say.

"Tales narrated across campfires and over centuries begin with an individual source—a seed. And from a single seed, roots will sprout and multiply. As such, nuances may be skewed, misinterpreted, and reinvented."

I cringe. This fact has never sat right with me, no matter the type of book. With the Fables alone, the mystical tales culled by those ancient scribes were repeated through generations. It had started with those initial wordsmiths, who'd crafted a duplication of their primary manuscript, which other scribes then repeated, over and over, passing them into the hands of mortals.

Because the Fables were replicated over generations, reproduced for humans to keep by their bedsides, certain gaps of information had accrued and were left unattended. Today, we're limited to reading an abridged version, the offspring of its ancestor.

"Long have centaurs repaid favors with the utmost care," Cypress announces, bumping me out of my thoughts. "Our kind gives what we believe is most wanted by the recipient. It is our way." He gazes at the concealed item, visibly acknowledging the consequences of his actions. "To play this game and hunt an animal that can't be hunted, perhaps you will need a firmer, richer knowledge of this world. Shall we say, the sum of its parts."

I wonder if it's a universal trait of centaurs, how he takes his time making a choice, then enacts it all at once. He extends the object to me around the fire. "You have earned this, moppet."

I accept the gift with my free hand, settling it on my lap. My heart jumps into my throat as I recognize the item's shape and weight. The apple core falls from my hand and rolls across the grass while I peel the fabric aside.

Vellum binding. Chunky spine. Brass hinges.

Brittle pages. A tome that belongs in an archive.

Fables eternal. I've never seen it, but I know what this is. There's only one of its kind, one that had vanished into the ages, along with its authors. It shouldn't be here, but it is.

The original Book of Fables.

17

Are my eyes deceiving me? They're not.

Is Cypress deceiving me? He's not.

Yet it can't be true. How did this book end up here, preserved in the centaur's possession?

Gold-leaf feathers, branches, and water droplets emboss the spine. Centuries have scratched and dulled the hinges. A menagerie of animals from each corner of The Dark Fables roams across the cover. Lions, panthers, bears, elephants, wolves, hares, and ravens.

I trail my fingers over the title, bathed in starlight and firelight. I touch the letters lightly, afraid this relic will crumble to ash at the slightest contact.

Book of Fables: Of Fauna and Fanciful Beings

A subtitle! The original has a subtitle!

That, more than anything, convinces me this is real. Behind my ribcage, something wondrous unfurls, fluttering from my chest to my head. I feel lightheaded, awestruck, dazed with hope. I would go so far as to call it a bookish high or an academic intoxication. My digits itch to pry open the tome and explore.

I lift my gaze to Cypress. When he gestures toward the book as if to say, "Be my guest," I don't need to be invited twice. I fish my spectacles from their protective case and jam the lenses onto my face. I press on the hinges' clasps, and they jolt open with a giddy click that matches the lurch in my pulse. Slowly, I turn from one page to the next.

My finger runs over the table of contents, then an introductory note from the scribes themselves, alongside their signatures—three of them.

Some Fables have the same titles as I'd been taught, whereas others diverge. I recognize many of the tales but not all.

Painted illustrations accompany the stories, as intricate as an illuminated manuscript I once saw displayed in the bookbinder's shop. I gasp at the depictions, smiling at the likenesses of owls, stags, and snakes.

While my sisters have coveted their own wishes—Lark, the ability to fly and perpetual orgasms; Cove, breathing underwater and a kindly world—I have fantasized about this book. I've imagined discovering it in a remote corner of the continent. I've envisioned it a thousand times, yet it doesn't compare to the reality.

Am I holding this book properly, respectfully?

I glance up, tensing. "How old are you? Were you alive during the scribes' era?"

Umbrage hardens the equine's face, which is distorted through the spectacles. "The centaurs did not steal this relic. However self-indulgent we are, thievery is against our custom."

Of all magical beings, centaurs are among the least documented figures, in addition to Pegasi, who went extinct after a battle with the southern dragons, and dragons themselves, who are impossible to get near. By comparison, the few existing Fables about centaurs have spoken of their hermetic nature. Sportive they may be—like all woodland Faeries—but centaurs remain the most reclusive of the Solitaries, despite their nomadic habits. Based on the latter fact, they must be prone to wandering alone. And in any case, few passages have been written about them as a result.

As to Cypress's denial about plundering this book, I believe him. While I turn the pages, he explains.

Centuries ago, three scribes traveled through The Dark Fables, collecting tales about magical beings. That much, mortals know. But there's a missing piece we haven't been privy to.

Cypress shares, "When two of the scribes passed on, and only one was left, she braved the Solitary wild, risking her life in pursuit of additional wisdom."

My head springs up, and I remove the spectacles. "She?"

When he nods, I grin. "What was her name?"

"She did not tell us. We merely referred to her as the scribe."

That's a disappointment. All the same, none of my people ever knew who the scribes were or what they looked like. I'm happy to learn at least one of them was a female.

According to Cypress, this scribe sought to fill in the blanks about centaurs, which is as far as she got in Faerie. She bargained and bartered her way through, cognizant of Fae treachery. When she finally located The Heart of Willows, the scribe conveyed to the centaurs who she was. Being nomads like her, the equines were willing to hear the woman out. She made a deal with them that the Book of Fables would never leave this land, providing she was allowed to stay and record tales about their kin.

By that time, the scribe was an elderly woman who'd wanted nothing more than to see the Book of Fables become as comprehensive as possible, whether or not humans ever read it. She lived among the centaurs, cultivated a rapport with them, and passed away here. The scribe died within this very land. At her behest, her ashes were sprinkled onto the soil, enriching the earth where the fauna graze.

Her accounts of Cypress's kin were never drafted into the replicas, and now I understand why. The centaurs have protected their society from such circulation and, worse, from being distorted by humans. Other Faeries are too blithe and arrogant about mortals to care. Centaurs are not. Nevertheless, they didn't object to one factual account existing, purely for the sake of it.

The scribe had bequeathed this book to the centaurs, the only Folk she'd trusted. Also, it was part of the bargain.

The centaurs had liked her, but they weren't sentimental about her passing. She'd been an anomaly. Otherwise, Cypress's kind believe as all Faeries do: that humans are the lesser beings.

I hold my tongue on the matter. The book's weight in my lap is too momentous to spoil by getting into a centuries-old quarrel.

Although Faeries repay favors in excess, this is too much. I have to thank Cypress, despite what he thinks of gratitude.

The centaur must see my intention because he shakes his head, his olive mane falling over his shoulders. "Do not bother, moppet. You may read it, but it will not leave these borders. Your scribe entrusted it to us.

Therefore, this gift is temporary—a loan."

"Oh," I stammer, my cheeks boiling. "Oh. Right."

"Five days remain until the Middle Moon Feast. We will grant you sanctuary for the remainder, or until you discover the whereabouts of your quarry. When you finish the book, it will remain here."

"Do the other Solitaries know about it? The ones outside of this territory, I mean?"

"We hide nothing from our kin. They are free to peruse the contents, so long as they do so here, in the presence of centaurs. Nonetheless, while they find it prudent to know what information mortals have on them, woodland Faeries live impulsively. Other than centaurs, the majority lack enough ambition to study the matter, for they have plenty of frolicsome antics to distract them.

"And apart from The Trapping, which they deem an isolated incident among a millennia of other chances to rebel, they believe mortals will never regain the upper hand again, no matter what intelligence they gather. Also, there is no account in the book about how to annihilate us, outside of iron, war, and the loss of our wildlife. Those options are no secret."

And they've already been exhausted. Since then, the Faeries have struck back with relish.

Still, I'm grateful for the Folks' lack of foresight. Perhaps if the Solitaries had investigated this book to their advantage, they might have learned supplementary ways to impose even harsher treatment on my world. "None of them have been prudent enough to take up the offer?"

Cypress's eyes kindle amidst the flames. "One has."

Well. I ought to have guessed. That makes Puck a more dangerous adversary.

The cautious side of me conflicts with a reckless and rather unwise side, one that warms from learning he's made an effort with this book. Of course, it also pinches me with jealousy, because he got to read the original edition first, long before me.

If my fingers cling to the binding, I have an excuse. Humans wrote this chronology. As such, it should go to my people.

However, the scribe had made a deal and went to her grave honoring that bargain. It's up to me to do the same. In the meantime, I'll digest every lost word and use them to prevail in this hunt.

"Why give me this leverage in the game?" I push.

Cypress's tail swishes. "I told you. When a centaur repays a favor, it must be something the recipient would most value. It is our way."

"Does this make you a traitor?"

"It makes me an honest player. Do not expect that from the rest of my brethren." He gives me a dispassionate look. "An advantage does not mean you will win."

It doesn't. Even though he'd told Tinder not to underestimate me, ultimately Cypress has misgivings that I'll prevail in the hunt. The notion sits plainly on his face.

I sigh. "Why make retaliation against humans into a game?"

I expect him to list something shallow and Fae-worthy, such as that it's fun. Instead, Cypress glances toward the hanging vines. His ears perk, sweeping outward as he listens to the sounds of life beyond the willow's confines. "Take that up with our ruler when next you see him."

I will. In the meantime, I have an ancient tome to acquaint myself with. Puck may have confiscated my notebook, but I've got something just as priceless now.

Since Cypress won't accept gratitude, I dip my head in acknowledgment. I'm desperate to begin reading, but I'm also famished, dirty, and smelly. He provides me with a platter of bread, cheese, slices of ham, a tankard of mead, and a jug of honey tea.

After filling my stomach and quenching my thirst, Cypress guides me to a secluded willow yurt where a pond ripples. A mound of furs, plus a chest, a ewer of water, and a candle outfit the interior.

When the centaur departs, I waver for a full ten minutes before feeling safe enough to strip, peeling the soiled dress from my body. I dunk myself into the water, the liquid warmer than it would be in my realm. I wash quickly, scrubbing my hair and skin, then rummage in the pack for my undergarments, socks, leggings, and sweater. The comforts of clean skin and fresh clothes has me sighing.

Resting against the tree, I adjust the spectacles atop my nose and open the book. The first pages spread with a thrilling crackle, the parchment dotted with age and creased in the corners, used to its fullest capacity. This isn't a perfect copy purchased in a bookshop but one featuring scratched-out words and notes in the margins, some legible, others smeared. It's a treasure trove, an artifact.

This book could be a lifeline in the game. It could bring me and my sisters one step closer to home.

Awe floods my senses, fizzing at my fingertips. The scribes of old had held this book, scripted these chapters. They traveled The Dark Fables with it, from the rural plains here in Middle Country, to the frostbitten castles in the Northern Frosts, to the sunset coasts in the Southern Seas.

An occasion such as this requires ceremony. I flip through without reading yet, examining the book as a whole. I introduce myself, saying, "Hello, my name is Juniper. I'm honored and will take good care of you."

Then I let the tome introduce itself to me. I tuck in my legs and read every annotation, every inked line. I study the illustrations of fauna and flora, of Faeries, elves, and dragons. I plunge into the Fables about butterflies, wolves, crocodiles, and leopards.

Where they deviate from what I've studied, I pay the utmost attention. Where they fill in gaps, I consume the information.

I scavenge for clues about an animal that can't be hunted—what it might be, where it might stray. The restless stars migrate. They skip industriously across the firmament, tossing beams of white, gold, and teal across my legs.

I shift from reading against the tree to reclining sideways on the grass with my head propped in my palm, then on my stomach with my legs crossed at the ankles. Eventually, I return to my original position, aligning myself with the trunk. My legs steeple, my knees pitching close to my chest as I balance the book on my thighs and flip to the next Fable.

A shadow drizzles over my shoulder, wrapping itself around me. A mischievous tenor slips into my ear, warm breath shimmying from my scalp to my tailbone. "Spoiler: Everyone dies."

I twist, my hair whipping across my chest. Puck crouches on all fours behind me. He must have crawled a distance across the grass like a sprite about to pounce. To prove it, a sneaky gleam alights his visage, as though I've been caught.

The satyr has also changed clothes since our parting, a new vest and breeches woven of chestnut suede clinging to his physique.

He takes a second look at the page. "Oops, that's the wrong tale. In this one, the prey escapes. How, you wonder?"

"I don't wonder," I say. "She gets away because she's smarter than the predator."

"A brilliant last-minute twist, but still. Where's the action? The drama? The fucking?" he laments. "When I read a book, I expect to laugh, to cry, to smolder."

"It's a one-page story," I point out.

"Nitty-gritty detail. Methinks if you'd been the author, you would have written a better ending." Puck's index finger extends toward my face, pushing the spectacles up the bridge of my nose. "That's quite a hearty scowl. Miss me, luv?"

Absolutely, certainly, definitely not. Though it would be impolite to say so, I have a feeling that answer would only make him laugh. And I don't want to hear that earthen sound. I don't want to feel its sultry effects.

What's he doing here? How did he know where to find me? What took him so long?

I evict the last question from my mind. Yet I fail to extinguish other stimuli from my body—an accelerated pulse and a blast of heat charging up my limbs.

It should not—it should *not*—please me to see him. I could kick myself. I will do so, when next I'm alone.

As for my spectacles, they must have slid down when I'd whirled to face him. His amused expression says as much, accompanied by an odd slant to his features, something subdued and harder to decipher.

I stare at him, deadpan. Puck wiggles his fingers as if he doesn't need an answer. "Yes, yes. You've been pining in my absence. I know, and I'm used to it. My kin say I'm the life of a party, and we throw plenty of those."

Should I wait out his speech? Stay quiet until he gets cross? The more I withhold, the more he says, the likelier he'll fumble, the crankier he'll get. The thought tickles my lips into the shape of a grin.

Fortunately, Puck doesn't notice the smile. "So here you are, in the land of the solitary Solitaries." He plops onto the grass right beside me. "Have you met everyone yet? Tell me Cypress has introduced you to his fellow equines. Or do I have to spank him? No? Excellent. I didn't think so anyway. We woodlanders are generous hosts, on many generous occasions, during a plethora of generous events."

Never mind. I snap the book shut. "Why are you here?"

"Because I can be," Puck says. "Being a ruler has its perks. I'm allowed to cause trouble wherever I want. Though even if that weren't true, the centaurs still wouldn't mind the disruption. They may be wanderers and soldiers and guides and keepers all rolled into one—custodians of the forest—but don't underestimate them. Cypress is as vicious as the rest of us, except he's dignified about it. Very unwoodland-like, but there you have it, and that's what I fancy about him. Consistency is ever so boring."

"So Cypress told you where I was."

The conclusion sours my tone, even though the centaur had made no vows about secrecy. He's still a member of the hunt, so perhaps it was his duty to report my whereabouts.

Velvet unfurls from Puck's mouth. "Now who said anything about Cypress playing the informant? He might be my best friend and first-in-command, but maybe I found you on my own, because maybe I know where to look, because maybe I've been hunting you."

"This is neutral territory."

"That it is. And look at you, being studious. I like your cozy camp. To top it off, I see Cypress has bestowed you with a bookish favor. And no, I haven't convened with him to hear the tale. I came straight to this spot, too greedy for the sight of your luscious glower. When you scowl, it does fabulous things to your mouth."

"Do you keep anything to yourself?"

"Why would I do that?"

It's not a yes or no, not an answer or a dismissal.

The satyr's eyes flick to the book. "Talk about a lucky favor. What happened to earn you this coup? Did you braid Cypress's tail?"

"I put a bolt in his flank and then took pity on him."

"My, my, my. You wild huntress, you. That'll do it, and you must be elated about the tome. You've been engrossed for the past ten minutes that I've been spying on you."

Heat creeps up my cheeks. "I see privacy is an afterthought to satyrs."

Puck just smiles.

The darkness has begun to recede, converting from a bruised blue to a lazy cornflower tinge. I had been so captivated by the Book of Fables I hadn't noticed twilight approaching, nor any sounds outside this enclosure. The centaurs must have retired by now.

I clasp the book to my chest. "As usual, you've pranced around my first question."

"As usual, you haven't accepted my first response. I don't need a reason to be here, but if you insist, I feel the urge to keep an eye on you, for when you step foot out of this safe haven. It's a naughty job, but someone has to do it."

"Despite the endless obligations and priorities of a ruler?"

His voice flattens. "This game is my priority."

"For what reason? I'm just another mortal to punish for crossing The Triad. Why bother yourself when a faun or leprechaun can do it for you? What makes this game so vital?"

The answer lingers behind his teeth, just out of reach. "I'll tell you later."

I can't decide whether to take that seriously. And what had I expected? That he would stop this game after our time alone? It had been a minor detour, however...friendly.

Yet I haven't forgotten that look on his face when we parted during the ambush. "Then tell me something else now."

"Humans first," he says, scooting backward and putting several feet between us. The distance requires me to remove the lenses while he drapes himself onto the grass like a showpiece, folding his arms behind his head as though we're comrades, as though we aren't on opposite sides of a deadly game. "Where does your passion for Fables come from?"

My gaze darts away from the muscles rising along his arms. "I wouldn't call it a passion."

"How would you define passion, then?"

His murmur reaches across the divide and sidles under my clothing. Warmth detonates beneath my flesh, gathering at a private spot between my hips. Lark would know what to do with this sensation, but I'm at my wit's end. I squirm for a comfortable position, hoping the satyr doesn't notice.

He does. He watches me absorb his words, watches what the question does to my complexion and posture, watches the disturbance travel across my body, watches the impact he has.

And I watch those eyes simmer in response.

My tongue yearns to give him a lashing. At the same time, it cleaves to the roof of my mouth, parched.

I latch on to his question about Fables, my mouth running away with itself. I tell him about the first day Papa Thorne brought me into his home, when I was ten years old, my hair oily and matted, and my bony limbs encased in moth-chewed rags. Papa must have smelled the staleness of sweat, the smokiness of a cooking spit, and the funk of the muskrat I'd recently skinned.

I'd wandered through the living room, marveling at the clean objects. When I halted at the bookshelf, Papa had smiled and asked, "Do you like books?"

"I don't know," I'd said, which had felt like the right answer. I kept exploring and found a specific tome braced on the shelf, with the cover facing out. "What's that one?"

"Oh." Papa plucked the book from the shelf. "Magic lives in this one."

When I first held that copy of the Fables, all the words had been blurry and smeared, nothing but puddles to my eyes. Yet I had felt the weight of those tales in my hands, the parchment brimming with life, a magical and perilous wilderness germinating inside. A tangle of branches had crept like a gateway from the margins, beckoning me into their forbidden world. The book had cast a spell on me, its cover becoming solid bark against my fingers, the pages as soft as fur.

There were lessons to be learned inside. I'd believed that if I taught my lips to form the letters, to string them together, one day I would know all the answers.

How to protect myself. How to redeem myself.

I could do better. I could be better.

Papa had noticed me blinking, squinting. A week later, he'd set a pair of spectacles on my nose. At which point, the book's pages cracked open like an eggshell, a yolk of shapes spilling out. The words evolved to squiggly configurations, arbitrary rows of symbols etched across calfskin vellum. They were clusters of circles and lines, dots and slashes, like a child's drawing. I couldn't tell the symmetry of A from the waywardness of K.

But then, Papa taught me and my sisters to read, and I loved every moment of it. The letters took shape—the potbelly of D, the illuminated candle of a lowercase i, and the mermaid's tail of Q. And I loved even it more when I understood the words, connecting them like strings of lights that brightened the world around me.

As for the Fables: Nothing is what it seems in Faerie, a notion that has always motivated me to know more. To make sense of the nonsensical. To see how different we really are—or how similar.

Finished, I glance at Puck. He's sitting up now and staring at me. An avalanche of red hair sweeps his broad shoulders, the waves unkempt, as haphazard as his personality.

He asks, "Will you do me a favor and keep talking?"

I don't rightly know how this started, but I find myself settling deeper into the tree. The satyr asks questions and confides what he thinks about the Fables. He finds them intriguing, unnerving, mostly accurate, sometimes incomplete, and occasionally false. We list the tales that have inspired us, agreeing on the ones featuring forest critters and simple agendas rather than grand, life-affirming ones.

On the other hand, we debate about the best stories. I prefer the ones that specify their lessons or morals without being sermonic, whereas Puck favors the ones open to multiple interpretations.

"Favorite Fable?" I broach.

He gives me a meaningful look. "I think you already know, luv."

Damnation. I do know. We had talked about this as children, but I'd wanted to see if his taste had changed, if we no longer had this favorite in common.

In unison, we recite, testing one another's memory.

"Once in the dark forest, a Stag hunted a Doe. Yet intelligence is the ally of intention and the foe of lethargy. Thus, both deer wondered, what if we thought wiser and hunted together?"

We watch each other while narrating. Once finished, we trail off to consider those lines in private. The Fable and this passage of time reminds me of our brief history, when we shared secrets in a forest, both of us wide awake while the world slept.

At one point, we segue to our families. I tell him about Papa Thorne. Middle-aged and finely edged, he's got a direct gaze, a loyal heart, and he calls me his tree of knowledge.

I talk about my sisters. I tell Puck that sometimes we dash outside and chase each other across a field, fighting angry, sibling angry. Or sometimes we fall asleep in the grass, huddling in a crescent until our papa rings the supper bell.

Riling each other up, throwing pillows, roughhousing—that's us. We do it as often as we cuddle or dab one another's tears.

If not Cove, Papa's the one to calm us down. "One time—I must have been eleven," I say, "Lark and I quarreled over a patchwork blanket, insisting it was 'Mine! No mine!' Our papa just about had it. To shut us up, he grabbed a pair of shears and cut that blanket right down the middle, then gave each of us half. Neither me, nor my slack-jawed sister, had thought of doing that. And by bedtime, it didn't matter. We'd crudely resewn the yards, so that we could snuggle together."

I chuckle at the memory, then catch Puck staring into space. He says to himself, "So that's a family."

This comes out quietly, attentively, as if such a life—a family cultivated—is foreign to him. I understand this, having lived without one for the first years of my life. For reasons having to do with my tattoo, I don't expand on that part.

Puck requests more family-orientated tidbits, soaking up the answers like a dish rag. His questions range from the profound—what are our traditions?—to the minute—who cooks?

Also, do we have inside jokes? What games do we play? How do we spend our mornings?

Nearby, a stream burbles. Remnant constellations hop through the sky, and a breeze rustles the willow vines. Whereas he and I remain still, caught in a recess between twilight and dawn.

The Book of Fables had been sitting on my lap. I set it on the grass and enfold my arms around my upturned limbs. "What about your family?"

Puck shrugs. "My pedigree's a short Fable, luv."

"Tell me anyway. Repay my favor."

The satyr sits upright and balances on one hip. It's a coltish pose, though he speaks to me in earnest, his tone one of sobriety. While conception doesn't come easily to Faeries, Puck takes it a step further, revealing there's another way to come into being. That's how it was for him.

For a start, he was born twelve-hundred years ago. That alone knocks me off balance.

Then he stuns me anew: He was born from a seed. Excluding the fauna, who procreate in the traditional manner, all woodland Solitaries are born from seeds. Moreover, all are born in the same place, in a dell called The Seeds that Give.

He averts his gaze, his profile a landscape of inclines—sharp and steep in their depths. "It's different from mountain and river, where the Folk hatch their babes the usual way, however infrequent. Lucky devils, they are."

"Lucky?" I repeat, but Puck doesn't expand on that adjective.

The satyr talks about growing up with the other Solitaries and Sylvan.

"She and I used to play hunting games," he says, fondness threading through his words. It's a sound I'd like to grab ahold of and tuck in my notebook for safekeeping.

"The doe back home loves to race me across our property," I say. "She always wins."

We trade appreciative grins. For someone so ruthless, this satyr has a tender spot for things I recognize: the flora and fauna of our lands. I've always known that as a fact, because all Faeries worship the nature in their environs. But until now, this idea hadn't been tangible. It hadn't felt real, nor on the same level.

Puck adds, "Years later, when I was a strapping young buck, I met Cypress. He became another friend."

"What about Cerulean and Elixir?" I inquire. "You refer to them as brothers of history and brothers-in-arms. Technically, that constitutes a family."

Puck's eyebrows vault into his forehead. "Not sure if you want to hear more about them, luv."

He's correct. I don't want to know a thing about the rulers who have my sisters in their clutches.

Yet he's wrong. I want to know everything, down to the last weakness. A noxious mood threatens to infest our surroundings. With one slip of the tongue, this could easily turn into an argument.

Puck probably senses it because he proceeds tentatively, seizing on a less destructive topic that has to do with his and his brothers' ages. He'd been a tad older than me when we met—the equivalent of a twelve-year-old. Certainly, he had looked that way, small and scrawny.

Yet after The Trapping, Puck had developed swiftly until he'd possessed the physical, mental, and emotional maturity of a male in his prime. He tells me his brothers had experienced the same transformation. They'd all been children during The Trapping, but after rescuing their kin, Cerulean, Puck, and Elixir began to change that same night. Literally, they grew into their newfound roles as leaders.

Instead of aging slowly like Faeries, they'd aged rapidly like humans.

In both looks and psychology, Puck's advancement became proportional to a mortal man of twenty-one years. At which point, the process slowed once more, and he resumed the normal pace of immortality.

None of the rulers know why any of this had happened. The catalyst remains a mystery.

That's all I can handle. I'll ask more about them later, when I'm able to swallow what I hear. I will ask when I can stomach the idea of Puck connected to Cerulean and Elixir in any manner, pledged to them in any capacity. In other words, when I'm able to reconcile this without the impulse to lodge a bolt in Puck's chest.

The satyr takes note of my expression and circles back to the centaur. "You know, when I met Cypress, he showed up at a rather inconvenient time."

Puck gives me a devilish look, and my gasp turns into a coughing fit. "He did not!"

"Oh yes, he did."

Just like that, a weight lifts, and the mood lightens. Puck feigns wistfulness. "The faun had been a fetching male. Older, with elk antlers as big my ego and a cock just as—"

I shove his hip with the sole of my boot. "I don't need a visual, thank you."

Puck chuckles. "When Cypress happened upon us, he'd been hunting his supper and accidentally misinterpreted the faun's groan for a howl. Needless to say, my partner ended up with an arrow lodged in his ass. The look on Cypress's face when he realized his mistake? It was precious as fuck." Puck shakes his head, rueful. "Shit. I can't believe I just told you that."

I chortle. "A satyr, aghast by his own admission?"

"Shh, don't tell anyone. We have our limitations, after all."

Yes, but very few. On that note, how many bed partners has Puck had? Is sex different for him between males versus than females? With Faeries in contrast to humans?

The notion chafes. I fall silent, mulling that over, blistering in silence for far too long.

I catch Puck surveying my reaction and snap, "What?"

His features ignite and darken all at once. Then he moves toward me.

18

The satyr gets on all fours and crawls across the grass, as he'd done when first approaching me hours ago. He stalks my way like a feline, his eyes fastening on to me.

I press myself into the trunk. Yet my limbs spread on reflex, permitting him entrance. The heady aromas of cloves and pine assault my senses, and his nostrils flare, inhaling whatever fragrance drifts from my clothing.

The Fae sidles into the vent of my pitched thighs and pauses. His breath coasts across my jaw, his visage inches from mine. He's wide and solid, all roguish leathers and provocative red hair.

Maidens would call him sexy. I would call him irritating, maddening.

He entices, "You told me what the Fables have taught you, what they've made you think. But what do they make you feel?"

"How do you mean?" I query.

"What do they make you feel?" The satyr leans forward, his head slanting toward my earlobe. "Delirious?" he whispers in one ear. "Blissful?" he whispers in the other.

I shiver. That voice sinks into a wretched, secret place tucked between my thighs. Each word coaxes that spot like a crooked finger, beckoning me to respond.

My pulse speeds up, smashing against my neck. When his mouth parts a fraction, my own lips ache.

It takes a phenomenal amount of resilience to pull myself from the haze. "Why haven't you been hunting me since The Passel of Boars? Why aren't you hunting me now?"

Puck tips his head. "Can't a satyr take a break? Rest his hooves? Unwind his antlers?"

"No. No. And no."

"Then how about this: Hunt is a relative term," the Fae intones, his fingernails digging into the grass as if locating its pressure points. "I can hunt you while sitting beside you. I can hunt you while walking beside you. I can hunt you from behind." He smiles. "Or in front."

"You can't strike me down in neutral terrain."

"Now who said anything about striking anyone down?"

As the riddling satyr pulls back, air gushes into my lungs. I glare while he rises to his hooves and crosses to the willow vines. Before he leaves, Puck clips his chin toward the Book of Fables. "Don't lose your spot."

The bastard struts off, callous and unruffled. I remain tacked to the tree, everything he'd said conspiring to burn several holes in my head.

At last, I break from my paralysis, get up, and march after him. Or rather, first I use a leaf to mark the page where I'd left off, then close the book and set it on the grass. And *then* I march after him.

My arms flay to the sides, batting the willow vines out of my way. I stride through, and with each step, I get my bearings. My laces snap around my ankles. Sometimes while hunting, I can tell the mood of my quarry based on its prints—hasty, frightened, or playful. As my boot soles punch the ground, I predict an aggravated trail branding the foundation behind me.

I find Puck sauntering across an arched bridge embroidered in willow leaves. Actually, not embroidered. One of the centaurs has crafted the bridge out of the foliage, a feat that would be unachievable in my world.

Fables curse these knaves and their liberties. Their arrogance. Their superiority. Their entitlement. Their smugness. Their belief that magic makes them better than we are—more empowered. Their inclination to have the last word, walk away, and assume the conversation is done.

It's not done. Not until I've had my turn.

The sun will rise shortly. Until then, the only illumination comes from a few remaining stars, candles lining the walkways, and the creek's reflective surface, eddying beneath the overpass. The centaurs are still sleeping inside their willow-strewn homes, the residences scattered across the pastures.

Is it possible to speak quietly in Puck's presence? Is it, when every unstable thing inside me has been making a racket since I met him?

I plant myself on one end of the bridge and speak to his retreating back. "Hey."

That's all. I haven't begun, haven't retaliated, haven't given my counter argument. Yet Puck halts at the opposite end. His vest contorts, toned muscles flexing beneath the leather, as if I've already given a full, destructive speech.

Turning on his hooves, he stalks my way. I pursue the bridge's center, swinging my arms as I walk, the planks cracking under my boots. A willow tree fans out above, its boughs forming a parasol of vines. In storybooks, this would be the ideal setting for romance.

A first touch. A first kiss. A confession. An embrace.

For us, it's the stage for yet another verbal duel.

I can hunt you while sitting beside you. I can hunt you while walking beside you.

Well. So can I.

We pause beneath the canopy. Under my breath, I promise him, "You're not the only one hunting someone. Watch your back, satyr. I won't make it easy for you."

And he tosses back, "Now who says I expect it to be easy?"

And I fire back, "And who says I care what you expect?"

Because a mysterious, mystical animal isn't the only target I'm after. I'm still hunting this satyr, the way he's hunting me. That hasn't changed. If he wants to bait me, I'll turn his words against him.

Overhead, a current rustles the branches. Below, the water lashes over stones. Around us, willow roots claw deep into the earth.

The waistband of my leggings cinches as tight as his own clothing. His scent and heat mingle with my temper. Any moment, I'm going to shout. And I never shout.

At my response, Puck's countenance breaks down before reinforcing itself. "She won't make it easy, she says." He gives that mock consideration. "Oh, but she never has." Then he dips his head, his tenor a low scrape of sound. "When we combated in the woods, I knew what you were about, hunting me back, tit-for-bloody-tat. In fact, your skills were effortless. So effortless that I know this much: You won't need to guess how to strike me down. You won't need to analyze my weak spots to target me. You won't even need to reach inside my head to penetrate those spots—because you're already there. You're there, taking up space in every corner. Every thought, every question, every grudge, every regret, every dream, every nightmare, every fantasy, every secret, every bad habit, every memory, and every fucking hope I have—it's all you.

"There's no point in me hiding, because there's nothing of me you can't access. There's nothing you can't take from me, except for one thing: my instincts.

"Awareness and action are two different skills, luv. That means you'll never know how I'll retaliate or what I'll do next, no matter how much you burrow into my skull. You might think you can predict my moves, but your bolt will always be a moment too late. And that's what it's like to lose the hunt, huntress. *That's* what it's like to be wrong."

My tongue fails to produce sound. Yet my teeth grate—outrage, longing, and an unforgivable jolt of heat sizzling me to the core. I'm feverish and livid, hot and wistful and shaking.

Puck murmurs a vow of his own. "You won't make it easy? Rest assured, neither will I."

And he doesn't. And I don't.

As the days unfold, we stalk one another. It's not about killing, and not only because we're restricted here. As Puck had said, the term hunt is relative, so we bend the rules. Instead of bloodshed, hunting one another is about being caught off guard. It's about traps and snares, each of us attempting to cage the other, to incapacitate or immobilize.

This keeps the game in motion. This also means getting creative.

Cunning Puck attempts that in spades, luring me by imitating foreign animal calls or baiting me with intellectual debates so that I'll lose my defenses, so that I won't see the net coming.

However, I do see it coming. Still, it's a challenge not to give in, because he knows what will draw me.

I stash myself in a thicket and aim for his antlers, intending to pin him against a tree. He dodges my pursuit with agile limbs, slick as he pleases. I fashion snares from branches and nets from vines, and he sidesteps them while tut-tutting me.

The satyr hunts with the zeal of a loose cannon, putting his heart into it. Whereas I hunt with my head, vigilant of his strategies. We each make mistakes that cost us the catch. Nevertheless, we refuse to underestimate the other, and that makes for a robust hunt.

What would happen if this were a partnership? If we were a team with a common goal?

The equines don't seem to mind my presence. Cypress has told them about my favor and his compensation. As for Puck, he's ruler and can roost wherever he wants.

When we're not hunting each other, we're still aware of each other.

Sometimes Puck catches me staring. He does so without having to look my way, his mouth crooking across his astute profile.

Sometimes I catch him staring. And I stare right back until his pupils swell.

Sometimes I feel that gaze in my knees. Sometimes I hope my gaze has the same debilitating impact.

Sometimes I wonder what sort of hunt this truly is. Sometimes I contemplate his question about the Fables: *What do they make you feel?*

I begin paying new attention to him. Over the rim of my book, my attention migrates toward fragments I hadn't noticed before. He makes Cypress laugh. He makes another male blush. He tends to his longbow beside the stream, oiling the yew while chatting with a female about the politics of distant Fae courts.

He plays with a foal. The centaur youth releases a whinnying giggle and bucks around him, the plaited cord of her chartreuse tail lashing about.

Later that day, the foal canters up to me while I'm reading. "You talk with a funny accent. Puck says you're a human," the little female reports, her eyes sparkling with curiosity. "I'm a filly. But someday, I will be a mare."

I close the book. "My name's Juniper."

"Puck said that, too."

"Did he now? What else did his snarky lordship tell you?"

The foal chortles and gallops off without answering.

The centaurs know what we're doing and sometimes gather to observe Puck's antics and my maneuvers. They're a regal audience. Their presence makes sense. This is a game after all, widespread through The Solitary Forest.

In between these skirmishes, I keep my distance, marveling at them from afar. They converse in Faeish while stargazing. They frolic as woodland Faeries do. They race, flirt, prance, and guide lovers and mates into secluded spots. They're promiscuous but less gaudy about it, unlike the debacle I'd witnessed in The Wicked Pines.

I try acclimating myself to the hours here. I attempt to sleep when the Fae sleep, to close my eyes when the sun rises, then open them as it sets. But while cloistered in my yurt, oftentimes I toss and turn in the furs. I worry about Papa Thorne and fret about my sisters.

The most annoying fits of restlessness come whenever I think about Puck.

Where is he sleeping in this place? What does he look like when he dreams? Does he breathe deeply or lightly? Does his heartbeat slow down?

What does he wear?

On a hiss, I mash my face into the pillow. I don't care what he wears. I don't care if he's wondering the same things about me. Anyway, I doubt he is.

For all I know, he vacates the premises while the land slumbers. He leaves and finds a willing nymph or faun to mount. How long do satyrs last without such…recreations…before they succumb to their baser tendencies?

One day, I sneak out of my campsite to find out. Merely for confirmation, to knot this loose end. No other reason.

It doesn't take long to hunt down his copse draped in willow vines. My feet swish through the grass. I nudge open the leaf curtain—and veer back, wrenching my head to the side and evading the provocative spread of his body.

Naked. That's how he sleeps.

Oxygen blasts through my lungs, irregular, shaky. I wait, wait, wait. Then I take another peek, careful not to stray anywhere phallic.

Skin and sinew fill my vision. Puck rests on his back, spread out like a messy blanket. One leg is propped up, the other outstretched. One arm is slung over his chest, the other flopping to the side. Red waves cover half his face, trembling with every push of his breath.

A single, tan nipple puckers above the slab of his torso. From the well-defined abdomen, sprigs of crimson hair taper between his hips. Below that, his humanlike thighs transform into thatches of fur at the knees, his limbs ending in hooves.

The sight causes a disruption in the general order of things. My fingers tingle to the point of discomfort.

Fables have mercy. However tempting, I avoid craning my head to peer at the rest, at the masculine part of him concealed behind his up-turned thigh.

The unconscious satyr groans and rolls over. The taut swells of his buttocks are as whipcord as the rest of him, fiendish divots flexing into the sides. This scene does something reprehensible to my pulse. I spring away and dash back to my yurt.

Belated shame creeps up on me. Puck hadn't given me consent to ogle him like that, and I don't consider myself a degenerate woodland Fae who would do so regardless.

Promptly, the insomnia gets worse. My body self-destructs, warming and aching in ways reminiscent of that time in The Skulk of Foxes, when his very words had penetrated my core.

The same physical sensations disturb me now. I envision the part of him I hadn't allowed myself to see, imagining its girth, its stiffness.

My hand sinks low, lower still, seeking relief beneath my skirt. As my fingers comb through the damp hair between my legs, his utterances from the pit vibrate in my head—whispered intonations about touching oneself. I think about the depth of his voice, the things he'd described. I follow those words, my palm encasing the sensitive flesh hidden within my thighs. A tiny jolt streaks through me, which multiplies into embers when my wrist rubs that area, creating a tremulous friction.

The ripples cause my lips to part in a soundless *Oh*.

Lark had gushed to me about this, but…but it's not…it's nowhere near…

Wetness coats the inner and outer walls of my center. My digits explore, searching, skimming. They trace the entrance, then—dear Fables—slip inside. I gasp, and my body ignites, seeming to know what it needs, what it wants.

Unbidden, visions of Puck flood my mind. His mouth, moving. His breath, stirring. His face, sleeping. That expanse of skin covering muscle and sinew as he slumbered, the athletic buttocks and that limb blocking his lower body from me—the male shaft that would have been limp, exposed.

My core dampens, permeated by heat and additional moisture. The fantasy unravels, so that I picture the satyr's face, had he been awake. That contagious grin. That predatory gaze. I imagine what his features look like while clenched with lust, his head thrown back, his mouth split wide and hollering. I picture him gripping himself, stroking himself.

I picture him thinking about me.

Embarrassment and guilt transcend into the very opposite. My touch becomes greedy, yearning. My fingers move of their own volition, plying into the heated channel of my body. They find a rhythm, probing the drenched cleft and pushing disjointed moans from my lips.

With every shove of my fingers, fluttery, rigorous sensations accumulate. I withdraw, my digits slick, and etch the pulsating kernel at the nexus of my body. At the slightest brush, the crest sparks, the stimulation erotic, overwhelming. My limbs fall wider apart, my heels grinding into the blanket.

I tease myself, circling my wrist on that spot, the result so intense my thoughts levitate. By the time my hand burrows back into the passage, I'm splayed and melting freely. I touch, and touch, and touch.

I see him, hear him. His hands become my hands, delving into the private space and extinguishing all sense of right and wrong. The tempo turns me into a wet mess, my hand pitching, striking a place that causes my eyes to roll back.

It builds, chases, and catches. I go still, my back snapping off the ground and my walls combusting, bursting. The orgasm hits. A blinding, hot flood releases from that intimate slot and courses from my head to my toes.

His name teeters there, on the tip of my tongue. A gritty, uncivilized noise threatens to spring from my throat. Yet somehow, I have the presence of mind to climax silently.

And instead of draining me, the onslaught feels powerful. A new type of strength.

I recall every time he's challenged me, all those *have-you-evers* compiling. Whether or not he'd known it, the satyr had been planting his words like seeds. To have an impact, he hadn't needed to lay a finger on me.

All he'd needed to do was open his mouth.

19

I can't lie. I had enjoyed what I'd done to myself, hadn't imagined it could be like that. However, I try not to dwell on what had inspired it—whose words had probed me to the core.

Concentration both rescues and torments my mind. I study through the following night and into the next morning, after the centaurs have retired. I should prioritize my rest, but the answer to this game might be in the scribe's book, sequestered within the pages.

All of us win—or none of us win.

Perspiration beads behind my earlobes. I read the same line a dozen times before thrusting the tome shut.

My forehead plops onto the cover. I instruct myself to breathe, breathe, breathe.

Hooves clomp into the copse, slenderer than an equine's. My head shoots up. Sylvan trots into the camp, the willow vines swaying around her, shamrocks encrusting her crown.

Perhaps she'd been expecting to find Puck?

She has shifted to her normal size. Cautious, I rise and tiptoe across the grass. When Sylvan remains passive, I reach out, thinking of the doe back home and every animal I've rescued. I let those memories overwhelm my being, hoping Sylvan will sense it.

The verdant shamrocks flare with color. Flecks of teal swim in those mineral black eyes.

Finally, I make contact, stroking her muzzle. And finally, she inches her head closer.

My eyes sting. An awed laugh bubbles from my lips.

The deer bumps my hand. She turns and lowers her rump. My chuckles amplify, proud, honored, because I know what she's offering.

I swing my leg over Sylvan and land astride her back. Without preamble, she takes off, springing through the willow trees. And now my laughter is a full-blown horn blasting from my throat.

My ponytail flies loose, my hair a flag whisking behind me. A button pops open in my blouse, the collars flapping. We race around trees and pass the bridge, surging into a wild chase across this land, from one end of The Heart of Willows to the other.

As the doe returns me to my camp, she eases to a halt. I pat her cheek and say, "Thank you."

"Never thank a Fae," a male advises.

The sun lacquers the area in tangerine and powdery blue. Puck stands at the hub of it, idling outside my yurt.

My face implodes with heat, wrought with images of him sleeping naked and how my fingers had reacted afterward. Moreover, I'm straddling his friend, my legs spread, my hair a riot of tangles, and my blouse undone below my collarbones. I'm flushed, panting from the gallop.

Nonetheless, quailing and blushing are useless reactions. I steel my features and jump off the animal, daring Puck to comment.

He just gazes at me, his eyes hooded as he traces my open blouse, my unkempt tresses, and my bare feet. I'd forgotten to don my ankle boots and cloak before the ride.

Sylvan ambles over to Puck in greeting. He pets her and whispers, *"Finnst fér jún kóde? Éck feit jfernick fade lídur."*

Despite the neighboring pond, she canters off to the stream winding through the valley. Likely, she's thirsty after our excursion.

I wait until she's gone. "What did you say to her?"

"It's confidential. You understand, I'm sure." Puck moseys my way. "Have a merry ride?"

"She offered," I explain, holding my ground.

He pauses a foot away—always, I'm aware of the precise distance between us. "The next time she does, have an apple ready. She fancies apples," he says, his inflection haggard, like he's speaking around broken glass. "And pat her neck. She fancies that, too. It relaxes her."

This tone of voice is new. It's poignant, troubling. "Puck?"

"Let her decide where to go. If you do that enough times, she'll eventually let you lead."

"Puck."

"Until then, wait for her to get used to you. Trust her, and she'll trust you back."

"Puck," I insist.

Distracted, the satyr admires my hair. He extends an arm, then halts to see what I'll do, which is nothing. I do nothing but swallow, and he takes that as permission, his pinky coiling around a lock of green. Air siphons from my lungs as he rubs the layer between his thumb and forefinger.

My tongue strays across my lower lip, catching his attention. His irises kindle, following the movement of my tongue, hunting its progress along my mouth.

"Why are you telling me this?" I ask.

Why is he counseling me on how to ride Sylvan? Why is he doing so as if this information is precious, imperative?

Puck recovers. He releases me and walks backward, then swings around and heads for the tributary where Sylvan had ventured. Before exiting, he stops. "The Trapping," he says. "I got to her before that snare could, but those mortal shitheads had already done a number on her. They tried working her to exhaustion, forcing her across tumbleweeds and around a minefield of iron jaws waiting to bite off a limb. I jammed my leg into that trap on purpose, knowing it would distract them from her, so she was able to get away. But Sylvan was never the same after that and never let anyone ride her but me.

"Once, she bit off a dryad's fucking hand when he got near her, even though he was a fellow Fae, not a human. So in The Redwoods of Exile, when I asked if she'd approached you on her own, I had my reasons. You're different, and that difference is a good thing for Sylvan. It's empowering her." The knob in his throat bobs, like an old mechanism that hasn't been exercised in a decade. "Thank you."

I stand rooted in place, long after he departs. Outside the copse, centaur hooves clomp. Among the emerald willows, a whiff of thyme sails past my nostrils. I notice all of it but process none of it.

All I can think about is the look on Puck's face when he saw me mounted on the deer, his admission, and his gratitude. I clutch my stomach, his confession nesting there. Puck had thanked me. He'd made the advice about Sylvan seem crucial because it had been. He'd provided this information, encouraging me to seek her out again.

If The Trapping has traumatized the animal, perhaps our ride is a sign of her recovery. It's feasible he'd like help with that, for the brief time I have left until Middle Moon.

It could be a ploy, a snare constructed by a master trickster. However, Faeries don't willingly exploit their fauna kin. I can't imagine Puck taking advantage for his own devices, nor manipulating the fauna to win a game. He hadn't chosen the hunt's terms. The forest had done that.

So perhaps he…trusts me. The thought punctures my chest, a chink breaking loose. Unable to cope with the aftereffects, I float to the ground, snatch the Book of Fables from the spot where I'd left it, perch my spectacles on my nose, and thumb through the contents.

I research for several hours, until midday leaks into the wild. Then I pass out.

At one point, two soft thunks nudge me from a dreamless rest. The weight of someone's eyes caress my skin. Groggy, I blink at the vines marking the entrance. They quiver, though there's no one there to disturb them.

It must have been the wind.

I awaken at twilight to find my lenses askew—and my notebook settled beside me on the grass. Somebody had done me a favor and returned it.

Initially, the sight of my notebook fuels me with indignation. However, I have no time for outrage, no matter how much I'd like to shove Puck into the creek for confiscating it in the first place. Giving back the tablet doesn't absolve him of that, but I pick my battles and let it go.

Instead, I dive into both tomes until my eyes ache behind the lenses. I pour over the Fables—the creatures, the morals, the illustrations—and compare them to my notes. I document theories about hunting, animals, and magical beings, then leave my refuge to stalk a wild hen for repast.

After that, I search for Sylvan. She has laid claim to a favorite grazing spot where I coax her into a ride. It takes gentle persuasion—me whispering to her, petting her neck, and bringing her an apple. As Puck had advised, it works.

During the ride, I don't reminisce about the sight of him sleeping. His nudity, splayed across the grass. His bare chest, a cliff of flesh and bone, teeming with unexplored landmarks. His mouth open, his breaths drawing in and out. His hips, twitching while he dreams.

I don't think about any of it. I don't ponder lots of things he's done and said. I don't agonize over how I've responded to those things, how my body has reacted.

Since I've ceased hunting Puck, I suspect he has elected to spend the remainder of this interim with Cypress, making plans for Middle Moon and collaborating on the hunt, should I venture beyond the veil prior to my deadline. The notion stings.

The trip with Sylvan soothes my headache, consoles my nerves, and fills me with wonder. Yet the spell is short-lived, failing to refresh my thoughts. This handful of days and nights have narrowed quickly, closing in on me like the walls of a cage.

I remember Lark's sassy grin and Cove's endearing smile.

When I return to the yurt, my eyes water. But crying will only dehydrate me. Besides, I haven't succumbed to tears in ages, and I'm not about to break down in this realm, and not because of my captors.

Also, the centaurs might hear it. Above all, they're still Faeries who might enjoy the sounds of my grief, however obliged Cypress is to reimburse my favor.

I think about what my papa and sisters have taught me. I think about what I've taught myself. I think about that and double my study efforts, then triple them, to no avail.

The eve of Middle Moon arrives. I've read through every original Fable and every annotation the scribe had penned. I've done so until my vision had blurred, until my spectacles had made dents in my face.

Yet. Nothing.

This, despite Papa calling me his tree of knowledge. This, despite the villagers of Reverie Hollow stigmatizing me as a know-it-all.

Come nightfall, I'll have to leave The Heart of Willows. Either I'll complete my tasks and win this game or not.

What will happen to Papa Thorne? What about Lark and Cove?

What will happen to the Fable Dusk Sanctuary and the animals who live there? What will befall the ones my sisters and I haven't yet rescued?

As the sun bakes in the sky, I go to sleep shaking, curled in a fetal position.

Later, a melody coasts into the thicket. It has weight and shape to it, brushing the hair from my temple. I stir, as bleary as a dewdrop.

Music flows from a single instrument. The tune carries the richness of soil, the resonance of a contemplative forest.

It's the sound of a cello.

20

I follow the tune, hunting its deep-throated notes through the willows. Before going to sleep, I'd changed into my leggings and sweater, the knit falling halfway down my thighs. A draft sneaks through the weave, pebbling my arms.

My hair hangs in a sheet over my shoulders. My bare feet step around fallen bracken, my heels brushing through stems of grass.

Hanging vines caress my shoulders as I pass from one coppice to the next, seeking the melody across the willow bridge. The music travels like a set of fingers, fondling the branches. It roots into the depths, burrowing under layers of earth and skin. It's the noise oak trees would make if they could speak.

Strong yet lush. Mournful yet soulful.

And slow like a heady, leisurely moan.

My heart thuds. In my village, I've attended jubilees and fairs, heard my share of fiddles and lutes. But this source is different, a particular assembly of strings that's unmistakable, playing a pivotal role in oral tales about three rulers of the Solitary wild.

One pipes a flute. One plucks a harp. One plays a cello.

The Fables say this: Beware of Fae music, for it will lead mortals to their doom.

I keep going. I keep hunting this instrument, pushing the vine cords out of the way, until I'm upon him.

Easing myself between two trees, I peek into an enclosure. And there he is.

He sits on a tree stump, his limbs spread around a tall, curvy piece of wood with strings affixed down the center. Clefts carve through the frame's belly, coiling at the ends. I see knobs at the top and a dartlike stand at the bottom.

Puck's head dips, wild layers of hair tumbling over his face. Those bladed ears spring from his head.

He doesn't see me, but I see him. Fables, how I see him.

Clad in umber breeches, his thighs are spread in a broad stance to accommodate the cello. It leans against his naked chest, jolting as he runs a wand-like bar across the strings. His arms flex, the muscles bunching, sweat glistening in his clavicles.

He plays with his eyes clamped shut. He plays with his whole body, putting his weight into it. He plays with all his vicious heart.

The satyr's right arm slides back and forth while his left digits vibrate over the cords. The pace is languid, at once seductive and yearning. The composition sways in one direction, then plunges low. So low that I feel it in my womb, and lower, and lower.

In one fluid movement, Puck lifts his head. His eyes open to find mine.

Air hitches between my teeth, getting trapped there. I grip the leaves on either side of me.

My cheeks roast with mortified heat. However, his expression doesn't change, nor does the music. His fingers move fluidly without pause, without tripping over the notes.

It's a vision worthy of anthology illustrations. *A satyr plays his cello, its seductive glamour luring innocent mortals into his lair.*

I linger. The music seeps in, its effects accumulating like sips of wine—potent, addictive. He plays, and he plays, and he plays. We stare, and we stare, and we stare. His melody dares me to stay, to listen, to find out.

The notes taper high, then quiver into a crescendo. Next, they descend once more, rippling to the ground and sinking in. The melody evaporates with a final shiver, leaving silence in its wake.

I step into the enclosure, folding my hands in front of me. "That was..." Splendid, dazzling, magnificent. "...exceptional."

When it comes to compliments, my deficiency rings clear. For once, I cringe at the tactless description. Exceptional? It was a sterling performance.

Puck lowers that stick apparatus, oxygen venting from his chest as if he's worn himself out. "You think so?" he pants. "I was going for tantalizing."

"No, you were not."

"No, I wasn't. For once."

Yes. The rulers of the Solitary wild have used their instruments to enchant mortals—to no benevolent end.

But not now. Not me.

Where did the cello come from? How did Puck transport it here?

Do I need to ask? Likely, he'd evanesced to retrieve the instrument, then materialized back here.

Puck assesses my unshod toes, the leggings clinging like film to my limbs, and the sweater covering everything else of notoriety. I feel his gaze penetrate beneath the material, no matter how heavy the yarn.

"It's past your bedtime, luv," he intones. "Need help sleeping?"

I refuse to answer that. "Where did you learn to play?"

The satyr drapes his arms over the cello. "Cerulean taught himself the flute. Elixir taught himself the harp. Not one to be left out, I had to keep up with them. That the instruments represented each of our worlds appealed to us, and I liked earning the skill instead of being entitled to it like a maudlin prince, or endowed with it like some extravagantly, long-suffering prodigy. I might have mentioned before, I fancy working with my hands."

"But now you'll ask, why the cello? I thought so." Puck drags his index finger down a string. "It reminds me of roots. The notes are immersive and resilient, the effect profound." He glimpses my face. "It reaches deeply."

I gulp, clench my fingers tighter.

"Also, the trees like the music, so to speak," he says. "And I'm ever at their merry service."

I have no idea what to make of that, but I'd like to know.

Puck adjusts the cello, shifts himself on the stump. "If you want another tune, your wish is my command. For a price, of course. My music doesn't come cheaply, especially with a ruler's schedule. Don't you see how very busy I am?"

He prattles whenever he's unsure of himself. "If you're so busy, where are the rest of your clothes?" I ask.

"I lost them."

A laugh bursts from me. "You're impossible."

"If I am, that makes the payoff more enticing. Don't you think?"

"And you're conceited."

"And that makes my redemption more engrossing. Don't you agree?"

My mirth disintegrates as abruptly as the music had. "I don't know what I think or agree with anymore."

Puck's voice thickens. "Neither do I."

Those offenses had just come out, my confession and his reply. I'm no longer surprised by this. Moreover, I'll have won or failed come eventide. I don't have a name for this culmination of emotions. It's a hodgepodge of terror, guilt, rage, desperation, resignation, hope, despair, frustration, incompetence, and resistance.

It's Puck's fault and the Faeries' fault. It's also my fault for being inadequate to the tasks thus far.

Still, I've never failed my family and won't allow myself to. But what am I overlooking? Where's the missing link?

"What did you mean, when you asked what I feel about the Fables?" I inquire.

Bracing the cello against the stump, Puck rises and saunters toward me. "You know what I meant. Back in The Wicked Pines, you were right about valuing the words of others, even though they don't come from oneself. I hadn't thought about it that way, but while I endorse the occasional quote, I want to know what you think. While I value what you think, I want to know what you feel."

I force myself to remain still. "This change of heart is awfully sudden."

Puck halts, looming over me like an oak tree—an enigmatic, imposing figure. "I would say it's nine years in the making."

"What brought this on?"

"You did, and I did, and we did."

My pulse has neglected to calm down since I got here. His riddling words don't help the matter. Me, and him, and us? So we're both to blame? How did this change happen? When, exactly? What's transpiring between us?

"Always analyzing. Always spoiling for explanations," Puck says. "Always smart, perceptive, observant."

"I know who and what I am," I snap. "I don't need you to appraise me."

"I'm glad of it. But remember when I said hunt is a relative term? It can be translated in many ways. Such as this…" He steps forward, his smooth torso grazing my sweater. "The farther you run toward something, the farther you run from something else."

"I should go."

I step around Puck. He whirls with me, his digits brushing my elbow. I freeze long enough for him to shift and block my path. Supple leather accentuates his hips, the breeches slung indecently low. The waistband leaves little to the imagination, the slopes of a V peeking from the pants.

"I didn't expose your hiding spot in the elms because I didn't want you to lose. I was trying to figure out how to keep you in one piece before it was too late," he says. "Tinder was there, and he couldn't know I was playing both sides. Cypress is another story, but suffice it to say, I was a misbehaving ruler.

"When we combatted in the wild, all the way to The Fauna Timbers, I held back because I didn't want to hurt you. Yet I prolonged the battle because I didn't want it to end, because I wanted to be near you, because I wanted to know how good you were—and fuck, you were good. I drew it out because I wanted to see my world as you saw it, to discover it as you discovered it. I wanted to be close to you, no matter how torn I was. You broke me long ago, but I just couldn't break you back."

I'm speechless. The confessions bring me up short, as much as the ragged texture of his breath. The heat of him. The wafting nips of spices and evergreens. Regardless, I've had enough of this particular game, and it seems he has as well.

"In the pit, I used my hands instead of magic to fix your shoulder because I wanted to touch you," he continues. "Later, I detailed the pleasures of touching yourself because I wanted it to be true for you. I wanted you to find that magic, to give yourself bliss. And selfishly, I wanted to be the reason you did it. I wanted my words thrusting inside you. I wanted to give you everything." His eyes peg me in place. "So have you touched yourself yet?"

I shiver, because he knows. He doesn't need to ask. "Yes."

His teeth flash, as do his eyes. "How did it feel?"

Immaculate. Staggering. "Powerful," I answer.

And he nods. "Please don't go."

His plea melts like wax, fluid and flaming, a slow ooze down my skin.

"What are we?" I ask. "Are we reluctant enemies? Forbidden friends?"

"We're not enemies. But like fuck are we just friends." Puck's timbre sneaks between my legs, reaching the seam of my thighs. "From the second you came back to me, I've been hooked. Your studious glower, your smoky voice, that determined huntress chin. Pink creeping across the tops of your luscious tits every time I made a wicked comment."

I wouldn't describe my bust as luscious. It's as flat as my visage, unless one counts my overgrown nose.

Not that I've wasted time mulling over these facets. My looks are immaterial to me. I don't need my face to do anything but see, smell, and taste.

Yet that's not the tone with which Puck describes me. Nowhere close to that.

"Every time you looked at me with the barest tinge of lust," he says. "Every time you put me in my place, and every time I made you laugh, it was glorious, and I could barely stand it. And these cruel, fucking leggings." He roves over the material clinging to my limbs. "They're going to be the end of me."

I can't move, can't breathe.

"But most of all," he continues, "seeing those smart, little spectacles perched on your nose has undone me numerous times. I've thought about you wearing them while astride my lap, jutting your hips and riding me to the brink of insanity."

"You're already insane," I utter.

"And growing madder by the hour," he agrees. "I've stroked my cock to fantasies of you, pumping myself hard to the memory of your laughter, your brusque scowl, the expression you'd wear while your body convulsed around your fingers. I took that self-pleasure last night, and I'll do again soon, and I'll do it so thoroughly—," he whispers, "—you'll feel when I come."

Moisture builds from within, pooling slick and warm from my body. I want that. He knows, I do. What he might not know is that I want to be there, watching him.

He murmurs, "My obsession will stop when I no longer care about you more than my kin. It'll stop when you quit consuming my mind, every hour, day and night. It'll stop then—which is to say, never. Unless you order me to stop."

My breath skitters out. "I should want that."

But I don't.

"What else should you want?" he wonders. "Educate me. Have you ever acted without thinking and then trusting where that took you? Flung your inhibitions to wind? Have you ever run naked through the forest?"

I haven't. One time, Lark had persuaded Cove to do it with her. I had disrobed only to my nightgown and only for them. I hadn't done it for myself.

I stare at him, refusing to shy away and needing to hear more. I know lots of things. But I don't know *this*.

Puck pushes the words out, as though his mouth is stuffed with cotton. "The leaves grazing your knees. The moon bathing your navel. The chill rushing across your nipples. Your hair, as free and wild as it is now."

He hasn't touched me. Yet we're panting, venting.

His whisper hits the ledge of my ear, then the column of my neck. My pulse leaps, rapping against my throat. Fables forgive me, but I want his mouth there, speaking against that delicate tempo.

"I know what you can do. I know what you're capable of," Puck mutters. "What I want to know is how you feel while doing it. I want to know what you're capable of feeling. I want so fucking badly to know, Juniper."

My name on his tongue. Three syllables puff against my lips, which part in response.

I understand what he's saying. How can I act with my head, if I haven't practiced acting with my heart? For once, I don't know. I've only relied on books to achieve something and hunted to atone for something else.

"Now." He tips his head lower, lower still. "Come. Here."

I want to, but it's my turn. "What about you?" I ask, my voice faint, a thin line of space remaining between his mouth and mine. "Have you ever taken a dalliance so seriously that you paced yourself? Have any of those consummations had a lasting effect, beyond immediate gratification? Have you ever had an affair of substance? Has it ever been that relevant to you?"

The questions probe his face, shifting it in a new direction. To all of my inquiries, he answers with a shake of his head.

"Have you ever hooked yourself around another body?" he asks. "Have you known what it's like to be filled sweetly, ridden hard? Your tits heaving, your sighs untamed, your core soaked? Do you know what it's like to bind yourself with someone, to unleash with them? Have you ever felt reckless, cresting to a pinnacle, then pitching over the edge?"

Other than when I slipped my fingers between my legs, no. But I sense it close, so close. Wetness coats the apex of my thighs, the nexus of which throbs.

My exhalations glide against his jaw. "Consideration," I whisper. "Significance."

"Passion," he insists. "Stimulation."

"Restraint."

"Rhapsody."

"Prove it."

"Show me."

We stand on a precipice, at the center of this enclosure. I don't know what's happening, but I know this: I don't want to leave.

We swallow, draw in air, and shove it out. My sweater flutters against his abdomen, but I do this: I press nearer, permitting, craving.

More, closer, now.

Puck's hands slide into my hair, clasping my scalp in his palms. A guilty thought sits on his face, and that same thought penetrates to the marrow of my bones: This is wrong.

This is so very wrong.

Our bodies slam together. And the satyr sinks his mouth into mine.

21

I had expected a kiss to make sense. I had expected it to be gradual, beginning with a prologue—perhaps an introductory peck. I had expected it to be methodical, something taught and learned. I had expected the kiss to be…expected.

What I hadn't expected was for this kiss to be a departure from consciousness. All body and soul. All hands and mouths. All taste and motion. All of it, proseful. This isn't a step taken, nor is it paced, but a wild leap into the fire.

Those wicked lips slant and fuse with mine. We fit together, our mouths folding in unison. He pries our lips apart, a humid blast of air colliding. I gasp at the temperature and flavor of it, balmy and gingered.

His fingers tangle in my locks, the heat of his palms radiating to the rest of my body. My flesh turns into kindling, then whips into an inferno, flames crackling.

The contact knocks me off my bare feet with the force of a quake, the earth shattering beneath us. I grab ahold of his waist for balance, my fingers digging into the leather.

At my touch, Puck shudders. A guttural hum vibrates from his throat and slips between my teeth. At the sound, an inarticulate noise spills from my own mouth.

And then his tongue sweeps between my lips.

My head dissolves into mist. He laps against me in a dizzying rhythm, pitching in and out. In and out. In and out. In and out. And oh, he tastes of forests and mischief.

His kiss spreads me wide, somehow impacting me everywhere, from my mouth to the slot between my legs. Both wet, both getting wetter by the second. I feel it there, and there, and *there*. My belly swoops with each swat of his tongue, another incomprehensible sound ripping from my throat. It ricochets across my tongue and travels to his. My fingers go rogue, knifing through his red layers and pulling on the roots. I need him closer, deeper.

Not enough. More.

Inhaling through my nostrils, I fill myself with the scandalous aromas of cloves and pine. Beneath the sweater, my nipples stiffen. My bust mashes against his naked torso, our hearts battering one another. The savage tempo causes my knees to liquefy.

Before this moment, I'd have assumed such a response would render me weak, reduce me to a damsel spirited away in the arms of a rakish satyr. Instead, the effect is empowering, primal.

My fingers feel indulgent, my thighs decadent, my mouth greedy. My body's a reckless, rebellious thing.

Sensations I hadn't known existed spring from my pores. Fuses ignite. Smoke curls through my blood. I'm a blaze, thrashing from its confines. He's the earth, fueling me to burn higher, brighter.

My arms sling around his neck, clinging for leverage. Then I match his cadence, lashing my tongue with his.

The satyr groans, long and needy. His fingers drag from my hair, one arm slinging around my lower back, the other clamping my head in place.

Our mouths are restless, hectic. Puck licks into me, over and over. His tongue thrusts against mine with deft strokes. I sketch the base of his antlers, then descend to the tips of his ears, thumbing the peaks.

And Puck snaps. On a hiss, he hoists me against him.

And the kiss erupts.

His mouth clings, riding my lips into a frenzy. My mouth rolls with his, the sensations coursing through my veins.

I also hadn't expected a kiss to feel alive—so very alive. I hadn't expected it to feel this right, this true. I hadn't expected it to be effortless and endless. I never thought it could be this way.

Instead of being satiated, my yearning expands. I want his mouth elsewhere, everywhere. I want it beneath my clothes. I want it in the passage between my legs, in the basin between my breasts, and beneath the ledge of my jaw.

I want my mouth to do the same. I want to provoke him, to see what it takes for this Fae to come undone, to see how far he'll unravel. I want to hunt for his vulnerable spots, his hidden spots, and his loud spots.

Puck peels his mouth away. Our foreheads press, our eyes locking. I move first, framing his hips and walking backward across the grass. He follows, letting me guide us to the nearest tree. Too impatient to wait, our mouths meet again. My back hits the trunk. The tenacious satyr takes over, pressing me into the bark, the plains of his bare chest flexing against me. I hitch a breath, welcoming those vicious lips, that fiendish half-grin.

We kiss deeper, harsher. His tongue strikes into my mouth, the strong movements of his jaw wringing sighs from me.

I'm kissing a satyr. I'm kissing the ruler of the woodland. I'm kissing the Fae from my past. I'm kissing Puck.

Experimentally, I wrap my lips around that infuriating, sarcastic tongue and suck. Puck shivers, gooseflesh popping across his arms. So I do it more, more, more.

The satyr mutters something in Faeish and palms my backside. I moan, his touch steaming through my leggings, his hands spanning my rear.

The woodland jolts as he hauls me off the ground. On reflex, my legs strap around his waist. That's when I feel something new, something long and firm rising in the gap of my thighs. Puck's stiff length wedges between us, rubbing against my center. Blood rushes to that private place, the intimate flesh throbbing, pounding, demanding.

I keen into his mouth, and the satyr devours the sound. My limbs splay around him, my knees steeple over his ribs, and my feet flatten on the trunk. He's taller, broader, able to bolster my weight.

We pant, softness molding with hardness. So much hardness.

If I'd had any chance before, it's over when Puck peels his mouth from mine and tucks his lips under my chin. He plies the tissuey skin under my mandible with open-mouthed kisses.

Another moan skitters from my mouth. The forest eats up the sound. My head drops against the trunk, my fingers wrenching through his hair again. With an erotic chuckle, he laps at me, his tongue swabbing my collarbones.

My teeth find his tapered ears and give a small nip. Unlike me, Puck barely handles it. He seethes and raises his drunken gaze to mine before catching my mouth once more.

Our lips tug, surging forward and retreating. Our arms hold tight, my thighs clutching his waist.

I also hadn't expected a kiss to feel joyous, riotous. If we don't stop, I'll run out of breath, out of heartbeats, out of my mind.

But I won't stop, because I don't want to stop. Please, don't stop.

I dip my head, my hair threading with his. I snatch his face, bite his bottom lip, and savor his sensuous growl. I kiss him, and kiss him, and kiss him back.

Our mouths fuse. Our tongues ply at one another, licking, sucking.

Yes, this is wrong. It will still be wrong when it's over. But the slam of Puck's heart against mine makes a counterargument: It's been wrong for a long time, so let it be wrong.

Let it be so very wrong.

22

We break away from the kiss at the same time. My lips wrench from Puck's, and his pry from mine on a gruff exhale. Our foreheads land together. Nails dig into rustled hair and mouths hang open, shocked and swollen.

For a split second, he and I remain bolted like that, pressing hard and scrambling for breath. For a split second, we're intoxicated. And for a split second, I don't mind.

Then we come to our senses and jolt apart, as though singed from the contact. I thrash from his arms, and he lets me go. Together, we yank ourselves out of the moment.

"Fuck," he mutters, stalking several paces from me.

"Fables," I gasp, launching backward.

My hands fumble, tidying the wreck he'd made of my clothes. Meanwhile, he's content to remain a shambles. The evidence of our kiss is smeared all over him—the damage my fingers have done to his hair, the fiery threads rumpled.

What. Have. I. Done?

Kissing the satyr had been different from my experience with that village buck. The embrace with Puck had exceeded a lapse in judgment. It's too profound, too staggering, too wretched to be reduced to a mere error. The emotions congest, a flurry of shame and something altogether exhilarating.

This lip-lock had been more than a mistake. It had *mattered*.

Puck whirls away, then abruptly spins back to face me, his expression severe. The aftermath of our kiss lingers in the influx of color rushing up his ears, the arousal firm under his breeches. Lust fattens his pupils, bloating them to the point where they eclipse his irises.

Is that how I look?

Yet all that ferocity begins to evaporate the longer his gaze adheres to mine. Once it vanishes completely, misery rises to the surface. I see it in the rickety bob of his throat.

Nearly every sensation I feel flakes apart, leaving only one behind. It's the only one I have room for, the only one that fits in my chest: betrayal.

How can he kiss me like that and still endorse this game? How can he look at me like that and still pursue this hunt?

How can I let him? And how dare I realize this too late?

I tense, my fists balling and my hair a tangled nest. I open my mouth to blast him with a question: Why?

No, a dozen questions. Why did he kiss me? Why is he doing this—all of this? Why won't they let me and my sisters go? Why is it so important to maintain this rift between humans and Faeries?

I've read the Fables inside and out until my eyes have blurred and my spectacles imprinted my face. Despite the morals and cautionary warnings, the fundamentals have never been addressed. Why does having magic make the Folk superior to my people? Why do they assume magic is restricted to tricks, curses, glamour, strength, speed, immortality, flawless beauty, and otherworldly links to nature?

Why do they assume mortals don't have magic of their own? Why isn't *being human* magical? And what isn't he telling me about the game?

Puck ejects a string of Faeish. He drags his palm over his mouth, shifts languages, and speaks quickly. "In The Heart of Willows, you asked what makes this game so vital? If I recall, I said I'd tell you later."

"You-you did," I stutter, aghast to hear my disjointed voice.

I'm not the only one. Never have I imagined witnessing Puck in a stupor, nor witnessing him sober with this degree of expediency.

I wish things were different. I wish we were allowed to savor this time rather than tear it to shreds. I wish the kiss hadn't been forbidden. I wish I could feel only pride for causing that flush in his complexion, that ripple effect in his body, that swell of his mouth. I wish lots of wishes that won't come true, not at the rate mortals and Faeries have been going.

Mostly, I wish I were a person who believed in wishes. Like Cove and Papa Thorne.

The Fae's prolonged silence speaks volumes. Whatever he's about to reveal, it's crucial, and I might very well despise him for it.

"Brace yourself, luv," Puck says.

Then he tells me. He tells me what my people don't know, how their plan to eviscerate the Solitaries during The Trapping had indeed worked. The villagers had reckoned otherwise, concluding that their rebellion failed when Puck, Cerulean, and Elixir rescued the surviving animals.

"But it hadn't?" I whisper.

"It hadn't," he confirms.

It hadn't because the wild began to decline after that. Having lost scores of its fauna, the landscape flourished less and wilted more. It's been weakening ever since: uneven foundations and brittle bridges in cliff peaks, shriveling leaves and parched soil in the woodland, and shallower water depths in the river, along with less rainfall and flora, and fewer abundant crops. Gradually, everything will fade into tendrils. The deterioration of their realms—the mountain, the forest, and the deep—means that Puck's kin are in danger of fading with it.

This is what my neighbors had hoped for. Unbeknownst to them, the Folk are stuck in a race against time. They've kept this knowledge from reaching mortal ears, though that couldn't have been grueling to accomplish.

Trepidation clots my lungs. That, and another unforgivable reaction. Fearing for the animals is one thing. Fearing for Puck is another.

Not only him, but Cypress. Not only Cypress, but the Fae children who play no part in the antics of their elders, because those children haven't been raised yet.

"How long do you have?" I ask.

Puck tells me, "Until the thirteenth year."

This number would be considerable for mortals. For Faeries who live forever, it's nothing. The Trapping was nine years ago; their window is closing.

I shake my head. "But what does this have to do with the game?"

Puck's gaze is tangible, an invisible thumb stroking my cheek. "Everything and anything."

He expands on the games his kin have played, how those games have been essential for the Faeries' survival. It's the loophole to their demise. His kin can't resurrect the Faeries who died trying to save their animals. But they can do something about the fauna. For each human life given to the Solitary wild, one of the lost animals will rise again. If all the fallen are restored, the land will thrive once more, and this world will endure.

A new emotion kindles, this one taking a hot bite out of the dread and worry I'd felt. I draw out, "What do you mean, a human life 'given' to the Solitary wild? What does 'given' mean?"

Puck's bleak grin delivers a blow to the nervous system. "Come, now. You're smarter than that."

"And you're gutsier than that," I scold.

But I know what 'given' implies. It means sacrifice.

Bile congeals in my mouth, and the betrayal I'd felt earlier recycles itself into repugnance. The Faeries are sacrificing humans to the wild, avenging what happened during The Trapping, compensating for what my people took from this land. That's what this hunt is about.

Puck tells me the rest. He tells me these sacrifices require rituals— games—as is the age-old custom of his culture. Each ruler of the Solitary wild oversees the proceedings and upholds its rules, which are unique to the environment.

Only one set of conditions is unanimous across the mountain, forest, and deep. If the human wins, they go free. If they lose, they die. If they die, another lost animal will rise.

Either the mortals perish from the game, the elements, or at the Faeries' hands. It depends on the game itself and how it's played. Apparently because my sisters and I had trespassed together, we suffer together. By suffering together, our fate is contingent on one another.

That's why I'm here. That's my purpose.

I'm here to die for Puck's survival, for the survival of an entire race. Either that, or I'm here to compete for his extinction and my sister's lives.

I stand there, quaking. Puck stands there, immobile.

Oh, I see the way my silence wrings him out like a cloth. I see the remorse, the hankering for forgiveness, and whatever else he hopes I'll feel. I see it's not about him, if it ever was. I see he's split like a fault line between his world and my life. I see that I've become more to this Fae than he'd planned. I see him snared, caged.

I see that he hadn't wanted to tell me. But he did anyway.

He'd been unable to keep this from me any longer. And I'm glad of it.

Because it means I can do this: I march up to the satyr and punch him in the face.

His head whips to the side. His body follows, twisting like a corkscrew. The mouth I'd recently suckled on spritzes red. Puck curses, his fingers shooting to his teeth, the ivories stained.

There's an extreme discrepancy between the strength of a mortal versus that of a Fae. Which means the circumstances must be exceptional for that mortal to do damage, to make the slightest dent. I'm wheezing, my knuckles smarting. Either I've caught him off guard or Puck had prepared himself for this scenario and loosened his stance. Both possibilities justify why the crack of my fist has a substantial impact.

Pearls of blood drip from his upper lip. He must have bitten the skin when my fist rammed into him.

Rage boils at the tips of my fingers, at the tip of my tongue. To say the least, my reaction is overdue, though I can't say which was a longer time coming—the punch or the kiss.

Yes, his offenses in the past had already warranted this response from me. He and these Faeries had forced my family here. He'd turned me into hunted prey. He'd made a game of it. Those factors validate more than my right hook.

By learning the reason behind this game, I understand his motives. But like hell do I agree with them.

My stomach curdles. "You eternal bastard."

Puck straightens. He waits for the rest, knowing better than to defend himself.

"You want to save your people, the fauna, this world," I grit between my teeth. "You want to restore the fallen animals. And who wouldn't? Who wouldn't battle for that?" I draw breath, scarcely keeping my venom in check. "But if you can't exist without this landscape, then leave. Seek out another wilderness or take refuge in one of the kingdoms. I'm sure the Unseelie Court would open its doors for the likes of you."

"Some have," he concedes. "The ones who weren't born in the Solitary wild have left, the ones who got the hell away from the Courts to begin with, wanting a life cloistered from political bullshit. But surprise, surprise, we merry natives belong to this land. We can leave whenever we want, but we'll be tied to this environment for eternity. Its fate is our fate. Leaving won't make a lick of difference."

"How tragic for you."

"What the fuck would you have me do, Juniper?" Puck shouts. "Tell me. What would you do?"

"Find another way!" My voice surges. The octave hits a plateau, a point of no return. I've never screamed like this at anyone, not even my family.

"And in what bountiful universe have Faeries historically cared about humans enough to do that?" Puck disputes. "They have zero qualms about eradicating mortals. Of all people, you know this."

Yes. I know this. I've lived this.

Still, I can't take this.

I stab a finger at him. "You claim to have this deep connection to nature. You say that because of this bond, you'll fade alongside the environment. How does that make you different from humans? My people wouldn't last without it, yet we find ways around that. We plant, we harvest, we build, and we make humane sacrifices along the way. We don't forfeit innocent lives."

That's incorrect. I realize this error instantly.

Puck seethes. "Innocent. Were your neighbors innocent of that massacre? Did they think of a way around it before deciding to butcher Fae striplings and animals?"

"You were terrorizing my people. I wish they'd sought another option, but they were desperate and scared."

"And to survive, they jumped into action. As did we."

"Survive, my ass!" I quote my younger sister. "What about this hunt? What you said about the forest choosing the game, basing it off my fears? Making me hunt an animal in this wild? If this is about restoring what's lost, then the hunt still doesn't make sense! Why trade a living animal for a fallen one?"

"Because sometimes nature's a royal prick," he says. "An ally lots of times, a prick other times. Either way, it's the price we pay for our future. The one consolation is that our lifecycle is only compromised when the fauna are slain and left to rot. If we hunt for nourishment, it has the opposite effect, preserving that cycle. That's why we'd planned to feast on the animal if you were successful."

I run a hand through my bedraggled hair. "What about my village? You're still harming humans! My people, my sisters, myself!"

"Not you," he stresses, quieting me. "That night years ago, I thought you led those villagers to me. I thought you betrayed Sylvan to them, and it broke my heart. And that night in the wagon, when you thought your sisters had vanished, and I'd baited you from the shadows? I'd hated you. And in The Wicked Pines, I'd wanted to stay hating you. I wanted to, so damn much.

"But the instant you stumbled into the candlelight, willful and brave and stubborn as hell, you wore the same expression as the moment we first met. All I felt was loss, and I wanted to punish you for that. And when I saw you in that redwood cage with Sylvan." He shakes his head. "The look on your face...the way she came to you...I didn't know what the fuck to do with myself. I couldn't hate you, but I couldn't let myself believe I'd been wrong about you. I couldn't let myself be that lad again. I couldn't make that same mistake twice.

"So, I fumed, goading the living shit out of you about The Trapping because I wanted to see how you'd react. I dreaded and hoped to find a spark of the girl I'd thought had been my friend. And I did see a flash of that girl, but not all of her yet. I didn't know what part of myself to trust or what part of you was real." He stares at me. "Until you shed that tear."

I remember that tear. I'd let it slip like a secret when beholding The Herd of Deer for the first time.

"Right then, you pulled me from my roots," Puck says. "I realized I'd been a fucking moron: You never betrayed me or Sylvan."

"No," I utter. "I didn't."

"From that moment on, I was all yours. No one else would get near you, but I couldn't make it obvious. Remember in The Skulk of Foxes, I said I'd used a Fae brew to strip the iron tips from your crossbow bolts; well, I did that because how the hell else was I supposed to wield them, to get the weaponry back to you without it seeming intentional?

"During the hunt, I thought I'd be sick, but pretending was the only way to make sure none of my kin touched you. I monitored and misdirected them, occasionally flirted and fondled them into distraction. To do that without arousing suspicion, I had to put up a front. They had to trust me."

"Keep your enemies close," I mumble.

Puck nods. "I'm sorry, Juniper. I'm so fucking sorry."

"Don't." My voice splinters, but I've changed my mind. No longer do I want my name on his lips. "I heard everything you said. I believe you, but it can't undo any of this."

"Juniper—"

"Why did you kiss me? I mean...*why* if you knew I'd have to die in order for your people to live? Why couldn't you leave my heart out of this?"

Puck hazards a step, but I thrust a warning hand at him. "Don't follow me."

I want to shriek and pull myself together. I want to throttle him and leap back into his arms. I want to go home. I want to stay right here. I want to fight. I want to flee.

I need to leave with dignity before I act on any of those impulses. Shoving my way past him, I slam out of the enclosure and storm down the willow passage to my yurt.

Once tucked inside the camp, I keel over onto the grass. My head bows between my knees as I heave for oxygen and fend off the roiling nausea.

However repellent, Puck's arguments about his kin are accurate. His people have never cared a wit for humans. Why would they start after The Trapping? Why would they fret over mortals who suffer during the games? Why would the Folk bother to change their methods?

Their survival is the priority. Preserving their existence is the goal. I abhor their tactics, but I'm cognizant of the roots.

As ruler of the woodland, Puck has a duty to follow through with this game. Keeping the Solitary wild alive is his responsibility. To do that, he has to vanquish me.

Yet the taste of him persists, its residue coating my lips. Yes, he'd realized the truth about our past. Yes, he wants to protect me. But no, he shouldn't have kissed me.

The Book of Fables rests on the grass. I snatch the tome and hurl it across the space. It flies and smacks into a mound of dirt, flopping open like a gaping mouth. Flecks speckle the parchment of a random page.

My remorse is immediate. I crawl over to the book and wipe my palm over the interior, wiping away the granules and streaking one of the words in the process. I retrieve my spectacles, and the letters solidify: *Immortal.*

And then. I stare.

I stare harder, closer. The stain lends a tilted quality to the word, which slants toward another noun several sentences down: *wild.*

"*Immortal wild,*" I mutter.

Another detail hits me—the penmanship of these two words. They've been written in a curvier style, diverting from the main one like a pair of snaggleteeth. The method is subtle, barely perceptible, but it's there. In fact, the results remind me of footprints.

My eyes broaden. I scan the Fable, then flip to the next one, and the next, and the next, until I land on a fresh word with the same rebellious calligraphy. Five pages later, I find another.

"*Immortal wild. Immortal land,*" I read.

The intermittent words link together like a chain, an unbreakable thing. It's the approximation of a hidden text. My digit runs across the leaflet, then seizes in place. "It's a trail," I whisper.

The scribe had stashed an uncharted passage throughout the book, accessible only by hunting for it. I pour over the tome. Each word I find, I pencil into my notebook. Hours later, I peer at the lines through my lenses. It's a secret Fable with a secret message, but this one isn't just for humans. It's for Faeries, too.

It's meant for both of us.

I reread the contents, mouthing the words to myself. At the tale's end, my head whips up, a grin sliding across my face. There's still a chance to win this hunt.

It looks like I'll be making a bargain, after all.

23

Eventide arrives. The last vestiges of daylight slip away, glossing my campsite in starlight—a cavorting kaleidoscope of white, gold, and teal. Dangling in the firmament is a chalky ring with a black pupil peeking through its center.

So that's what the Middle Moon looks like. I stand beneath it, the vision reminding me of a target marker, with its obsidian bullseye.

Middle Moon is the annual cycle marking the historical, ancestral birth of the Fae fauna. In The Wicked Pines, Puck had imparted the abridged details, how every environment in the Solitary wild celebrates in a different way.

Since I refuse to speak further with him, I locate Cypress and probe the centaur for additional information. From night to morning, the landscapes belong to the animals. Only they may roam their environments. This means whatever game the latest human is playing—if they haven't perished by then—comes to a temporary halt.

Until the sun rises, Faeries must remain idle, short of attending the revels.

In The Solitary Mountain, the Folk host a masquerade. Because they're a lofty bunch, that event is forbidden to mortal players, though I doubt that's a point of contention. What human would want to frolic with their captors?

Unless that human is my reckless sister. Before we'd parted ways, I had warned Lark to behave herself, but I wouldn't put it past her to sneak into the masquerade and spy.

As for what happens in The Solitary Deep, I miss out on the specifics. I don't get the opportunity to wheedle them out of Cypress because it's time to leave. It's time to depart from The Heart of Willows and step into the lion's den: The Middle Moon Feast.

Unlike in the mountain, the Faeries have solicited my presence. They want me trapped amidst their revelry and shaking in my boots. They want me as the centerpiece. This feast will be the site of my "reckoning," where I'll win or lose. Since they're used to it, they anticipate a gruesome end for me and a triumphant one for them.

The hunt has ended, the mysterious animal unidentified and unaccounted for. But I'm not done playing.

An entourage of centaurs guides me from their territory, a procession of equines parading in a straight line with their prisoner in tow. It's a spectacle of vivid coats, intricately braided tails, woven leather belts, horned helmets, and laurel circlets.

We take a considerable shortcut that I hadn't known existed, reducing travel by days. Apparently, undisclosed bends will dump an individual far from where they'd been, sometimes at the opposite margins of these woods. Not that Cypress imparts knowledge of those avenues to me.

With each landscape, species of trees transform from lacey to prickly. The fauna meander among us, threading in and out of niches like a living canvas. A stag with seedlings growing from its antlers stands proud, watching us from a distance. Bobcats shift to the size of panthers and slink through the murk. Voles with sage fur scamper into thickets.

After the shortcut, we progress down a main thoroughfare. I sit astride Cypress, a state of affairs that's more about keeping me in check than keeping me comfortable. I'm the quarry, the trophy, the sacrifice. They're the bastards who mistake savagery for splendor.

My limbs hang like cords on either side of the centaur, and my hips jut from side to side, in sync with his steady gait. He moves consciously, pacing himself. His pensive silence tells me he's measuring my own.

I press a hand to my shoulder, feeling for a strap that isn't there. Cypress had ordered me to leave my crossbow, notebook, and the rest of my possessions at the yurt. If I win, they'll be returned to me.

If I lose, he hadn't said what happens to my stuff. He'd just given me a conciliatory look.

My burgeoning fondness for the centaur has waned, though my feelings toward him had already been dwindling since the fight with Puck. Their plight should inspire me to empathize, but the satyr had made it clear that neither he, nor his people, had strained themselves to find an alternative. While I can't fault the Solitaries for trying to save their world—I would slay a dragon to save mine—I can neither digest nor condone the solution. Especially not after the passage I'd excavated from the Fables.

In any event, that Cypress is transporting me with little-to-no resistance is a stark reminder of the truth: We're not allies. We're not even friends.

As for the satyr, I can't go there. I don't have the energy to sift through those conflicting emotions, fluctuating as they do like shawls of wind.

Cypress broaches, "They will not request fulfillment of your tasks until midnight."

In other words, it's not over yet. There's still a chance for me. His assistance hurts. It hurts because he's on their side, not mine. No matter what, he won't intervene if the Faeries close in on me. Will he?

What will Puck do if it comes to that? Although he's been safeguarding me since the hunt began, he can't do so forever. If he has to choose between me and his world, where will he ultimately draw the line?

Well. I won't need to find out. I don't intend to roast on a spit tonight.

I would prefer to lash Cypress with a retort. Instead, I ask, "When humans lose, what happens to them?"

In The Redwoods of Exile, Puck had said any disobedient mortals confined in the trunk cage—instead of playing the game—end up getting eaten by wild fauna. Either that, or they deteriorate from the passage of time.

I've been reminded enough that mortals who lose the game also perish. But how?

Cypress hedges. Too soon, and not soon enough, the equine breaks the silence. He gets it out swiftly, saying, "They burn."

Disgust is the least of what I feel. I shudder, my thighs digging into his sides. That's why they want me at this feast, which commences with a bonfire. Outside of Middle Moon, they must light alternate flames for this purpose. Perhaps torches or a cauldron. That means I have the pleasure of being a special occasion.

The foal I'd seen playing with Puck travels amidst our group. She canters about, chatting animatedly with a mare.

I glower and jerk my chin toward the foal, although Cypress can't see the motion. The accusation in my voice is unmistakable, dry and flammable as lumber. "You let the youths watch?"

"We do not," he's quick to answer. "We send them home beforehand. We do not subject our youths to carnage." With a defensive edge, he adds, "They have seen enough of that."

The Fae children who weren't captured had nevertheless witnessed The Trapping. I cringe, then scrub the visual from my mind and focus on the task at hand. There's no guarantee my bargain will be accepted. But if I know anything about these knaves, deals are irresistible.

I'm gambling on their zeal for surprises. Deals presented by desperate humans are an added garnish. This bargain in particular is sure to whet the appetite of a certain satyr who shall not be named.

We bypass scattered cabins embedded in various tree trunks or perched high in the branches. Moss drips from the roofs, and log chimneys cough smoke. Several doors are built flat into the ground, flush with the earth and leading into some type of underground residence.

Fae homes. These are Fae homes, spread out at significant distances befitting Solitary lives. Aside from revels and bacchanals, the Folk appear to live in considerable privacy.

Additionally, I glimpse shops tucked into recesses. Signs hang above the doors, indicating a bakery, a pottery, a teahouse, and an establishment peddling "Lively Mushrooms."

Darkness fills the windows. Everyone's at the feast.

We arrive in a setting populated by lush, fernlike trees. An archway of fronds leads to an invisible location, light simmering from within. The music of lutes, fiddles, and several foreign instruments—something with a twang, something else with a multilayered vibration—oscillates through the air, collaborating into a jaunty tune.

As we halt at the entrance, a bevy of nymphs swarms us. They skip from between the trees in a tide of perfume and intolerance. One of the males bends over to pet the foal, who relishes the attention. The male offers the little one a cube of sugar, a treat that results in a jubilant squeal.

Foxglove heads my way, her clique sashaying on either side of her. Based on previous experience, I have an inkling of what's about to happen.

As a hand wraps around my ankle, I grip the centaur's mane. His ears swing backward, and he grunts at the clan. "She will dismount on her own."

I hop to the ground, tossing Cypress a reluctant but grateful nod.

The hive spirits me away, the same ritual that began the hunt ending it as well. They shepherd me to a steaming pool, where I bathe. This time, I don't have to negotiate for privacy. They simply leave me there.

Did Cypress tell them to mind their business? Or did someone else?

They're back within minutes of me emerging from the water and securing myself with a towel. They carry baskets of fabrics—canvases, twills, velvets, furs, leathers, wools, and flora.

"Puck said you'd want to choose what you wear," a female pouts.

Did he, indeed? But at this point in the game, what makes him think I'd have been polite and let them outfit me in anything to the contrary?

If I'm going to play the centerpiece, and if I'm going to bargain, and if I'm going to deceive a congregation of Faeries, I might as well dress the part. I stride over to the baskets, rifle through the contents, and find my armor.

Swinging around, I hold up my choices. "These."

Aside from my drawers, I've chosen three key pieces.

First, a verdant skirt woven of leaves, the jade foliage overlapping. The leaves are tapered, with finely-serrated tips, and the floor-length hem brushes the grass.

Second, a white cotton camisole with crisscrossing straps along the belly, the buckles made to cinch tightly.

Third, a wooden band with antlers flaring from the sides.

I slip the camisole over my head before any of the group members touch me, the maneuver covertly shielding my tattoo from sight. The nymphs don't notice. They simply get to work, primping and grooming me with dizzying, otherworldly speed.

Five minutes later, I'm ready.

My feet stay bare. The antler prongs spear the night while my hair hangs loose.

The nymphs admire their handiwork, pleased by an attractive, well-dressed sacrifice. They like their mortals ornamented while screaming for mercy.

As for me, I like my Faeries dumb.

I'm an apt pupil. One new thing I've learned is this: It takes a wild one to hunt a wild one. The Fae may think they're done with me, but I'm not done with them.

I'm not done with him.

They call it The Bonfire Glade. The path leading there pulsates with light and heat. On either side of me, small fire pits lick the air like miniature infernos.

I walk straight and proud. Yet my heart clatters like cutlery—cold and sharp.

I'm nervous. I use that to my advantage, the way I've used it during hunts as a child, and during rescues as an adult. I mold my fear into a tool, keeping me vigilant, focused.

Only my knees liquefy, shivering under my skirt. I'm human, after all.

The flames writhe, snapping and popping along the lane. Beyond the erratic blazes, a funnel of smoke coils into the fringed canopy. Raucous cackles and elated giggles accompany the lusty skip of fiddles. One could get inebriated from the sensory overload. And that's before the whiffs of a feast permeate my nostrils, a mishmash of savory, smoky, gamey, and sweet.

I return to the frond archway and pause. Parties are my least favorite things. Combine that with a party hosted by shameless woodland Faeries, in which I'm the doomed main event, and that feeling magnifies a thousandfold.

"You are bold," a baritone observes from the sidelines.

I twist, the leaf skirt fluttering. Like a majestic ship, Cypress emerges out of nowhere, the firelight bathing his olive coat and dark torso. He evaluates my choice of accessory, the antler headband encompassing my scalp, and mild humor creeps into his voice. "Very bold, indeed."

"I'm a huntress," I answer, by way of explanation. "That's how I came here. That's how I'll go out."

"The book did not help," Cypress presumes.

Oh, it helped. It most certainly did.

But because I don't correct him, the centaur appears more troubled by my imminent demise than I'd expected him to be. Despite his hard-boiled exterior, an almost indiscernible pang stretches his features in two directions. He may not want his world to expire, but he doesn't want it to happen at my expense. Since we haven't had time to bond, I'm unsure where this is coming from.

"Like you said, there were no guarantees." I soften my tone. "But like you also said, they won't interrogate me until midnight."

Cypress's ears perk. The ink markings around his navel shimmer tonight, the Middle Moon's rays enhancing the designs. A spurt of hope bolsters his posture, then he gazes toward the archway, his features cramped, wistful. "He does not want to lose you."

My spine goes rigid. My heart does something else—something defiant. "He told you that?"

"He did not have to. I have tolerated the brat for years."

The centaur says this with affection. "Long ago, he confided in me about your past together. With all your devotion to Fables, did you know it is rare for satyrs to have mates?"

The idea of Puck finding a mate produces a hollow inside me. I wish it didn't, but it does.

"They are lovers and seducers, misfits and mischief makers. That is the makeup of their promiscuous lineage," Cypress continues. "It is rare for satyrs to form an amorous bond, rarer still for them to fall in love. Be that soul a fated mate or a partner by choice, when a satyr does find that other half, the satyr's love becomes as fierce as hate."

My brows stamp together. "That doesn't sound pleasant."

Amusement puffs from the centaur's nostrils, jostling the leather hoop. "I will amend my explanation."

"Please do."

"As the most licentious of Faeries, affection confuses them. And because love is rarer still, if it does flourish, it is exceptional. You might say, profound. The intensity of a satyr's devotion will be intrinsic, as heightened as their senses. Therefore, they shall be prone to rashness and mishaps. That will render them vulnerable." Cypress glimpses me from a steep, sideways angle. "Puck is shrewd. He is cunning, but he is not immune. If such a connection were to blossom, he would act with his heart before his head." The equine lowers his voice and inclines his chin toward the archway. "Be careful, moppet. We Faeries see many things."

I want to assure him that nothing of the sort will happen between me and Puck. We're not in danger of being caught in a tryst. But protesting will sound guilty.

"I would like you to live, without us dying. If you can find a way, find a way." Cypress offers me his bulky arm. "I will escort you inside."

Since the kiss, I've cast aside whatever connection I'd shared with Puck. It's a relief to know I have one companion left, one other Fae in this realm who wants me alive instead of served on a platter.

It takes maneuvering on our parts, the equine leaning down and me straining upward, but I manage to link my arm with his. Cypress snorts with dignity, his tail flicking. Together, we stroll through the archway into The Bonfire Glade.

And into the Middle Moon Feast.

24

The scene is a vision out of a storybook—a cautionary one, a graphic one.

A throng of Faeries gathers in full force.

Pointed ears and ink markings. Badger tails and boar tusks. Porcupine quills around their wrists and ankles.

Briars wind around one side of a dryad's skull. A faun's complexion shifts from maize to champagne down his unclothed torso. Nettings of rosemary intersect over the arms and legs of a blonde nymph.

Oaken chairs and a banquet table weave around the space, meandering and wayward in its direction, like an unraveled spool. Candles snake down the middle, threaded with fern garlands. They weave around platters overflowing with a variety of meats, as well as pastries, confections, and fruits so plump with juice they're about to burst.

Brownies carry jugs of wine and tankards of ale, chirping to one another in their language.

Leprechauns cackle, dressed in layers of wool and choking pints in their fists. Their bearded or stubbled faces are ruggedly attractive, like roughhewn farmers and timberland loggers who spend hours plowing fields and chopping wood.

Nymphs and satyrs dance through the glade. Groups hold hands and bound through frond bushes and around trunks, their heels kicking out a series of intricate steps.

Another mixed group forms a prancing ring around an inferno. The great bonfire hisses and sputters embers, churning in hues of red and gold. It rises to an impossible elevation, yet the fern trees remain impervious to the flames.

I think of fairy tales and folktales. I think of their grisly beauty. I think of their morals and warnings. I think of how they're true and untrue.

I think of this world, living and breathing the elements. Wind atop the mountain peaks. Water in the river. Earth and fire across the woodland.

Here, mortal victims suffer amidst the soil. Then they burn.

Cypress and I make our entrance. According to him, the scribe was banned from recording this sacred night while living with the centaurs. Upon my entry, I expect the revelers to swerve in unison and lick their gums. I expect them to tackle and place me on a pedestal for exhibition. However, the woodland Faeries' version of ceremony involves a lot of rambunctious shouting. They register us and clamor, clapping their hands or raising their goblets and toasting to our arrival. They chant in Faeish, their complexions flush with libations and vibrant with gaiety.

It's mayhem. Until they notice the antler crown.

Levity, alcohol, and a surplus of cake must have muddied their senses. But now they see it, and the mood alters. Some sneer, others seethe. Some gaze at the crown with fretful creases, others with slitted eyes.

Tails whip about. Claws jut from fingers.

Yes, the nymphs had offered me the headband, among other accessories. And perhaps the gesture had been a spoof, a jeopardous temptation meant to incite this very reaction.

What scrawny mortal dares to wear the traits of the fauna, as if I possess Fae origins instead of human ones? Who am I, to do such a thing?

Does this mean I've arrived victorious? Are the antlers the sign of a winner? An act of defiance?

Am I being ironic, tactical, or just stupid?

Conversely, several of the Faeries smirk. My cheek intrigues them, but it doesn't concern them. Either way, I don't regret my decision to wear the crown.

Their interest shifts. As if someone has endorsed them to carry on, they whirl back into the frenzy.

"Don't worry about them, luv," a tenor whispers. "They're just jealous because you wear it better. As am I."

Masculine heat swelters across my shoulders. I turn on my bare heels, dirt grinding into my sole.

He's wearing an ankle-length vest of buttery leather dyed black. A ladder of buckled tabs descends from the collar to the waist, at which point the vest flares open like a gaping door around his breeches.

To be sure, Puck's sporting fewer clasps than usual. Though, this isn't saying much for him. His fashion choice still exhibits an abnormal amount of closures, particularly the ones running down the outer seams of the pants.

That aside, he's more polished than I've seen him before. Less uncouth, less rustic. With a twisted patch of caramel-dyed velvet at his throat, peeking from the valley in his collar, he's the picture of a vicious gentleman. That is, if he were human.

We have an audience. The Faeries observe our greeting, and though I'm aware of their attention, I don't feel it. What I feel is Puck's gaze as it skims my jade leaf skirt and white camisole, the upheaval on his face when he notices the buckles strapped across my own waist. Those orbs expand, great black reservoirs holding my reflection inside them.

He strays to my antler crown, a grin ricocheting across his face. Recollections of the kiss surface as I watch that damned mouth slide upward. His lips had partaken of my sighs. His tongue had wrung other noises from me, too. Thinking about it causes tremulous sensations beneath my garments.

Be careful, moppet. We Faeries see many things.

I fold my hands in front of me, my digits fusing together. At the same time, Puck fastens his hands behind his back.

"My, my, my," he murmurs. "You drive a hard bargain."

"I haven't started yet," I reply.

The satyr can't know what I mean by that, but those scrupulous eyes alight, flecks of amber dancing in reams of sable brown.

"By all means," Puck invites in that husky Fae accent, then turns to the congregation. "Behold, our merry guest has arrived!"

The Faeries cheer. Evidently, I'm supposed to pretend this is normal—that *any* of this is normal. I'm supposed to obey like a good little prisoner, like happy prey. I'm supposed to be complacent and indulge them, so they don't have to waste their energy on glamour.

If Lark were here, she would tell these Faeries to go fuck themselves. Of course, I'd have to slap my palm over her mouth.

A gambit is imperative. I have my plan. Until then, if they want me to be their sacrificial lamb, so be it.

Puck moves aside and gestures toward the bonfire. He falls in line with me, and we step into the candlelight. We keep our distance from each other, avoiding the slightest contact. Yet the air feels magnetized, roused with energy.

And it hurts. It hurts that he's willing to go through with this, that he sought no other choice. It hurts so much.

My ribs splinter, on the verge of cracking open. If that happens, what will leak out of me?

Under my breath, I hiss, "I will never forgive you for this."

From the corner of my eye, Puck stares ahead. "Now who said anything about forgiveness?"

Not a stutter to his voice. Not a hitch in his reply.

His gait is another matter, faltering at my words. It's scarcely noticeable unless one is a huntress, attuned to how creatures move. It's hardly discernible unless one knows this satyr, unless one has tasted him, touched him. It's nothing unless one has spent time stalking him.

The Faeries resume dancing. I spot the young male with orange eyes and that marten tail, which swats about in enthusiasm. He drives his tongue into the mouth of a dryad.

The foal from earlier joins the festivities, skipping amidst the trees. Fiddlers pluck and lute players strum. One musician runs a daggerlike tool across a stringed apparatus resembling a paddleboard.

The revelers have donned gowns woven of daffodils or flowers I can't identify; jackets of leather, suede, or moss; canvas tunics embroidered in vines; and leggings sewn from lichen or cowslip petals.

The rest flaunt their nudity. I avert my eyes from bosoms and exposed genitals. The only knickknacks embellishing these exhibitionists are anklets and bangles, since the Folk adore their trinkets as much as they adore themselves. The baubles chime with the Faeries' movements as they whirl about.

My digits stray to my arm, around which a bracelet of gold leaves had once twined. Once, before those wenches called nymphs took my sisters' gift from me.

Does Lark still have her thigh cuff? Has Cove managed to keep her necklace, with its waterdrop pendant? Or were my sisters forced to surrender those precious talismans, in order to make deals?

Puck notices my fingers resting where the bracelet should be. I snatch my hand away.

The feast is extravagant. It's a gluttonous spread of smoked game in beds of squash, pea pods, and greens. To say nothing of the desserts—dumplings oozing steamed plums, apricot tarts garnished with toasted nuts; miniature cakes coated in mirrored chocolate glaze and encrusted with golden seeds; and on, and on. The overabundance of sugar would make any baker in Reverie Hollow swoon.

Puck leads me to the head of the table and pulls out the chair. I bite my tongue and sit. At which point, the satyr covertly bumps my crown, then leans over to straighten it and whisper, *"Once in the dark forest, a Stag hunted a Doe…"*

Just like that, my ribs do crack. They burst open, a landslide of emotions gushing out. I gawk at the table in a trance, then hazard a glimpse of him walking away. He claims the opposite end of the long, winding table, far away from my chair.

Lounging back, the satyr kicks his hooves onto the surface and crosses them at the ankles. Not sparing me a glance, he chats up an inebriated dryad. Suddenly, he acts as if I'm inconsequential, expendable to him and his kin.

It's a simple gesture and an infinite declaration. It's good and bad. It's wrong and right. It's dangerous and safe.

I could pummel him. I could kiss him.

Yet intelligence is the ally of intention and the foe of lethargy. Thus, both deer wondered, what if we thought wiser and hunted together?

Ally. Intention. Together.

It's a ruse. He's still playing his role, still choosing me over winning. But more than that, Puck wants to find another way out of this mayhem. He'd heard my argument, loud and clear. And he's in.

I duck my head, allowing myself a few precious seconds to relish this connection, the magnitude of his pledge, then shove my reaction back into its cage. I'd wanted this from him, yet I shouldn't. This development complicates things, from our allegiances to the game itself.

There's nothing for it. I have to move forward, no matter how Puck feels, no matter how I feel. I pin my features in place and raise my head.

The Faeries sitting nearby insist I sample the delicacies they set before me.

"Try this, human," they say.

"And this," they tempt.

"But not this," one titters. "It'll scald your nipples off."

They roar with laughter. I waver, auditing the fare for signs of manipulation and enchantment. Some of the dishes, I know to avoid from the Fables, whereas other servings are debatable.

When the Faeries present me with hazelnut cake soaked in honey—a potentially distrustful course—my eyes flit to Puck. He's still chatting with the dryad, yet the satyr taps his fork on the rim of a plate. He'd once described himself as hands-on, so I recognize the private signal: This dish is safe.

Throughout the meal, I exercise judgment when I can. For the rest, I check the genuflections of Puck's hand. The hearty rye bread with butter is edible, as is a fig-shaped bulb with a vivid yellow rind.

However, a faun rummages through a cornucopia of fruits and extends a blushing orb sprouting florets instead of stems. Puck's index finger wags covertly. While laughing with a group of brownies, he swings that digit back and forth along the edge of his goblet. I catch the pantomimed warning and politely decline the fruit.

The satyr and I continue this charade until I've ladened my plate with harmless options, and my neighbors have grown bored of testing my tastebuds. En masse, they dismiss my presence and rise to enjoy the music.

Cypress had vanished the moment Puck appeared by my side. Now I see the centaur has confined himself to his brethren. Every so often, he casts furtive glances between the satyr and me.

Meanwhile, Puck holds court with a group that eyes him like a succulent roast. A pretty male faun wiggles onto Puck's lap. A female satyr with elk antlers tucks a lock of red behind Puck's pointed ear, then pops a turquoise berry into his mouth.

He chews slowly, deliberately, while looking at me. The rotations of his mouth have a palpable effect, reaching across the divide to probe my inner flesh. I squirm, but the friction doesn't help.

Another berry goes into Puck's mouth. This time, the floozy, female satyr dabs juice from the crook of his lips.

I snatch my fork and spear the flaky crust of a pie. Steam blasts from vents, and the crust crumbles to reveal a whole lemon inside. A river of butter and sugar drains from the pie, then dissolves on my palate as I slip the fork into my mouth. I feel his attention, his gaze on the tip of my tongue, where the sharpness of citrus and sweetness of sugar blend together.

My chest pumps. I flit my gaze to where Puck lounges, one arm slung across the table, his fingers suffocating the stem of a goblet.

He stares, watches, waits for more. The faun and female satyr are gone.

The ghost of a smile threatens to expose me. I choose my fare wisely, savor it thoroughly.

My younger sister is skilled in the art of temptation. I'm not. Yet based on the heat of his gaze, the obsessive clutch of his fingers around the goblet, it doesn't matter.

I refuse to bat my lashes, simper, or swoon. But I know how to eat.

When I sink my teeth into the crisp skin of a rabbit, syrup glaze dribbles at the corner of my mouth. I lick the remnants clean, wetting my lips. A glossy cherry is next, trembling on my tongue before I purse my mouth around it and bite.

The bonfire thrashes. It flings orange hues across the glade.

I don't have to look. I know the weight of those eyes, the slashes of white and black lining them. I know his breathing has quickened. I know he's coming close to snapping that goblet in half.

I know he got his leg caught in a mortal trap when he was a child. I know he did it to rescue a deer.

I know he has a soft spot for baby boars and a camaraderie with foxes.

I know he plays with centaur foals and makes them giggle. I know his best friend is a centaur, too.

233

I know he plays the cello because the skill is hands-on, earned instead of inherited by magic. I know the music reminds him of roots—immersive, resilient, and profound. I know he plays with his eyes clenched shut.

I know he wants to know what I think, rather than what I can recite. I know he wants more from me, all of me, every inch of me.

I know he's vicious. I know more than that, better than that. I know it now.

By the time I pluck a nectarine slice swimming in cream from a bowl, I detect a goblet turning over, liquid splashing onto the table. Despite the boisterous music, I hear this.

A huntress knows the sound of her prey.

Because yes, I'm still hunting him. Because like he'd said, hunt is a relative term.

I swallow the cream, vanilla spilling down my throat. I catch his entertained expression, a proper reaction from a sordid Fae, which won't alert anyone. For all they know, he's attempting to intimidate me while I eat, to make me blush for his own gratification. But the covert drag of his thumb across the rim of his drinking vessel says otherwise.

This is perilous. However subtle, we're playing a terrible game in plain sight.

I turn away and finish the rest of my meal.

The Middle Moon bleeds pearlescent light into the glade. Platters and cutlery flash along the banquet table. Candles bloom from the trees.

It's midnight.

My pulse hammers. Puck gives me an imperceptible nod, anticipating whatever I have in mind. With that, he rises, and the music halts.

"Woodland kin," he announces. "Shall we get on with it?"

The guests erupt. They whistle and pound the tabletop.

From his end of the feast, Puck directs his attention to me. "So, luv. You've led us on a merry chase through this weald. Do you have three successful tasks to present to your rowdy captors? Have you triumphantly hunted down an animal that can't be hunted? Can you tell us a Fable we've never heard before about that animal? And can you prove the moral is true?"

I stand. "No."

Pandemonium results. The satisfaction this elicits disgusts me, but their reactions right afterward make me feel a whole lot better.

"I have a bargain instead," I say.

An extravagant silence follows. It whooshes through the glade, amplifying the rampant sounds of the bonfire. The inferno fumes, its talons scratching the air.

Then commotion ensues. The Faeries glower, some braying in Faeish, others whining like adolescents, their voices overlapping.

Cypress's mouth twitches. *Bargain* is the irresistible, indispensable magic word.

Puck flicks his hand, quieting the protesters. "You have our attention."

I formulate my proposal with care. "I'm willing to bargain for more time: I'd like one extra week of my life. In exchange, I'll reveal a passage hidden in the original Book of Fables." I recount the details of Cypress owing me a favor—my bolt injuring him, my hands nursing him, the tome he'd leant, and the scribe's secret text. Some have heard reports from the centaurs about what I've been up to, others not.

"The text indicates there's a second way to preserve your land," I announce.

The uproar resumes. The stupefied Folk exchange looks of disbelief. They whisper, scoff, and fling superior or insulted glares my way.

In the midst of that, Puck's face slackens. This, he hadn't foreseen. His eyes blaze with astonishment, then sparkle with ambition.

The text had said a link exists between humans and magical beings. If it can be identified, it will open another door for the Faeries, another means to restore the lost fauna.

I speak cautiously. "If you grant me this week, I'll share the passage."

"My, my, *my*," Puck says, quieting the hubbub. "You've exceeded our expectations tenfold and many times over. Except how did this mortal scribe know about a 'second way,' if we don't?"

"I have no idea," I answer honestly. "But I think someone told her. An ancient Fae during her time, perhaps? Someone with an incentive?"

They contemplate that. The notion is hardly far-fetched, taking into account the Folk's desire to barter and haggle. For the right price, a Fae of old could have informed a mortal of such vital information. If the scribes were industrious enough to traverse the continent and forage for knowledge about magical beings, why wouldn't they be savvy enough—and daring enough—to make a deal?

I want to find out the source, but I have to be alive to do it. Survival comes first—mine and my sisters'.

Puck likes what he's hearing. After several moments, so do the others. They don't want to lose this game, but the odds imply that isn't at risk, considering my track record thus far. What's the harm in an extra week? Seven days of watching me struggle? That allotment of time is nothing to immortals.

And again, they do love surprises.

I take a deep, courageous breath and play another card. "One other condition. I will reveal the scribe's text only when my extension is up, whether or not I win."

"Faristn brakde," Foxglove says to Puck, her face crimping with suspicion.

"Jún ketur lokide," Tinder presses, his tone disruptive.

Cypress shoots the pair a combative look. *"Jannsji er jún fade ejji."* Then he faces Puck, his voice turning flexible, companionable. *"Jfade fá?"*

I recognize the sounds of a debate. Based on the angles of their words, I take an educated guess. The other two must have raised skepticism that I'm tricking them, lying to them. Whereas Cypress must have shot that down with a crucial point: Why wouldn't they want to know if there's an alternative to restoring the fauna and saving the Solitary wild?

The satyr and centaur swap a look that borders on elemental, ingrained. Puck's on my side, so I have no misgivings that he'll agree. Yet he and his friend make a show of deliberation, locked in wordless communication.

After a moment, Puck's eyes flit to the Faeries, then to me. He slouches like a disheveled monarch, his arm resting on the table, fingers rubbing together.

Beneath the facade, I see pride. The woodland may have chosen this game, but its ruler has the authority to approve of the extension. I had dislodged that bit of information from Cypress before we'd left The Heart of Willows, when I inquired about the varying Middle Moon celebrations within each segment of the wild.

Hundreds of guests await their ruler's response. Puck skims his audience and tosses up his hands, "Why the fuck not?"

Other than Foxglove and Tinder, a chorus of elation surges through the glade. My proposition excites them, catering to their sportive nature. Cypress lifts his brow, impressed.

Amidst the hoopla, Puck gives me a wry bow. To them, it's mockery and perhaps pity. To me, it's an alliance.

Under my skirt, my knees threaten to give out.

The Middle Moon Feast continues. Again, Cypress's gaze clicks between Puck and me, monitoring us.

A brawny leprechaun elbows me, saying, "A fine hunt you were, lass."

A nymph fluffs my hair as she passes, then winks.

A disgruntled brownie clears my plate.

I approach the bonfire while a pair of devilish eyes trail my movements. Coronas of orange warm my leaf skirt and unshod toes. I'm unafraid of the flames, although my captors had initially meant to toss me inside the blaze. I have plenty of other things to fear. There's no room left for more.

I welcome the heat. I crane back my head, spread my arms, and let it seep inside. Among my enemies, I do this.

Perhaps because of that, because I don't act timid, they leave me alone. My tears might have delighted them, but my rapture has the same influence. They like when this world seduces mortals, whether or not by enchantment.

When my head lowers, he's there. Across the bonfire, he's there still watching, still waiting.

My loose hair tickles my clavicles. My skirt brushes my thighs.

The Faeries flirt with each other in low tones, or dare one another to do daring things, or reminisce about their favorite fauna. I hear them express awe for bears, admiration for foxes, affection for rabbits.

Outside this glade, the animals roam. Outside this glade is where I want to be.

I'm not alone in this. Puck might dress the part of a ruler, but the role will never suit him. Not because he isn't strong or smart enough, nor devoted enough. I've learned how much he loves this world. But this satyr belongs to the branches and roots. He belongs to the does, hinds, and stags. He belongs to the earth.

He's the soil. I'm the fire.

We Faeries see many things.

But they don't see. Not right now. Not this evening. They're too giddy, too drunk, too self-absorbed, too tempted by others to see. They've stolen into their own lusty corners. They've set their sights on other diversions.

And I'm done with rationalizing, done with thinking. For tonight, I'm so very done.

Puck is, too.

We belong away from here, in a place where they can't find us. We belong in a corner where we can strip ourselves bare, down to the flesh. We belong naked in the grass, his body on top of mine, his body filling mine.

I want that. I want this.

Which is why he turns, saunters through the archway, and exits the glade. Which is why I follow him.

And so it begins—a forbidden type of hunt.

25

I wait the appropriate amount of time. Then I wait for the optimal moment when the sloppy Faeries start singing about their fauna, getting lost in themselves and the Middle Moon. After that, I exit through a slot of fronds.

It doesn't take long to catch sight of him. The satyr detours off the main path and weaves through shadows. His black silhouette slips in and out of shrubbery, the ferns tapping his arms. He blends into the wild until all that's visible are the sharp bones of his antlers—a Solitary stag of the weald.

Yet he's left an evident trail.

I know how this Fae moves. I know how he struts across this land. I know how the foliage bends around him. I know the depth and size of his hoof prints. I know the patterns of his tracks and the pace of his swagger.

And he knows not to mistake me for an amateur. Because I also know what he's doing and why he's doing it. I know when my quarry is aware of my presence.

This target wants to be found.

I step lightly, picking through the dense woodland. I squat behind plump bushes and spidery brambles. I peer through outcroppings and monitor his progress.

He halts in a single beam of Middle Moon light, the spectral glint perching on his shoulders. A breeze rustles the wanton red of his hair. When his head slants a fraction, I imagine that evocative smirk. He knows, that I know, that he knows. Because I'm not the only one hunting.

He keeps going, and I keep following. From leagues behind us, music tapers through the wilderness—the languid strumming and deft plucking of strings. Sounds of the revels pursue us from The Bonfire Glade until those disappear as well.

Fronds and fern trees recede, the landscape unspooling into a compact dell of fruit trees. Branch candles temper to a dim glow in this area. The chief source of illumination comes from the orbs huddled between the leaves—some type of strawberry-shaped Fae fruit, the flesh golden and glittering. They leak warm, gilded shadows onto the ground.

Basil mingles with a candied fragrance wafting from the fruits. Untamed overgrowth surrounds us, with a small oval bed of grass in the center.

I step over a patch of basil, then stop. He's gone. Yet he's here.

I twist and flatten myself against a trunk. A ridiculous thrill eddies through me, my mouth lifting. I tuck a lock of hair behind my ear and listen.

Then it really begins. When I hear those hooves, I duck into the nearest shrub. When the satyr hears me, he bounds from one shadow to the next. When he does that, I crawl into a neighboring hedge.

This would be much easier in leggings. A few times, the leaf skirt snags on twigs until I learn to maneuver with the garment. It's a minor inconvenience. The material camouflages my lower half, the antler band splays from my head, and this midnight escapade sets my heart to pounding.

I've hunted to do harm. I've hunted to rescue.

I've hunted to live. I've hunted to save a life.

But I've never hunted my own desires.

I'm a mortal, stalking a Fae. I'm a wild one, an earthen creature on the prowl.

We've broken the rules of this sacred evening. Only the fauna are allowed to ramble tonight. Yet here we are, hoping they'll forgive us, pardon our intrusion.

Regardless, I find no traces of animals. No eyes glowing in the muted light, nor agitations in the foliage. No thunk of paws or scratch of talons. The dell is quiet, secluded.

A scintillating ripple of fear tracks down my vertebrae. It's nothing short of magnetic, this pursuit. Our outlines skate around each other, moving in tandem to one another. His slick figure prances from corner to corner. I spring from recess to recess.

Like the fauna, he moves instinctively. Also like the fauna, I move systematically.

He aims, and I target. And we strike true, finding our mark.

When I maneuver from the dark to snare him, he leaps from the light to catch me. We collide in that oval, in that tiny heart of grass. Encompassed by herbs and several fallen fruit, we grapple for balance, his hands gripping my waist, my fingers clinging to his hips.

"Gotcha," we pant at the same time.

The word punches out of us, exhilarated, effervescent. For the first time, I hear the smoke of my voice as it mingles with his sultry tenor. Our chests heave, my pulse thrusting against his. My eyes stagger into a set of irises gleaming with every shade of soil.

Puck. My Puck.

Mine for tonight.

We inhale, exhale. And then we chuckle, breathless, delirious.

But the mirth ebbs. In his pupils, I think my own eyes reflect every shade of tree. He dips his head to marvel at my features—my ears, my chin, my mouth. His attention is restless, riveted.

So is mine. From the streaks lining his eyelashes, to the white freckles dotting his nose, to the crook of his lips. This close, I discover a chip in one of his antlers, then gaze at the iron scars on his furred calf.

As my throat bobs, his thumb traces the movement. My eyes drift closed, and my breath quickens, compromised by that touch.

My digits press into the leather breeches hugging his solid hips. Puck hisses, and my eyes flare open just as his clench shut. The sound and sight of him like this probes a tender, palpitating spot between my legs.

To say nothing about the feel of him, all taut muscle and polished skin. What will it be like to strip him down and sketch those private contours? Which will be pliable? Which spots will be rigid?

My fingers stray across his waistband, drifting to the buckles at the front. Puck sucks in another gust of oxygen. His mouth parts to speak, but I set my fingers over his lips, afraid he'll break the spell I have over him.

If he does, I won't know how to proceed. As it is, I've never done this before.

Puck snatches my fingers and curls them into his palm. "No Fae touches like this," he puffs out.

Wounded, I'm about to reel back and bluster that I'm not a Fae, in case he's forgotten. But then his voice registers, afflicted and overwhelmed.

Affection confuses satyrs. That's what Cypress had said.

I comprehend that look of inquisitiveness, of bemusement. I recognize the mystery of inexperience, of not recognizing something and wanting very much to know what that something is.

Puck isn't discounting or belittling my touch. He's awed by it, mesmerized by it. For all his vast acquaintance with seduction, the satyr is unaccustomed to this kind of contact.

My fingers sizzle at the tips. I'm not the only one stumbling through this moment.

No Fae touches like this.

"No," I agree, licking my lips. "But I do. I touch like this."

As my digits sweep aside a red forelock, he squeezes those eyelids tighter. "And like this," I say, drawing an experimental line with my pinky across his eyebrow.

"And like this," I continue, running that finger over his cheekbone and sliding to the edge of his jaw.

Puck's exhalations grow shallow, becoming thinner. My inhalations reach deep, becoming uneven.

Fire erupts in my belly, spreading from my navel to my toes, to my scalp. I don't know how to touch a male, have never touched a male, only touched myself, and only once thus far. So I hunt for the right direction, following his reactions like a trail, a route to *yes, more, there.*

And like this, I explore the cranks of his antlers. They're hard and smooth like the rest of him must be under those clothes.

And like this, I glide my fingernail along a vein in his arm, down that tributary to his wrist, where his pulse hammers.

And like this, I knit our hands together.

And that's when his eyes flip open, clarity brightening his mien. "And I touch like this." His strong arm slings around my middle, hauling me against him. His head slants and dips to my earlobe.

"And this," he entices, flicking his teeth over the delicate flesh.

I gasp. My arms hook around his shoulders for balance, my nails imprinting his vest collar. The hot scrape of his ivories runs along my ear, teasing the shell until my thoughts melt into putty.

"And this," he whispers into the canal, his mouth skimming, coaxing.

"And this," he mutters, those lips parting, latching around the lobe and sucking on it like a disc of butterscotch.

Fables help me. The wet tug of his lips feels so good. My bones go limp, yet my body ignites like dry kindling smoking to life.

Puck pulls back on a ravenous groan—"And like this," he seethes—and plies my skin with open-mouthed kisses. He scorches a path from the base of my ear, to the trench beneath my jaw, to the column of my neck.

I keen, the sound as chipped as porcelain, on the brink of shattering. I don't know what's become of my faculties, but my body doesn't care. It acts of its own volition, grasping onto him, clinging for mercy's sake.

My head falls back, the antler crown tumbling to the ground as I grant the satyr access. He nibbles and kisses his way along my clavicles. "And like this," he hums into the basin, then dabs the spot with that vicious tongue.

Puck alternates between licking and suckling there, his tongue swabbing rhythmically, then his lips suctioning me in, exerting pressure. The backs of my knees thaw, and my flesh pebbles, the foreign sensations rendering me speechless. Where have these avid, physical reactions come from? And where have they been hiding all this time?

I can't take this. How does anyone take this?

My hands don't know what to do with themselves. They shoot into his hair, but that's not right either. I scramble to frame his face, then map out his biceps, then strike back into his waves. My fingers tangle into the threads, making a mess of him. Still, it's not enough.

I'm riled up, fed up. All I want is more, then more, and then even more.

I wiggle, squirm, and grind myself against the satyr. "Puck…"

He peels his mouth from my neck, veering back and jerking me into him. "Puck, what?"

We chuff against one another, stare at one another. The length of his body aligns with my own, my breasts mashing into that ample chest. Our height difference brings my stomach in contact with his pelvis. His length is erect and wedged between us, creating that friction I'd experienced when we'd first kissed, and even before that, when the fantasy of him had pried me open.

Air compresses in my lungs. My flesh sears where he's kissed me—and where he's yet to kiss me. I quiver from the need of it. I've never been this unsteady in my life, never this unbound.

Puck senses this disruption, the upheaval inside me. He cradles my face and cranes it to meet him halfway, then leans down and brushes his lips against mine. "You have a question for me?"

I do, before this goes any further. "Can you…can we…?"

He translates the rest. "Ah. Not to worry, luv. Like I said, my forest kin are born from seeds. And even if we fuck others from outside this weald, I've never heard of a woodland Fae conceiving. We're safe there."

I had suspected that. Still, I'd needed to be sure.

"What else?" he asks. "Tell me, luv."

At present, I'm barely able to stand, let alone articulate myself. I shake my head, unsure what to appeal for. Thus, the admission falls from my tongue. "I-I don't know what to do."

Satyr or not, only he can manage a smile that's simultaneously carnal and sweet. "You will."

"How?" I ask.

Puck pecks my lips. "Trust yourself."

I hesitate. He gathers me closer, his hands palming my rear, possessive, feverish. I was wrong earlier. Even as a huntress, I don't know all the ways he moves. Not yet.

The very thought causes my eyelids to flutter. I might be a novice at this, but I have a flirtatious younger sister who's lived a rather social existence. Thanks to her, I'm aware of the mechanics.

As for the rest, I'll trust myself. I'll trust the drum of my heart. I'll trust the furious throb between my legs. I'll trust the wetness building under my skirt.

Encased in Puck's arms, my body takes over once more. I follow its lead, balance on my tiptoes, and angle my head. I speak privately against his mouth, so that not even the fruit trees can overhear. "I want you inside me."

I want his body above mine, surging into mine. I want that stiffness lodged to the brink. I want all of him within all of me.

That's it. That's all I say.

Puck's face darkens. His features contort, his pupils swell, and his nostrils flare.

And then he snaps. The satyr hauls me into him, sweeping me off the ground. His head swoops down, and his mouth seizes mine. On a moan, my mouth yields under him, welcoming the nimble flick of his tongue. It slips past my lips, flexing into me.

The kiss splays wide, our tongues lapping together. I open myself to every lick of heat, every stroke.

I snatch the caramel velvet cloth at his throat, divesting him of the fine material and casting it aside. After that, my shaky fingers plummet to the neckline of his vest. I fumble with the clasps, but the cursed things won't release. An incoherent noise rattles from me, ending on a growl.

Puck chuckles, the masculine timbre pebbling my flesh. I muster a glower that doesn't fit across my face. Despite the ravenous buzzing in my stomach, my expression inevitably slackens with humor.

Now I know the motivation behind this excessive amount of fastenings. It's an enticement. The more difficult it is to access him, the more tempting. The harder one must work, the more eager one becomes.

Puck breaks the kiss and locates my digits. "Like this," he says, placing my hands on the right spots.

We work the buckles loose. One by one, we burn a path down his torso, revealing plates of flesh, all creamy pectorals and tan nipples. From there, the long garment shivers apart, black leather splitting at his abdomen. The muscles bunch and stack there, foothills of skin intersected by fibers of dark red hair between the slopes of his hipbones.

He sheds himself of the attire, chucking it to the grass. My stomach swoops at the vision doused in lunar light and the golden shimmer of fruit. He's a part of this magical place, where the world is recognizable and unrecognizable. This place, where teal shadows saturate the landscapes and candles accent the trees. This place, where the fauna roam on jewel-colored paws, their tusks inked and pelts resplendent, clovers perched on their antlers, and their metallic whiskers twitching.

And for once, I feel like I was meant to be here, too. I was meant for this moment. I was meant to find this dell with him.

I belong here as a human, not as one of them. And that's precisely how he wants me.

I bask in Puck's naked torso. Smooth plains of flesh wait at my disposal, a blank page meant to be covered with my marks. My knuckles curl and release, restless, unsure.

He takes a step nearer, our foreheads bumping, and nods. I bite my tongue, and my huntress hands resume their exploration. I sketch his shoulders, his ribs. I run wild across the veins of his forearms. I slide across his navel. I scale his chest and aim for the heart.

Under my palm, that organ beats like a man's, like an animal's, like my own. The tempo goes mad, thrashing in sync with my pulse.

Puck watches my progress. His eyelids shudder as though drugged or glamoured. In spite of his escalating heart rate, he appears to have the sensual patience befitting his kind. As masters of seduction, I imagine satyrs don't rush things.

Curious, I test that theory. When the pads of my thumbs catch his nipples, his upper body hitches. The sensitive crests toughen under my ministrations, and my lungs tighten as well.

We inch closer while I fondle him, our sighs filling the hollow. As he disarms me, I show him a new kind of restraint.

Then again, perhaps I was wrong to assume he could endure. Puck's resolve collapses. He snakes his arm once more around my midriff and thrusts me into him. And like this, he introduces me to euphoria.

His mouth skims my wrist, then works its way up my arm. We move in tandem, my head arching as he reaches the plunge of my neckline, then higher to the left strap.

When he hooks on to the cord of material, it urges me out of the trance. The poacher tattoo inked into my lower back tingles as though in warning.

Even if I trust him, I still can't let him see the marking. The only ones whom I've shared it with since childhood have been my family.

I get my bearings and straighten, the movement giving Puck pause. He halts, dazed. I blink at him, equally hazy. Somehow, I manage to communicate without speaking, my fingers landing over his: My clothes stay on.

Confusion surfaces, then vanishes. These Faeries may think me prissy, but he knows better than that. He knows better than to assume I'm self-conscious about my body.

Yes, I long to be naked with him. But no, that's not possible.

I take his hand and rest it on the neckline, inching the material down. "Like this."

Whatever conclusion he makes about my preferences, a secret sort of aspiration darkens Puck's irises.

He lifts me off the ground and lowers us onto the bed of grass. I land astride him, my thighs splayed around his waist. The skirt trembles up my calves, the jade leaves shivering around his leathers.

Puck wastes no time. His fingers curl into the bodice and stretch it down. My left breast pops from the neckline, blooming fully in the half-light.

On a hum of appreciation, he admires the swell of flesh. *"Éck ferde ade smajja fade."*

My cheeks flood with warmth, but not from embarrassment. No, the lusty weight of his stare causes frustration, and the lilt of his language causes excitement. Both fuse together, driving me to my wit's end.

My nipple is a hard stud under the onslaught of his gaze. With his arm fixed around my waist, he bends forward. And his mouth seals around the bud.

I splinter apart. Crying out, I clutch the back of his head. My spine curls so far back that I see the branches quivering above us. Suspended like this, my moans vault into the swirl of white, gold, and teal starlight.

Puck balances me with that single hand, his other one braced...I don't know where. I don't know anything—not a damn thing. His tongue swats the nipple, licking and then drawing the apex into the cavern of his mouth. Every gentle tug wrings another captivated moan from me.

At last, he strains the bodice, freeing the other breast. His lips work me into a stupor, sucking and pulling on the tip. His tongue sketches me, drawing around the bud, then flicking against it.

The disorder progresses from one stimulation to the next. Puck shifts direction and, in one heated stroke, laps across the underside of my breast. He wanders from there, kissing his way back to the crest, his lips spreading around my nipple and towing it into his shameless mouth.

The material's ruined. It's limp, exposing the fall of my breasts.

And well. I just don't care.

He yanks me back to him, our mouths colliding. As our lips fasten into a pent-up kiss, the dell rotates. Puck reclines me atop the grass, the blades yielding beneath my weight. Sprawled before him, with my knees upturned, the skirt rucks up my thighs.

The Fae holds my gaze. He works on his breeches, thumbing the buckles free. It's an exercise in self-control, for all I'd like to sit up and shred those pants to ribbons. At the same time, I savor the patches of flesh revealed to me, the tantalizing exposure of it.

The waistband loosens. The closures flap open. And that masculine part of him rises from the vent.

A gentle wheeze fans through my lungs. I lie there, glimpsing the narrow waist and steep inclines of his hips. The trail of red leads to a firm mast at the center of his body. His length is erect and hard, the crown ruddy.

To be sure, my fantasies had been liberal. Nevertheless, it's bigger than I had expected.

My calves quaver, the split of my legs widens, and slickness gathers in my core. "Closer," I plead.

With a devious grin, Puck crawls my way. "Closer, like this?"

His body lands over mine, filling the valley between my limbs. I make a tremulous noise from the weight and broadness of him, anticipation shimmying through me. This is what it's like to be enveloped, to have a male above me.

He frames my face and kisses me, parting my mouth with his tongue and coaxing a sigh from us both.

I'm nervous. Yet I'm not nervous at all.

Also, my digits can't resist nor wait. I wiggle between us and search for that intimate part of him. His startled growl hits the back of my throat. Strapping my hand around his phallus, I marvel at its temperature, its size, its shape.

Puck's back caves in. He tears his mouth from mine. "Like this," he encourages.

Molding my fingers around him, he shows me how to grope and rub, how much pressure to use. Then he releases me, letting me figure out the rest on my own.

In the space between our bodies, I wring my hand around him. He's hefty, the circumference torrid. I swirl my thumb around the head, etch the slit at its nexus, and observe the anarchy this causes. Puck's face crimps. He likes this. So I do it more, charting that small incision at the crown, brushing the line until it liquefies, a bead forming there.

I collect the droplet, sweeping it over the crown. Tremors rack Puck's body. Emboldened by his broken moans, I intensify my grip. My wrist glides up and down, stroking his length from the base to the tip, pumping him into madness.

As his shaft thickens in my palm, moisture drenches my undergarments. I ought to be mortified. But I'm not, because it feels right. Everything about this feels right, from the heat racing across my skin to the siphoning motions of my hand.

My sole flattens on his calf, brushing the fur. My toes outline his hoof, then skid upward again. My heel locates the iron trap scars and caresses the marred flesh.

On a suffocated groan, Puck tugs his shaft from my ministrations. "Wider," he mutters.

My legs comply, spreading for him. The skirt rustles up to my waist, revealing the thin, skimpy drawers beneath, which he plucks and drags down my form. They, too, land on the grass.

A breeze winnows through my open limbs. I'm splayed out, bare and wanting.

Puck's molten gaze scrolls down to the thatch of curls and the slickness accumulating there. His expression turns savage, devouring what he sees. That aperture aches, thudding hectically from his attention. Unforgivably, I need him there.

Once more, the satyr prowls forward and hovers over me. His substantial figure looms, the very picture of a chimerical being, cast from a dark and prohibited folktale. I wrap my arms around his neck and hook my legs over the width of his hips, giving permission.

He nudges his waist between my thighs, flattening his palms on the grass for leverage. His earrings swing past his hair, the bronze strands vibrating, and his breeches slump low around his pelvis. The crown poises at my entrance, setting that place aflame.

Puck's pupils dilate into twin pools of black. He takes me in, holds me in.

Then his hips rock forward. The tip probes, slipping through the curls. A strangled sound leaps from my tongue. "Oh."

Puck circles his hips, prodding my walls apart with short, shallow juts. He moves at a languid pace, barely inside me. Yet already, my hands abandon his neck and surge into his breeches. I clasp his buttocks, feeling the dimples contracting.

He grunts, "Warmer."

Flames course from the spot where he teases me apart. The satyr works gently into me, opening the soft folds. With each leisurely swat of his crown, my knees pitch higher, clamping his sides.

His lower body rocks in a spherical motion, plying at my wetness and then retreating. The effect is torturous, stunning.

Astonished moans stutter out of me. Haggard moans grind out of him.

Puck braces his arm under my right leg. "Wetter," he rumbles.

My body reacts, flooding his mast. I sink my fingers into his gyrating backside, beseeching him to go deeper, so very deep. The friction is an agony, as if I'm chasing something that will never be caught.

I seize his rear, pressing him down. At last, Puck releases my leg and sinks closer. His elbows bracket atop the grass, his feverish length sliding out and radiating with heat at my center.

"I'm going to fuck you now, my luv," he prompts "And when I start, don't hold back. Let me hear that sweet fire."

I roll my hips once, nestling him there. "It's going to hurt," I predict.

He quirks a fiendish eyebrow. "On the contrary. I'm a satyr."

And with a forward swing of his hips, he thrusts fully into me. My back vaults off the ground, my cry tumbling into the dell. Oh, my Fables.

Puck groans, low and long. He roots himself in and moves in earnest, pivoting his hips, snapping his pelvis. The momentum is even, controlled, yet delirious.

I moan, weep, plead. I chant nonsense.

"Yes, Juniper," Puck growls. "Teach me how to fuck you."

And I do. Like this, our bodies pitch across the grass. Like this, he increases the rhythm. Like this, I shout into the void, in tune with the jutting piston of his body.

His breeches flare open around his waist, shameless and sexy. Glimpsing us like this, I see his abs clench, his body hefting into mine. I see a flash of his length entering and withdrawing.

Again, he lifts himself and watches my reactions. He follows the sounds, the gestures. Spurred on, he whips into me, sheathing to the hilt before retreating again.

In and out. In and out. In and out.

My hands scale the ladder of his spine and claw at his flesh. My touch pleads *yes*, and it says *there*, and it wants *more*.

I snatch his face, urging him to hunch, our foreheads stamping together, his body plowing through mine. "Teach me how to finish you," I demand.

Puck unleashes. He falls atop me and grapples for my bottom. Achieving a firm grip, he charges with swift, tireless thrusts.

I whine, practically sobbing in cadence with his shaft. My bust jostles, and the camisole straps fall down my shoulders. I'm so drenched, the prow of his length plunges effortlessly.

We grunt, holler into one another's mouths. I don't know what's coming, but it's coming rapidly, that flame hitting a plateau, hastening toward it. Like this, and this, and this.

"I never forgot you," I whimper. "Every day since that night, I thought of you."

"I thought about you, too," he pants. "Always and endlessly."

"I hadn't wanted to."

"But I did."

My nipples pit into his chest, rubbing against him. Perspiration beads his torso and across my stomach. His pelvis hauls into mine, working me into the grass. I dig my heels into the ground and ride him back, lurching my core up around his length, until he can't go any further, until I can't

251

reach any higher.

But I need to. Fables help me, I need to have more, take more.

My plaintive whimpers multiply, splintering from my throat.

"What's the matter, luv?" Puck entreats. "Want my cock to go faster? Hmm?"

"Yes," I whine.

He obliges, hoisting me firm against him, his palms spanning my rear. His waist slings forward with abandon. He pumps into me, shorter, shallower now. The tip of his hardness hits a spot that threatens to shatter me, to break me into a million radiant pieces. Somehow, he lodges himself deeper, deeper still. The crest of his body strikes that place again and again.

Puck hugs me to him, dashing forth, sweating. I clamp my mouth around his and catch our moans.

Our hips slam together. Over and over and over.

And like this, we find our mark. Peeling back, our gazes lock, and our mouths fall open. Puck stills, and I still, and then a great spasm releases. The climax detonates from where we're joined and swarms my being.

I scream, wild, hysterical. Puck roars, feral, passionate.

My inner walls convulse around his shaft. Warmth pulsates into my womb as Puck shudders. Like this, we root ourselves and ignite together.

Puck sags atop me, and I crumple to the grassy bed. Around us, the trees gleam, dripping with gilded orbs. The scents of fruit and basil envelope us.

We struggle for breath. The satyr lies between my legs, his length filling the cleft of my body. His face presses into my cheek, but he angles himself carefully, lest his antlers jab my skin. I drag my foot over his furred calf and comb my fingers through his red layers, speechless, astonished.

Well. Speechless for all of a minute.

Perhaps this is glamour. Perhaps this is what happens when a mortal spends too long in Faerie, too long in the company of a satyr. Or perhaps this is something else, something more.

So when Puck raises his head and shows off that glorious Fae smirk, I realize I do have something to say. I knot my legs around him and whisper, "Again."

26

My wish is his command. Thus, *again* happens.

This time, we face each other while stretched out on our sides. Puck fastens on to my knee, hitching my right thigh over his waist as he plies me with temperate thrusts. Our pelvises rock together, gyrating in a leisurely manner.

Though, I'm feeling anything but lethargic. My whimpers coalesce with his groans, the sounds punctuating every soft beat of his waist. He strokes into me fluidly, my wetness coating his length, my walls gripping around him.

I keen into the night and cling to his nape, letting myself be ridden.

Puck watches me through slitted eyes. His mouth hangs open, heavy breaths rolling off his tongue. The muscles of his abdomen clench, bunching as he angles himself into my body, his hips slinging gently between my thighs.

The climax builds just out of reach. It coils into that narrow place where his shaft glides within my core, the cadence so euphoric, so good that I'm trembling.

"I'm going to…," I pant, "I'm going to…"

To which, Puck shakes his head. "No, luv," he husks. "No, you're not."

Not yet. Not if this satyr can help it.

With that, his hand drops to my backside, his palm fixing me in place. And then he slows the tempo even more, the sluggish grind of his length heightening my moans, coaxing them out until I'm pleading for it to end, until I'm hoping it will never end.

An eternity later, I shatter on a long-suffering cry. I arch into him, engulfed by a vehement profusion of bliss. Puck tenses, then joins me as we climax in one collective holler.

And on it goes...

By the time Puck's done with me, and by the time I'm done with him, neither of us can move. We deflate into the grass, languishing like a pile of exhausted, sweaty fools. During our final tumble, he'd drawn out my orgasm yet again, persevering for so long I'd nearly passed out.

Now he rolls over, cradling me to his side. The muskiness of sex coils with the essence of fruit, herbs, and leather. Rumpled together, we suck in air.

The satyr and I rest in a slash of moonlight, sprawled atop slender blades of glass spritzed in gold from the trees. As we stare at the sky, Puck's index finger skims the margin of my neck, and my arm drapes across his stomach.

Tingling warmth flows beneath my skin, as if someone has injected a mixture of tea and wine into my bloodstream. A drowsy sensation takes over. I wonder if being drunk feels remotely similar.

This moment seems as intimate as when he'd been inside me. My arms and limbs, sticky with perspiration under the garments. My breasts, swollen from the pressure of his mouth. My core, damp from his thrusts. His arms, hot and bare. His limbs, tangled with mine. His calf scars, pulped and covered by my toes. This is us in the aftermath, raw and ravaged.

"My, my, my," Puck says, his voice thin from all the noise we'd made. "You *are* a fast learner." He swings his head down and taps his freckled nose against mine. "That explains the rather confident grip you had on my ass."

Smug bastard. Then again, I frown at him. "Past tense? Does that mean we're done for tonight?"

"Fables have mercy!" He throws back his head and bellows with laughter. "Woman, I've made you come three times in the last hour."

"You're a satyr," I point out.

"Bloody true, last time I checked, but even we have our limits of stamina. Faeries can go on for a very long time, but after that many victory laps, certain appendages need a break." For emphasis, his eyes tick down to the unbuckled vent in his breeches. "Just ask it. I'm sure it will agree."

Scandalized mirth rolls across my tongue. "I'm not going to ask it anything."

"You sure? This is a rare opportunity."

I'm tempted to smack his arm. Unfortunately, his rich tenor wends its way into my belly, seeping into the chinks. That, and the expression he slants my way, a potent blend of fondness and amusement.

Curse him and that contagious grin. Curse the indecent sprawl of his body.

He twists onto his side, facing me while his thumb runs up and down my hip. This position allows me to maintain my hold on him while addressing important business.

Puck reads my expression with playful skepticism. "Wait a minute. I know that look," he accuses, hoisting himself on his elbow. "That's the List Look. You're assembling a mental roster of how many positions there are to check off."

I match his pose and slap the grass. "I am not!"

"How many?"

He's far too eager to know. I compress my mouth into a disapproving plank, then grunt, "Four, thus far."

"Egads. I've created a merry monster." Delighted with himself, Puck dives in and snatches my lips. He kisses me until I'm sinking into the forest floor, the upper half of his frame covering me. The naughty imp nuzzles under my jaw, his muffled voice chanting, "Nom, nom, nom, nom, nom."

I chuckle. How does he do this? How does he make me laugh when there's nothing to laugh about?

Puck pops off me. "On second thought, that's a pitifully low number of positions in Faerie," he admonishes. "Wherever did you come up with it?"

"Lark," I answer.

For a proper list, I'd consulted every graphic detail she's ever shared with me and Cove. Our younger sister has clogged our ears with enough tales to permanently plug them.

I want to expand on that, to share more anecdotes about my family. However, Lark's name is a gust of cold wind slicing between us. I've imparted tidbits about my sisters with this Fae, back when the stakes were already high, and he had less right to know anything about them. But the reminder of Lark and Cove is a brutal dose of reality, snuffing out my mood. Contrition worms into my gut. I'd had sex with the woodland's ruler, the enemy of my people, the antagonist of this Fable.

Sometime during the hunt, he'd stopped being a villain and become my friend. Sometime during our friendship, he became more than that.

Rawness assaults my throat, depriving me of speech. Puck notices, his brows crinkling. "Juniper—"

"Don't say I did nothing wrong," I warn him, turning away and speaking around a mouthful of remorse. "I...I've..."

I've betrayed them. I indulged in this night at the expense of the ones who mean more to me than anyone else in this world.

All of us win—or none of us win. Our lives hinge on each other.

I'm the stringent one of our trio. I'm the righteous one. Yet I'm the one who gave myself to my captor. I did so multiple times tonight. I did this—*me*, not Lark or Cove.

Puck reaches out and catches the strap of my camisole, which has slid down my shoulder. While tucking it into place, he dips his head until I face him, then his roughspun voice abrades the night. "Sorry, luv. I have to disagree. You did nothing wrong."

"I went to bed with the ruler of The Solitary Forest."

"Actually, we're not in bed."

"That's not funny," I clip.

"Of course it's not," he replies. "If I had made a jest, you would have laughed."

"Puck—"

"Are you still playing this game?"

"Yes."

"Are you still planning to win?"

"Yes."

He gestures mutely, as if that explains everything. I study the inclines of his cheeks, the lacquer of his irises. I glimpse no self-serving agendas, nor devious intentions on his part. Not that I would expect them at this point, however much he wants to save his world. We've left the duplicity behind us, otherwise I wouldn't have trailed him here in the first place.

And it's true. I'm still in this game. I'm still aiming to win.

But if I win, he's one step closer to fading. He and an entire race.

Where does that leave us? What happens next? How can we compete against each other, without competing against each other?

"Do you want to leave the dell?" Puck offers.

Yes. No. Now. Never. "I don't know," I whisper.

My voice wobbles, the words tripping over themselves. My intonations sound as though they're made of pebbles—small and unstable. I feel repentant for that as well, because not once have I ever let my resolve slip.

I stare at our fingers, which have absently begun to thread together. My digits weave with his, bunching and forming a globe—or a combined fist—between us. Speaking of family, I'm not the only player letting their siblings down.

Puck examines my features. "And that, right there? That's the Q & A Look."

Yes, it is. I need to keep talking, keep asking questions. If not, my mind will stagger to places I don't want it to yet.

He coaxes me to turn, linking himself around me from behind. Our legs plait together, his calf fur stroking the backs of my knees, my heels brushing his hooves. His torso rises and falls, his heart knocking into my spine like a ticking clock, steady and sure.

I escape into that rhythm, into this moment. Because once it's gone, I don't know what I'll do. Once my thoughts readjust, I don't know how I'll feel about what's happened.

Perhaps if I don't budge, reality won't surge in. Perhaps I can prevent that avalanche for a few more minutes.

Puck rests his chin on my shoulder. "You go first."

"What about your brothers?" I ask. "What if they find out we were intimate?"

"Ahh, them." He's quiet for a while. "They know me for the shallow but savory rake I am. Satyrs don't draw the line at humans, as the rest of our kin do. It's not a common fetish, but we don't object to pleasuring the ones who are willing. I doubt my frisky actions will startle Cerulean or Elixir.

"Now don't scowl at me over your shoulder like that—satyrs don't beguile humans into bumping hips. We're monsters, but we're not *mon-*

sters. In short, we force no one. Our partners come voluntarily, no pun intended."

"So, you've bedded other mortals."

"Only the emboldened, fanatical ones who've ventured just outside our border, searching for a thrill. Several males. No females. Because they didn't step beyond The Triad, and because I didn't intentionally lure them into trespassing, they weren't condemned to play the game. Therefore, we had a merry time together." He entwines a lock of my hair around his pinky. "I like this color on you."

"Lucky for me, since it's the only hair color I possess."

"You don't happen to have a pair of matching unmentionables, do you? Ow!" he yelps, his chest rumbling with humor when I twist and slap his arm.

He grabs my hand and nips my knuckles. "Behave yourself. Now where was I? Oh, yes. My rakishness and the infamous brothers. If they find out I've been a bad boy, they won't be surprised. Annoyed, but not surprised." Puck bites my middle finger. "Now ask me if I give a shit what they think."

As much as I like hearing that last part, I give him another dubious look over my shoulder, and he tells me, "We each have our vices and limits. We each have our breaking points. Cerulean hides behind his candidness, which is rather clever, since no one suspects him of concealing anything. As for Elixir, he doesn't hide a thing, because he doesn't believe he has to—or that he can. It's the world that hides from him."

"How does the world manage that?"

"Quite easily, though you'd have to see for yourself. And me? I nurture my secrets by planting the seeds and letting them grow for the world to behold. I deny nothing."

Puck says that while his brothers care for one another and have a pact to remain loyal, they have their own rules, in their own environments. Neither can tell the other what to do, only trust they're working for the same end result.

He detours, breaking down the regions. Mountain Faeries are of the wind and air; they're lofty and elegantly unpredictable. River Faeries are of the water; they're transparent and fluidly lethal. Woodland Faeries are of earth and fire; they're primitive, untamed. They're boisterous, provocative, and sexual.

Speaking of landscapes, I have no idea where we are. "What is this place?"

Nostalgia fills his voice. "This is where I came from."

I jolt in realization, glimpsing the compact dell and its fruit trees anew. "The Seeds that Give."

Puck's silence is enough. This is the place he had spoken about, the place where woodland Faeries are born from seeds. This is where he began.

He kisses my nape. "I wish I could see where you came from."

"I was a foundling," I remind him.

"That's how you started, luv. That's not how you ended."

The gap in his tone is unmistakable, the bereavement of it. The notion of being born from a seed might sound romantic and whimsical, but it isn't. Not to him.

If he knows how to interpret my expressions, I know my way around his words. So that's what he'd meant during our talk in The Heart of Willows, when he'd called the mountain and river Folk lucky for their ability to reproduce, however seldom.

I scoot around, catching Puck's expression before he has time to conceal it. On the other hand, he doesn't fight to hide the signs.

I lean on my elbow, my breasts about to spill from the drooping camisole. "You said you deny nothing. You said you plant your secrets and let them grow for the world to view. Number one, that negates the definition of a secret. Number two, trees have roots."

Roots that no one can see unless a person searches deeply enough.

Puck's face twitches. "Smart woman."

"Know-it-all," I correct. "Puck?"

"Yeah?"

"More than anything, who do you want to be?"

"Someone's son." The answer comes out slowly. "Someone's father." The satyr grins, the humor failing to reach his eyes. "Hell, at least I've never been told to do my chores or morphed into some starchy, overprotective parent."

All this time, he's lived as an archetypal satyr of folklore. All the while, he's compensated in the roguish, flippant way expected of his kind, indulging himself in harems and orgies. When, in fact, he wants something more. Something I had managed to find with Papa Throne, Cove, and Lark.

Satyrs may not need love. But that doesn't mean they don't want to be part of a family.

Puck flits his digits. "It's not as dire as it sounds. As for the rest, Cerulean and Elixir are my brothers-in-arms, Sylvan is my sister, Cypress is my best friend, and everyone is my lover. I fancy sex as much as the next Fae and get plenty of attention. There, you see? I keep myself merrily busy."

"And what am I?" I ask.

His eyes consume me. "*Minn ó feijleiji*," he whispers. "My weakness." "*Minn ó stürjur*," he adds. "My strength."

The answer enfolds me like a blanket. And then he says, "I was going to manipulate the rules, to give you extra time. Only as a precaution, in case you didn't come up with anything at the feast. Though, I'd wagered you would. That was a precious fucking bargain, luv." He peers at me. "Is there really another way to preserve our land?"

A question tucked within a question. I encode his meaning. What am I leaving out of this bargain? What am I not saying?

A breeze sneaks through the trees, rustling the shingles of leaves.

I want to tell him but can't. I can't because the bargain has been made; it's set and binding. He knows this, just as he patently suspects I had disguised my words while making that deal.

He's correct. Although I can't outright confide this to him, there's no harm in alluding to it. Is there a second way to save his world? One that doesn't involve sacrificing my people?

"The book says there is," I answer.

Puck absorbs my reply, converting it to its true meaning. "Such foxiness."

Yes, there's another way. The Book of Fables just doesn't give specifics. Precisely what this alternative option is, well, that's yet to be figured out. In the meantime, I had only promised to show the Solitaries the trail I'd found.

"You'll just have to wait and see," I say.

"Hmm," Puck muses. "Lucky you, immortals are patient." He drags his mouth across mine and murmurs, "And I'm not going anywhere."

I sigh into him. "What are we doing?"

"We're becoming partners," he negotiates, plastering me to him. "What say you?"

He means it. And because he means it, I pull back. "How?"

"So we've progressed from a list of sexual positions to a list of contingency plans, have we? You would think between my satyrness and your smartyness, the solution would be a given. Did you think I was going to give up on you once we left this dell? Not an option." His voice flattens, and he slants his knuckles across my chin. "We'll find a way."

I think of Cypress's first warning. *If such a connection were to blossom, he would act with his heart before his head.*

I think of Cypress's second warning. *We Faeries see many things.*

But I also think of what this could mean, what Puck and I might be capable of together. Then I deliberate beyond that. Even if I win, the Faeries will go after another innocent human, and another, and another. This strife will never end unless we find another way.

I shift closer, so that our limbs tangle. "That's a deal I'm willing to make."

27

We become a secret. With urgency, we throw ourselves into it, spurning the rules and consuming every window of opportunity afforded to us.

On the pretense of being an impersonal ruler, Puck designates a campsite for me, located near a warren of rabbits and a field of juniper trees. "Wise guy," I say while admiring the area.

"Hey now," he defends. "I have no idea what you're talking about. The trees were here first."

He'd wanted to give me a vacant cabin, but such comforts would have been seen as preferential. He may reign over his woodland kin, but he can't control what they think or how they act. Nor would he be expected to try. If we want to protect our bond, he needs to play out this role.

Nevertheless, Puck declares any intervention upon my camp prohibited. With the hunt over and my bargain set, nefarious acts would flout those terms anyway. But Puck doesn't take chances, and neither do I. One never knows if a bored leprechaun or faun will be in the mood to bait or glamour me.

As an extra precaution, Puck beseeches Sylvan for her help. He hadn't been sure if she would, but the doe honors me by obliging, bedding down in the vicinity. With her there, Faeries are even less likely to seek me out for a prank.

Cypress delivers my archery and supply pack from The Heart of Willows, along with the scribe's tome. I keep to the camp half of the time, researching the Fables and comparing my notes to the scribe's. After discovering the hidden message, I read with fresh eyes, foraging for additional clues—camouflaged notes, coded trails, or anything I hadn't seen before. I read between the lines and anthologize whatever comes to mind, whatever does or doesn't add up. I pace and babble to myself, trying to connect the evasive dots. I pull off my spectacles and scrub the fatigue from my eyes.

Meanwhile, the satyr does his own reconnaissance. He revisits the history of his people and charms his kin into telling their tales, their memories of centuries past. He searches for a loophole, a way for us both to win this game.

The other half of the time, we meet in private. As archers and hunters, Puck and I follow one important rule: We cover our tracks. In a vast weald populated by Faeries, we rendezvous in various spots, never meeting in the same area twice.

We walk that perilous line with care, designating halfway points and venturing to them on the cusp of dusk, after we've rested but before his kin awaken. Though, sometimes we reunite in broad daylight, with none but the animals to bear witness.

Whenever we reunite, we compare and debate notes. Then we formulate further theories and possibilities…

Well. This isn't precisely the first thing we do.

I step into a shrouded glen. He's already there, his back facing me, his frame clad in olive leather pants and a tight, matching shirt that clings to his physique. He's so robust, the fabric threatens to rip at the seams, or perhaps that's due to the tension in his arms.

We'll talk first, I tell myself. Of course, we'll get to the critical things first. They take priority. Naturally, they do.

He whirls when I enter the space. The instant we spot each other, my skin flares, and his eyes glow. He shakes his head and growls, "Fuck it."

Puck and I drop our bows and pounce.

Ten minutes later, my thighs shake like jelly around his head. His red hair burns brightly between my legs, his antlers perilously close to poking my navel if I don't calm down.

However, I can't calm down. I can barely think in a straight line, barely recite the alphabet.

My leggings have been peeled off and chucked to the grass, along with my ankle boots and undergarments. My sweater drapes over my belly, the only thing concealing my tattoo.

I writhe on the ground, my naked limbs falling widely apart. The satyr clamps his hands around my thighs, spreading me open while his tongue lashes at my core, stroking the private crest rising from the thatch of hair. With each teasing lick, the peak swells. It pulses, aches. It scales higher, higher—an excruciating crawl to an unreachable summit.

Thankfully, my companion's weary of drawing blood. Experience has taught him which angles will prevent his antlers from clipping my skin.

Puck hums into my walls, open and wet for him. He laps up the moisture, his mouth pulling tremors out of me. My cries shred through the wild. At one point, this forces him to cover my lips with his palm.

I whine and groan into his hand, my hips bucking, demanding. He makes an appreciative noise against my center. His tongue rides up the drenched slit, then lunges inside me in a devastating sequence of pumps.

I had assumed it would feel similar to when I'd used my fingers, or perhaps when his length had filled me. But his tongue is different. So defiantly different.

It's utter chaos. I grapple for leverage—the grass, tree roots, his scalp. Finally, I go still and stifle my breath, which allows me to feel his ministrations even more.

He strays again, strapping his lips around that sensitive little bud and sucking. And even his hand can't block the cacophony, an unearthly climax tearing me in half. I break down, calling out like a wild creature.

When the stress threatens to puncture a hole in my head, he finds me hunched into a ball at my camp. Crouching before me, Puck unfurls my limbs and extends a hand. "Come with me."

In a pasture, he challenges me and Cypress to an archery contest. Blackbirds with iridescent beaks swing through the branches. Squirrels shrink to the size of pinecones and nest up there, munching on nuts.

The satyr, centaur, and I line up—their longbows versus my crossbow. We loose our weapons. Puck wins the first round. By the next bout, my joints have relaxed, as well as my aim. I focus on the markers engraved into the tree trunks and claim the following round. Then Cypress outshines us both, striking true for the final three stretches.

My sisters accuse me of being a sore loser. But I don't feel that way at the moment. Tonight, I'm simply content to let it fly.

As far as appearances go, it's a fine ploy. The contest engages the Solitaries who gather on the fringes to watch. The exposure distracts them from keeping a closer eye on us.

Cypress pretends to store his arrows in his quiver. Only the centaur notices me mouthing covertly to Puck, *Thank you*. Only the centaur notices the confidential—and intimate—nod Puck gives me. Only the centaur turns away, doing so abruptly.

And so, I'm only the one who notices the bob of Cypress's throat and his fixed grip on his weapon.

Puck takes me to The Clan of Badgers, excited about introducing me to "all the nocturnal badgery." They live in an expanse of hickory trees. As always, a nimbus of candlelight pours onto the shaggy trunks and broadleaves.

As we watch the critters digging for supper, I gawk at their honeydew-colored tails.

One of the badgers shifts to the size of a pony and trots up to us. It rolls on the ground and makes itself comfortable, and Puck ruffles its fluffy tail.

I find courage to do the same, smiling as the animal wiggles against my touch. All the while, I feel the satyr's attention on me.

After the badger scampers away, Puck and I exchange tidbits about the creatures, the characteristics and habitats from his land and mine, the things we'd known and hadn't known.

"I rescued a badger once," I tell him. "The little one had been so dehydrated, I'd had to feed it every two hours for days."

I hadn't let it show in front of my sisters, but I was terrified the cub wouldn't survive.

"But it did," Puck predicts.

I glance sideways at him. "It did."

I race from his grasp, dashing through the trees with my blouse unbuttoned, my hair untethered, and my skirt flying around my limbs. He chases me through dew-covered foliage, condensation spattering with our movements.

When a scream resonates through the wild, we halt and listen. Puck and I stare at one another as the cavernous yip travels from the west.

We smirk and blurt out in unison, "Foxes."

Puck is the adventurous one. I'm the cautious one. Yet this infectious creature finds ways to turn me inside-out, inspiring me to spontaneity.

And while he's shrewder than he lets on—vigilant of his kin and expertly flippant when we're in the company of watchful Faeries—there are times when he pushes the boundaries.

He's there to disarm me. I'm there to steady him.

Puck hefts me off the ground, dumps me on a low-hanging branch, and yanks up my skirt. Astride him and clad only in my blouse, I tear into his breeches so violently the closures rip. As they flap open, he stands within the split of my body and lunges into me.

I yelp with pleasure, eternally stunned by this. I'd never known what my body could accomplish, what response I could elicit in a male.

Puck's shaft pitches to the hilt, pivoting in and out of my wetness at a frantic pace. I spur him on, gripping his buttocks and thumping my groin with his. The rhythm is swift, hectic, and glorious.

"Don't tell me to stop," he pants.

I shake my head. "Don't tell me what to do."

A passionate chuckle rumbles from his mouth, which collapses into another groan. All the while, we watch each other.

After crescendoing, Puck carries me to the nest of furs he'd prepared. I fall asleep in his arms and awaken later to the rich thrum of music. The notes wind through the area, rousing me from dreams.

Daybreak filters through, illuminating his bare-chested frame perched on a tree stump and straddling his cello. He glimpses me while sliding that wand-like bar across the instrument.

I want to ask him what the various parts are called, such as the knobs at the top. Except all I can do is watch him, watching me.

His fingers vibrate atop the uppermost strings, causing the melody to shiver. Around him, the trees glint as though soothed by the notes. Several blooms flounce their petals toward the sound.

"Afternoon, luv," he says. "Fancy your wake-up call?"

I curl into the furs and use my hands as a pillow. "Did you compose that?"

The bar glides over the strings. "It's the only thing I've ever written. All the rest are folkish ditties of old."

"Does it have a title?"

"I was thinking *Sexy Masterpiece* or *The Hottest Solo Ever Composed.* Or maybe *Sylvan.*"

To the last option, I give him a brisk nod. "Approved."

"Then it's settled." He jerks his chin toward the pack containing my notebook, both of which I'd dropped when Puck had grabbed me earlier. "Why haven't you thought about writing your own book?"

The question is so random and unprecedented, I scoff. "Very comical."

"What now? What's that face?"

"I'm not a writer," I insist. "I'm a reader."

"In my world, that's the first step to becoming a writer." He plucks at the strings, changing the tune. The composition sharpens, quickens. "You've researched the Fables, their theorists, and their emulators. Why not write something of your own? Try it. Give it a merry whirl. See what happens when you put pencil to parchment."

I sit up, fish the notebook from my pack, and exhibit the tablet. "I already do that."

I'd scripted my latest set of notes and had planned to share them, but our bodies had gotten distracted.

Puck drags the bar across the cello. "Yes, but I'm talking about a text that's completely yours. Create something from your mind. Explore, ponder, and scribble whatever comes out. That's all storytelling is, isn't it? It's just making something of your own. Write for yourself."

"Compose more music," I volley.

Puck stops playing and grins like a devil. "Wanna help me?"

He uses the bar to tap his thigh, inviting me over. I shake my head but smile. I can't help thinking about what he's suggested, can't help the leap in my stomach.

Me, writing a book of my own.

I bite my lower lip, to which Puck smirks persuasively. "You like my idea, don't you?"

"Which one? Your first idea?" I rise and prance toward him. I'm feeling bold, nothing like myself and every bit myself. Settling on his lap, I speak against his mouth. "Or the second?"

He shifts me between his thighs and sets the cello in front of us. We twine ourselves around the instrument, and he arranges my left fingers on the strings, then my right digits on the bar. "Like this," he instructs and sways our arms together, the melody rising to the trees.

His breath hits my ears, and he names each note. My eyes fall shut, and I coil into him. As he shows me the basics, his whispers shimmy down my spine, causing an outbreak across my skin.

The cello tosses music into the air, and I toss my head back to find Puck's lips descending. He pries my mouth open, kissing me as we keep playing, keep making something of our own.

We explore The Swarm of Rats. In an entrancing hollow of maple trees, seeds litter the floor, perfect for rodent-hoarding.

I grin at what Puck calls "rattery antics." The females move constantly, flitting here and there, balancing on their hind legs to sniff the air, and grooming themselves with considerable regularity. Meanwhile, half a dozen males get cozy in leaf hammocks suspended in the branches, the rodents sleeping in puddles of whiskers and whiplike tails.

Their squeaks peal through the wild, as shrill as tin whistles. In my world, humans often can't hear the sounds rats make, barring the occasional peep. In Faerie, their vocalizations bounce off everything.

According to Puck, they rarely shift sizes. These creatures like their routine, excluding when a predator lurks nearby.

"They're pragmatic," I observe to Puck. "Like me."

He snorts. "Bragger."

I elbow him in the ribs, then get distracted by a pup with sea-glass pupils who chases its siblings up a maple tree. Wistful, I watch the trio for an hour.

Puck runs a thumb down my arm. "You never told me what happened to your bracelet."

He had inquired about the winding leaf bracelet before, prior to the hunt's commencement. I'd never answered him.

I still don't, because I would rather pretend the nymphs never took it from me. I'd rather imagine the trinket from my sisters still clings to my arm, unbroken.

Puck clasps my hips under the skirt and tugs me into a languid tempo. My thighs split around him, straddling his body as I revolve back and forth. He demonstrates the rhythm, then eases his grip as I catch on.

He's naked, his torso clenching in the drowsy starlight. My breasts tumble from the unbuttoned blouse, the only stitch of clothing I'm wearing.

That, and the spectacles.

I'd finished reading aloud a passage from the original Fables when Puck had stalked toward me. Because we'd failed to draw from the tale any passages of consequence or significance, he'd suggested we take a break.

The kiss had turned into caresses. The caresses had escalated to bared teeth and my nails raking through his hair.

Every time I tell myself it'll be enough, it never is. Every time we think we've learned one another's bodies, we discover another way to touch. Every time I extract a groan from him, he plucks a sigh from me.

As I'd scrambled on top of him, my fingers had extended to my spectacles. But Puck had rasped, "Leave them on."

My belly had swooped. And now, here we are.

It's barely dusk, barely time for the Faeries to skulk from their homes and make mischief. The satyr and I gyrate, the pace sinuous and patient. I brace my hands on his shoulders and buck into his lap. We bow our heads, watching our hips collide, my waist swatting his.

Tapered ears perk from the satyr's hair. He looks wickedly rumpled, so much so that my toes curl on either side of him. I can't stop wanting this Fae. It's an endless craving, this thing called desire.

Puck licks beneath my ear. "You hear that?" he says over my cries. "That's the sound of me fucking you. And it's beautiful, luv. So beautiful."

"Puck," I keen, grinding onto him.

"Listen. Do you hear it?"

Yes, I hear it. I hear so much of it.

Encouraged, I accelerate the pace, lurching up and down on his length. Puck joins my movements, his pelvis swinging into me, spreading my thighs further.

The incense of cloves and pine curls into my nose. I chase that scent while slamming my waist with his. In response, his shaft thickens. It passes into the wet clench of my body, into a spot that has me chanting.

My head flings back. I take the brunt of his length, take it, take it. His growls collide with my moans, and the noises swirl into a frenzy.

We charge faster, louder. The friction is maddening, the exertion astounding.

Finally we convulse, my center contracting around him. It goes on, and on, and on. By the time we slump together, my spectacles have gone askew.

He chuckles with exhaustion, and I grin in spite of myself. At the same time, we straighten the lenses.

Puck is correct. There are more than four positions.

Solitaries they may be, but these woodland dwellers enjoy their share of communal escapades and chatter. As I bathe and replenish my water-skin in a babbling creek, I overhear brownies gossiping nearby. Puck has rejected one of the nymph's offers for a tumble. Although he'd flirted to appease the male, Puck seldom says no.

Later, at a crossway leading to a secluded teashop, one of the dryads glances at me for a few seconds too long. And from another cavity, fauns and satyrs tip their heads in my direction, following my trajectory while I pretend not to notice.

We read the Book of Fables together. Encasing me from behind, Puck noshes on my ear.

I reach back and rap his hip with the book. "Stop it."

"Stop what?" he mumbles into my skin.

"You're up to no good. I'm well-versed in the signs."

"I should hope so, know-it-all."

When I laugh, he pauses. "Do that again."

"Catch you in the act?"

Another brief pause. "Laugh."

Halfway through my third day, the fear increases. Puck and I sit across from one another at midnight, the Book of Fables and my notebook resting between us. It's a risk to be awake together at this hour, but I'm getting desperate.

I must appear miserable, because Puck stands and sets his hand against the nearest tree. Minutes later, Sylvan trots into the coppice we'd chosen for tonight. I totter to my feet, the sight of her pulverizing the weight on my shoulders to ash.

The Fae engages in silent communication with her, then knocks his head toward the deer. "Fancy an adventure?"

He settles behind me and leads us through the woods, the regal creature galloping around trunks and across hills. She moves seamlessly, as if she knows every nook and cranny of this forest.

Puck encircles my middle, securing me to him. The landscape is a montage of color, flying by on either side of us.

We slow to a canter and emerge into a glade of oak trees. They resemble the giant standing vigil at The Faerie Triad, as well as the arcade from when I'd first arrived in this realm.

In a neighboring field where acorns carpet the ground, a dozen silhouettes graze. Their antlers crank outward, the racks and crowns blooming wisteria, cascading with water droplets, and simmering with flames.

I soak in the pastoral view. The last time I'd seen these beauties, the hunt had been about to begin.

The largest oak stands in the center, its branches sprawling with candles. The trunk carves through the roof of a log cabin nestled at the base—a circular, two-story structure that wraps around the tree's neck. One would think the house and oak have grown together, germinating from the same seed.

"What is this place?" I ask.

"The Herd of Deer," Puck says. "My home."

28

His home. The Herd of Deer is his home.

The great oak hovers above the log cabin, a vast umbrella of branches fanning over and beyond the residence, the roof dripping with broad-leaves. Bucks, does, and hinds forage amidst the trees, the creatures' spindle legs carrying them from one patch to the next.

Puck speaks over my shoulder. "There hasn't been a safe time to show off my humble abode, but with all our researching and fucking, I figured now was our best bet for a palate cleanser. I know it's a trifle size for a ruler, but then I've never fancied myself, ahem, the fancy type. I told you I was hands-on." He clears his throat. "Don't keep me in suspense, luv. Do...do you like it?"

"Like it...," I trail off.

Once upon a time, I had assumed his kin lived indulgently. But similar to the other Faeries' homes, Puck's cabin is unassuming and rustic, picturesque in an unrefined way.

In all this time, why haven't I thought to ask where he lives?

I twist to find him awaiting my reaction. Candlelight trickles through the glade, dusting the grass and embossing his hair in red-gold.

"It's wonderful," I tell him.

Satisfaction dances across his face. "Then come inside with me."

I drop my forehead against his jaw, a sigh whooshing from me. I hadn't realized I'd needed this—we both need this escape. But can we truly indulge, even for a few hours? How long will it last before this game catches up with us again?

"What are we going to do?" I mumble.

Puck slides his mouth across my temple. "We're going to step inside, then you're going to let me cook for you, then we're going to sleep."

The answer pricks my chest. Being here and seeing this place, I think about a normal life filled with simple things—breakfasts with steaming coffee, productive afternoons planting a garden, intimate nights reading and talking…and not reading or talking. I think about preparing a meal together while reflecting on our day and sharing news. I think about keeping animals here—ones that need our help, if any. I think about a life divided equally, allocated between time spent in his world and in mine, between his kin and my family. I think about that life, wild yet peaceful.

I adore and resent him for this brief sample. But no matter what, I'll take it. If we don't know what will happen tomorrow, I'll take as much of it as I can have. I'll take it until the last second, until the last drop of time when I have to resume this game.

Puck hops down and offers me his hand. We dismount Sylvan, who leaves to join the herd. The satyr welds our fingers together and leads me through the double doors.

Inside, oaken beams run across the low ceiling. The foyer tunnels to a living room with the oak's trunk at its heart and a fireplace carving straight through the bark. Puck has outfitted the place with a masculine, robust flair. A supple leather sofa upholstered in warm sepia rings around the trunk, strewn with an abundance of plump evergreen cushions. Overgrown plants spill from pots lining the windowsills, the glass partitions interspersed by doorways leading to the kitchen, larder, dining room, bathroom, and closets.

Puck hooks my cloak, archery, and supply pack—with the book tucked inside—on to wall pegs, all in a row. He gives me a tour of every chamber except the bedroom loft, telling stories about the deer who meander outside these walls.

My attention falls on the panorama artwork affixed to the trunk and extending around its circumference over the fireplace. It's a landscape painting of birches at dusk, coated in chunky swabs of green, blue, and saffron. "Who painted this?"

Puck brackets an elbow on the mantle. "Cypress."

I startle. "He paints?"

"And bloody well, too. It's a rendering of where we met."

"The place where you and the faun…"

The satyr rumbles with mirth. "Yes, but there's more to that memory. Cypress and I ended up lingering afterward, having our first chat. How swiftly we connected surprised us both. It was marvelous." He considers the likeness. "The talented bugger was spot on with every aspect, down to the angles of light and specks of dust."

For some reason, this gives me pause. However, Puck just admires the depiction fondly, then ushers me into the kitchen. Apple and onion bushels stand beneath a vine of sausage links hanging from the ceiling. In addition to the wood stove—wrought from some obsidian element native to this land—a cauldron squats in the belly of another fireplace. Crockery clutters the exposed shelves, and an island presides in the room's center, along with a pair of stools.

Puck extracts potatoes and carrots from the larder. I sit on a stool and watch him putter about. "Behold: Satyrs can cook."

"This satyr can." He flips a peppermill in his hand. "I can cook, spice, and grind."

He waggles his brows. An undignified snigger hops up my throat, about to skip across my tongue like a stone. But instead of letting it out, I roll my eyes. However, Puck's cavalier smile indicates he knows I'm struggling to hold back.

It isn't long before I march to his side and judge the amount of salt and herbs he uses for a stew recipe. He tries to shoo me away, but I examine the assortment of ingredients and declare, "That's too much" and "That's too little."

"Bossy woman," he says.

"I'll have you know, I'm a fine baker back home. My family loves my pies."

"I'll bet I would, too," Puck flirts. "But we're not baking."

We'll see about that. This menu requires an addition.

We end up cooking together, hovering side by side at the stove. He stirs, I chop. He insists we include an acidic component, declaring it one of the pillars of flavor. And I insist we use measuring spoons.

To thicken the pot, we add extra potatoes, then mix a quick batch of biscuits. Impulsively, Puck flicks granules of flour at my chin. I maintain a blank, deadpan expression. Without missing a beat, and without looking away from my task, I scoop a handful of flour and lob it at his antlers.

And so it goes. By the battle's end, powdered flecks mottle our clothes and skin, and we've gotten flour everywhere.

It takes effort for me to keep a straight face, whereas Puck's snicker fills the room, and my temperature rises from the sound. It takes even more effort to control myself when he pins me against the counter and seizes my mouth in a hot, flour-coated kiss.

This feels effortless, normal. The cabin feels like a home, especially with him here.

After cleaning up, we feast on the stew, Puck watching me lap fluid from my spoon. Based on the way he chokes his own utensil, it's a wonder I don't find myself sprawled on the island.

We pull ourselves together long enough to eat and talk. Settled on the stools, our conversation jumps from one topic to the next, mostly about the animals of my world and his.

The sprawling comes later, when talking segues to touching, then to fondling, then to more kissing. Thrusting his arm across the countertop, Puck swipes our dishes to the floor and hauls me out of the seat. Ceramics clatter and roll across the planks as he deposits me on the island and drapes me across its surface. He hunches over, his lips seizing mine, his hips grinding between my legs.

Our pelvises rub through the clothes. In that position, we don't last long. I'm halfway to a climax when Puck lifts me into his arms, my limbs hooking around him. The top floor is the loft where he sleeps. I barely have time to register his cello case propped in a corner and the bed covered in furs before we're stripping one another.

Minutes later, I'm moaning into the mattress. Divested of everything but my sweater, I rest on my stomach while Puck's naked torso bends over me from behind. My backside pitches into the air as his length thrusts inside, his hips slinging into the apex of my thighs. He calls out my name, and I call out his, my walls squeezing him to the hilt.

Like this, always like this.

He rides me into the blankets, the bed jostling, until I've unleashed to the point of hoarseness. Then he lets himself go, hauling me upright and driving his shaft high. The firm crown lunges inside me, stroking out and then striking back in. Rolling my bottom into his pelvis, I reach back and cling to his nape, astonished cries still vaulting from my mouth.

And like this, I bring him down for a kiss. And like this, I taste his release.

Lying in a tangle of arms and limbs afterward, we whisper tired things that make no sense. Puck gathers me to him and nuzzles my throat, making it his mission to draw a laugh from me. "Look at you, thoroughly fucked and pleasured, all relaxed and radiant and—" he kisses me, "—alive."

We mumble until my eyes drift shut, aware of what's happening before tumbling into a well of peaceful black. Finally, we sleep.

When I come to, the brink of dawn floods the room, splotching the walls and blankets. We've been unconscious for hours. Along with the languid shades of early morning, candlelight from the oak branches pours through the windows.

Puck rests on his side, lost in oblivion while his arm links around my midriff. Curled into him, I count the white freckles speckling his nose.

"Look at you," I whisper. "All mischievous and merry. For all that, such a deep dreamer."

Thus far, he hasn't questioned my desire to keep at least one article of clothing on while having sex, nor has he pressed me to be fully nude with him.

Part of me wants him to ask. Part of me dreads that he will.

Outside, critter noises vie for my attention. Eager for a peek, I slip out of bed, my sweater hanging midway down my thighs. I shuffle into my undergarments, socks, and skirt, then steal another glimpse of the sleeping satyr. His muscles expand and contract rhythmically, the furs barely covering his pelvis, red fibers of hair trailing from his navel. Damn this prig. He has every idea what he does to his conquests but no idea what he does to me.

My heart winces, tenderizing in pain. If I don't leave now, I'll crawl into the blankets and wake him up.

I pad downstairs for my boots and step into daybreak. Rose gold splashes across the sky as I venture across the grass, hoping to explore The Herd of Deer. The oak stands proud, candle wicks sizzling from the boughs. A chipmunk leaps from its burrow, and twin hedgehogs with parsley-colored spikes waddle into a bush.

I tuck a lock of green behind my ear and watch the animals roam in their habitats. A current of air rustles my skirt. My clothes and hair are weightless, untethered. I tilt my head back, inhaling the crisp, earthen scent of dew on the hedges.

Look at you, thoroughly fucked and pleasured, all relaxed and radiant and—

"Alive," I echo.

Puck's loyal companion lounges on the ground, but she rises when I spot her. Shamrocks jingle from Sylvan's antler crown as she trots in my direction. That she trusts me enough to do this floods my belly with warmth.

I step toward her, then stumble. The ground jolts, rupturing across the soil. Branches crack, acorns raining from the boughs. Roots burst from the soil, spitting chunks of dirt.

My palm presses to the deer's side for balance. The small critters have already fled, having sensed the quake and scuttled off.

Is it truly a quake? I tense, scanning the perimeter for signs of an incoming creature. Perhaps one of the wandering fauna has shifted to a behemoth size.

Yet the sound doesn't seem to be coming from within the woodland. No, it's coming from above.

I crane my head to the heavens. Through the oaken mesh, distant mountain peaks spear the air. The chiseled bluffs and pillars of The Solitary Mountain loom beyond the forest valley like sentinels, clearer than I've ever glimpsed them. Amidst the range, one summit appears to be…moving…broadening.

Holding on to the doe, I peer closer. The peak is shooting toward the clouds.

It's growing. And it's growing fast, faster than any landmass should. It vaults from the earth, a craggy monolith spearing toward the heavens. The woodland vibrates, the turbulence uprooting flora.

I cling to Sylvan while she remains steady, her hooves stamped firmly into the grass. We stay like that for a few minutes, then I break from my stupor and glance at the cabin. This mayhem is sufficient to wake the dead, yet there's no sign of Puck. He can't possibly sleep through this pandemonium!

Or yes, he could. I want to run inside and shake him from his slumber, but if I move, I could trip and snap my neck.

Sylvan nudges my elbow and offers me her back. I recognize the invitation from the last times we've ridden together, those times when she'd sprung through the wild as though she could travel through it while blindfolded. This isn't a bid to escort me indoors but elsewhere. Perhaps she senses my agitation, because any occurrences having to do with that mountain mean only one thing to me. Only one person.

My head swings between her and the cabin. Puck will have to wait.

I heft myself onto Sylvan's back, and she sprints into the trees. I lean over as the deer hurtles around trunks and over bushes. Despite the ground rumbling, she moves with velocity and focus, like a flying lance.

We come to a dale with a gap in the canopy, which offers a clearer view. Mounted atop Sylvan, I witness the pinnacle spearing into the air. It launches past a strange network of platforms, what appears to be bridges intersecting and overlapping to form a jigsaw of crossings—like some bizarre maze.

Again, a single face blooms in my mind. "Lark," I whisper.

The name surges from my breast, where it's been tucked safely away, protected like a nut inside its shell. It's been thirteen days since I last saw her, but it feels like thirteen times longer.

What's happening up there? Where are you? Are you all right? If I holler, will you hear me? If you hear me, will you answer? Can you answer? Please?

Fear thrashes in the hive of my chest. Perhaps a sixth sense is overtaking me, hyperawareness snarling around my gut. Either way, I'm done evaluating.

I feel my sister up there. I know she's on that peak. I can't say how, but I do.

The pinnacle keeps rising like a sharp tooth. It bypasses every crest—then stops. Everything ceases. The jolting comes to a standstill.

Whatever caused that peak to grow, the impact has dislodged parts of The Solitary Forest from its hinges. Fallen branches inundate the ground. Several holes pockmark the floor, and speckles of dust filter through the creepers.

I dismount, my boot soles thudding to the ground. I take a tentative step forward. That's when the foundation gives a final, episodic shudder, an aftershock scrolling across the earth. I stumble, thrusting my arms out to the sides and catching the doe.

She braces me. I pat her in gratitude, my palms trembling. On reflex, I glance down to make sure my limbs don't collide with hers. My entire left foot lands in one of her hoof prints, my boot fitting inside the wedges. In my world, this wouldn't be possible. However small, my foot would never fit inside the impressions of even the largest deer.

But this is no ordinary creature, and she comes from no ordinary world. Size-shifting aside, she's a big female who would dwarf any buck in the human realm.

My brows furrow as I study our prints nesting together. The sight is familiar, jogging my memory. I slip into the past, to a succession of evenings when I was ten years old. I met a young satyr for the first time, disliked him, and then became friends with him. Nearly a fortnight later, I quarreled with that Fae and stormed off, leaving him behind.

Shortly after that, his deer had come to retrieve him, to take him home. That's when two villagers—a farmer and glassblower—had caught up with me and snatched my crossbow, then hustled after the magnificent creature. I'd given chase, racing after the men only to find them targeting not only the doe, but the satyr as well.

Both ethereal beings had gotten away, had fled to their magical land. But before they'd left, that young Fae had noticed my weapon in the glassblower's possession. And the satyr had glared at me with contempt.

It hurt so much, I'd crumbled against the tree. After he was gone, I'd mustered a step and caught sight of my little foot pinned atop a hoof print, a marking made by the very same animal that stands beside me.

As a huntress, I've conditioned myself to remember such things. As a reader, I've taught myself to bookmark other things, such as the contents of a Fable. As the spinster know-it-all everyone accuses me of being, I've learned to bear things in mind.

The rules of a game, for example. Also, the objective of that game: Hunt an animal that can't be hunted.

The details gnarl together, the hints and implications that have permeated my mind since my first day here. Original Fables, replicated Fables, and hidden Fables. They've taught me countless lessons, one of them being this: Appearances can be deceiving here, just as much as words and deals, bargains and favors.

The rules of the game aren't exempt from this. I've been taking those rules too literally, starting with my first task.

Puck had said so himself. The term hunt is relative.

Hunting an animal that can't be hunted isn't a transparent quest. It never was.

"It's a riddle," I say.

Puck had also said he and the Faeries don't know the answers to my tasks, that they would only know when I did. Yet for all his cleverness, and all my studiousness, neither of us had considered this.

Why hadn't we considered this?

I feel stupid, ignorant. Then I pull myself together and think, think, think. Riddles constitute a reexamination of words, an investigation of double meanings. I ruminate on the nature of hunting, the definition of it. To hunt is to search. To hunt an animal that can't be hunted, is to search for an animal that can't be sought.

My heart stops. It stops as quickly as that mountain peak had stopped, as swiftly as the quake had stopped. There's only one quarry that can't technically be sought. Not if it's inches from your face.

You can't hunt an animal that's right in front of you.

29

My eyes lift to Sylvan. The deer gazes at me, unaware. She watches me with the kind of trust she hasn't given anyone else but Puck. This creature, who was traumatized by The Trapping, haunted by what mortals had done to her fauna kin and the satyr. This animal, who nevertheless learned to put faith in a mortal—a human, after so long.

"No," I insist. "No."

My limbs carry me backward, putting distance between us. I shake my head, whipping it from side to side. No, no, no, no, no, no.

Desperation rattles me to the core. If the term hunt is relative, then I'll fix this.

I'll revise the riddle. If I can't hunt an animal that's right in front of me, that also means I can't hunt an animal in my line of sight. Or instead, I can target any other creature I lay my eyes on. It doesn't have to be her. Isn't that correct?

No, it isn't. The rules had been set in stone. In the beginning, Puck had told me that once I identify the animal, I'm not permitted to change my mind.

But if an animal can't be hunted, it can't be hunted. That's a riddle, too. Isn't it?

True, if it weren't for the infernal rules again. Puck had also said that once I find my target, I have to take action on its life. Simply trapping her in a net or harness won't suffice.

I have to do this, but I can't do this. *I can't.*

I fight to untangle these rules, to find a loophole or another cryptogram. But there's nothing, absolutely nothing. So much for being well read.

Puck. On that horrific night when we were children, he'd falsely believed I helped the villagers target his kin, including the doe he loves. He had been wrong then, and he knows that now. But if I hurt this deer, he won't be wrong about me this time.

I think of the tattoo branded into my lower back. The X of crossbow bolts. The marking of a trade poacher, the last secret I've kept from the world.

My stomach roils. I scuttle away from Sylvan, but she steps toward me, sensing my urge to flee. I raise my hands, palms up. "Don't," I plead. "Shh, girl. It's all right. But please, don't come any closer."

She stalls, her ears pricking. Rather than danger, she senses torment. At least I hadn't armed myself with the crossbow. At least, that.

Despite the past, and despite my tattoo, I want to rush back to the cabin. I want to tell Puck what's happened, figure a way out of this. But I can't just yet. I can't because the news is still curdling in my belly.

I'm going to be sick. Whirling, I sprint into the trees. As I pump my arms and legs, acorn shells snap under my boots. I run blindly, my pulse hammering.

Opal eyes flash from an overhead bough. An unknown dweller rustles inside the womb of a shrub. Several leagues away, a marsupial hisses in my direction.

I'm weaponless. Thus, I'm being senseless.

An eternity later, the oaks vanish behind me. I must have crossed the dividing line into a new location, because these trees possess narrow, tubelike trunks and slender leaves that remind me of splinters. Likely, this species is native to Faerie.

I stagger in place. I just need a moment before figuring out what to do. I need this moment. I need to…to…

My body topples to the ground, where I hunch over and spew into the grass. The contents of my stomach splatter the neighboring plants. Flattening my palms on the ground, I empty myself.

Wheezes peal from my cracked lips. I think of Cove, who would rub my back and console me, urging me to breathe, breathe, breathe.

Another noise floods the atmosphere. From a distance, the faint hum of a cello glides into the forest. The music reverberates in my ears, stroking, tugging.

I wipe my mouth with my forearm and hobble to my feet. "Puck?"

I trail those notes through the foliage. The melody evades me like a mirage, out of reach no matter which way I swerve. An object squashes under my boot. At the same time, the cello music evaporates, swallowed by silence. Deceptive, eerie silence.

I halt in confusion. Then I see it—a ring of mushrooms.

The fungi surround me, but they aren't the teal-and-white dotted toadstools I'd encountered beyond The Faerie Triad. A slimy film coats these caps, their arrangement far too orderly to be natural, their placement methodic rather than organic.

Of my entire family, I'm the only one who's bothered to peruse the Fables' appendices. Among the notations, several address the disparities of time between worlds. The hours run parallel but for one hiccup. If anyone steps into a Fae ring, time stalls. While trapped in the confines, the captive exists in a void where the seconds stagnate. Whereas outside of that ring, time will proceed, so that what seems like minutes is actually days. What feels like days is weeks, in reality.

A Fae ring steals time.

If I was sick before, it hits critical mass now. The woodland tilts, and a hazy sensation clouds my head. As I sink to the ground, my head lands in a pillow of vegetation.

Baffled, I replay the music in my psyche and realize the fraudulent tune hadn't come from Puck. And while it had been a stringed instrument, it hadn't been a cello.

From someplace nearby, laughter coils through the trees, mirth honed at the edges of filed teeth. I claw at the grass. I mumble and lick my lips. All the while, my audience titters.

When I recover, I will put a bolt through those chortling mouths. I will find my mark. But first, I'm so very tired, so very cozy. It's time to rest…time…time…lots of time.

My eyes droop, but I smile and snuggle into the grass. So this is what it's like, being glamoured. One really does learn something new every day.

30

I'm lying on my belly, concealed behind a bush and waiting for the animal to emerge from its hiding spot. I'm cocking my tiny finger over the crossbow's trigger. I'm hoping, dreading, gulping.

The creature's pelt will fetch a decent price. But its claws...those will secure a fortune, a month of meat, bread, and cheese. Perhaps a fresh pair of socks.

Inside my boot, my big toe wiggles through the gash in my stockings. New socks. Now that would be a luxury.

The men lurk behind me, scrutinizing my posture, my aim. If I get this wrong, I won't live it down.

They won't let me. They rarely do.

My knees quiver. I can't take another round of name-calling, another bout of them yanking on my hair and barking into my face to get my act together, to suck it up, to learn. Why did they pluck me off the streets, if I'm useless to them?

I'd like to flee from this gang. I want to, but where would I go? What would I eat?

That's the thing my stomach can't handle—another night without food.

"You'd better not fuck this up, urchin," one of the men says under his breath.

Really, the lout should muzzle himself. He ought to be quiet, lest he foil this hunt. They'll blame me for that, too.

I drag my arm across my brow, mopping away the sweat. A stunted whine builds on my tongue. In the distance, leaves shiver like cymbals, tossing a great green wave of hush-hush-hush through the field.

As to their threat, the men are bluffing. They like me because I'm small, because I can fit into small places, and because I make small noises. The kinds of noises animals are less likely to hear. Animals worth a fat sack of coins to trade poachers.

Even if I could run away and find the means to live, these brutes won't let me go. They'll track me down, catch me. That's what trade poachers do. Like an animal, I'm worth a little something.

Sure, they'll eat the meat. But that's not really what they're after. They want the ligaments, fangs, tusks, antlers, and coats that patrons will display in cases, mount on walls, and wear as accessories.

The high grasses rustle. A fluffy tail pops above the stalks, then a snout swims between the blades, followed by a face. The female looks at me through the glass beads of its eyes. I see myself reflected in those pupils, a little girl scuffed and famished.

Then I see the litter traipsing behind her, a gaggle of fluffs trotting and yipping her way.

Cubs. She has cubs.

I sense the gang tensing, festering like an infection. The muffled echo of a curse jabs my ears. Hunting takes patience, poaching takes an iron stomach. Yet she's in my direct line of sight. If I've learned anything about using this weapon, I've learned this vantage point is foolproof, easy to strike true.

What am I waiting for?

The cubs encircle her. She bristles, registering my apprehension, my indecision. The creature bares her teeth and growls, the noise scraping from her end of the field to mine, then to the dusty pack of males bringing up the rear.

Another crossbow locks from several leagues away. Because if I can't finish the job, one of them will.

No. I shake my head, whipping it from side to side. I can't, I can't, I *can't*.

I could scare her, make her flee. But if I do, they'll see it. My belly's an empty well, and if I muck up this target, it will stay empty for another day or so.

I'm sorry, I'm sorry, I'm sorry. Whimpers teeter on my lips and form the words, "I can't," but I don't know if that's directed to the gang or the mother.

Tears leak down my cheeks, the field and those beady eyes blurring. As my finger curls, a bolt flies free.

And I thrash awake. I lurch upright, my limbs flailing. "I c-can't," I stutter. "I can't, I can't—"

Hands cup my shoulders, wrestling to steady me. An earthen tenor speaks rapidly over my babbles, "Juniper-Juniper-Juniper!"

A stag materializes. Flaming red hair whisks around his visage. White and black streaks line a pair of wild, worried eyes.

The world sharpens, bringing him into stark relief. "Puck," I say.

The satyr hunches before me, violet sickles lurking beneath his eyelids. "It's me, luv," he professes. "It's me."

I leap into his arms. They strap around me, pining me tightly to him. It was a dream. It was only a dream, a nightmare.

Puck combs through my hair and murmurs in a language I don't understand, the words causing me to sag in relief. I pull back, bleary.

I'm curled into a ball against this Fae, his longbow and quiver resting beside us on the grassy floor. Instead of a field, a weald of strange tube trunks surrounds us, as straight as pencils, as thin as sticks. If I concentrate on them long enough, they remind me of the bars of a cage.

Then I remember. My trembling body reminds me of the forest convulsing earlier. An uncharted peak had sprouted from The Solitary Mountain. When that happened, I'd discovered something else, something awful—something I *can't* do.

Puck cradles my jaw. "Are you hurt?" He looks exhausted, his hair unkempt and his vest half-clasped, the leather stained with dirt.

I shake my head. "I-I don't think so. Did you feel the quake? Did you see the mountain?"

He gives a start, as if this question is old news. "It's all my kin are talking about." His voice dampens. "Among other things. Are you sure—"

"I'm fine."

The satyr deflates and musters a sleep-deprived grin. "So you couldn't have waited until after I'd made pancakes to disappear? Give it me to truthfully: Is this a delayed reaction? Did you flee the smutty scene because you panicked? All because you've been Pucked?"

"I didn't run away," I stammer. "The mountain was...and I found out...I have to tell you—"

"Where the fuck have you been?" he bites out. "I've been searching for—"

He leans forward to embrace me once more, and I lean forward to explain. But a circle of fungi catches our attention. We freeze, thrust our palms toward each other in halting motions, and blurt out in unison, "Wait!"

The circle loops around me, separating us by inches. Puck hadn't crossed over, but he could have. While hugging me to him, he could have made that mistake.

Horror drains his complexion. From certain angles, the fungi vanish and reappear, camouflaged into the landscape like an invisible snare. Hunters we might be, but these diminutive caps had hidden themselves well.

I recall this part now. Before losing consciousness, I'd raced through these tube trees and keeled over, sick and vomiting. When I noticed the mushrooms, I'd barely had time to register the consequences before darkness overtook me.

That's why Puck looks the way he does. That's why he'd asked me where I've been.

Terror lodges itself in my throat as I meet Puck's gaze, which has transformed from shock to wrath. "Fuck," he spits.

"Puck?" I croak. "How long have I been asleep?"

The muscles of his face twitch. "Three days."

But it's the wrong question. "What about on your side of the ring?"

He mutters another oath. "Three weeks."

"Three weeks?" Hysteria pitches my voice high. "How could I have been asleep for three days and lost for three weeks? What about Lark? What about Cove? What about the bargain? You're a hunter! How could it have taken you this long to find me?!"

"Fae rings are Fae rings because they don't want to be found. And if they don't want to be found, good luck identifying them quickly unless you're already trapped," he says. "I woke up during that chaos in the mountain, and you were fucking gone. Your cloak and supplies were still in my cabin, so I knew something was wrong, but when I caught up with Sylvan, we couldn't locate you. Juniper." He draws out my name. "These rings don't grow just anywhere."

He stalls in awareness, then mock-sighs. "Shit."

A saw-edged dagger appears in my periphery, the hilt attached to a groomed hand. I know how Puck would have finished his sentence. The Fables' appendices invalidate an old belief that Fae rings burgeon when the Folk dance. The truth is, Fae rings don't grow like that.

"They're planted," a feminine voice says.

Foxglove must have recovered the dagger I'd taken from her. She brandishes it while her clan slinks from the trees, hemmed in by a fleet of woodland Faeries. Leprechauns, dryads, fauns, satyrs, brownies, centaurs, and nymphs stalk forward. They close in, wielding their bows, staffs, hammers, axes, blades, and throwing stars. Tinder stands among them, too.

I recall the stares Puck and I have gotten since The Middle Moon Feast. Cypress had warned me that Faeries see many things.

They know about us. We'd been so careful, so tactful. Still, they know. They know their ruler has betrayed them.

Foxglove confiscates Puck's longbow and quiver, tossing the items to a faun with goat horns. "Get up, gorgeous," the nymph says to Puck.

He puffs out an inconvenienced breath. "And just who the fuck invited you?"

"I said, get up."

He complies with a lazy air, swaggering to his hooves. He exhales dramatically—then whips into motion. In a flash of arms and limbs, he twists, ducks, and rams his fist into an encroaching dryad.

Faeries spring into the fray. Puck whirls around the nymph, yanking her arms behind her and swiping the female's blade, then vaulting it toward a leprechaun who grunts and goes down, his shoulder spraying blood.

I jerk, reaching for my crossbow on instinct and coming up short. Like a dimwit, I hadn't brought it with me.

Veering, Puck snatches his longbow from the faun and shoots, his arrow pinning a fellow satyr's hand to a tree. As the Fae howls, Puck rotates and tumbles, loosing a series of arrows with each turn.

Tinder snatches throwing stars from the harness at his thigh. His marten tail flits, and his orange eyes gleam with several fluctuating emotions—hurt, betrayal, disillusionment—as he aims for the satyr.

"Puck!" I shriek.

Hooves pound, a massive equine body storming into the scene. With a deafening roar, Cypress smashes his way through the quagmire, his livid features strung tightly. He nocks his longbow, the arrow plumes glowing. Tinder swivels and casts himself evasively to the ground before he can throw the first star, so that Cypress's weapon misses the youth's leg.

The brownies have scattered, taking shelter in the bushes. The centaur bucks his hindquarters, punching a dryad in the chest.

Damnation! I scout the area for something, anything to help the equine and satyr. Then I freeze, the tip of an arrowhead nipping at my ribs.

"Care to give up?" Foxglove says, targeting my side while regarding Puck.

The satyr goes still, his chest puffing. Cypress falters, enabling a trio of leprechauns to confiscate his bow and harness him in restraints.

Puck's expression contorts. He catches my eye, his fists on the brink of causing mayhem.

The intensity of a satyr's devotion will be intrinsic, as heightened as their senses. Therefore, they shall be prone to rashness and mishaps. That will render them vulnerable.

Covertly, I shake my head. Puck hesitates, then lowers his archery and sneers, "My, my, my. I do fancy surprises, but this is a tad overdone."

"Is it?" the nymph questions. "Funny you would say that, considering everything that's occurred since The Wild Peak. We began to sense a certain trend between rulers and humans."

My gaze jumps between them. What is she talking about?

"I was merely having fun with the scholarly huntress," Puck deflects. "What can I say? I have a thing for reading spectacles."

"Nice try." The female arches a brow, a gradient of yellows and greens dusting her upper eyelids. "Tragically, though, we've realized how much fun you've been having with this human."

She uses the arrow to pat my backside. Somewhere within me must dwell a bit of Lark's moxie. Either that, or I've had enough.

My fist flies, ramming into the Fae's perfect cheekbone. Her head cracks sideways. She hisses and rights herself, backhanding me across the face so hard my body staggers and hits the grass.

Puck roars and surges toward me, but a troop of satyrs and fauns shackle his arms. One of the fauns uses a staff, delivering a blow to the back of Puck's thighs. Cypress growls, struggling against his restraints as Puck's knees slam into the ground.

"Stop!" I scream. The nymph's foot lands on my profile, shoving my face into the dirt until I'm gagging. I hack and wriggle, wads of soil clotting my mouth. Any more of this, and she'll cut off my oxygen supply.

The Faeries grab Puck's hair by the roots and jerk him upright, forcing him to watch. The nymph's weight bears down on me while I paw and scratch at her limbs. As long as she's not fully inside the ring, it can't trap her. I grapple for her calves, hoping to either free myself or yank her into this snare with me, but her limbs have been molded from marble. She's too strong for me.

"Yes, I'm sure your prick was having fun," she tells Puck, indifferent to my scraping fingernails. "With your prowess, I imagine she was an enthusiastic conquest—a little human pleasure toy—and who can fault you there? However, you left out the part where this dalliance evolved. We're concerned your heart has gotten carried away. Poor timing, gorgeous."

"You can't rig the game like this," I cough out. "We made a bargain."

"You were still given the time you asked for," Tinder assures me, falling in line with Foxglove. "You just didn't make use of it."

Fables curse them! They glamoured me into this ring, where I slept through my deadline.

Except... Unfortunately for these lots, they're not the only culture skilled in twisting their words. I remember the phrasing of my deal, the verbiage I'd painstakingly strung together for the feast. "I didn't sleep through my time," I expel into the dirt. "At the feast, I asked for a week of my life—*my* life," I stress. "Not yours or anyone else's."

Three days had passed before I'd stumbled into this ring, and while three weeks might have lapsed for them, it has only been an additional three days for me. That means I have one day left.

A scheming grin wreathes across Puck's face. Cypress quits struggling. Tinder blinks, and Foxglove's foot eases from my profile. Anger crinkles the Faeries' features as they process this error.

"Fine," the nymph grumbles. "We'll wait it out. As for Puck, he can join you in the nest."

"Clever, indeed," Puck compliments, because the consequences of entering a Fae ring aren't exclusive to humans. It impacts the Folk as well, which is a crafty way for them to punish or trick one another.

"And what if I refuse?" the satyr asks.

Foxglove releases my face, so that I flop onto my back and suck up air. Calmly, she aims the bow at my heart. "Ask me that again," she dares him. "I promise, I'll have an answer for you."

"Such viciousness," Puck muses. "First, let's get my visceral response out of the way. Touch my woman again, and I'll peel the exfoliated flesh from your bones. As for my delayed response, here it is: Juniper's essential to our future, which means harming her is futile."

Correct. They can't restore their fauna and their world if I'm dead— not before the deal is honored and the game officially reaches its end. Suffocating me or planting an arrow in my chest isn't an option, and doing impermanent damage necessitates her getting inside the ring.

Therefore, she can't threaten my life in order to make sure Puck behaves himself. Getting him to cooperate simply won't work that way.

Foxglove blanches, her features torn as she considers her options. Whatever alternative she's weighing, a certain destitution compromises her features, which gives way to a pang of resignation. She nods with effort, flagging as if slathered in tar. "Okay."

Then she redirects her arrow to Cypress. And she shoots.

31

It happens in slow motion, then all at once. The arrow spears into the side of Cypress's torso, a fountain of blood spritzing the air. A terrible sound erupts from his mouth, his front hooves buckling from the impact. It's like watching a redwood capsize, his enormous body crashing to the forest floor.

I picture the centaur sitting across from me in a yurt, quizzing me about the various parts of a tree, inquiring which is the wisest part. I picture him handing me a book, honoring his favor. I picture him advising me shortly before I'd stepped into the Middle Moon Feast and his surveillance of Puck and me during the revels. I picture the centaur and me on the cusp of a tentative friendship.

A scream lodges in my throat. Puck makes enough noise for us both. He howls, wrestling with his captors. It takes half a dozen of them to overpower him.

The sorrow in his voice pierces the woodland, the source of which rings clear and harrowing. Not only is his best friend bleeding in the grass, but the nymph had targeted the centaur with the satyr's weapon. She shot Cypress with Puck's bow.

Several of the Faeries gawk, including Tinder, his orange eyes bloating from his face. Presumably, this hadn't been part of the plan. Yet they stand there, refusing to intercept. Without extracting the arrow puncturing Cypress's abdomen, the clan applies extra tethers to the centaur and hauls him away. A crimson brook follows in their wake, marking a path to wherever they're taking him.

I lack my archery, much less an artificial slingshot. My hands are empty, useless. So I grab the only thing in reaching distance—a broken branch from one of the tube trees, sturdy yet wieldy. Cove excels in fighting with a spear, her choice of weapon since we were children. My skill doesn't measure up to hers, but she did teach me a few things, such as where to aim.

I swing the bough and pummel the nymph off balance. She vaults forward and goes down faster than Cypress had, the staff clubbing her in the rump. With a shriek, Foxglove hits the grass in a pile of long limbs and yellow petals.

However, she's up and seething in my face before I can blink. Her arms fly, but I block the strike. She rushes at me, a whirlwind of fists and elbows. It takes everything I have to stay on my feet, thrusting and parrying the branch to thwart her complex sequence of punches. She tries to sideswipe me under my feet. I leap in place, then catch her in the shoulder. Now that she's concentrating, she barely budges, hardly flinches from the impact.

Puck unleashes a deranged string of Faeish. He thrashes, forcing an additional three Solitaries to shackle him. One of them shoves a gag into his mouth, plugging his shouts.

I switch tactics and bait Foxglove to come closer, to cross the Fae ring and get cozy with me. With their powers, any Fae should be able to overtake me in seconds. But their egos are defect—being too confident when pitted against a human must make them lazy. Moreover, Papa Thorne says an angry fighter is a sloppy fighter. I dodge Foxglove's moves, hoping such manipulation will frustrate her.

It does, but not enough. She jerks to the left, then doubles back, a bluff that costs me. The female snatches the branch and breaks it in half over her thigh.

Well. It was worth a try.

Because she had dropped the bow when Cypress went down, someone tosses the female her dagger. She catches it, flips it between her fingers, and tips it against my ear. I stall, gasping as she etches the rounded shape, so different from her pointed ear.

She regards me with fresh eyes. "I can see why he's smitten. You must be one hell of a quality fuck." The nymph glances over her shoulder toward Puck's livid gaze. One of the fauns unplugs the satyr's mouth, allowing a single word to punch from his lips. "Why?"

He's not asking why they would attack us. Fables eternal, their world is at stake. But why had it come to this? Why had Foxglove seen fit to target Cypress?

The nymph's gaze strays to the blood trail, a wince twitching in her face like a broken mechanism. Regret? Sadness? Weariness? A moment ago, I wouldn't have said the emotions would fit inside the margins of her countenance, yet they do now.

For all this violence, I don't think she had intended to hurt anyone. At least, she'd hoped otherwise.

"If you want us to provide a remedy for his wound, you'll get in the ring," she demands.

So that's why she'd done it. Yet Puck ignores the ultimatum. "That's not the whole answer."

Foxglove belts out a humorless, wounded laugh. "Before you met this human, what would you have done? If anyone of us had betrayed you like this." Quietly, she enunciates, "What would you have done, Puck?"

He doesn't answer. Everyone knows what he would have done, had another mortal stepped into this domain and beguiled another Fae.

Except I did come here, and we did reunite. Nothing is the same anymore. Not for any of us.

Foxglove nods to herself, the petals in her hair trembling. She holds the dagger to my heart, then gestures to one of the leprechauns who jabs an axe toward Puck.

"In you go," he says. "There's a good lad."

"Come now. You know better than to call me good," Puck remarks dryly.

I shake my head, imploring him not to. But he crosses the distance and steps into the ring with me.

It's midnight, an hour since they dragged Cypress away. Puck and I huddle on the grass, my back aligned with his chest, his limbs bracketing mine. My feet lean against his hooves, and my head rests on his shoulder.

All of the Faeries have disbanded, barring a handful of guards. The fauns, dryads, and leprechauns who had restrained Puck presently stalk the perimeter, keeping watch beyond the tube trees. Tinder has volunteered as well. Every once in a while, he glances our way, his brow corrugating.

I stare at that crimson trail raking through the woods and sense Puck doing the same. "Foxglove missed a vital organ," I whisper.

Of course, she had. Cypress had been a pawn. But in spite of the redundancy, I'd needed to say it for comfort.

The satyr nods. "If they've staunched the blood quickly enough, he'll survive."

"Then what will they do to him?"

Puck gives me the worst answer I could possibly hear, my least favorite answer of all time. "I don't know."

I clench my eyes shut. Cypress will be all right. We have to believe that.

My attention diverts to the mushrooms and tube trees. Puck folds his arms across my collarbones and interprets the silence. "Time is passing quicker for them, although it doesn't look that way. As to where we are, this is The Roots that Take."

"What do they take?"

"Depends on the visitor. Sometimes the earth takes away a Fae's anger or pain, on the condition the Fae never feels that emotion again. It's a hefty price. Sometimes Faeries come here to take something from one another, either in a bargain, a scrimmage, or a colossal hissy fit. I say, it's a pretty fitting location to plant a ring. Anything else you want to know?"

"Give me five minutes, and I'll have more for you."

But in truth, I'm unsure whether I can handle more information. Every minute we spend in this trap, time zips past us. What does that mean for my sisters? What does that mean for this game? Try as we might, neither of us has contrived a solution, a means to get out of this ring.

"By the way?" Puck says. "You forgot to take this with you."

He clamps a delicate object around my forearm. I gasp at the gold-plated bracelet adorned with leaves, the surface tarnished from age.

After that bath in The Wicked Pines, the nymphs had picked apart the band, divvying up the pieces. Yet the bracelet is intact, as if that had never happened. My shaky thumb sketches the bauble. "How?"

"I'd planned on giving it back while we were in bed, once we'd slept off the delights of fuckery," Puck says. "Early on, I caught the nymphs wearing snippets of your bracelet. Seems you bargained with them at some point, yeah? I thought so. Basically, I waited until they got tired of your offering, then made a deal—the bracelet pieces for several of my leather buckles. I told them I wanted the bits for a new pair of earrings. What can I say? I'm a sentimental sap."

I brush my mouth against Puck's knuckles to thank him.

"P.S.," he mumbles, shivering from my touch. "I met your feisty sister."

Lark! The name unfurls in my chest like a pair of wings. I twist, my pulse jackhammering. "You met her?" Then I shove him. "Why didn't you tell me?"

"I'm telling you now. I couldn't for the last hour, with our audience too close and both of us recovering from the brawl."

The floodgates open. I whirl from Puck's arms and face him. "Where is she? Where did you see her? Is she all right? If you saw her alive, does that mean she won? Or is she still playing her game? Why aren't you answering me?"

He frames my face. "Prepare yourself. Are you sitting?"

Does he ever stop making jokes? I glower but wait.

Puck gets serious. He assures me Lark's perfectly hale and hearty, then recounts her sojourn in The Solitary Mountain. Puck hadn't known the details before, but Lark's game had ended while he was searching for me. As such, the news had reached the forest valley.

Lark had been tasked to solve a mountain labyrinth. And she had won!

My relief morphs into confusion at the next part of this tale. "It appears your sister and my brother found time to fall in love while she traipsed through the labyrinth," Puck says. "But wait for it: They're also mates."

My jaw unhinges the instant that odious word tumbles from his mouth. "What?" I demand. "What do you mean, they're mates?"

I stare at him, awaiting the punchline. When it doesn't come, a pang of betrayal cleaves through me.

No way. There's no feasible way. Lark is impulsive and has a penchant for male company, but my sisters and I had sworn never to turn our backs on one another. She wouldn't consort with the ruler of the sky.

"She would never do that to me and Cove," I insist.

Puck arches his brow. "Would she say that about you?"

I fall silent. He's right. Of all of us, Lark and Cove would brand me the least likely to do what I've done with Puck. Lark doesn't know that story yet, just like I don't know hers. If I jump to conclusions, what does that say about the bond between me and my sisters? What does that say about our trust in each other?

I can't let this news destroy that. If I know my sister at all, I should know nothing will ever come between us. We won't let it.

In any event, the union between the Lark and Cerulean had spread. Puck tells me about The Wild Peak—the one that had soared past the other promontories. He tells me how being Cerulean's mate has rendered Lark immune to the Faeries' retribution. It has given her a power she hadn't had before.

Moreover, Lark and Cerulean's bond has granted them an extended life together, the midpoint between a short lifespan and immortality. As such, they've dedicated themselves to campaigning for a truce between humans and Faeries. Since the game's end, they have vowed to find an alternative to sacrificing mortals, one that will nevertheless ensure the Folk's survival.

So far, they've been hard-pressed to rally support outside of a handful of Solitaries, but that hasn't stopped them. They've become quite the renegade pair.

Pride wells inside me. Now that's the Lark I know.

Yesterday, Puck had cornered Lark near The Faerie Triad. At that point, it had been three weeks, and Puck still didn't know where I was. He'd taken a chance, approaching Lark in case she had information on my whereabouts.

However, with his kin in the vicinity and potentially eavesdropping, Puck couldn't outright tell Lark the truth—that I was missing. As much as he'd wanted to, the satyr had to be tactful, to see if Lark showed the remotest sign of knowing where I was.

This hadn't been easy, since my sister openly hated him on sight. He'd decided to play off that, riling her up in order to loosen her tongue. Puck riddled his words, made her think I was still his enemy, a performance that would satiate any onlookers hiding in the shadows. Because by then, Puck had understood his kin were leery. By then, he'd suspected my disappearance likely had something to do with them.

But first, he'd needed to rule out Lark as a possibility. Unbeknownst to my sister, her profanities and threats to slay Puck if he hurt me proved Lark didn't know where I was.

So Puck had kept searching. Shortly after, he'd found me in this spot.

The link between Lark and Cerulean has insulted the mountain Solitaries. As for the inhabitants here, news of the bond alarmed the woodland Folk, heightening their budding skepticism about Puck and me. Hence, their actions tonight.

"You want my guess?" Puck asks. "Naturally, you do. My guess is your sister and my brother have been conspiring as we speak, searching for an outlet that will enable them to come here and save you, all without jeopardizing the rules of this hunt and, thus—"

"Endangering me further," I fill in.

"My heart-to-heart with your sister must have inflamed the love birds. But being of the mountain, they don't know the actual game or what its rules are, which means they have no clue what they're dealing with yet, much less what my motives are. I'm known to be a tad unpredictable."

"Where did anyone get that idea?" I quip, fatigued. "Puck?"

"Luv?"

"I like that you're unpredictable." I might not get the chance to tell my sisters one more time how I feel about them. But I can tell him. "I like you a lot," I whisper, tracking my fingers across his jaw.

He leans into the touch. "I like you, too," he admits. "No Fae touches like this."

I remember the last time we'd exchanged this sentiment, and a tiny grin steals across my face. "But I do."

"That, you do. Always, you've exceeded my expectations. I couldn't have stayed away from you if I tried. And I did, trust me. But when I was a lad, I beheld the most captivating of sights—you with sticks and leaves in your hair, with round cheeks and rounder ears, with wide-set eyes and a smoky voice the likes of which I'd never heard before. If I hadn't already been snared on the ground, seeing you would have done me in, knocked me on my perky ass." Puck holds my gaze. "Every time you spoke, you took my fucking breath away."

"No satyr talks like this," I muster.

"But I do." His lips find the space between my brows. "Just don't tell anyone, or you'll ruin my reputation."

When I stammer out a laugh, he points at me. "That, right there. The weight of your hand in mine, or your lips on mine? Those are my favorite feelings. The sight of you happy or about to come around me? Those are my favorite sights. But hearing you laugh? That's my favorite sound. When we were striplings, I made it my life's mission to get a chuckle out of you—a challenge, if there ever was one. Every time I succeeded, it intoxicated me. I adored your laugh as much as I relished your scowl. Greedy Fae that I was, I wanted both of them. You were so familiar and strange, like I really saw you but hadn't yet seen everything."

"That makes no sense," I breathe against his chin. "Puck?"

"Luv?"

But I don't say anything, because I can't say anything. That last bit he'd just imparted is a harness roping around my throat, my heart, my everything. Back then, he had seen many things about me, but he hadn't seen everything.

He still hasn't. And I'm tired of him not knowing.

I take Puck's hand and slide it to my lower back, slipping his palm under my sweater. When I reach the tattoo, I settle us there. Although the marking has no texture to humans, his face transforms from quizzical to skeptical. The tips of his fingers traipse across the X of crossbow bolts, his Fae senses kicking in, somehow attuning themselves to the presence of ink.

His eyes narrow, then widen. The rest of his features follow, slackening. "You're a..."

"Was," I correct. "I was."

The Faeries standing post have traversed farther into the tube trunks. They're gabbing, perhaps out of boredom. The distance isn't sufficient enough for us to speak freely, but it is enough to protect our whispers.

Yet no matter how hard I try to bolster myself, my voice comes out tissue-thin. "I was a trade poacher before we met."

Puck gawks, his pupils jumping all over my face like a skipping stone. Then his visage crimps into fury. "What happened? Who did it to you?"

So, I tell him. My birth parents had given me up when I was an infant, and I was passed from home to home for the first six years of my life. Then one day, the family presently hosting me surrendered the responsibility and dumped me in a carriage headed for a workhouse in some far-off town.

I'd scurried out of the vehicle and into the forest. Eventually, a trade poaching gang caught me snaring an animal and saw an opportunity. I tell Puck about the years I spent with them, how they taught me to use a crossbow but forced me to exercise it in a way I hadn't expected. I tell him it was either that or starve, or worse—and *worse* had hurt a great deal. Sometimes they'd twisted my arm or pulled on one of my canines until it felt like the tooth would rip from my gums. But mostly, the threats were enough to scare me. They didn't have to do much more.

I recall cackles slipping through the cracks of stained teeth. I recall orders spitting from a chapped mouth and the burlap texture of one male's voice. I recall another set of eyes, the shade of a bruise.

I recall their tattoos—the same poacher marking that taints my lower back. I tell Puck about the last time I targeted a creature for them and how she'd had cubs with her. I hadn't been able to go through with it, so one of the men had done it instead.

That's when I'd screamed. That's when my scream had turned into a roar. And that's when I quit.

While the poachers had slept at our camp that night, I'd swiped the necessary provisions and bagged the animal. Then I went searching for the cubs and found them in their burrow. Together, we buried their mother.

I had stayed with them all night. The next morning, others from their pack came sniffing. To my relief, they didn't reject the cubs, and I was able to leave them without worrying.

I'd stumbled through the wild for a few days until coming upon a house in the woods, just outside Reverie Hollow's square. I took shelter on the property, inside an old wagon parked beneath a willow tree.

By sunrise, I awoke to the sight of a little girl my age, kneeling and staring down at me through a cloud of white hair. "Who the hell are you?" she'd chirped.

Those had been her first words to me. And because I would never let anyone look down on me again, I'd sat up, brushed a twig from my hair, and rolled my dignified shoulders. "I can spell seven words."

Those had been my first boastful sentence to her. To which, she'd thrown back her head and hooted, then called out, "Papa! Can I have a sister?"

After that, I became part of a family. But I never forgot what I'd done for those men. I've since rescued hundreds of animals with my sisters, but it hasn't atoned for the creatures I took down before that, the ones targeted for their pelts and claws, the rest of their carcasses left to decay.

I tell Puck all of this.

He's quiet for longer than I'd thought him capable. "Look at me, luv."

"I can't," I mutter around a congested throat. *I can't.*

"Yes, you can," he says. "You can do any fucking thing. I've seen that."

"I can't—"

"Juniper." He frames my cheeks. "It wasn't your fault."

My face crumples. And I cry. The sobs wrack my form, quite tears pouring out between us.

"Ah, luv." Puck holds me fast. "You were a wee sapling, and those men were a bunch of fuckwits. They gave you no choice. You had to survive."

"I h-hurt them," I choke out. "I h-hurt them all. The w-way they c-cried out from the b-bolts. The sounds they m-made in the tr-traps."

Other memories surface—delivering animal parts to the highest bidder, to homes where fauna heads had decorated the halls, to manors where ligaments had been displayed in glass cases. Those people had shown no interest in meat or furs. They hadn't paid us to reduce the overpopulation in forests, so that other species could share the wild.

Rather, they'd wanted decorations for their parlors and embellishments for their carriages. They had wanted to make fashion statements and show off their wealth. I had given that to them.

Puck's hushed words reach my ears. "But then what happened? How does this story continue?"

"I left," I say.

"And what happened after you left?"

I found a family, so I'd never be alone again. I learned to read and write, so I'd never starve again, never be desperate again. I studied the Fables, to ensure I never underestimated an enemy again, never felt inferior again. I saved animals, so that I'd never regret my actions again.

Never again.

The satyr thumbs my tears, and our foreheads meet. We stay like this, my breaths growing steadier as the seconds tick by.

By contrast, his grow haggard. "Fables and fuck. That's why the forest chose this hunt. It knows your fear."

It does. But now that I've drained myself of that fear, a new thought dawns on me. Magic got us in here, but it can't get us out.

No. This is going to take human skill.

"If it knows my fear, the woodland also knows my strengths," I conclude. To emphasize, my eyes click over to where the Faeries stand vigil.

Puck contemplates that. "Are you thinking what I'm thinking?"

"The odds are sound. I am a know-it-all."

After a moment of silent communication, a grin slides across his face. "Sounds like a merry plan."

32

Our heads jerk toward the best candidate with whom to engage. This whole time, Tinder has been stealing glances at us, his gaze torn between resentful and wounded. While spying on him and Puck by the elm trees, I'd noted that the youth had looked up to the satyr.

Taking the direction of Puck's gaze into account, I know he has drawn the same conclusion. Across the tube trees, he catches Tinder's eye. The satyr and youth had been close until now. Perhaps not as close as Puck and Cypress, but close enough that guilt pinches the young one's face. He may not have liked the centaur, but I don't think Tinder had wanted to hurt Cypress. I don't think Tinder likes hurting Puck, either.

"Wait for it," Puck says to me.

On cue, Tinder marches in our direction. As the Fae approaches, the satyr turns my way. "Let me speak first?"

I nod, recognizing the culpability in his voice. He cares about Tinder.

We swivel as the youth crouches in front of us, a froth of black curls framing his jaded features. Tinder's the very picture of disillusioned hero worship. But because he maintains a righteous sneer that doesn't match the fragility in his eyes, it's hard to tell whether he wants an apology for Puck's treachery, or if he wants to apologize for betraying Puck in turn.

"Ready to grovel yet?" Tinder asks.

"Come now, luv," Puck says. "I'm hardly dressed for groveling."

"Then what are you staring at?"

"A friend."

The male sniffs in a belligerent, you'll-have-to-do-better-than-that manner. "You're only saying this because you want out of the ring."

"Sure, that'd be nice. I do want out of this ring, but that's not why I'm saying it. I don't loan my longbow to just anyone."

The youth winces, his eyes flashing with hurt. To bolster himself, he crosses his arms, not sparing me a glance. "Then why her? Why her over the rest of us?"

"Now who said anything about me taking sides? Can't a satyr have his cake and eat it, too? Maybe I want both parties to win, and maybe this is the way to do it. But if you're asking why I adore her in the first place, that's a long Fable. Have you got time?"

"More time than you two," Tinder affirms, his obstinate expression testifying that he's unwilling to be convinced.

"Marvelous," Pucks says, patting the ground. "Get comfortable."

The youth doesn't get comfortable, but he does listen as Puck tells him our story, how we met as children. Tinder's expression thaws little by little, like pebbles loosening from a rocky facade. It reminds me how stories can change one's perspective, how they can make a person see the same scenario from a new angle. If the tale finds the right audience and strikes true, it can inspire empathy or even change.

What I hadn't expected was for such a tale to influence a Fae. Yet when Puck finishes, the youth's eyes have mellowed from simmering orange to ripe persimmon.

"Choosing Juniper was inevitable for me," Puck dares to say. "You might accuse me of being mad for her, aptly wooed indeed, but here's the thing: It doesn't lessen the way I feel about this world or you. Do you seriously think I would forsake that? Do you think I've stopped fighting for that? Have you forgotten how clever I am? Remember, there's another way to preserve this world, without anyone from her side having to die. That's what this bargain is about."

Tinder glances at the other Faeries who have noticed our huddle. He turns back. "I'll let you out," he says to Puck, then cuffs his head toward me. "But not her."

This is hardly a surprise to either of us. As much as he'd appreciated the story about Puck and me, we can't expect an abrupt transformation.

A seed has been planted. That's all for now.

Thus, I take my cue. "Then we'll play a game for your help. A guessing game, involving trivia." I lean forward, resting my elbows on my knees. "You ask me a question about your world, and I'll ask you a question about mine. The one who takes the longest to answer loses. If I win, you let me out with Puck."

The youth snorts. "I've already got you where I want you. Why would I play? What do I get out of it?"

Also, expected. "In addition to my staying in here? Fair point. What would you like? Name your trophy."

Temptation alights his face. He won't risk his world or his survival, but his problem is the same one all Faeries have: He doesn't believe I'm a formidable opponent. Additionally, he's going to make sure the price is something that protects this land, should I happen to win by sheer luck.

His comrades start toward us, sensing trouble. The youth needs to accept this match before they get here, otherwise it won't be set in stone.

He glances between Puck and me, then makes his request. "You choose the next human."

I force myself to keep a straight face. If I fail at this match, I'll have to select the next mortal who gets sucked into this world, into a game tailored for them by the forest. Whether I free myself or burn, I'll carry that weight on my conscience.

Puck opens his mouth. Tinder and I move in unison, clapping our palms over his lips while taking one another's measure.

"Deal," I say, pearls of sweat beading in my armpits.

"What's going on?" a leprechaun grumbles when the clan approaches.

We release Puck's mouth, allowing him to get cheeky. He gloats, casually revealing the most recent events, to which the Faeries curse and bark at the youth. Again to his credit, Tinder seems unruffled, his confidence buoyed in front of the satyr.

Nonetheless, they gather around and rub their hands as if this is a baiting ring and they're about to place bets. That they capitulate so quickly is rather comical, making the satyr's lips quirk with irony.

Faeries. I'll grant, they're consistent.

They agree to keep tabs on the time, alongside Puck. Each of them vows explicit honesty, void of duplicity.

"Ask away," I invite, because there's no way I'm going first.

The youth deliberates. "What is Puck's name?"

Damnation. Once more, I keep my features in check. I had counted on trivia, but his question veers off that default path.

Puck draws in the slightest intake of breath. I sense his impending panic, his desire to warn me through a hand gesture or a covert glance, which would constitute as cheating.

We mustn't do that. Besides, I know what he'll say: It's a trick question.

Tinder isn't asking for the obvious. The canon about humans possessing a Fae's true name and having power over them applies to fellow Solitaries as well. That's what this is about.

It's an impossible question to answer. If I know and share Puck's true name with Tinder, the youth will acquire power over the satyr. But if I don't know the name, not only will I lose, but it will serve as a belittling reminder that I'll never know Puck fully.

Under benevolent circumstances, the satyr might be impressed. This inquiry attacks from multiple angles, backing its recipient into a corner. Tinder might be busy idolizing and impersonating Puck, but someday he won't have to. He's intrepid enough on his own.

All the same, ambition sits unsteadily on Tinder's face. He's taking this risk not because he wants to preside over anyone. I think he wants to validate himself in front of Puck. I think Tinder's close enough to the satyr to conclude he wouldn't share this information freely with me. I think the youth's certain I have no clue what the answer is. I think he wouldn't have gambled otherwise.

But if Tinder is betting on a sensitive female, he hasn't been paying attention. I understand why the satyr hasn't revealed his moniker to me. And in my eyes, he's always been just Puck. That's all I need him to be.

Soon enough, I sense Puck rationalizing this, his muscles unwinding.

Not long ago, I would have felt degraded by this exchange. But now, I feel the merit of my answer. I tell them, "I don't know."

The Faeries gnash their teeth, and Tinder's face falls, all of them disappointed by the lack of drama and my swift response.

My turn. I hadn't known what to ask, but it comes to me while recalling those initial days in which I'd reminded Puck that he doesn't know me, that none of them do. Sometimes, the simplest questions are the hardest to answer.

I ask, "What is it like to be human?"

Tinder's eyes widen into saucers. He twiddles his thumbs and thinks, thinks, thinks. It's not a trick question, but it's not an easy one. At the very least, he would have to know a human as a friend, not as an enemy.

After quite a while, his nose twitches in annoyance. "I don't know."

Technically, it's an answer. Despite the Faeries keeping time, it's clear he had taken much longer to reply.

A moment of silence ensues. Puck grabs my hand and squeezes it. Rather than a gesture of pride, it's a cautionary touch. Although our captors must honor the deal and let us out, they possess weapons. We don't.

Puck and I rise. I glance at the tube trees, checking the perimeter while Puck levels his gaze with the Faeries.

"Fine," the leprechaun snarls around the copper stubble of his jaw. "Go ahead. Leave."

Tinder's features spasm with indecision, his fingers faltering over the throwing stars. Pity and compassion well in my chest. He's no different from a human boy, one who reveres the satyr yet has a world of peers hovering at his back.

Puck gives him an understanding look. "Not to worry, luv. Just remember what I said amongst the elms—what I told you about the foxes and the elks. Heed that, and you'll do fine."

The Fae swallows and nods. The others spread out.

My elbow taps Puck's. We swap a quick glance—a quick plan—then we spring forward. I dive across the ground and roll through a dryad's tall limbs. With the heel of my boot, I thwack his lower spine and send him careening into a tumbleweed. In my periphery, I catch Puck delivering a sequence of punches and kicks that take down the rest.

The youth skitters backward, a throwing star in his grip. I spare him the burden of having to choose and swipe my leg under his feet. Tinder smacks into the earth, and I lean over him. "Stay down."

They won't notice if they think he's knocked out. After that, it's up to him whether to pursue us.

He gawks at me, stupefied. I lurch up as Puck seizes my hand and hauls me into the trees. We barrel between the trunks while livid voices holler behind us.

A mile later, we jump over a winding creek. The shouting fades, and conifers usurp the tube trees. Based on the needles growing in single limbs rather than clusters, I gauge them to be fir trees. We vault into a clearing and then jog to a halt, pinecones shivering around us.

Puck hoists me off the grass. He snickers and twirls me in a circle, as if we've emerged victorious. "That's my woman," he cheers, planting a swift but hard kiss to my lips. "Giving them as good as they gave. I knew you were smart, but that question damn near castrated them."

"Puck," I gasp. "They're coming."

"Ugh." He sets me down and heads for the nearest tree.

I waver in place. I want to ask what the plan is now. I want to ask where Cypress is being held and where our weapons have been taken. I want to ask why in Fables Puck is going near that tree!

But anxiety thrums in my veins, because I know exactly what he's doing and what he intends. For a while, I'd forgotten. Now that we're free, reality comes rushing back.

"Puck," I spurt. "Puck, wait."

"I'd be delighted to, but there's no time for a quickie." He kneels, reaching for one of the trunk bases. "Faeries can only transport themselves, so I can't evanesce us both out of here. If we want to keep ahead of the posse, we need to hitch a ride."

"Don't call her," I plead. "She shouldn't—"

"Don't worry, she'll come. The Gang of Elks isn't her terrain, but she'll travel quicker than we will on foot. I'd summon an elk, but they're an unpredictable bunch, with all their unpredictable elkish ways. Better if I call out to Sylvan."

"Puck," I snap. "Please, stop. Puck!"

He swings around, exasperated, peeved. "What?"

"I have to target her!"

The words fire out of me, shooting into the cloister of trees. Fir needles shake, as though my outburst has shocked them. Perhaps I've shocked myself, too. Somehow, speaking the truth makes it more final. I can't take it back.

Puck goes rigid. He peers at me, stumped. His confused expression reminds me of when we were children, when I tended to his injury and later, when we stood on opposite sides of a field, separated by the carnage of Faeries and fauna. During those last hellish moments, he'd looked at me with such raw disorientation. He looks at me that way now.

Then it sinks in. He staggers upright, his hooves tilting off balance. I've left him speechless several times, but not like this.

"The first task. I solved it," I say, rushing to get it over with. "You can't hunt an animal that's—"

"No." He shakes his head. "No."

"You can't hunt one that's—"

"No, Juniper."

"That's right in front of you." The answer ends on a dry sob. "We rode out to view The Wild Peak. I stumbled into her footprint, and then I looked up, and…and I knew." My voice cracks. "And there she was."

I could have sought out another animal in the vicinity, but there had been none. My gaze had floundered. It had landed upon Sylvan at the moment of realization, and I hadn't been able to turn away.

The color drains from Puck's face, a sickly pale green splotching his complexion. The bulb in his throat bobs, however nothing comes out. Nothing but a guttural noise.

The satyr collapses, his knees hitting the carpet of pine needles. He hunches over and clamps on to his thighs, his fingers clenching, his knuckles bleeding from the fight we'd left behind. I dart over to him and drop by his side, threading his digits with mine.

He's in danger of losing his world. He might lose Cypress, if he hasn't already. He will lose Sylvan, if I'm to win.

Any human would say it serves him right, that it's the least of what he deserves. This Fae has done horrifying things to my people. He and his brothers had separated me and my sisters, then dumped me into this hunt.

Yet I've forgiven him. Not long ago, I would have cited Papa Thorne's mercy and Cove's compassion as having an influence on me.

Now it's more. Puck's more. We're more.

I want to say I won't do it. Instead, I bend my forehead and rest it against his. Oxygen grates from his mouth, beating onto my lips.

My palms grow clammy. The rules are indisputable: I have to take action on the animal's life. I think about aiming my crossbow once I've recovered it. I think about taking that shot. The forest knows what I fear. It knows *I can't.*

It also knows I have to. For my sisters, I have to.

"Breathe," I instruct. "Breathe."

I repeat this mantra, pacing it until both of our heartbeats slow down. Puck's fingers crawl over to mine. He welds us together, sealing our hands into fists.

"We'll figure it out," he says.

It's not enough to convince me. We haven't deciphered how to win on equal sides. All the same, I force myself to nod and echo, "We will."

There has to be a way out of this, to win this game without either of us losing, to unravel the scribe's message, to find that second way of fortifying this land. It's the first and foremost step to a peaceful future between our worlds.

We're a fierce couple. More than that, we're a smart one.

All the same, his eyes tremble, and my mouth trembles. Because part of him knows, and part of me knows, there's a greater chance we'll fail.

"Don't call her yet," I say.

Fear stalks across Puck's countenance. His reaction says enough. I'd blurted out the truth too late.

She's on her way. And she's not the only one.

The ground rumbles as it had during The Wild Peak. Except this quake vibrates toward us, not toward the sky, produced by dozens of pounding feet and stomping hooves.

We lurch off the ground. The fir trees writhe, shedding pinecones.

A pair of antlers crops up through the creepers, the crown's serrated rims thwacking branches out of the way. Then another pair of spokes appears, and another, and another.

Bows twang. Blades and axes flash. Staffs and hammers club the foliage.

Puck had called this place The Gang of Elks.

A legion of Faeries charge in our direction, including Foxglove and the troop who'd guarded us in the Fae ring. Half of the attackers are mounted on giants—elks that have shifted to twice their usual size.

The satyr and I reel, catapulting into the firs. One of the riders—a faun—breaks from onslaught and wallops in our direction until he's parallel to us. Raising his arms, he aims a throwing star and targets my throat.

Puck leaps to get in front of me, but another flying object beats him to it. A thin spear-like projectile whizzes through the air, plummeting from the sky and stabbing the ground.

We skid in place. The javelin startles the rider, who loses his grip on the elk's reins. Then another weapon whisks from overhead—one that I recognize. The golden whip snaps, catching the assailant's weapon and knocking it into the trees.

At which point, a feisty, feminine voice growls, "Get the fuck away from my sister!"

33

My heart stops. It stops along with everything else, every sound, every movement. Time goes still, the world suspending itself. A winged silhouette dives from the sky—a nightingale the size of a dragon, its wingspan threatening to decapitate the trees.

I see her. Astride the nightingale, a female figure brandishes her whip. She twirls the golden cord into a loop above her head, whisking it into the air.

Lark.

With another lash, my sister's weapon snares a leprechaun's waist and yanks him off a charging elk. The nightingale veers, twisting vertically and slipping between two trunks. Righting itself, the bird careens downward and prepares to land.

Lark doesn't wait. Midflight, she swings her legs off the bird's back and plunges to the forest floor. At the same time, the nightingale shrinks, its body reducing to the girth of a falcon.

My sister lands with a thud, her ankle boots walloping the ground, a storm of white hair gusting around her face. She wears a slate gray dress that buffets her limbs like a gale, with feathers ornamenting the short sleeves. Frantically, she casts about, searching among the drove.

Is this a farce? Have one of the Fae enchanted me?

Her eyes stumble across mine and freeze. The instant those irises flash like silver coins, flaring with recognition, I know she's real. And she knows I'm real.

Time resumes, along with the fight. Faeries fling themselves off the incoming elks and whip out weapons. It's a smaller mob than I had originally thought, but it's sufficient to outnumber us.

A dryad pounces on Puck. The satyr rotates out of the Fae's chokehold, his arms thwarting the dryad's staff. They battle with inhuman speed, delivering blows too fast for me to monitor.

It's over in a matter of seconds. By that time, the dryad's bleeding on the ground, and Puck tosses me the staff. "I've got you," he says. "Go!"

When I swing back to Lark, love floods my being. We break from our stance and sprint ahead. She and I battle our way toward one another, exchanging blows with Faeries, dodging their fists and evading their claws. Relieved of their riders, the elks pound off into the fir trees.

Puck covers me, opening a path for me to travel. He swipes the axe that had tumbled from the leprechaun's grip when Lark unsaddled that Fae. Flipping the weapon in his hands, he barrels in front of me and collides with a pair fauns. He head-butts one of them and rams the axe handle into the other's stomach.

Lark executes a deft series of flicks, slashing her whip across necks and limbs. Using both ends of the cord, she corrals two nymphs and gives a sharp jerk, hammering them into one another. Their heads crack together, and they fall just as Lark leaps over them and jockeys my way.

The staff's heavy, bulky. I manage to avoid the attackers, mainly out of reflex, ducking and dodging like a slippery critter.

A petal dress materializes in my periphery. I swerve to evade Foxglove's dagger and spin behind her, clubbing the staff against the backs of her knees. The collision rattles my teeth. With a yelp, Foxglove topples over, but my luck won't detain her for long.

I accelerate my pace, but too many Faeries pack the clearing. And they're too strong, too quick.

So quick that a centaur snatches me from behind. For a foolish instant, I mistake the equine for Cypress. However, the arms are thinner and lack his dark complexion.

Lark squawks as the female centaur hauls me off the ground—then drops me again. With a grunt, I hit the grass. Batting the layers of green hair from my face, I gawk as an invisible force knocks the centaur off her limbs and hurls her into a trunk. It's as if a cyclone had catapulted the female off the ground.

Overhead, a shadow passes. A masculine figure dives from the sky, mantles of midnight blue plumage splaying on either side of him. He plunges headfirst, then swoops at the last moment and snatches a javelin from the soil—the weapon I'd seen earlier, flying out of nowhere and impaling the earth. It must belong to this...this...who is he?

The male slingshots, circling above the quagmire in a flurry of billowing clothes and windswept blue-black hair that matches the dark pigment of his lips. He catches sight of Lark, and his eyes suffuse with protectiveness.

Oh. That's who he is.

Cerulean. Ruler of the sky.

He lands beside Lark and joins the fray. Like Puck, he throws down anyone who blocks her path to me.

Lark and Cerulean's lips move, exchanging words I can't hear. Based on their expressions, it's something snarky from her, something elegant from him.

So much happens at once. Too much happens.

Another smaller Fae flutters into the scene, topaz eyes flashing in her spunky face. Her diminutive, papery wings fan and whirl, slapping Faeries out of the way while her runty fists do the rest.

Lark's nightingale companion bares its talons against several leprechauns, shredding their burly forms. Meanwhile, another raptor appears from the heavens, a great owl with tufted horns and a single aquamarine eye. With a cavernous hoot, it plucks Foxglove off the ground. The airborne nymph, who'd gained her feet and been homing in on me, shrieks as the owl zooms into the wild, conveying her to who-knows-where.

Another centaur skulks into the thicket. He cranes his moss-green arm and targets a figure with scalding red hair.

No! I skid in place, my heart vaulting into my throat. I open my mouth to yell Puck's name—and out comes a volcanic roar. But it doesn't erupt from me.

An outline gallops into the clearing, leaving fir trees shuddering in his wake. The incoming figure charges, his face a mask of fury.

Cypress. A sash of bandages speckled in blood encases his torso, and his dark skin has lost its richness, but he's alive. He's alive and here.

He nocks his bow, the arrow's plume glowing like a beacon. With a twang, the projectile rends through the branches and lodges in the other centaur's hindquarters. The Fae buckles and crashes to the ground.

Puck pivots and registers what just happened. His gaze leaps toward Cypress, who merely stares back with a raw, uncensored look I can't place.

Puck sees it as well. His features twitch, then a grin races across the satyr's face. "It's about fucking time," he drawls while combating a dryad, then flings a comment across the divide toward Cerulean. "That goes for you, too."

The ruler of the sky tsks. "Call me fashionably late, brother. It has a loftier ring to it."

The scrimmage thins out. The last of the Faeries evacuate, collecting their injured company on the way out.

At length, silence descends. With my route unhampered, the vision of white hair lights a match beneath my feet. Lark runs like the wind, and I match her pace like a brush fire. The distance narrows, narrows, narrows.

Under the vicious stars, we drop our weapons and smash into one another. With cries, or bellows, or both, my sister and I collide, roping our arms around each other. I inhale the fragrances of rain and crisp morning air as we cling to one another, on the verge of crumbling to the floor. One of us whimpers, but I'm not sure who.

"Juniper," Lark gasps.

"Lark," I say.

Lark leans back to plant kisses all over my face, as she always does to annoy me. I'm not the mushy or precious type, not like a certain older sister who isn't here. But right now, nothing in this world compares to the sight of Lark puckering her lips to smother me.

We clasp one another's cheeks. We're grimy and threadbare, with lacerations marring our skin. And we smile and sniffle through it all.

Movement behind me seizes Lark's attention. Recognition and rage blasts across her face like a tempest. She sidesteps me and bolts toward Puck, who's a vision of torn leather buckles, a cracked antler, and an inappropriate smirk.

Belatedly, I catch my sister, strapping my arms around her midriff while she flails. "You son of a bitch!" Lark squawks. "Stay away from her, or so help me, I will end you!"

"Lark." I stagger in front, gripping her shoulders. "Lark, stop."

"Try it." She points over my shoulder. "Just try it, and I'll have your nuts strapped in my whip."

"Lark!" I grab her face. "It's all right. He's on our side."

"What the hell?" She calms down, gaping at me like I've grown horns. "Him?"

"Yes. Him," I say, giving her a sibling-worthy look.

As the meaning takes root, quiet permeates the weald. Finally, Lark's countenance morphs into shock. "You've got to be shitting me."

I shake my head, because when have I ever not meant what I've said to her?

It takes my sister a while to get her bearings. She dumps her fists on her hips and regards me with adoration and bafflement. Then she scoffs at Puck. "Quit grinning like an asshole. Don't go thinking this gets you off the hook. One word from Juniper, and I'll make good on your nuts."

"Believe me, luv," Puck vows. "Your sister's already got the monopoly on those merry nuts."

"Be very careful." In one hand, Cerulean twirls his javelin with deliberate slowness. "Call my mate 'luv' again, and I'll help her string you up."

"Such affection." Puck winks at his brother. "Enough pleasantries. Tell me how much you've missed me."

Cerulean's javelin halts midrotation. He huffs with mirth and responds in Faeish, whatever he says widening Puck's smirk.

Lark pinches my elbow. "You've got explaining to do, hussy."

That's going to be a long story. I nudge my head toward the masculine source of my sister's own indiscretion. "That makes two of us."

Her face knits, transforming from irate to sheepish.

Cerulean's wings have retracted and disappeared. He steps nearer, a tall specimen in loose linen clothing and a long coat that buffets the wind. His hair and lips are the color of a midnight sky, and despite the Fae's shorter shag of layers, a single braid dangles longer, falling into the plunging V of his neckline. Lastly, a set of golden plume caps adorn the tips of his ears.

317

I'll grant, it's no wonder Lark went rogue with him. Cerulean's just her type—male and pretty.

It strikes me that he hadn't moved to stop Lark from charging at the satyr. He'd simply stood by while she took the initiative, as if he'd known better. Or rather, because he knows Lark's choices are her own, and he's not about to change that, especially since they'd both suspected Puck of treachery.

Lark's mate speaks to me with an eloquent slope to his accent. "We haven't been introduced. Call me Cerulean."

"Juniper," I return before my sister can rectify the situation.

"A sharp tree, indeed," he interprets. "At some point, let's get better acquainted, shall we? Say, when my glorious mate isn't eager to castrate your lover?"

"Agreed."

Although I'd like to start the conversation now, we have other pressing matters. And yes, my sister needs to calm down. Plus, I wager she's hungry. She's insufferably cranky when she's hungry.

Puck swaggers up behind me, enveloping me in his warmth. A lump buds in my throat. Suddenly, appropriately, I'm overwhelmed. He must know, because his chest flanks my back, bolstering me as I lean into him.

He's alive. Lark's alive. They're in one piece.

We all are, for the time being.

From the sidelines, Cypress averts his gaze and makes a show of harnessing his archery. I'm about to spring his way and startle him with a hug, but Lark's mate cuts off the impulse.

"By the way, you'll have to excuse our tardiness," Cerulean says. "Brawls are so inconvenient, always occurring at random."

"Speaking of which," Puck interjects. "How did you know? I didn't call out to you."

I swing my head between them. "Then who did?"

"That was me," a female voice chirps from her perch on a tree branch.

That scanty Fae with the papery moth wings sits among the fir needles and pinecones, her limbs swinging back and forth. Her topaz eyes sparkle, the vibrant hue matching the finely spun nest of hair piled atop her head. She wears a gauzy gown as pale as her complexion. For what it's worth, the pint-sized female looks to be Tinder's age or a bit younger.

"Ah, if it isn't Moth of the Cantankerous Committee," Puck says. "Charmed to see you."

Her head swats in the satyr's direction. "If it isn't Puck of the Prick Brigade. I thought I smelled something toxic."

"Actually, that would be my charisma. It emits a sexy but dangerous incense. Didn't anyone-who's-anyone warn you of its addictive properties?"

The Fae named Moth holds up a snooty palm, blocking out Puck while she addresses Cerulean. "If I have to join forces with a satyr, I'll want my dignity back when this is over."

"Mountain Faeries," Puck sniggers. "Those soaring elevations really do inflate your heads."

Moth gives him a phony smile. "Forest Faeries. Playing in the dirt really does turn you into heathens."

Cerulean rolls his eyes. "Moth, my childhood friend and sibling-at-heart." He loops his arm between the sprite and me. "Juniper, Lark's huntress sister."

The wee one bounces her head toward me. "Oh, yay. Now there's two of you."

I match her dour expression with an upright one of my own. "Soon to be three."

To which the female lifts an impressed eyebrow. "So you're not as obnoxious, crass, or snarky as your sibling? I just might like you."

"I just might approve of you," I reply, somewhat congenially. "Once you acknowledge my sister's finer points."

Nevertheless, Lark snorts. "Ignore the whippersnapper. It works for me."

"Humph. You're just jealous that I have wings," Moth answers. "I knew it from the moment your ugly face darkened the doorstep of our world—ouch!" she carps when Lark approaches and playfully snaps the Fae's ankle, as if she's a precious pest.

Their bickering camaraderie reminds me of, well, my family. Me, Lark, and Cove. The scene is so familiar that it stings until Lark winks at me with nine years' worth of love, washing away my envy.

Cerulean watches them with fondness, his blue eyes smoldering when they land on my sister. It's an unconditional look, armored and indestructible around the edges.

He loves her. The ruler of the sky loves my gutsy human sister—brashness, audaciousness, and all. That wins him a point with me.

Yet I still don't understand how they ended up here. "But how did you know what was happening?" I ask Moth. "If you called out to Lark and Cerulean, who called out to you?"

"That was me," a baritone voice announces.

Our band wheels toward Cypress. The moment we do, his olive eyes jolt away from Puck, whom he'd been observing.

At last, I break from the huddle and rush toward the centaur, ignoring his grunt when I throw my arms around his bulk. With our height difference, I barely reach his pectorals, but I don't care.

Awkwardly, he pats my shoulder. "Cease, moppet. All is well."

I step back, note the bandage at his waist, and feel that lump grow bigger in my throat. "Damnation. They dragged you away."

"As I said, I am fine now."

"You'd better be," Puck murmurs. He reaches us, his eyes saturated in an affectionate shade of brown. "You scared the shit out of us, luv."

Cypress's eyes slide toward Puck. "The feeling was mutual."

Lark shuffles over to me, and we strap our arms around one another's waists. According to Cypress, he'd been unconscious for the entire trip as the Faeries dragged him away. After they'd deposited him in an herb patch, the centaur had resurfaced from the haze long enough to clasp a root and contact The Solitary Mountain. Since he hadn't been able to reach Cerulean, he'd called out to Moth.

Then Cypress had blacked out once more, only to awaken with Moth's face hovering inches from his. The sprite and centaur exchange respectful nods, indicating they've built a long-established fellowship with one another, despite their conflicting personalities.

"Communication takes a while from the roots to the wind," Moth supplies from her perch. "Otherwise, we would have gotten here sooner."

"Wait." Lark takes in my appearance, noticing something for the first time. "Where's your crossbow?"

Cerulean asks the same of Puck. "And your longbow?"

Puck and I speak in unison. "We were trapped—"

An owl's hoot pierces the sky, slicing above the canopy. The horned raptor and nightingale have returned. Presently, they circle overhead, the owl's cry alerting Cerulean first, then Lark. They listen to the birds, then bank their heads north.

The rest of us follow suit, whipping our gazes toward the place from which the stampede had come. The Faes' tapered ears perk, and their features pull taut. They feel it nearly a full minute before I do: earthen tremors.

It's the same cacophony from the first battle. Only this time, the onslaught magnifies tenfold. It ripples into a quake, shaking the ground off its hinges and flinging candlelight across the clearing.

The owl and nightingale dive our way while shifting, their bodies contorting into larger forms.

Moth pops into the air. Her bare feet slap atop the branch as she crouches into a fighting stance.

Cerulean draws his javelin, rotating it into a windmill of movement. He spins the weapon behind his head and goes still.

Lark unspools her whip. Cypress nocks his bow.

Puck arms himself with the axe he'd take from the leprechaun. I retrieve the staff I'd dropped.

Beside me, the satyr clicks his head to loosen a kink. "Guess we'll find out what happened to our archery."

I concur. The Solitaries must have the bows in their possession, and they're presumably about to use our weapons against us.

Earlier, they weren't retreating. They were gathering reinforcements.

The soil ruptures beneath our feet, and the dawning firmament thrusts my memory to the surface. Puck's profile blanches, the recollection hitting him, too. His attention veers, landing on me. It's the last day, with minimal time remaining to fulfill my three tasks.

Hunt an animal that can't be hunted.

Hunt Sylvan, the doe who isn't here—but whom Puck had summoned.

My stomach plunges. It's a visceral free-fall, dread threatening to bowl me over.

Firs split as armed Faeries spill into the clearing. Leprechauns swing axes and hammers. Centaurs, fauns, and satyrs wield their weapons and surge across the divide.

Cerulean spins the javelin and hurls it into the air, skewering an attacker and tacking him to the nearest tree. Cypress looses his arrow, his expression placid, steadfast.

I peek at Lark, who mutters to me, "Love you, hun."

I hike up my chin and mouth the same words. *"Love you back."*

With that, she twists ahead. Our gang charges, including the raptors. I hear Puck's frenzied breath pumping next to me. "Remember, luv," he pants. "I've got you."

And I've got him.

We race faster—and collide. Razor-sharp noises explode around me. The world swirls with movement, arms and limbs interlocked, hollers in my language and in Faeish, arrows flying, and steel clanging. Blood splatters the ground. I whirl and duck, block and parry. Something hard rams into my side, and something pronged rips through my sweater.

My vision jolts into focus. Lark and Cerulean fight back-to-back. Moth clashes midair with a clique of nymphs balancing on the branches. Cypress ejects a succession of arrows. Puck's got his hands full with leprechauns.

Foxglove hasn't returned, but Tinder has. The youth blasts into the scene and scans the mess. Locating Puck, Tinder hurls a throwing star with a backhanded thrust that pierces the neck of Puck's adversary.

The satyr pauses, then gives the youth a grateful nod. In the midst of that, a lone elk gallops through the clearing as if startled by the cacophony, then swerves back toward the firs. At which point, Puck also notices something within the crowd and grins. He runs toward the departing elk, bounds onto the animal's rump, and uses the momentum as a springboard to catapult into the air and plummet into the horde.

For a moment, he drops out of sight. Then he emerges at my side, his archery attached to his back, and tosses me a familiar crossbow and quiver.

"On the count of three?" he suggests.

Side by side, we jump atop a boulder between two firs. I count, then we let the weapons fly. They strike true, felling the Faeries who get near our gang.

After fastening another bolt in place, I aim—then stall.

The doe gallops into the scene, shamrocks budding from her antlers. From across the scrimmage, Sylvan's head turns and finds us.

My pulse drums. I will her to move, but she doesn't. Instead, she pauses within range.

Right in my line of fire.

34

I'm seven years old, poaching an animal.

I'm thirteen years old, rescuing an animal.

I'm nineteen years old, hunting an animal.

The memories coalesce. Every regret and atonement, every haunting and rewarding incident wheel together, the vignettes blurring into a spectrum of images and color. I watch them spiral, around and around and around.

When the funnel ceases, I behold her again. The doe recognizes me, the black coins of her eyes reflecting a battle between allies and enemies. Somewhere in that collage, her pupils must reflect me aiming the weapon, pointing the bolt at her.

Sylvan remains idle. I want her to flee, need her to flee, to take the choice away from me. But she doesn't. The deer won't move because I'm the only soul besides Puck whom she trusts. This mystical creature doesn't anticipate an attack.

My lips wobble. A silent scream skids across my tongue.

When I was little, I couldn't decide what was worse—when they just stood there or when they tried to get away, tried to save themselves once realizing a predator was near. Me, that huntress. Them, in range. I remember the ones who'd grunted, howled, squeaked, and cried in pain or alarm.

Puck had reminded me: I'd done it to eat, to live, to survive. And by now, I've saved more animals than I've harmed. Yet I've never forgotten.

I had once told Puck I have no use for fear, thinking myself impenetrable, as if that were a good thing, a valuable trait. I'd been wrong. I was scared when parting from my sisters. I was scared when this game began. I'm scared now. I'm petrified, horrified.

The fight recedes, the hollers muffling. Sweat slickens my palms, compromising my grip on the crossbow. My fingers spasm on the trigger.

Then I hear my name. Then I feel a masculine body next to me, and Puck becomes the only other thing in focus. I chance a quick glance. His profile turns ashen as he registers Sylvan on the opposite end of the divide, prevailing among the fir trees. He had called, and she'd come.

Anguish mars his features, but he drags his gaze to mine and shifts to stand behind me. What is he—

Puck aligns his arms with mine and cups his palms over my knuckles. "I'm with you," he cracks out, his voice splitting in two.

He's with me. If I have to do this, and he has to let me do this, then we'll do this together.

We aim. I shake my head, whipping it from side to side. No, no, no, no, no.

"Juniper," he prods. "Juniper, please."

My chest breaks, my heart shattering while violent shouts boom around us. I keep shaking my head, keep shaking it.

The satyr encircles me and presses his cheek to mine, his digits trembling. "Juniper!" he bellows in my ear. "Do it! Now!"

"I can't!" I screech.

I can't.

My sister whirls in my direction, because perhaps she'd heard me. Those gray eyes find mine, and although she doesn't know what my game is or what I have to do, she knows me. Her gaze flares with concern—and love, and life.

If I don't strike true, I'll lose her. I'll lose Cove. I'll lose Papa.

But if I strike true, someday I might lose Puck. And if I strike true, will I also lose myself?

Myself…

I loosen my grip on the weapon as my mind swirls. The rules of this game jumble together in my psyche, coupled with a mishmash of experiences and lessons. They remind me that I'm smarter than this.

There must be another way. There *has* to be another way.

But what am I missing? What haven't I considered yet?

I can't do this. Or rather, I can…but I won't. I *won't*.

Not again. Never again.

Behind Lark, one of the male dryads notices my sister. The Fae halts, momentarily disengaging his longbow. His attention transfers from Lark to me, then he sees Puck stationed at my rear, and then he gauges my crossbow's trajectory.

The doe stands frozen, caught in my aim.

Understanding dawns across the dryad's countenance. In a manner of seconds, the male recognizes what I'm about to do. Like all the Folk, he knows what my task is. The bereavement in his expression gives way to panic, which segues to desperation.

And it happens. The dryad raises his longbow. An arrow fires, slicing through the maelstrom of bodies.

Sylvan doesn't see it coming. She groans, her limbs buckling. The weapon pierces her fur, spearing into the paunch where crimson sprays on impact.

The sound she makes penetrates my breast. When she crashes to the ground, so does my archery. The crossbow clatters to the boulder, then skids off the edge and thunks into the grass, still loaded with its bolt.

The battle ceases, everyone jolting to a standstill. The combatants process the magnificent deer sprawled on her side. Blood leaks from her wound, where the dryad's arrow lodges.

As he gazes upon the fallen animal, the male's face mirrors determination—right before he collapses to the ground, his weapon slumping beside him. Prone on the grass, he tenses, bloats with air, then caves in and goes still. Red spritzes from his back, pierced by a saw-edged dagger.

At the fringes of the clearing, Foxglove rises from her throwing stance, her eyes fixed on the dryad. The nymph must have returned from wherever the owl had dumped her and seen what the Fae intended. She'd sought to prevent it by hurling the blade.

Too late.

Heads swivel from the nymph to the dryad, then to the deer. Gasps and shrieks fill The Gang of Elks, the calamity of noise dicing through the wild.

Tinder gapes. Foxglove teeters in place.

A myriad of emotions sears across Cypress's features, each of them clashing.

From their respective corners, Lark, Cerulean, and Moth pause, arrested by the scene.

A sob hefts from my mouth. I press a fist to my lips and stumble backward into Puck.

He unleashes a strangled noise that tears through me. We break from the paralysis and leap off the boulder, hurling ourselves toward Sylvan. Our knees slam into the grass. The doe gargles for breath, her stomach pumping, disjointed exhalations puffing from her snout. Shamrocks droop over her antlers, and the russet hue of her coat dulls, its luster waning.

Puck's hand quavers as he touches her neck, stroking the fur with his thumb. *"Eck er jérna,"* he says. *"Eck er jérna."*

When she nudges his fingers with her nose, all semblance of restraint snaps. Puck draws in a suffocated breath and lets it out, a choked cry grating from his lungs. His head bows and lands on hers, sobs racking his shoulders.

The deer casts me a glance, her eyes crawling to meet my gaze. Heat scorches my face, and my eyes water, beads leaking down my cheeks. Rivulets cascade to my jaw and drip on my sweater.

Footfalls approach. Lark kneels and embraces me from behind, tucking her chin on my shoulder. Her presence brings more tears to the surface. I weep silently while Puck weeps openly, his body rocking over the doe, the animal he considers a sister.

Puck, whose only wish is to have a family.

Faeries and fauna gather around us, some lamenting and sniffling, others hissing and braying. Cypress lowers himself and closes his eyes, muttering words in Faeish, chanting what sounds like a hymn.

Cerulean and Moth prostrate themselves, watching the deer with mournful gazes. Although I haven't imparted the game or its rules to them yet, they must guess. Based on their expressions, and the expressions around them, they guess the essentials correctly, if not the complexities of the game.

The hunt, which I've lost because I hadn't pulled the trigger.

I'd refused to let the bolt fly, striving instead to think of an alternative. In that interim, the dryad had endeavored to stop me from winning. And he'd succeeded.

Despair eclipses my terror. While I may not have struck Sylvan down with my own weapon, if I hadn't targeted her in the first place, the dryad wouldn't have noticed.

"I-I'm sorry," I blubber, resting my hand on Sylvan's jaw. "I'm s-so sorry."

In the blooming light from the branch candles, she does something none of us anticipate. She nuzzles my palm, as if in forgiveness. The contact fills me with tenderness, with humility, with grief.

The gesture incites a collective disquiet among the crowd. I sense the Faeries' astonishment that one of their own would target their fauna, even out desperation. And that an animal of their land would show me affection, would want me near during these final moments. Particularly this beauty, whom Puck had said tolerates none but him, who lets no other rider mount her.

This, they hadn't foreseen. Neither had I.

That a Fae creature would form such a bond with a human. That a mortal would have such a kinship with their living fauna.

Living fauna...

I startle, my hand pausing atop Sylvan's coat. A thought creeps through my mind, kindling a spark.

If the term hunt is relative, what if I'd interpreted it wrong? All this time, what if the forest hadn't designated this task simply to plague me? Instead of using my fears against me, what if the purpose had been different? What if the objective was never for me to relive who I used to be—but rather, to remind me of who I've become?

A rescuer. A rehabilitator.

"You can't hunt an animal that's right in front of you," I whisper, my brain toiling, working.

In my peripheral vision, a myriad of faces ticks my way, including Lark and Cerulean. Puck raises his head, his eyes raw on mine. The sight throttles me—and reinforces me.

I'm wiser than this. I can fix this.

"You can't hunt an animal that's right in front of you," I repeat with vehemence, and Puck straightens, listening, waiting. "But neither can you hunt an animal if...if..." I jerk my head toward him, "...if you rescue it instead."

The rules had stated I needed to take action on the animal's life. But they had never said in what manner.

The answer courses through me, simmering in my blood. When I was a child, trade poachers had targeted a mother guarding her cubs. Back then, I'd been unable to save that creature.

But I'm older now. And I can save this deer.

I whirl toward my sister. "Lark."

"On it," she says, unspooling her whip and handing it to me.

Lark understands my intentions. We're used to this process, because we've done it before with dozens of animals.

"Keep her calm," I tell Puck.

Awareness and a hopeful glimmer dawn across his face. He bends over the doe and whispers in his language.

Blood dribbles from the crater in Sylvan's flesh. I assess the arrow and gauge its depth, its placement. The tip hasn't punctured any crucial organs or arteries.

I clamp on to the weapon's stem and pull, extracting it fully. The doe grunts, a seizure rolling across her body.

Lark mentions that Cerulean has the ability to purge wounds of infections. He did it for her atop The Wild Peak. But with regret, Cerulean testifies what I already know. He can't take direct action on the animal's life.

That's my job. As the player, I have to be the one administering Sylvan's care. Still, it's within the game's bounds to ask for help in other ways.

"All right." Mentally, I rifle through an anthology's worth of Fables while pressing my thumbs to my temples. "In...in *The Fox and the Fae*, the fox sanitizes its wound with...with something called a violet willow. I need a violet willow!"

Cypress evanesces and returns with a purple, eight-bladed leaf. "Place this onto the cleft."

I do as he bids, settling the plant against the gash. But after unraveling an errant thread from my skirt, dismay catches up with me. Sealing the injury requires a needle or anything similar that will penetrate Sylvan's flesh.

Puck catches on. He removes a leaf charm from one of his earrings and detaches the clasp.

"Give me that." Moth snatches the makeshift needle and pinches the loop just so. This narrows the gap, refining it from a crude fabrication to a workable tool. She hands it over to me. "My parents were tailors."

I loop the skirt thread into the hole and press it through Sylvan's fur. Puck continues whispering to her while I stitch the wound closed, blood smearing my fingers. Lastly, I use the edge of Cerulean's javelin and cut the arm of my sweater. After wadding the material onto the stitches, I cinch everything in place with Lark's whip. Then I join Puck, petting the deer and waiting.

And waiting. And waiting.

The crowd inches nearer, scarcely making a noise. At last, dawn burns through the canopy, soaking us in burnished hues of goldenrod. The wind filters through the trees while candle flames spring higher, drenching the clearing in additional light.

Sylvan stirs. Her breathing evens out, her pallor brightening to rich russet once more.

Impassioned sighs multiply through the area. The Faeries' voices overlap, shaken and intermingling like a thousand leaves breaking from their stems.

Lark clamps on to my shoulder. "Hell yeah," she utters in a choked voice. "You did it, woman."

Tear streaks dry across my skin as I fixate on the deer. Tension leeches from my muscles, and a torrent of relief surges through me.

Puck's eyes rove over Sylvan. When she nudges his hand again, he cradles the deer's face. "Fables and fuck," he sob-chuckles, then sweeps his attention to me and says with gruff affection, "Smart woman."

A small, weepy laugh spurts from my throat. I rub Sylvan's back, gazing at her until certain she won't disappear.

She's all right. She's all right now.

But I'm not done yet. As if my actions have pried open a gate, additional thoughts swarm my consciousness. That long-ago discussion when Cypress gave me the scribe's tome resurfaces. Before handing over the original manuscript, he'd asked me which is the wisest part of a tree. I'd said the sum of its parts.

That's what knowledge is—the sum of experiences. That's the knot, the heartwood.

I think about The Wicked Pines, where Puck had ordered me to tell a story, but I'd flubbed. I think about my notebook and Puck suggesting I write a book of my own. I think about trusting the value of my own words. I think about how often I've been wrong in this land and how I feel more knowledgeable because of it.

The second task had been to tell the Faeries a Fable about this animal—one they've never heard. I won't find it in the Book of Fables, neither in the original nor my own volume. That story has to come from me.

All at once, I know how it goes and clear my throat. *"Once in the dark forest, a Stag hunted a Doe."* I swap a definitive look with the satyr, then recall everything that's happened since our reunion. *"So she hunted him back."*

I speak from the pit of my stomach, infusing my fears and loves and hates and desires into it. I recite with experience and inexperience, with curiosity and humbleness. I narrate randomly and imperfectly, and somehow, the pieces string together.

The moral is this: Even a human has magic, worth, and strength. Even a human has a deep connection to nature. Even a human and an animal can heal each other. Even a Fae can recognize this. Even a human and Fae can share an unbreakable bond.

Sylvan. Puck. Me.

When I finish the tale—our tale—I complete the third task. To prove the story's moral is true, the only necessary act is a gentle one, profound in its simplicity and sincerity.

I brush my lips against Sylvan's forehead, and she nestles against my hip. Then I swipe the final tear from Puck's face. And he reciprocates by taking my fingers and kissing them.

But like a typical Fae, the satyr pushes that gesture a step further and exceeds what my heart can bear.

Puck clutches my hand and then releases it. And he whispers tenderly, selflessly, "Go home, Juniper."

35

It was always going to happen, always going to end this way. Winner or not, I was always going to lose him.

His words rob me of speech. That devilish smirk hasn't lost its artifice, but it has gained a wistful slant.

Inside, I crack into brittle pieces. Outside, I go numb.

Yet somehow, I manage to nod. And somehow, he manages to grin.

What transpires over the next few hours requires concentration and perseverance. With the presence of my sister anchoring me, I manage to readapt.

Because I've won, I don't need anyone's blessing to leave. The only potential tragedy left is if Cove loses her game. Since there's been no news of that, I'm free to go. I can leave with Lark or return to Papa. It's my choice.

But not yet.

The Faeries collect their fallen—including the dryad—and deposit the bodies beneath a spruce tree, where the lifeless figures fade into the earth. Most of the Folk remain in this clearing afterward, save for Tinder and Cypress along with a handful of volunteers. They offer to transport Sylvan to The Herd of Deer, where she'll recover.

Puck inclines his head toward Foxglove in gratitude. Though, the gesture isn't without reservation. From what I've gathered, the nymph hadn't gleaned why the dryad had targeted Sylvan. Her interference had been merely instinctive.

Regardless, Foxglove had attempted to spare the deer's life. I won't forget that.

Before the convoy departs, I stroke Sylvan's head once more. Puck whispers to the doe in Faeish, his tone that of a promise.

I want to accompany Sylvan to her home, but current events demand my presence. Privately, I vow to see her later.

Puck appeals to the Faeries, advocating a ceasefire. Negotiating to abolish sacrificing mortals is jagged terrain, especially after the tumult with so many wounded, bereaved, dumbstruck, confused, and perhaps ashamed by the dryad's actions. The latter proves that, when in a vulnerable state, even Faeries can lose their connection to the fauna, whereas a mortal's bond with that same animal might strengthen. It's a difficult conclusion for them to digest.

The satyr's proposal for an intermission affords our opponents time to reflect. Alongside Lark and Cerulean's story, this game has challenged the beliefs the Folk have harbored about humans. Plus, there's the original Book of Fables to consider.

Unfortunately, Puck and I still have no idea what exactly the scribe's message about preserving the Solitary wild is referring to. I had sworn to reveal the passage, promising to share it. Since I don't have the book with me, I recite the contents:

"*Immortal wild. Immortal land. Dwellers of the mountain, forest, and river. You are born of eternal nature—of the wind, earth, and water. Yet that which is everlasting is not unbreakable. And should you wither by the hands of others, look not merely to sacrifice, for another path to restoration lies in wait. Therefore, follow your Fables, heed your neighbors, and look closer.*"

The crowd stares at me, expecting more information. But there isn't any. When I had made that bargain with them, I'd been twisting my words, because I'd never said the contents would yield specifics, much less a solid answer.

Lark, Cerulean, and Moth—to whom I'd recapped the details after caring for Sylvan—respond with mystified grins, impressed by my nerve albeit disappointed about this cliffhanger.

As for the rest of my audience, protests flare across The Gang of Elks. Notwithstanding, they can hardly deny my tactic emulates what they would have done in my position. In fact, several faces reevaluate me with a modicum of respect.

Even Foxglove relents. Her eyes still flash my way, but a grudging appreciation curbs the nymph's resentment.

Amidst the hubbub, Puck sighs and snaps his fingers. The fervor dies quickly.

"We have a chance," he tells the battered crowd. "Given time, we can figure out this merry riddle. If there's another way out of this plight, I like to think we've got the knack. We're crafty Folk, after all."

A fraction of the mob accepts Puck's words and departs in peace, agreeing to conference once they've tended to their injuries and regained their strength. Others stomp away or merely evanesce, their anger burning a trail through the flickering fir trees. After centuries of seeing humans as inferiors, consensus can't be achieved overnight, not in any region of The Dark Fables. It might take a lifetime to reach some measure of accord.

Puck watches through cautious eyes as they leave. At the onset, everyone had reached a temporary understanding and disarmed. Now, a segment of his kin may as well have denounced him as their ruler.

Cerulean leans into Puck and murmurs, *"Feir joma vvjótleka aftur."*

Puck nods, his gaze pinned to the Faeries' backs. "If that happens, we'll be ready."

And just like that, I know: There's no going back to Reverie Hollow. Not for me. Not yet. As much as I want to race to my family's sanctuary, to fling my arms around Papa Thorne, our father would understand my decision.

If Lark's here, I'm here. If Cove's here, I'm here.

And if Puck's here…

My ribs contract. Well. If anything, I can stay with my sister and Cerulean. They've offered me a room in his tower, situated on a promontory in the mountain, a haven tucked within a wildlife park.

The satyr is anxious to see Sylvan. In the gleam of candlelight and sunlight, he glances at me once. He's a Fae, and I'm a human. Not for the first time, my practical side knows such a combination has no future.

Lark and Cerulean are bonded, but the satyr and I haven't been graced with that luxury. Puck will live forever, and I will age. He belongs in this realm, among the stags and foxes, and I'm destined for Papa and the Fable Dusk Sanctuary, where I'm needed. When this battle is over, when his world is preserved, and when Cove wins her game—dear Fables, let her win—the chasm between me and this Fae will widen. We'll fight as allies from this point on, but that's all.

In spite of this, Puck's body angles my way, about to defy the rules once more. I know him too well. He wants to say, "Fuck it," and grab me.

My yearning to let him is so overwhelming, I step back. If I have to choose between suffering now or later, I choose now. Gingerly, I shake my head, pleading with him to be sensible, rational.

A muscle ticks in his jaw. He shrugs. "It was worth a try," he says, his eyes warm on mine. "See you later, luv."

And he fades into a wisp.

I'll wait until the coast is clear. I'll be patient until the satyr has finished visiting with Sylvan, then I'll take my turn.

In the meantime, Cerulean has gone with his brother, needing a private word. Lark and Moth huddle under a fir tree, talking in hushed tones. My sister hasn't approached yet, having sensed I'd needed a precious moment alone.

Now that the scrimmage is over, several elks appear in the vicinity and graze among the firs. I sit beside a sparkling creek, where the water flops over stones, the surface reflecting midday. After washing my hands and removing my boots and socks, I dip my feet into the babbling stream, eternally marveling at its lukewarm temperature. It feels good, though I can't wait for a bath.

A sack lands at my hip. I jolt to where my supply pack rests.

"Do not thank me, moppet." A baritone voice fills the void, and a hulking figure looms beside me. "It was a trivial errand."

Leveling my hand like a visor to blot out the sun, I gaze up at the centaur. Although the broad horn helmet shields half of his visage, the radiance of his dark complexion implies his wound is healing at an expedited rate. That same flush of exertion also certifies that he's been busy, conveying Sylvan to The Herd of Deer and then fetching the pack from Puck's cabin.

When I gesture to the ground, the centaur lowers himself next to me. For a while, we observe the marigold rays spearing through the needle leaves and pelting the water's surface.

"The Book of Fables," I begin. "I left it in Puck's cabin, too."

"I have retrieved it for my territory," the equine replies. "It has served you well." He shuffles as if uncomfortable, as though he's hunkered atop a patch of loose gravel. "Do not go."

My head swings toward him. "What?"

"I crossed paths with Puck when I was leaving Sylvan with the herd. He informed me of your plans to settle with your sister and her mate. I would ask you to reconsider this. Do not go. Stay here."

"Why?" I blurt out. "My sister's in the mountain, whereas I have nobody here." My voice clangs steadily when I say this, even though I feel anything but stable. "I can be an ally to you and Puck from the safety of Cerulean's tower. Puck and his brother talked with us about establishing a hub, a meeting place where the mountain and forest intersect. It's settled."

"It is not settled," Cypress disputes, unleashing a huff that jostles his leather nose ring. "I would not beg this of you if I did not believe you truly wished for it. Am I wrong?"

He's not wrong. I let my expression verify that, telling its own story for Cypress, knowing he'll understand.

Satisfied, he forges ahead. "You would be safe in The Heart of Willows—or in Puck's cabin with the herd. After what happened to Sylvan, my kin would not dare to penetrate that area. I vouch for this and shall guard you with my life, as will Puck. He will never push you, never press such a burden on you, so he keeps this to himself: He does not want you to go."

"Puck told you that?"

"He did not have to. Do not leave him. Please..." Cypress swipes off his helmet and thrusts it to the ground, then shoves the words out. "Your feelings for one another are matched. You need each other."

I swallow. "Why are you saying this?"

The centaur is quiet for a long time. He contemplates the water, his profile rigid, strung tight. Then like a band stretched too far, it releases. His voice tapers to a whisper. "I want him to be happy."

I blink at this tremendous being hunched over, his mane cascading around his profile. That austere face carved from granite collapses, its scaffolding breaking down. His brows crinkle with protectiveness.

With heartache.

Realization pummels me in the chest, sympathy and shock colliding. Every previous interaction with the centaur takes on a new shape, gaining new clarity.

At the hunt's onset, I'd hidden in the elms and eavesdropped on Cypress, Tinder, and Puck. The satyr had given his longbow to Tinder not only to foster trust, but to encourage the youth to leave, to keep him from registering my presence. Indeed, the centaur and satyr had known I was there but hadn't exposed me.

Now I know why. Now I know the impetus behind their silent communication, that look between them while discussing my whereabouts after Tinder had departed. The pair had been checking to see if the other knew I was hiding nearby. Once they'd confirmed it, Cypress had wordlessly waited to see if Puck would take action. When the satyr hadn't, the centaur understood that Puck didn't want to reveal me. The game could have ended then, but Cypress had played along. He'd done that for Puck.

Before the bonfire, Cypress had warned me to be careful with Puck. He'd already known something was brimming between me and the satyr, and Cypress had sought to safeguard us from being discovered. That's why he'd watched us carefully during the feast. He'd taken stock of our behavior, checking to make sure no one else noticed or suspected.

In The Roots that Take, Cypress had charged onto the scene with a vengeance, knowing Puck and I were in danger. And during the battle, he'd roared when a Fae had attempted to strike Puck down.

I recall each look that stoic face had aimed Puck's way, including the reluctant grins Puck was able to inspire in him. I recall Cypress's painting affixed to Puck's living room wall, depicting the place where they'd met. I recall how Puck had stared at the rendering with fondness, but nothing more.

Puck is scarcely a clueless fop, yet... "He doesn't know," I say.

Cypress's throat bobs. "I told you once. Amorous devotion confuses satyrs, and it is uncommon for them to feel that degree of ardor.

Oftentimes, they are not equipped and cannot recognize that level of passion or fidelity in partners. Not unless the feeling is requited on the satyr's part." The equine drags his face to mine, the movement arduous, as if he's breaking through a layer of plaster. "You are the exception, moppet. He is in love with you."

"Cypress." I trail off, because what can I say to comfort him? I've never excelled at soothing people like Cove has. Worse, guilt pinches me for being the one Puck wants. "Cypress, I'm sorry."

"I am not," the centaur replies. "Long have I loved him, and I shall continue to love him, for that is my right. It is *my* heart—my own," he stresses. "He may not echo the sentiment but loving him is woven into my very marrow. It is a part of me that I am grateful to have. It is a privilege."

I marvel how Faeries and humans are more alike than they'd care to admit. Both feel love and live with heartbreak. They can be violent and brutal, but they can also be selfless, affectionate, and loyal. Each world begets heroes, not just villains. If that's possible on both sides, surely we can find a common ground.

I do what feels right and take the centaur's hand. "I like you, Cypress of the willow trees."

He startles, frowning at our clasped fingers as if it's a foreign gesture. After a moment, a divot appears in the corner of his mouth. When he looks my way, his irises shimmer with something close to friendship. "And I like you, Juniper of Reverie Hollow."

Peace washes over me. We sit together, studying our reflections in the water. His imploring request lingers in my head, that he wants me to stay.

That Puck wants me to stay.

36

Cerulean returns. He descends from the sky, the plumed mantels of his blue-black wings crimping and seeping into his back when he lands. Under normal circumstances, my curious mind would inquire about such a trick. Instead, I merely observe the spectacle that is my sister's lover. Her mate.

Lithesome and statuesque, he possesses the type of frame that manages to be slender yet toned. Whereas his brother is cinched and sturdy, Cerulean is billowing and aerial. With the low V of his linen shirt exhibiting his chest to its best advantage, this Fae is the epitome of lazy elegance, appearing as though he's just tumbled out of bed.

Moth and Lark break from their conversation. My sister rushes to Cerulean and frog-leaps into his arms, strapping herself around him like a knapsack. The Fae bands one arm around her waist and cups her scalp with his free hand, crushing her to him. Their mouths meet in a searing, unabashed kiss.

My brazen sibling has never been coy or discrete. It appears, neither is Cerulean. Her lips clamp over his blue ones, their tongues plaiting.

The occupants of this clearing—myself included—turn away, giving them privacy. Several emotions congeal in my gut. Relief to see my sister alive and presumably happy, jealousy over that happiness, and a certain sorrow I refuse to dwell on.

Well. If only one of us can be so lucky, I'm glad it's my sister. Between us, I would have chosen that for her anyway.

Cerulean has recovered Lark's whip, indicating Sylvan's injuries must have received upgraded treatment. My sister, Cerulean, and Moth join Cypress and me by the creek.

As they settle across the water from us, a lanky surprise appears: Tinder has also returned from The Herd of Deer, materializing from thin air among the trees. The youth teeters like a pendulum, his orange eyes casting an uncertain glance at our small party.

Cerulean speaks to him in their language, his tone encouraging.

My sister pats the ground. "You gonna just stand there or keep us company?"

But Tinder isn't paying attention to her. He's busy studying Moth.

The sprite lances her gaze toward him, her papery wings beating with rigorous snaps. "What are you gawking at?" She bats her lashes and mock-simpers, "See anything you like?"

The youth scrunches his epicene features, his marten tail swatting the ground. "I prefer woodland Faeries, thank you very much."

"Suit yourself." Moth shrugs. "I don't bother with forest dwellers, anyhow."

Cypress angles his countenance toward the female. "Since when?"

To that, Moth's wings slow to a flutter. She flits her eyes to the centaur, her topaz irises glowing like fireflies and daring him to invalidate her statement.

"Settle down, Miss High and Mighty," my sister teases while snuggling into Cerulean's chest.

"You settle down," Moth jabs back, a half-smile tilting her face.

"See what I mean?" Lark swings her gaze my way. "She likes me."

"Who wouldn't?" Cerulean whispers into the cloud of Lark's hair, a breezy chuckle filling his voice. He has the same accent as Puck, only less rugged. By comparison, Cerulean's casual inflection is vaporous, a well-ventilated intonation that sweeps through the air like the wind itself.

Tinder catches my eye, then Cypress's. As we nod and welcome him into our huddle, a ribbon of pink creeps across the youth's cheeks. He lowers himself adjacent to the centaur.

It's a picture I've never dreamed of taking part in. And only two faces are missing.

I feel Cove's dainty, lace-edged absence in my chest. I feel the loss of

Puck in too many places to count.

Although partial introductions had been made in haste before the battle, our group eases into the preliminaries: where we've come from and who we are to one another. Shaken, bruised, thirsty, and famished as we are, it's a much-needed respite. Everyone slurps from the creek, bathes their wounds, and contributes to the conversation, each of us telling our story. As the sun arcs from morning to afternoon, our differences in culture seem to disappear and amplify at the same time.

We exchange fortified glances. Hope burgeons among us, that humans and Faeries can communicate like this.

My spirits lift, hardly minding that Moth has found extra time to nose around in my pack. She's confiscated the posey of dried bluebells—the last of my bartering trinkets—and tied it to her dress like a broach. The ornament incites a peep of glee, so I let her keep it.

Without Puck, our band refrains from conferencing about defensive strategies or where we go from here. Nonetheless, the goals are evident. That much, we acknowledge.

We'll need to rouse allies from the mountain and forest. We'll need to find out what's become of Cove and the status of her game in The Solitary Deep. And we'll need to unravel the scribe's message, to decipher the second way to preserve this wild.

Cerulean and Lark have been working on the former. Though to my bafflement, Cerulean informs us that he no longer rules the sky. The mountain fauna have that distinction now, because when Lark's game had ended, she and her mate had achieved this realization and announced it to the Folk.

But if that's true, why don't the woodland fauna rule this land instead of Puck?

Cypress discloses the answer. "The mountain fauna possess a vaster awareness of the feud between humans and Faeries. They have an expansive viewpoint from which to assess their world." He checks Cerulean for confirmation, and when Cerulean nods, the centaur continues. "Woodland fauna are cloistered and have evolved to be less cognizant. Though, it is not merely that. By nature, they are indifferent to the rift that divides mortals and immortals. As for the river fauna, it becomes even more claustrophobic."

"I've always considered myself to rule beside the fauna, not above them," Cerulean adds. "That was my choice. In every decision I made, I sought their guidance. Particularly, The Parliament of Owls."

"Cerulean needed only to stand down, and the fauna adopted their roles organically. That is their way," Cypress elaborates. "This is not to say the forest fauna may not rule, for they indeed possess the spirit for it. Cloistered they may be, but woodland animals will defend their packs and territories with vigor. So for the transfer of leadership, Puck must not only concede, he must offer the honor, and it must be accepted." Cypress shifts. "But there is a quandary."

"Without grasping this dispute between worlds, the woodland fauna cannot lead as Puck can," Cerulean provides. "He's willing to relinquish his title to the fauna, but it would make no sense for what's ahead. The mountain fauna have the mindset to rule amidst this crisis, yet my own influence has been diluted; gaining support has been a slow progression. We need Puck to exercise his authority."

That stands to reason.

As for the scribe's message, Cerulean rubs his chin. "Puck, Cypress, and I exchanged a few theories at my brother's home. We suspect the answer will be simple yet anything but."

"Two sides of a coin," Tinder translates.

I mull over riddles, loopholes, and relative terms. Certain Fables suggest the answer is often simpler than it seems. With regard to Tinder's statement, other Fables advocate for perceiving things from conflicting angles. "If sacrificing humans is one solution, perhaps this other way is its opposite," I volunteer.

Cerulean nods. "To take revenge on mortals or—"

"—to unite."

Our group hedges. If that hunch is correct, it's a key hidden in plain sight. The conundrum is our small band has, in fact, united. Yet nothing has changed, which means there's a ligament missing. A complicated one.

"Unite in what way, though?" I question.

"That is where we left off," Cypress says.

But Cerulean's blue lips press together. "Not quite."

Five heads swerve toward him. Moth crosses her arms. "Care to enlighten us?"

Cerulean addresses the centaur. "You'd left by the time Puck conjured another theory." Then his expression grows distant. "There is one Fae who might have the answer. It's possible he knows what manner of unity is required."

My sister's mate doesn't spell it out, because he doesn't need to. From the way his eyes jump between all of us, only one being comes to mind.

Elixir.

The creek slithers through the grass, the water channel thrashing over the rocks. I glower at the turbulent ripples, picturing Cove suffering at the hands of that monster. According to Puck, that bastard is the most venomous of the brothers.

Even Moth tenses, worry cramping her face. "You can't be serious."

Tinder blusters, "Pick another option."

Cypress grunts, massaging the bridge of his nose. "Elixir will not help us."

"There's no way in hell," Moth concurs, balking at Cerulean. "You know what that wanker is like. Not only is he a soul-sucking fiend without a redeemable fishbone in his body, but he has a thirst for power, a hunger to rule. Annihilating mortals isn't just about vengeance and preservation for him—it's primal. And guess what? His subjects are practically a cult. None of them will turn against him."

"Oh trust me, I'm aware of that." Cerulean spears an elegant hand through his hair. "But we might not have a chance without him, which means we'll have to be careful where he's concerned. Very, very, careful. Puck made a shrewd point: Elixir sees what none of us can see."

"Is he a seer?" I inquire.

"Quite the reverse, actually."

Done with riddles, Lark flings up her hands. "Oh, I give the fuck up."

Cerulean cradles her tighter. "I'd be clearer, but I'm not allowed. None may divulge Elixir's capabilities or limitations. One may only witness them for oneself. It's a rule he lives by, so to speak."

The magical members of the circle accept this, whereas Lark and I fester. Our conversation dissolves. The Faeries take note of the yearning look between me and my sister, and they excuse themselves.

Before disbanding, Cypress says, "For the eternal wild."

We echo that sentiment to one another. The ancient saying has existed since before our time, an oath of loyalty and camaraderie, a well-wish between allies.

Tinder retires, but not before tossing Moth a sneer, which she mirrors.

With a scoff, the wee Fae pops into the air. She clips her head at me in acknowledgment, then addresses Lark and Cerulean. "I have animals to feed. See you at the tower."

Because it's unsafe to leave us completely alone, Cerulean and Cypress elect to stick close. They depart to a location amidst the firs where they can stand post, out of eyeshot and hearing range yet near enough to patrol the area.

Cerulean gives me a half-bow. "Lovely to meet my mate's precious family."

"Charmed," I say, somewhat willing to give him the benefit of the doubt.

He kisses Lark's temple. "Until later, my mutinous love."

She fists his collar and purrs, "Rule or not, I'm going to give you so much shit tonight for your secrecy."

"I look forward to it," he flirts, then joins the centaur.

Only the horned owl and nightingale remain perched in a tree, keeping surveillance from a candlelit branch. Although the latter hasn't revealed its name to anyone, Cerulean had introduced the former as his father, Tímien. This explains how the owl's lone, aquamarine eye had reflected patience and devotion for the couple, particularly for his son.

At last, Lark and I are alone. I twist back to my sister, about to throttle her with questions when I stumble across that naughty sibling grin.

Fables almighty. Here it comes.

"Hot damn," Lark exclaims, biting her tongue with glee. "You've been Pucked."

In the past twenty-four hours, this isn't the first time I've heard that term. I swear, Lark and the satyr might as well have been born in the same rowdy tavern.

I snatch a pebble and chuck it at her, the stone bouncing off her hip.

"You couldn't resist, could you?" In spite of myself, I huff. "And yes, I might have been. In a manner of speaking."

To which Lark squeals, the giddy noise splintering through the fir trees. She scrambles to my side and clasps my hand, explicit thoughts hopping across her face. "Tell me everything," she demands. "How is he in bed? Is he a good lover? What's his *dick* like?"

"Lark!" I grouse, smacking her arm. "You would never answer that if I inquired about your—" I gesture to the spot where Cerulean had exited, "—your mate."

"You'd never grill me about Cerulean that way. And no, I wouldn't tell because while he's candid about many things, my bloke is private about us. But Puck of the Filthy Mouth doesn't strike me as someone who'd mind if you blabbed to your dear ol' sister about the size and skills of his pecker."

"You're shameless."

Lark nods with gusto. "You bet I am. Not sorry about it, but I hated the arrogant fucker when I met 'im. I reckon he told you about that?"

"He gave me a summary."

"But if Puck's achieved the impossible and wooed you, I'm willing to give 'im another once-over. Not that it'll be hard. Nobody trumps Cerulean, but I've got two eyes: You've nabbed yourself one hunky satyr. And because I love you, it's my duty to make sure you're a well-satisfied woman."

We might as well be tucked back in our wagon, sharing secrets, squabbling, and laughing. Although a million things have changed, this hasn't.

Fine. "Puck is rather…enthusiastic. We're quite animated together and…," discreetly, I scratch with the side of my neck, "…energetic." I peek at my engrossed sister and feel a mortified grin sneak across my face. "Truly, I had no idea there was such variance to the act. And such vitality." Getting ahold of myself, I square my shoulders. "I like sex. I like it very much…with him."

Lark beams, a big, fat *Hell Yeah* alighting her features—right before she tackles me. We roll over the grass, wrestling and tickling and chortling, her dress tangling with my skirt. For a moment, this is all that exists, all I need.

Flopping over and gasping with mirth, we lie on our sides and face one another.

"Let me look at you." Lark bunches our hands between us. "I missed you like hell."

"I missed you, too," I say. "So much."

Then she gets serious and asks something Papa Thorne isn't here to ask. "Does he treat you right?"

"He does now." And my face crumples. "He does."

At the sight of my tears, Lark appears stricken. "Oh, hun." Then she does something Cove isn't here to do. She gathers me close, wringing her arms around me while my shoulders shake.

I inhale rainfall and crisp air. When I've wept myself dry, we whisper as if we're still in our wagon, lanterns illuminating our shadows.

Lark tells me about her journey with Cerulean. She tells me about his wildlife park and their history together. She tells me about their bond, invoked through a single kiss when they were children—the purest of kisses.

I wince, reassessing my embraces with Puck. Why hadn't that worked for us?

Lark reads my expression and tucks a lock of green behind my ear. "Hell, the Fables don't cover everything. Papa Thorne would say just because it was the purest kiss, that doesn't make it the most meaningful. The lip-locks I've had with Cerulean since? Those are raw, with all the crazy complications, all the good and bad between us. I like to think those matter more." She thumbs my tears. "You hear me?"

My chin steadies. "I hear you."

We sit upright and huddle together, our arms entwined as we watch the eddies flow. Late afternoon paints the woodland in teal and amber. A distant elk call rumbles across the landscape.

"And now?" Lark ponders.

"Now we get Cove back," I say.

"Can't breach her game without knowing its rules."

"We won't have to. She's going to win." For once, I hear what others hear: the smokiness in my voice, crackling like a pyre. "But just in case she doesn't, we'll hunt down those rules and get her back anyway."

Also, I have an idea. Thank Fables Cypress had returned my supply pack. Extracting my notebook and pencil, I compose a message, one that our older sister will recognize, one she'll understand.

Lark catches on and plants a hearty, wet kiss on my cheek. "I knew you were smart for a reason."

After signing our names, Lark folds the paper into the shape of a boat. We set the missive into the creek and let it go, watching the vessel sail down the conduit and vanish around a bend.

All waterways converge in The Deep. If Cove's alive, the boat will find its way to her.

When Lark's ready to leave, all she needs to do is get to her feet. Cerulean appears like a shadow, his wings splayed as if he'd taken to the sky and been scanning the area from above.

I want to travel with them to mountain, but I've yet to see Sylvan. At first, Lark refuses to let me walk alone to Cypress, who has staked his vigil some thirty paces away. It takes three rounds of bickering before I persuade her and Cerulean that I'll be fine walking the minuscule distance.

What I don't say is that I need a moment to myself.

At last, the pair gives up. At Cerulean's signal, the raptors dive off the branch and coast into the firmament. I had expected one of them to convey Lark, but Cerulean sweeps my laughing sister off her feet. Pressing a kiss to her temple, he pitches into the sky. Lark waves, the wind lashing behind them, their departure scattering needle leaves and hurling candlelight across the clearing.

For a while, I sit by the creek and reflect on my conversations with Cypress and my sister. Specifically, our discussions about Puck.

What do I want? What's the wise choice? What do I feel?

It's unfair to keep the centaur waiting too long. I slip on my socks and boots, then haul myself up. Several steps into the dense firs, something winks in my periphery. It hails from a different part of the estuary that winds from The Gang of Elks to other regions of this forest.

I consider flagging down Cypress, but the shimmer of light draws my attention to its source beyond the coppice. The illumination glitters into a single bead, reminiscent of a pearl...or a waterdrop.

Just like the one Cove wears from a chain.

Intuition creeps up my limbs. I break into a run, slapping my way through needled branches and pinecones. I skid to a halt beside the grassy bank where the creek widens. Streams are usually shallower than this, yet the current darkens into an obsidian well, suggesting a considerable depth.

That winking bead pulsates among wildflowers and stems of green. I kneel and track the droplet's radiance, brushing my fingers through the undergrowth.

My hand freezes. Everything in me freezes.

Tucked inside the vegetation is a stray necklace, resting there as if abandoned or lost, with a pendant shaped into a waterdrop.

The bauble is unmistakable, as familiar as the cuff around Lark's thigh or the bracelet entwining my arm. Cove would never relinquish this gem. Not unless she'd been forced to or had gotten hurt. Or not unless she's too dead to care.

"Cove," I whisper, snatching the gem.

Some sort of tide courses through the stream, marking the path of a fish. On the opposite end, the serpentine current narrows and glides into the forest.

What sort of creek makes this much noise? It sounds more like a river.

The hairs on my nape stand on end. Instinct catapults me to my feet, but I'm a huntress. I know when it's too late. I know when a predator has spotted me first. Which is why a masculine hand punches through the watery surface, seizes my ankles, and yanks me under.

37

The well swallows me whole. A ruthless funnel suctions my body down, shackling my limbs and pulling, pulling, pulling. It drags me into its maw, water clogging my lungs and nose, a school of bubbles frothing around me.

I flail my arms and kick my feet, trying to reach the surface, which sparkles overhead like liquid glass. The flood sluices down my throat. My lungs burst into flames, struggling for oxygen. In my family, only one sister can hold her breath underwater for an expert length of time. And that sister isn't me.

A savage tug alerts me to the fingers banded in a vicelike grip around my ankles. Something—or someone—forces me down. My frantic mind conjures up crocodiles, sharks, and reptilian sea creatures. But then I remember the human-shaped digits.

It's not an animal. But whatever it is, whoever it is, the monster's hold migrates to my knees and fastens around them. The current accelerates, a whirling blur of teal blue slamming into me as though I'm made of parchment—frail, shreddable. I may as well be trapped beneath a tsunami, in a raging vortex hundreds of leagues under the sea. The flux impairs my vision, blotting out my predator. I can't see its figure, only feel those steely, ferocious hands strapping me in a boa's clamp.

It feels as though we're traveling, surging into oblivion. Then suddenly, the profusion stops. I float, whiplashed in place.

As I force my eyelids to open, a masculine outline ripples from the murk. I claw at the giant silhouette, to no avail.

A mane of oil-black hair cascades to his hips, all other details obscured from the waist below. Olive skin burnishes his naked chest, the torso wobbling like a watercolor painting. Metallic scales encrust the joints—elbows, knuckles, and cheekbones.

A water Fae. The creature comes into hazy view, the manifestation of a hard, angular countenance. From below, a tapered tail lashes the water, then disappears.

Not like a merman or siren. No, like a cobra.

Or like a sea serpent.

Terror and oxygen deprivation constrict my lungs. I feel my eyes bulge, my gaze slamming into a pair of pitiless orbs. They flash gold, their intensity unlike anything I've ever beheld, as if I'm gawking into the sun while it detonates. Before I can fully register the spectacle, a terrible light blasts from his face, from those blinding irises.

I swerve away, dots swimming in my vision. One of his hands links around my neck, and he slams me into a foundation. My back rams into a spongy wall where stalks of teal seaweed jostle like tentacles.

Lightheadedness fogs my brain, my view turning fuzzy around the edges. I feel myself suffocating, dying. I'm on the verge of going limp, so that he won't need to choke me anymore.

Those dazzling eyes make it impossible to focus, impossible to punch him. My thoughts sail to Lark's face, Cove's face, Papa Thorne's face.

The satyr's face.

Summoning the last vestiges of my strength, I thunk my boot against the serpent's tail. He hisses, the slippery noise loaded with venom. He snaps that whipcord tail against my ribs, striking so fast I go dizzy. The scales dappling his temples glitter, as visibly sharp as a blade's edge.

His free hand snatches my arm, as if he's about to shake me. But he stops, jerking to a halt. I gauge his blurry profile, which is easier to discern than his eyes, accessible without impairing my sight. He's staring at the leaf bracelet blossoming around my forearm.

Actually, no. He isn't staring. Not directly.

His attention skates in the bracelet's general vicinity, the effort wayward, unfocused. The Fae traces his digits along the leaves and coiling stem, mapping out their shapes. His eyes slit as though in recognition, which doesn't make sense.

His grip on me loosens. Attuning himself to other sources, the Fae's head flings toward the surface. He glares at the forest above, as if listening to something rather than actually seeing it.

Whatever he detects, it causes him to seethe. Those spiteful fingers snap open, releasing me as if I'll contaminate these waters. The viper swipes at my hand. Then he executes a backward loop, flipping upside down and diving into the abyss, the spiked tip of that serpent's tail vanishing behind him.

Listless, I descend before remembering to beat my limbs and stay afloat. I pump my arms, but it's too much. I'm too heavy, and I'm too deep, and I'm not going to make it.

I'm drowning. Yet everything's on fire, from my gullet to my muscles.

As if in reverse, another masculine hand punches into the creek. Fingers search, swiping madly at the water, reaching, straining. I recognize those digits, the ones that play a cello and wield a longbow of yew wood.

I thrust my arm and catch his wrist. The satyr yanks me out of the depths. I break the surface, a geyser of water spraying the grass. Strong arms sling around my waist and hoist me onto the bank, where I collapse into Puck's body, wilting against the hard basin of his chest.

Shivers rack my frame, although the undertow had been lukewarm. Drenched to the core, I wheeze for breath, the noise sawing from my lips. It takes a long time for my lungs to relax, for the charred sensation to fade. The gasps dissolve into blubbering sobs.

"I've got you," Puck grates out while rocking us back and forth, his fingers in my soaked hair. "I've got you now. I've got you, luv."

I sputter into his collarbone. "P-Puck."

"That's what they call me."

Yet his cavalier voice has lost its veneer and withered to a dry leaf, brittle and jittery. I fling my arms around him, and we stay like that, huddled on the ground until his heat radiates through my clothes, and my muscles unlock.

Puck helps me sit up, my movements sluggish. He grasps my cheeks, his features wild, terrified. "You all right?"

I nod, dripping all over his leathers. "H-how did y-you know w-where

I w-was?"

"Cypress. He got to the bank just as you went under. Poor fool went out of his mind and called to me through the roots." Puck drills a hand through his red waves. "When he told me what happened, I knew who had you and where you were headed. Your captor travels faster than any of us, and he always uses this route. If I hadn't been going crazy, I might have alerted Cypress to follow suit and manifest here, too."

I glance around, discovering the creek isn't a creek anymore. It's a lake. And instead of fir trees, spruces occupy the landscape. We're tucked beneath a tree closest to the bank, where the musk of wet soil mingles with a floral aroma, the latter possibly emanating from a cluster of strange, teal water blossoms peeking from the surface.

In the distance, a burly groan rumbles from a copse. A four-legged mass of fur trudges to its den, followed by a trio of cubs.

This must be The Sleuth of Bears, which is too far south from where I'd been. At least, that's what Puck once told me.

At my bewildered expression, the satyr runs a thumb along my chin. "Let me send Cypress a message before he continues to panic. I'll tell him to go home, and we'll get your pack and archery on the way back. Oh, and don't worry about the bears. They'll tolerate our presence, so long as we don't show interest in eating their offspring. It's a matter of bearness, you understand."

Puck leans over and rests his palm on an exposed root, channeling a message to the centaur. A minute later, he turns back. After taking one pained look at me, rage strings his features taut. The satyr regards the lake and slams his hoof into the water, splattering the area.

"Fucking Elixir," he growls. "I'm going to kill him. Next time we meet, his ass is mine."

"That…was…Elixir?" I heave.

Puck drops beside me. He crouches, anxiety marring his countenance. "Did you see him?"

"Only parts."

"Which parts? What did you see?"

"Gold," I blurt out. "So much gold."

Puck frowns, as though that's incomprehensible. I realize why. But of course, it was Elixir! In the oral tales that circulate through my world, only one villain possesses gilded eyes that threaten to blind all who look upon him.

"I glanced away," I assure him. "It hurt too much to focus, so I glanced away."

His body sags with relief. "Seeing as you can still distinguish my handsome face, I was about to either commend you on your hidden powers or conclude your reflexes had kicked in before it was too late. Smart woman."

"He heard something. Whatever it was, he let me go."

Puck shrugs. "Let's just say he knew I was pissed."

Oh. That makes sense. If Puck knew Elixir had taken me, the satyr must have called out to Elixir, ordering him to let me go.

But that's not the only enigma. The ruler of the river had registered my bracelet—its shape, at least. He'd sketched the leaves and stem without truly perceiving them. One would think my accessory had been shrouded, the vacancy in his eyes suggesting Elixir hadn't known how to exercise those muscles. I'm about to inquire about that, but the memory of my bracelet brings to mind another precious object.

My fingers lurch open, my palms empty. During the skirmish, I'd clung to Cove's necklace. In a frenzy, I pat myself down, rummaging in my skirt pockets and under my sweater. It's gone. I'd had a piece of her, but it's gone now.

Bereavement hardens my jaw. When I describe what happened, Puck deliberates. "You said he swiped at your hand before he took off?"

"Yes." I blink, reconsidering Elixir's errant gaze. "Can he see?"

Puck hedges. "His tactile abilities are stronger."

Typical Fae response. But then, Cerulean had mentioned something about none being permitted to disclose his brother's capabilities or limitations, that one may only witness it for oneself. If Elixir's vision is impaired, perhaps he'd felt the jewelry in my grasp.

I speculate, "He must have taken the necklace."

Puck nods. "Then she's alive, luv."

"How?" I plead. "How can you be sure?"

"If your sister loses her game, we'll know. News doesn't travel from a region until its game is over. Them's the rules. Since we haven't heard reports, she has to be alive. Besides, I might have interrogated the shithead point-blank, from my roots to his depths. That is, after I told him to get his fucking hands off my woman."

I bleat, "What about her eyesight? If she looks upon him—"

Puck shakes his head. "It won't go that far. As instinctive as Elixir is, he can control that effect, and he'd be a dumbfuck to impair the one who's playing a game. But to be sure, I asked if Cove was in one piece. He spat two words: 'She is.' Elixir's never been a chatty one, but you'll be pleased to know that was a direct quote."

As for how the pendant ended up in the grass or why Elixir stole it, both remain mysteries. And how does he rule the river if he can't exist above the surface?

Or can he? Can Elixir breathe air?

I'd investigate further, but right now, all I care about is that Cove's alive. To be "in one piece" can imply many things in Faerie, but I won't allow myself to go there. Catastrophizing will accomplish nothing. No matter what, my older sister is living, breathing, and surviving. I need to keep faith in that.

My relief is fleeting, giving way to an awkward silence between Puck and me.

I'm exhausted, overwhelmed, and a mite sheepish. In the near future, the past few weeks will likely trigger a delayed bout of trauma. But that's not all that consumes me. That's not all I'll continue to feel.

Plump clouds roll in, dragging a storm with them. Amidst an incoming tempest, the sight of Puck alleviates the harsh sensations, enabling me to register other feelings. Softer ones. Gentler ones. By some miraculous feat, these impulses reinvigorate me.

In the backdrop, one of the bears swats at its tapered, otherworldly ears. Its fur brightens to an incandescent green at the paws, which matches the swirl in the animal's pupils, visible from this vantage point. Maybe it's the same wandering bear we'd heard during our intermission in the pit.

The pit, when we'd been stuck together, when everything began to change.

Puck and I rise and stare at one another, his eyes roving down my sodden form. I must resemble a pale fish with spinach-green strands of hair. Yet he admires me as if I'm the tallest, broadest, strongest tree in the woods—monumental, unwavering, and resilient against the elements. Also, wild and able to grow on its own, to outlast the fiercest of tempests.

Including the one that falls from the sky. Rain cascades in a pattering shower, then surges into a full-fledged downpour. Sheets of water douse the foliage, the spruce trees glistening, the teal afternoon darkening.

In spite of the deluge, branch candles twitch with restless spurts of fire. The flaming wicks accentuate the cut of Puck's jaw and the rich hue of his irises. Rivulets bind the breeches and vest to his form. The garments leave nothing to the imagination, defining the hard thighs and stacked abdomen beneath. Not far off that mark, my clothes are a sopping mess. The sweater and skirt hang off me like heavy drapes. That doesn't stop my rakish satyr from mentally peeling off the fabric from where he stands. His features strain, his decadent thoughts on evident display.

That look jumpstarts my pulse. Desire blossoms low in my belly, paired with another devastating emotion—unconditional, unequivocal. It burrows into me, with no intention of vacating anytime soon. Like the rain, I welcome the onslaught.

I want him. I need him.

I love him.

Fables help me. This impish, swaggering Fae with the most scandalous mouth I've ever encountered has stolen my heart.

My judicious side rehashes why this won't work. The renegade side I hadn't known existed stands at a precipice, ready to leap off the edge. I can't be without him another second.

I don't know what will happen tomorrow. I don't know where we'll go from here, nor do I care. Today, I just want to be happy.

Puck misreads the expression on my face and grimaces, as if I'm afraid of him getting too close, since we'd agreed it was over between us. Anger, pain, and lust scrunch his visage into a ball. Then his instincts kick in, his countenance flexing into a sarcastic smirk. "Well, shit," he mocks. "How impolite of the weather, don't you think?" He spreads his arms and executes a half-bow. "Time to get going, luv."

"Puck," I say.

He rotates toward the tree looming over us. "Let's see which fauna are in a merry mood to give us a ride."

"Puck, wait."

"Though, if you want to see Sylvan before heading to the mountain, it's best if we travel by air."

"Puck!" I snap, nervous and annoyed. "How…how do you say…'I love you'…in Faeish?"

He stops. Under the torrent, his hooves jolt in place, and his shoulder blades pinch together. I wait forever, the rain pelting this world, splashing the leaves and lake's surface.

Slowly, the satyr turns. The storm pastes his hair to his profile, darkening the waves to a shade of claret. His eyes blaze with astonishment and a new kind of fire, one that's never kindled there before.

Yes, it's rare for his kind to fall in love. Yes, satyrs can't recognize the emotion unless it's requited. And yes, I let my feelings reflect back to him, exposing them for him to catch, to share.

Finally, he prowls my way. Closing the divide, he halts an inch from me, our chests brushing. Droplets plunk from his antlers and land on his eyelashes.

The Fae tilts his head, his gaze searching mine. "You want to learn my language? That'll take time."

My voice cracks with joy. "I'm a quick study."

"Bloody true."

"Even so, I don't care how long it takes. Now stop tarrying and tell me how you say—"

"*Eck elsja fick,*" he murmurs, his accent gruff and sensuous. Then he repeats himself, drawing out the syllables as though for the first time.

"*Eck elsja fick.*" I pronounce those three words, returning them to him, offering them in kind. As I do, his eyelids hood.

Submerged in the rain, we go still. I glimpse his parted mouth—wet and hovering—while Puck's own gaze stalks my lips. Then a ravenous, guttural snarl builds in his throat. He shakes his head—"Fuck it"—and grabs me.

His arms band around my waist and haul me into him. On a cry, I fling myself against his body, my fingers spearing into his hair. Puck yanks me off the ground. His mouth clamps on to mine and pries my lips apart, the heat fueling higher, harsher.

The kiss explodes. Our tongues collide, striking at a frenetic pace. He licks into me, the hot flat slipping in and out, making me dizzy. I kiss him back, taste him back.

My soaked breasts mash into his torso, our wet garments rubbing in a glorious friction. One of his palms braces my scalp, fixing me in place while our lips fuse, rolling together. Like this, I shiver and burn with him.

We break apart only to switch angles, gasping into another smoldering embrace. His vicious mouth folds with mine, his tongue darting along the seam and then flicking between my lips, plunging and retreating and licking.

I feel his touch everywhere, yet everywhere isn't enough.

I want to kiss him more, and more, and more. I want my body rocking above his. I want us naked—wild and untamed. I want to make him howl. I want to love him.

I whine when the satyr peels himself away, my eyelids flapping open to behold rings of decadent brown. Puck speaks against my swollen mouth, his sultry breath coasting across my skin. "I've got an important question for you, luv."

Delirious, I can only nod. "I like questions."

"No, you like answers. I like questions."

"What do you want to know?"

A fiendish grin slides across his face. "You hungry?"

38

With Sylvan recovering, Puck corresponds with another creature through the roots. A majestic buck arrives, the spruce trees quaking under its weighty approach. The deer looms before us in its larger shape, the scopes of its eyes reflecting our drenched forms.

The bears grunt from their territory, the feral sounds indicating it's time to go before they take the buck's presence as an intrusion or a potential quarry. This similarity between my world and Puck's fills me with reassurance. The fauna are mystical, but they retain territoriality and hierarchy here, equally resplendent and grisly.

The deer's antlers blaze with flames in spite of the downpour. The animal's towering height must account for how quickly it has reached us across the forest. It shifts, enabling us to mount. Once Puck settles behind me, securing his arms around my middle, the creature shudders back into its massive form. It grows tall enough to cover more leagues, yet small enough for us sit without tumbling off his sides.

I find myself hovering a considerable distance from the ground, nearly to the tops of the trees. Excitement flutters through me. The buck leaps into a gallop, causing the wind to buffet our hair as the animal surges forward. At this range, I have a clear prospect of the valley, with its assortment of candlelit trees and the mountain range pulsating with light beneath sheets of late afternoon rain.

I inhale Puck's scent mixed with crisp precipitation and the deer's wet fur. Its antlers are a vast fortress of bone, its crown a blazing torch. I'd like to whoop as Lark would or sigh as Cove would.

Instead, I marvel in silence. And perhaps I smile.

Puck rests his chin on my shoulder and identifies every landmark I point out. In this way, he gives me a tour from a panoramic perspective. Miles pass in a fraction of the time it would have taken to cross The Solitary Forest on foot, embarking from the southeast to the north.

On the way, we detour to retrieve my archery and pack from The Gang of Elks. At last, our trio arrives at The Herd of Deer just prior to evening. His log cabin glows from the inside, orange simmering from its womb. I savor the view, a familiar nostalgia stirring from within, akin to how I feel about my family's house.

I can belong in two places, if I want to. But do I?

The deer shrinks, enabling us to dismount, then trots to the field where its kin reside. I grab fistfuls of my skirt and dash to the rear expanse. Hinds with waterfalls springing from their crowns nibble on vegetation. Stags with seedlings encrusting their antlers take shelter under broadleaf canopies.

A doe with shamrock antlers lounges beneath one of the oaks, a fresh bandage dressing her wound, likely provided by Puck or Cypress.

"Sylvan!" I sink to the grass and sling my arms around the deer. She nudges me with her muzzle, the affectionate gesture squeezing a place in my chest.

Puck kneels and cups Sylvan's cheek. "There's my favorite doe." He glances around, then whispers to her, "Don't go bragging about that." He knocks his head my way. "Not like this overachiever."

I smack his arm. We stay with her for a few minutes until I begin shivering. The doe is faring well, and the herd is with her.

Puck takes my hand. We run to the cabin, rain pelting us from a slanted angle. The fireplace kindles to life, puddles of gold filling the interior as we spill inside. My cloak is still hanging on the wall peg, where I'd left it the last time I was here. Cypress must have overlooked it when collecting my possessions.

Puck closes the door. My teeth clatter, and I unlace my boots while the satyr tracks up the stairs. He returns several heartbeats later with spare clothes, tossing me a small pile. "They'll dwarf you, but they're warm and smell like me."

The rascal. He just can't resist teasing, even when he's serious. Puck moves without hesitation, unbuckling his vest and shrugging it off. I go still, immobile as the muscles carved into his torso contract, skin and sinew bathed in fiery hues. With the blaze as our only source of illumination, shadows and scorching light enhance his body. The tan nipples and taut ribcage, the square jaw and sopping red hair.

And lower. Fables eternal, he twists and drags his breeches down his limbs, his buttocks dimpled and flexing only inches from me. His spine curls, and beads of water slide down his frame, into the divots of his lower back.

And I. Can't. Move.

True, I've seen him naked multiple times. I've felt that solid body against mine, thrusting into me.

And true, we'd kissed in the rain. And true, we as good as admitted we love each other.

But this is a new sort of intimacy. I don't know how to proceed, and with Puck disrobed like this, he's not making it any easier. I lack the faculties to pace myself, much less to pronounce a single, comprehensible word. Fables, there's so much of him, all that soused, masculine flesh.

When he bends and steps into fresh pants dyed the color of cider, my nipples pit against my sweater. Of course, Puck chooses that moment to wheel toward me. His gaze drops to my chest, catching those nipples in the act. They're so stiff, even the thickest wool clothing wouldn't succeed in concealing them.

Puck's eyes swell. His attention trails from the green hair plastered to my cheeks to my bare toes. I'm dripping all over his floor, clutching the garments he's given me.

Inside, logs crackle and hiss. Outside, the storm batters the windows and roof.

We idle in the foyer, bordered by an open doorway. He grabs the overhead lintel with both hands and leans forward, knolls of muscle bunching across his arms. The position urges those pants to slump lower down his waist. Another pearl of water sizzles into the path of red sprigs descending between his pelvic bones.

Poised like this, he flaunts all that roguish splendor, emanating sexuality. I gawk. Then I scowl, my body humming with frustration. Dammit, he's doing this on purpose.

"What are you hungry for?" Puck murmurs.

My eyes lurch from his mouth to those evil eyes. "Thirsty."

His lips slant. Fondness, amusement, and something altogether wicked flit across his visage. He releases the lintel and juts his chin toward the living room while sauntering past me. "Make yourself at home, luv."

Puck disappears into the kitchen, taking his scent and half-clad body with him. I hustle out of my clothes and into the dry ones. It's a miracle he owns a textile other than leather in his wardrobe. The loose cotton vest falls to my knees. The pants sag around my frame, puddling at my ankles; I cuff them about four times before they suit my height.

Padding into the living room, I collect pillows from the sofa and arrange them atop the fur rug. At last, my joints slump before the hearth. The fire toasts my feet and blooms a marmalade hue on the walls.

I listen to echoes of the satyr puttering in the kitchen, crockery and spoons clinking. He returns, settling beside me and offering a steaming mug. I take a sip, milk and melted cocoa pouring down my throat.

"You have hot chocolate in Faerie?" I ask.

"Come now," he says. "What do you take us for?"

Indeed. Dairy and sugar. Two delicacies that Faeries covet.

Puck guzzles his chocolate in one throat-pumping swallow. Setting down his cup, he scoops my feet into his palms and massages the toes. "Cold little piggies," he croons. "Poor things. What have you done to them?"

I can't help laughing, then sobering as he circles his knuckles into my heels. When he hits a particular spot, I sigh.

"Better?" he rasps.

I nod and focus on his strong fingers rubbing, pressing. With every touch, lightning streaks up my limbs until my body's buzzing. My eyelids shudder, then flap open as he releases me.

Puck rises abruptly and stalks back to the kitchen. I blink from my stupor, my blood raging, my thoughts feverish. He makes a great deal of noise from the other room, his agitation evident in the clash of pans and cutlery.

I don't overthink it. I simply get to my feet and shuffle to the doorway, where his back faces me. Something fries in one of the pans, emitting the aromas of butter and maple syrup.

Distracted, I inch closer and take a peek. "Pancakes," I exclaim.

Puck gives me a sideways smirk. "Like I said in The Seeds that Give. You didn't give me the chance to whip up the batter before getting yourself glamoured into a mushroom trap. Inconsiderate of you, luv."

He hands me a plate of three cakes, then helps himself. Instead of perching at the island, Puck leans his hip against the counter and spears the food with his fork, shoving in mouthfuls.

My stomach lurches, and my mouth waters. I feast on the pancakes, inwardly moaning at the flavors, both mortal and immortal. The sugar is richer, the syrup smoother. Yet the salted butter is everything I remember from my world.

I finish before he does, my belly sated—the rest of me decidedly not, especially when I peek at the Fae dominating this kitchen. The lattice of his abdomen. The final droplet trickling down his temple. The beat of his pulse, thudding like a button in his neck.

Never once have I witnessed Puck avoiding my gaze like this. It's as if he doesn't know what to do with himself and needs to keep feasting, to keep swallowing, to consume anything but me. I sketch the tension in his wrists. The tick in his jaw.

An ache builds in the nexus of my thighs. My heart pumps, savage and erratic. Moisture pools between my thighs as I will the satyr to look at me.

I want his attention. And then I want the rest of him.

I want his lips on the wet cleft of my thighs. I want his body surging into mine, his hips going wild between my legs. I want my lips strapped around his length, sucking on him until every sinful word he's ever learned skitters helplessly off his tongue.

I fixate on Puck's bent head and the movements of his mouth as he chews—then stops chewing. He goes rigid, his nostrils flaring. I realize the instant he's scented my arousal.

The air thickens in this cabin, while fierce creatures roam outdoors. The rain splatters the windowpanes, blotting out the landscape.

Slowly, his throat siphons down the last of his meal. Then his head drags toward mine, his gaze darkening, targeting.

I'm brimming, vibrating everywhere. My breasts hang heavily, my palms sweating, my lips parting. I can barely stand this prolonged silence.

"You're throbbing, luv," he says.

I lick my lips. "Yes."

Yes. The word seeps into the air, begging, demanding.

It's all the invitation Puck needs. He chucks the plate aside. My breathing hitches when he swaggers in front of me, bracketing his bulky arms on either side of my quavering form.

Embers glitter in his swollen pupils. "Where else are you throbbing?"

We stare at one another while I hitch my right leg off the floor. My sole plants on the lower cabinet door behind me, my knee flanking his hip. "Find out," I pant.

With an appreciative hum, he dips his hand into the front of my pants. Those hot, long fingers scroll through the patch of hair between my thighs—and a small gasp tears from my mouth. The satyr scrapes lightly, delicately across my slit. He hunts for that kernel of sensation, dragging out the sounds braced on the tip of my tongue, the sensations teetering at the fringes of my center.

Our foreheads land together, our mouths dangling open. Sable brown consumes my vision, the whiff of leather, cloves, and pine enveloping me. His digits circle my opening, coaxing a tide of wetness from the slot. Then he glides those drenched fingers to the place where I throb. He presses onto the delicate nub, sparks igniting from that protrusion of skin.

I quaver, dizzy with need. "I want you there, Puck."

"Which part of me?" he inquires. "My finger?" He crooks a digit between my folds and slides it high. "My tongue?" He draws that tongue up my throat, urging my head to loll back until my hair brushes the countertop. At last, he whispers into my ear, "Or my cock?"

"All of you," I implore. "Give me all of it. Give me your body."

With a growl, Puck claims my profile with his free hand and hauls my mouth to his. The satyr's tongue pries me apart. I moan, kissing him back, our lips fusing.

My hands dive into the back of his breeches, spanning his rear. He groans, licks the crease of my mouth and plunges in again. All the while, his fingers whisk into the soaked cleft of my body, pumping up to his knuckles and matching the pace of our kiss.

I'm going to faint. Either that, or I'm going to tear him to shreds.

If he doesn't stop, I'll climax right here. I peel my lips away, snare his waistband, and walk backward, leading him into the living room.

He gives me a fiendish grin and trails, his pants captured in my grip. We cross to the fur rug spread before the fireplace. As I let him go, he moves in tandem with me. I turn, giving him my back, and he prowls close behind. Those rugged hands seize my hips, making me shiver. His bare torso—as wide as a shield—presses into my spine, and I recline against him.

Puck's lips descend first, hot and pliable against the crook of my neck. My eyelids shut at the contact, and my head rocks back to land on his shoulder, giving him better access. I reach behind, clamping his nape beneath the curtain of hair.

He drops open-mouthed kisses in that sensitive nook. My mouth unhinges, falling open on a silent moan. The satyr has barely started with me, yet he raises gooseflesh across my skin. My fingers dig into him, holding fast, requesting more.

Puck obliges. A smile lingers in his kiss—I can feel it—which yields to an appreciative growl. He sucks on me, drawing my flesh into the humid cavern of his mouth. A noise reminiscent of a cry leaps from me. I curl into his solid frame, my bottom fitting against the erect ridge of his groin.

This feels like a hunt. Every motion and gesture are in sync, each of us taking turns as hunter and prey.

He's everything I never wanted, never thought I'd desire. He's mischief and sensuality, viciousness and impulsiveness. He's a taunting smirk and a chain reaction of unpredictable words. He's my blush, my scowl, and my laughter. He's cleverness and candidness. He means what he says. And once he loves you, he puts everything into it, and he doesn't falter.

Once you're his, he's yours.

This impish Fae is lightness and darkness. So am I.

Puck's tongue tracks along my shoulder, then licks up the side of my throat to my ear. He suckles the lobe until I'm a shambles, quivering and gasping and utterly out of control.

This is what it's like to be seduced by him. This is what it's like to steal his heart.

My roguish Fae returns to that crook in my neck, kissing it as he would my lips, lapping and tasting until I can't take it any longer. I step away from him, tarry for a moment, and make a choice.

I'm nervous, my pulse accelerating. Although we've done this numerous times, in numerous ways, there's one thing I've never done with him. But I will now.

The fire lashes from the grate. Facing that small inferno, I slip out of the pants he'd given me. Then I take a deep breath and peel the long vest over my head, kicking aside the garments. I stand before him, fully naked.

My tattoo sits on my lower back, exposed to his gaze. I can't see the marking, but I feel it. The X of crossbow bolts. The ink I'll never be able to remove. It's my regret, yet for the first time, the guilt hurts a bit less. If I hadn't gone through that era of my life, I wouldn't have become who I am now.

So, I reveal this part of myself to him. I do so without shame, my nudity on display. I've never disrobed for anyone. Tonight, I do it not merely for him. I do it for myself.

Puck remains quiet. I sense his gaze, avid on the tattoo while the blaze sputters.

He breaches the distance. In the firelight, I watch his shadow kneel, his fingers sliding down my sides. Lowering himself on the floor, he sketches the marking with his thumbs.

Then his lips follow. When they do, tears spring to my eyes. I clamp my eyelids together, my chin stern but shaky. Puck maps out the tattoo, planting kisses atop every dab of ink, until he's covered the whole rendering.

Suddenly, my features smooth out, solace easing my stance. I don't set the tears free, not because I refuse to but because I feel like smiling instead.

Finished, he rises. As he does, his lips peck their way up my form, searing a path to my mouth.

I twist my head to find his lips, a second before he hisses, "Now kiss the shit out of me, luv."

With a sigh, I claim that mouth. My tongue skates across the ledge, then lunges inside. He makes a gravely sound while parting his lips, yielding them above my own, our tongues sweeping against one another.

Though I haven't wheeled around, I reach behind to assist him. We fumble with his pants, shoving them down. Briefly, I glimpse his length, thick and high, the head flushed. But then Puck deepens the kiss, the force of which causes my head to fog.

He walks us forward. At the mantle, he grabs my wrists and pins my hands to the shelf. The sweltering flames throw heat at my breasts and core.

He breaks the kiss, seething against my lips, "Don't move."

"I'm not going anywhere," I vow.

While nuzzling the opposite side of my neck, his palms cup my breasts and circle the nipples with his thumbs. More noises skitter from me. I'm kindling, sparking to life. The crests tighten, perking under the ministrations of his fingers. The hands of a cellist, an archer, a hunter.

He pinches and teases my nipples, the buds darkening. From behind, he torments each swell and recess of my body. It's an erotic test of my restraint. He samples the backs of my knees, the insides of my elbows, the cleft beneath my earlobe, and the canal of my ear. His tongue travels, scorching me from head to heel.

Wetness seeps from my center, aching for friction. The tiny bud of sensation pounds like a drum.

At last, Puck's whole body aligns with mine. "Spread yourself wider," he instructs. "I'm going to need lots of room to fuck you."

I broaden my position, parting my limbs further. "Hurry."

His sultry chuckle ripples up my scalp. "That's one promise I can't keep."

Fables curse this imp. By now, I'm moaning nonstop, damning him for pushing me this far to the edge. Puck secures one arm around my midriff and my right hip with the other, angling them just so.

The tip of his shaft probes, expanding my walls. Languidly, he teases me to the brink with gentle, shallow juts. I whimper in cadence with his movements, my head falling once more atop his shoulder. Experimentally, I roll my hips with his. Puck buckles, his grunts hoarse and deep.

Little by little, his crown slides in and retreats. Again and again. Inarticulate phrases tangle on my tongue, unable to get out, and he doesn't sound much more coherent. It's so unbearable that I whine, and he pushes out a strained breath.

We shift into place, mindless, desperate. And then he launches into me, his entire length pitching high and hard. I cry out. Puck bites my shoulder, a guttural noise breaking from him as he buries himself into the narrow clench of my body.

I'm soaked around him, clamping around him. I feel every inch, long and firm. I feel the temperature of his shaft. And then I feel more as he begins thrusting, the lazy cadence of his hips pushing moans from my open mouth.

Puck laps slowly into me, circling his pelvis. He withdraws to the crest and plunges in, in, in. I tilt my bottom for more, taking each flick of his waist. He puffs with exertion, drawing it out, prolonging the anguish.

But it's not enough. I'm greedy, and he's just too good at this.

Either he registers my need or hits his breaking point. Whatever it is, Puck releases my hip and grabs the mantle beside my own hand, using the shelf for leverage. Then he charges forth. With his other arm fixed around my middle, he holds me in place and whips into my core.

Puck flings himself against me, putting his whole frame into it. I keen at the snapping of his waist.

I manage to swerve and gasp, "How are you? Happy?"

The satyr gives me a salacious grin. "Ecstatic," he grunts. "Agonized. Fucking besotted." He pecks my lips. "And in love." Then he whispers, "With you, I feel love."

The last word punctures my heart. "I want to see you."

He knows what I mean. Nodding, he withdraws. I spin and press on his shoulders, urging him to the ground. It's my turn.

We hunker to the rug. My palms shove him back, reclining the satyr across the floor. Stretched out, his torso gleams with sweat, his length smooth and wet from me.

I waste no time climbing onto Puck, my thighs splitting around his pelvis. He helps me, grabbing himself and pointing it to my entrance. Then I take over, sinking onto him with an elongated sigh.

Flattening my hands on his pectorals, I swirl my hips. Puck hisses, his head flinging back, his fingers gripping my backside. His bronze earrings flash in the muted room and emit a short, tinkling tease of noise. A needy, ravenous expression cleaves his face.

Seeing him like this fuels me to action. I hunch over and gyrate my body, stroking his length with sharp jerks. The satyr disintegrates beneath me, his moans frayed and so very primal. My confidence grows, expands. This is new for me, but I find my rhythm, stalking after his pleasure, hunting it down. And in this way, I seek my own rapture.

He's mine. His ragged groans are mine.

I undulate my hips, burrowing him deeper, so deep. My head flings back, my hair brushes his thighs, and my breasts bounce. The fire licks my skin as everything inside me coils, tightens.

"So gorgeous," Puck rasps. "That's it, luv. Ride me until you come."

The satyr has stamina. I know this from previous endeavors, but it never ceases to amaze me. Whereas I'm about to fracture into a million pieces, he's not done. Snatching my hips, he advances our movements, tugging me back and forth. He meets me halfway, his waist lunging with urgency.

I sob with need, with ecstasy. We move in haste, rocking together, driving faster, faster. My fingernails puncture his flesh, my waist beating against his. Puck's length hits another glorious spot and hammers there. Rapture and tension converge where he pumps into me.

I bend over and grab the fur rug for support, my hips racing. "Oh," I scream.

"Come on, luv," he urges.

It happens. We lock together, then unravel. A white-hot sensation condenses and then blasts from our centers. My walls contort around him, bliss and warmth gushing to the tips of my toes, to the peak of my skull.

Moans pour from my throat and scatter across the living room. Puck hollers, his length pulsating, emptying inside me. The release goes on and on, endless, boundless.

We slump, panting for air. I collapse, falling atop Puck. He catches my lips in a tired kiss, his fingers lurching into my hair.

The fire sways. It brushes gold across the room, illuminating the perspiration at my bust and across the grid of his stomach. I nestle into Puck's chest while he palms my backside. Like this, we listen to the rain tapping against the panes, gentle and steady now.

I smell the leftover pancakes and the musky aroma of our bodies. That's when I know for sure. With him, I'm home.

Puck mutters against my scalp, "By the way, have I complimented that spectacular fable you composed?"

The fable. After the battle, the tale had flowed as if it had been building inside me, storing itself away until then. Perhaps I ought to write it down. Thinking of the blank pages left in my notebook, a thrill flutters through my chest.

I fold my arms across his collarbones and rest my chin there. "It was a start."

"And a fine one." The satyr runs his knuckles down my ear. "What are you feeling, luv?"

"I want to stay," I tell him. "I want to stay here with you."

His eyes jump all over me with hope and repentance. So I ask, "What about you? What are you thinking?"

"Same thing." Yet he sighs, combing through his hair. "But—"

"I don't care. I don't care that you're immortal, and I'm not. Do you?"

"Don't fucking go there," he says tenderly. "You know me better."

"I'll grow old and die someday. You'll have to watch it happen. Can you take that?"

"You'll destroy me whether you leave or stay, Juniper. Either way, it'll always be you. Just you forever, and ever, and ever, and ever…" He thinks about it. "And ever." And he nibbles on my neck. "And ever." And my shoulder. "And ever."

I chuckle. "Then I'll stay—"

But Puck grabs my face and kisses the last of my words from my lips. I smile, because although I don't like being cut off, I'll forgive him this one time.

Perhaps I'd made my decision a long time ago. We may have begun in different worlds, but I don't want it to end that way. I want my realm and his, my family and his arms. By some measure, I want both, even if it means dividing my time between here and where I came from. That's what Lark's planning to do, so I'll do it with her.

Puck lives out loud, and I live within the boundaries. But those differences strengthen us, which means we're capable of making this work.

I'm not giving up, and neither will Puck. We're too stubborn for that.

Impulsively, the satyr peels his mouth away. "You sure, luv?"

"I'm sure," I promise. "I want more of this—more of you."

The words prompt a thought in his head. I see an idea flittering through that cunning mind. "In that case, why wait to start?"

Thusly, Puck gives more of himself to me. He brushes my lips with his and whispers something against them. It takes me an educated moment to decipher the word: His name.

It's a quick but hearty trio of letters, two vowels and a consonant. It's a throaty sounding moniker that originates from under the soil. It's the name of the tree standing vigil outside this home.

When the satyr pulls back, I can't disguise the astonishment in my face. Though, Puck only shrugs. "Two reasons. One, you might need it if you ever play another guessing game with Tinder. Two, I still owe you for freeing me nine years ago."

"But I didn't do that so you could owe me. And besides, you repaid me in gratitude. When I unlocked the trap, I remember it clearly." I had freed his leg from the iron jowls, and he'd said, *"Thanks, luv."*

"Ah, that," Puck recalls. "I was being witty, so it doesn't count."

I crumble into stunned laughter. Technically, that must be true if he can't lie. And while he was born with a wonderful name, I like the one he's chosen better. That's the satyr whom I'd met, befriended, and shared my heart with.

"Sooooo." Puck gathers me to him. "You've got me by the balls now, huntress. What are you going to do with me?"

Again, I need a moment to reflect on what he's alluding to. "I don't need or want power over you. I can simply rescind that, correct?"

"Come now," he insists. "If you have power over me, you can take power from me. There must be something. Be greedy for once in your misbegotten life."

"I've got what I want." To illustrate, I wiggle my hips around his waist. He groans, reminding me we're intimately attached. And, dear Fables, he's still hard.

After that discovery, it's a wonder I'm able to articulate my thoughts. "I'm human, and that's all I need to be. That's what your world needs to see. They need to see we have our own form of magic." I gasp as he attacks my throat with enthusiasm, and our restless hands begin to wander once more. "I only want you, for as long as possible."

Just like that, Puck halts. "Oh, shit." In a flash, the satyr sits up.

He brings me with him, my thighs flanking his hips. "What?" I breathe.

"For as long as possible," Puck repeats and then frames my cheeks, inspiration brightening his mien. "So, take that from me." At my quizzical expression, he rushes out, "Take power from my immortality."

I freeze, my mind clicking into place. "Do you mean—"

"Take half of my life."

"Can…I do that?"

His lips slant into a clever grin. "Yes, luv. You can."

Fables! In the firelight, we stare at one another. If I take half his immortality, we'll live, what? A prolonged life? Like Lark and Cerulean?

If we do this, I won't have to leave him bereft, nor Lark. They needn't endure the grief of outliving me.

He and I can be together. As it is, there's enough to plague us, enough to worry about for the future. This is one less threat in the fight that lies ahead, one extra blessing in this cabin.

This is happiness. This is us.

"How about it, Juniper?" Puck tempts, setting my hand on his warm, wicked heart. "Want to give it a try?"

My mouth wobbles. "Sure." Then I clear my throat and rest my palms on his shoulders. "How does it work? I've never read anything about it. Is there a ritual? An act to perform?"

Another devious smile. "There is. We cement it by performing an act that expresses your will—that which you desire from me."

What a sneak. "Such as?"

"I can think of one." I yelp as Puck rolls me over, his body fitting atop mine, my legs slinging over his waist. "But it'll take time," he purrs, those stag antlers illuminated by the flames. "A lot of time."

I strap myself around him. It's a good thing I have plenty of that now.

Epilogue

Puck

Fables and fuck. It's early, on the rumpled edge of dusk. Twilight rustles through the window and tangles itself into the bedroom loft, fondling the sheets with a hybrid of teal and black.

I groan out of sleep and stretch my limbs, already grinning like an asshole. It's a queer phenomenon to wake up like this, knowing someone takes up valuable space next to me. Body heat. Entwined limbs. Her breath stroking my neck. Her ass tucked against my groin. That adorable scrunch of her brows when she sleeps, like she's scolding her dreams for not making a damn bit of sense.

How magnificent to have a partner claim the better half of this house, filling it with new smells and sounds. Her pencils and quills littering the tables. Her clothes folded on chairs and in the wardrobe. Her crossbow mounted beside my longbow. The smell of ink, parchment, juniper berries, and campfires. I haven't told her she emits those scents, that they've seeped like water into my bed.

Our bed. I fancy the sound of that word—short, uncomplicated, and sexy.

Ahh, my bookish woman of words. My scholarly huntress.

She's an intoxication, a chemical reaction, a rush of blood. She's verbal battles and pursed lips. She's the green of spruce trees, from her hair, to her eyes, to the beautiful patch between her thighs. She's willpower and intelligence. She's righteousness and primness. She's hidden desires and bossy opinions. She's candid and says what she means.

She strikes true. She's all mortal, all raw inspiration, all mine.

And I'm hers. Fuck if I'm not all hers.

I flop over to grope my favorite parts of the huntress, nibble on the rounded edge of her ear, and continue where we'd left off hours ago. But instead of skin, my fingers cup a pillow.

Stumped, I blink.

Nobody else has ever rendered me speechless. But she's done that.

Nobody else has ever gotten my heart to pump at critical mass. But she's done that.

Nobody else has ever left me alone in bed. But fuck, she's done that, too.

Her side of the mattress is vacant. This blanket is smooth and devoid of wrinkles because she likes to make the bed seconds after rising. I know the Fable quote she uses to express why, touting a moral about clean homes and clean minds. It's a darling penchant of hers.

On the flip side, the many times I've enticed her to chuck that routine and destroy the bedsheets with me dabs a smirk into the corner of my mouth. It's a glorious balance of habit and impulse, in which we both tip the scales. I fancy that, too.

My cello case leans against the corner beside the writing desk, which the huntress has dubbed as her own, claiming it like a parcel of land. I don't mind. I'll give her whatever the fuck she wants. And I have, countless naughty times.

As for the cello, my temperature scales to a combustible degree when I recall yesterday. I'd played for her. Then I'd hunted her through this cabin, stalking her laughter from the living room, to the kitchen, to this loft.

And oh, then. I'd gotten that divine female to touch herself. She had been tentative at first, sheepish but curious. Sprawled on the mattress, with her legs spread like the pages of an erotic novel, she'd pressed and probed and panted.

I'd watched in mindless, helpless delirium. Blood had rushed to my skull, my fingers itched, and my pulse detonated with the spangled light of an exploding star. Not to wax poetic, but she'd looked so fucking pretty—so real. I'd watched this unparalleled woman give herself power.

She came, her smoke-edged voice striking the rafters. Afterward, she'd tossed me a demand: my turn.

Who was I to deny her? I'd gripped myself while feeling her gaze on me, exerting a delicious pressure that had undone my very soul.

Naturally, she'd upped the ante. Tugging my fingers away, she'd lowered her head, and I'd gone mute. And Fables, she'd clamped her studious lips around my cock, sucking the sanity out of me.

Happiness. That's what got me to holler and release. She makes me happy.

But it's more. It's that I make *her* happy.

By some lopsided miracle, not only do I make her climax. I make her smile. I make her laugh. What else is there?

I roll onto my back and keep grinning like a moron at the wood-beamed ceiling. My torso inflates and deflates, letting the sensations fuel me like oxygen or a merry goblet of wine. The crackling of flames tickles my ears, the sound lined with the crisp flip of a page.

With another hearty rumble, I swagger out of bed and get to my hooves. Mellow candlelight and eventide shadows trickle down my naked body. I won't lie—because I can't, ha—but one appendage has been fully awake since before I'd regained consciousness. If I don't learn to calm it down, my cock will be perpetually stuck this way, knocking shit over as I track through the house.

I do myself a favor and scrape my fingers over my ribcage and abdomen, a relaxing, lazy migration that settles the phallus in question but wakes up the rest of me. Most importantly, my brain. I won't last a second in the huntress's presence without that.

I snatch my breeches off the floor and step into them, letting the waistband slouch like a troublemaker around my pelvic bones. It's a cheap trick, a racy maneuver to get her attention, and she'll see right through it. But then, I like when she calls me out.

The planks sag under my weight as I saunter down the staircase, book-ended by a pair of walls. At the bottom, the passage twists like the end of a fox tail and dumps me into the foyer. Around the corner, I swank into the living room—and go still.

Shit. I don't just go still. I go stupid.

The couch is a crescent around the fireplace trunk. A sumptuous vision perches sideways across the cushions, mortal toes gilded by the blaze writing on the grate. The compact shape of her body takes up only a fraction of that sofa, yet she's the largest, vastest thing in the room.

Juniper's profile ducks toward an open notebook propped on her up-turned thighs. Her pencil flies across the page as if it's got wings. Only she possesses the type of steadfast grip that makes a writing tool look like a weapon. She bites her tongue in concentration, her brows crinkling with the productive prowess of an ancient wordsmith.

She's writing. Did I mention she's also naked?

Probably not, since my thoughts have melted into sap. And that's only half of my body's evident response. My shaft twitches, thickening in my breeches.

Flames douse her calves in hot shades of orange and red, while her green hair hangs gloriously unkempt around her cheeks. She's a candlelit tree, resistant to fire. The half-moon curve of her hip nestles into the cushions. Her oh-so-pretty tits inflate with each breath, capped in rosy little nipples.

She's writing naked. She's writing naked, with a pair of spectacles on her nose.

Fuck. Me.

My prick loves what it sees and wants what it sees. If she weren't already stripped, I'd do the honors with, well, honor.

Here I'd been attempting to impress her with my bare torso and low-slung pants. Here she is, stealing my thunder, outdoing me as she often does.

Fables almighty. How she owns me.

I whistle, the noise swooping from my end of the cabin to hers. But the huntress already knows I'm here, because she'd heard me coming, and she knows my pace. Yet she doesn't turn my way, a fact I'll need to rectify.

Her perceptive lips tilt. "*Kott jföld*, satyr."

"And a good evening to you, too," I intone, savoring her mortal accent.

She's been soaking up Faeish like a sponge. I've taught her a few basics of the practical and filthy variety. When this woman puts her mind to something, she devotes herself to it, devouring it whole. I like to think we have this in common.

Although I'm fond of my antlers, I don't mind pretending to be a panther now and then. I step into the firelight, prowling slowly, my gaze fixed on its quarry. That aside, one of the bountiful traits Juniper appreciates about me is my directness, which matches her own. We don't mince words with each other, a fact that gets me into trouble with this huntress as much as it causes her breath to quicken.

I murmur, "Look at me, luv."

Her pencil ceases its voyage across the parchment. She removes her spectacles and swings her head my way, those evergreen eyes warming on my face. How I adore being one of the chosen few who elicits this sort of gentle response from her. Pride oozes through me. The achievement is as rewarding as getting her to chuckle or moan with pleasure. I've decided to add it to my nonexistent list of top three life accomplishments.

A thorough inspection of my pecs, arms, and navel causes a ravenous shift in her features. She's caught sight of the waistband and everything straining beneath it. I haven't fooled her.

Desire leaps to the forefront of her face, a firestorm suffusing her throat and lips in swaths of pink. That, right there. That's the Passionate Look. That's why I came down here half dressed, indulging in my addiction to that expression. I have an eternal thing for her stare, her eyes holding me in a way no other being ever has.

Is this feeling ever going to end? I hope to fuck not.

In my present erectile condition, it's a wonder I can walk without hobbling. I take a step toward her—and the fucking teakettle shrieks, blaring like a scandalized matron. We jolt toward the shrill noise, then twist back to each other and break into contrite laughter.

I wrestle to control the goofy, pubescent smile on my face while the kettle continues to squeal and throw a tantrum. I stride into the kitchen and shut the damn thing up, pouring a mug for Juniper and adding a dollop of the berry syrup she likes.

Returning to the living room, I set the cup on the coffee table, then make my useless self actually useful and stoke the fire. Behind me, Juniper clears her throat. Based on the sound, it doesn't take a genius to know she's indulging in a sneak peek at my ass.

"I suggest we start over before this gets out of hand," she proposes.

"I like when things get out of hand," I remark.

But I know what she means, and she's right. If we don't learn to keep our hands off each other for more than three minutes, we'll never make it out of this cabin again.

I straighten and lean against the mantle. "Hey there, huntress."

"Hello, satyr. Did you sleep well?"

"I do it better with you. How about yourself?"

"Ten hours."

I must have worn her out. "Hmm. I hate to bring this up, luv." I flick my finger toward her figure. "Seems you've misplaced your robe. What was the point in commissioning Moth to tailor you a wardrobe if you're not going to embellish all those delectable curves?"

"I don't have curves."

"I've found plenty of them," I flirt. "Not that I'm complaining about your current outfit, but I've been eager to see your tush in those cruel new leggings." While Juniper shakes her head in amusement, my nose twitches in a belated reaction to the overdose of butter and spices wafting from the kitchen. If it weren't so difficult to concentrate on more than one thing at a time around her, I would have noticed the aroma while shushing the kettle. "What's that smell?"

"Apple pie."

"You dared to bake without me?"

"It's for Cypress."

That's...nice of her. I quirk an eyebrow, a fresh batch of warmth sloshing through my stomach. "Such plentiful kindness. What's the merry occasion?"

She hesitates, her attention flicking to Cypress's painting behind me. Some remote, confidential emotion softens her features. She and my best friend have gotten chummy, but that look goes beyond, as if she knows something I don't. Something fragile—a word I'd never associate with Cypress.

In fact, the look resembles empathy. How peculiar.

Why do I get the feeling she'll clam up if I ask more?

Case in point, she just answers, "It's comfort food."

Ah. I'd expected it was something like that. Cypress has recovered from his battle wound, but the pastry must be a sympathetic gesture. Very human, indeed.

I sniff the air. "You used too much cinnamon."

Her eyes thin, her chin jutting like a stubborn fist. "I have not."

"Did you add—"

"Lemon? Yes." Juniper scoots into the cushions, making room as if there weren't miles of couch leftover. She cradles the book to her chest like a secret while curling her limbs beneath her. It's such an endearing, fetching pose. "I've been thinking," she begins.

"Indeed?" I recline across from the huntress. "Let's hear it."

She rethinks her posture, discards the notebook on the table, and sweeps a throw blanket over her lap. Then she rests her feet on my hooves and tucks a lock of hair behind one of those cute ears.

It isn't like her to fidget. Is this about her father? She and Lark are planning to see him, and I know she's antsy over that. The closer that reunion looms, the more shelves and cupboards she reorganizes. She'd started with the bookcase, her default coping mechanism.

I think my hunch is right, albeit with a twist. When she still doesn't answer, I lean forward, cup her knee, and croon, "Yessssss?"

Junipers quits twiddling and lifts her chin as though she's about to negotiate a pact. "I want you to come with me."

I blink. "What?"

"In The Seeds that Give, you said you wished to see where I come from. After Lark and I visit our papa alone, I want you to join me for the next trip. I want you to meet my father, and I want him to meet you."

I...don't know what to say. My throat does something rickety, fear and awkwardness contorting there. She wants her father to meet me. She wants to show me her home. Every corrupt decision and foible I've ever been responsible for flashes before my eyes like an omnibus of monster stories and cautionary folktales. Her father will rip my fucking head off. He'll despise the shit out of me, which will hurt Juniper.

He'll say what I've known since I met her. She's too perfect for me. She deserves better. She deserves a human with human legs and a human heart, not a riffraff Fae who's done more damage than not.

Juniper interprets my silence and whatever expression warps my face, and she gives me a terse look. "Don't you dare, Puck. He knows me better than that, and so do you."

"Bloody true," I remark in a daze.

Fables know why, but Juniper will disagree with her father about me. She knows her own mind and owns it fully, with grit and tenacity. It's one of the many traits that had initially attracted me to her.

I remember her standing in the rain, asking me to translate three pivotal mortal words into Faeish, the request squeezing my heart and then releasing it, letting the blood rush back in. I'd just about passed out from the impact.

This huntress knows the good and bad of me, the shards of redemption and surplus of viciousness. Yet she's still here.

My heart clenches, an extraordinary sensation dominating that pounding slab of arteries and tissue. I've felt this every day since Juniper stepped into this forest, except I hadn't been able to name it until our kiss in the rain, until I'd spoken to her in my language.

I love you.

Queer thing, being in love. It's a hodgepodge of emotions that regularly changes its melody, from terrifying as hell to baffling, exquisite, consuming, infuriating, intimidating, thrilling, erotic, tender, simple, complicated, soft, hard, and a stack of other words Juniper would know to list.

But one thing stays constant: the way my pulse stalls every time I look at her, hear her, touch her. No need for bargains or games anymore. No favors or repayments. When I'm with Juniper, it's absolute and unconditional.

It's not about me. It's all about her.

"So, um, what do you think?" she presses. "Will you meet him? Will you be part of my family?"

A family. Again, my tongue flops in my mouth. "My, my, my," I whisper. "I think you've left me speechless."

Her mouth quirks, joy blazing across her face. "Then *show* me what you think."

That, I can do. I swipe aside the blanket and snatch her. Dragging Juniper onto my lap, I seize her grinning mouth and tease the seam until she parts on a sigh. My tongue flicks into that precious cavern, licking and scooping out more delightful noises. Her fingers trickle into my hair, her thighs splayed around my pelvis, emitting heat.

Keyed up, I slant my head and kiss her with an intense sort of softness, tasting the forest on her lips, sucking on that mortal tongue with deliberate slowness. She keens, the sound driving me wild. Her wetness slickens my waist, that sweet root rubbing against my cock.

Then and there, my brain dies a full death. I harden to the point of pain. My mouth tugs on Juniper's lips, her tongue swerving with mine as I turn, my back flush with the sofa. I adjust Juniper atop my waist and drape her spread legs over my shoulders.

She gasps, the sound tilting in an upward, adventurous slope. We haven't tried this position yet. She clasps my nape for balance, her clit bracing against my shaft, dislodging a groan from me.

The flames undulate, gilding her jaw and tits, the nipples ruching beneath my digits. I sketch the tips, watching them toughen into stones, relishing the sight. When that's not enough, I thumb that tiny, swollen nub between her hips, swirling my fingers until she's on the verge of convulsing.

We pant, fed up with waiting. Clutching her ass, I find her entrance with my tip and give a gentle snap of my hips. Juniper moans, her warm walls clutching tightly around my prick. I pitch my waist, pistoning into her with measured thrusts.

I watch her jutting above me, her mouth open. Fuck, she's everything. This is everything.

Our hips roll, bumping together. Her head drops, and she hunches to brush my mouth with hers. I lunge into the soaked grip of her body, my efforts relentless until I feel her seizing up, on the brink of release.

Heat charges up my thighs and straight to my crown. With each pass of my hips, my cock plies her deeply, thoroughly, languidly.

Like this, we growl against one another.

Like this, I fuck her slowly. Like this, she fucks me back.

Juniper arches and cries out, her hair brushing my knees, where fur and skin meet. As the room burns, she comes around me, and I shout to the rafters.

When the aftershocks subside, I lower her legs from my shoulders, and she curls against my chest. We catch our breaths, an intense calm washing over the room.

Home is what this feels like. Her, in the cabin. And Sylvan, in the glade.

I've never lived with anyone before. I've never shared tasks with a partner, both of us flexing our muscles—her brain, my tongue—on a regular basis while learning how to fit our lives together like keys into latches, seeing which ones fit and which will open doors to other raptures. How I look forward to more of it.

I drag my finger up and down her spine, from the peak to the tattoo below. It's official, I've got a Juniper hangover. I've been talk-drunk and sex-drunk over the past few days since we'd shut ourselves in this house, determined to know one another inside and out, from our demons, to our griefs, to our moans.

But after hours of fucking, sleeping, bickering, teasing, confiding, debating, bathing, and eating—not always in that order—it's time to come up for air.

It's going to be a long couple of nights. Lark and Cerulean are expecting us in the mountain, in their wildlife park at The Fauna Tower. After that, we'll segue to Cypress's yurt in The Heart of Willows, apparently with Juniper's apple pie in tow.

Moth will be there, along with Tinder. With simmering tensions among the Solitaries and increasing animosity toward our small clan, a shitstorm is brewing. I've felt it in the roots, and my brother has sensed it in the wind. We're meeting to discuss a game plan.

I've got a feeling Foxglove will come around. Call me a hypocrite, but despite her attempt to save Sylvan's life, she shot Cypress and tried to suffocate Juniper in that Fae ring. Whether I'll be able to stomach the nymph's company while moving forward, I have doubts.

Nevertheless, if Foxglove does convert to our side, my tongue will do its best to behave and act civil. I'll only be sarcastic and moderately threatening half the time—cross my scoundrel heart.

As for Elixir, I'd like to shackle my fingers around his jugular for attempting to drown my woman. But that would probably work against the greater goal. The river Solitaries are ruthless and don't pace themselves.

They'd retaliate fast on his behalf.

Besides, I'd been just like Elixir not too long ago. I'll have to keep that in mind if we have a prayer of getting through to him. Between Cerulean, myself, and our serpentine sibling, Elixir's the most visceral, which means he'll be the hardest to reach. He's a viper for a reason—swift and venomous. And like I'd told Cerulean, Elixir sees what others can't, which is ironic given he's blind.

One thing at a time, I guess. Juniper will have the rest of this night planned by now, divided into time slots. But I'll wiggle in a few of my own, starting with breakfast. I'll make her a dish that's native to my culture, something orgasmically palatable that'll blow her tastebuds to smithereens. I flatter my roguish self, but I wager she'll love it so much, the huntress will forget to gobble the food in her preferred order: sides first, main course second.

Then maybe we'll take a ride with Sylvan before heading to the mountain. Apparently, Tímien is coming to get us. I can't wait to see the look on Juniper's face when she realizes we're flying to the tower. More than that, I can't wait to see her reaction when she discovers this world from those heights.

Juniper gasps, the noise tugging me out of my reverie. One of her palms lands on her stomach, a stumped expression distorting the huntress's features.

"What is it?" I ask. "Everything okay?"

After a second, she relaxes and nods with a bemused tilt of her lips. "Yes, I just…felt a little lurch. It's nothing. I must be hungry."

Huh. Sounds like it.

I'm about to pluck her off my lap, so I can make good on breakfast, when the notebook catches my eye. Suddenly, I recall that riveted, zealous look on her face from earlier. "What were you writing?"

Juniper raises her head, her cheeks mottling. "I was working." With an impulsive energy wholly out of character for her, she twists to collect her notebook and spectacles, then faces me. While straddling my waist, she plops the lenses onto her nose and flips through the pages, her fingers jittery with excitement and a smidgen of self-criticism. After finding the spot she'd been looking for, Juniper peers at me with eyes made of spruce.

"I've…," she begins. "I've been writing something. I thought you might like to hear it?"

My lips wreathe into a smirk. "Is this 'something' what I think it is, luv?"

Juniper purses her mouth to hide the smile. "Maybe."

"In that case." I gather the throw blanket and wrap it around us, caging us in warmth. And then I speak against her lips, "Tell me a story."

Get ready for Elixir & Cove…

Vicious Faeries #3

CURSE THE FAE

Want new release alerts, exclusive content,
and wicked details about new books?
Join my mailing list at www.nataliajaster.com/newsletter!

Author's Note

Fables eternal! This has been one hell of a wild journey. Puck and Juniper's story took me on a bunch of twists and turns that I hadn't expected—and it was worth it. From the moment they first interacted, the chemistry between them ignited. I related to Juniper on so many levels, and I adore her bookish heart. And I have to say, one of my favorite experiences writing this one was the epilogue, when I got to explore Puck's wicked mind. His voice flowed effortlessly—and roguishly—and I grinned the whole way through it. He's one epic ride.

I fell in love with this pair, and I hope you did, too.

I'm feeling blessed to have an ensemble of folk who have helped along the way.

To Esther Gwynne, for proofreading this monstrously long book to perfection.

Many thanks to Juan, for another stunning cover—including that antler crown! And to Noverantale, for taking my rough sketch and turning it into that jaw-dropping map.

To Lela, for not only helping me with this release but for your heartwarming support.

Hugs to Michelle (the cello-playing goddess), Jessa, and Candace, for your beta prowess and kinship. I'm lucky to be friends will each of you.

To my family, for whom I'd battle any Fae.

To Roman, my naughty and beloved mate.

And my amazing readers. To my ARC team, the Myths & Tricksters FB group, the wonderful community on bookstagram, and everyone who has opened my books. Thank you, wholeheartedly.

See you in The Solitary Deep. Elixir is waiting…

About Natalia

Natalia Jaster is a fantasy romance author who routinely swoons for the villain.

She lives in an enchanted forest, where she writes steamy New Adult tales about rakish jesters, immortal deities, and vicious fae. Wicked heroes are her weakness, and rebellious heroines are her best friends. She's also a total fool for first-kiss scenes and fanfiction.

Her series include Foolish Kingdoms, Selfish Myths, and Vicious Faeries (set in The Dark Fables extended universe).

When she's not writing, you'll probably find her perched atop a castle tower, guzzling caramel apple tea and counting the stars.

Come say hi!

Bookbub: www.bookbub.com/authors/natalia-jaster
Facebook: www.facebook.com/NataliaJasterAuthor
Goodreads: www.goodreads.com/nataliajaster
Instagram: www.instagram.com/nataliajaster

See the boards for Natalia's novels on
Pinterest: www.pinterest.com/andshewaits

Printed in Great Britain
by Amazon